Also by Rob Edwards

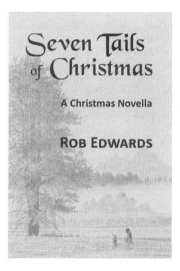

Seven Tails of Christmas

A Christmas Novella

ROB EDWARDS

Threads of Life: Book One

PRISONS
A Novel

Rob Edwards

Copyright © 2020 Rayn Media
All rights reserved.
ISBN-13: 978-1-7340656-2-6: ebook
ISBN-13: 978-1-7340656-3-3: paperback

For Mom, Dad,
and Dayna Marie

Prologue

Noah Higgins stared at the bricks on the side of the school building, his eyes following the endless lines jutting out in every direction. He heard the scraping of the chalk sticks across the asphalt, and two kids arguing over the color blue.

The other children in Mrs. Schucard's first grade class drew trees or monsters on the blacktop. But Noah concentrated on the bugs on the window, then the tiny holes that dotted the wall.

"No, Adrian," Mrs. Schucard called out. "We don't eat chalk."

A flash of red caught Noah's attention. Looking out toward the playground, he saw a big red ball bouncing around among a group of kids. He wanted to go to the ball.

"Spit it out. Come on, spit."

Noah stepped off the blacktop onto the grass. The change in texture under his foot stopped him. He looked down to examine the difference from the hardness of the blacktop to the softness of the grass. The bouncing of the ball grabbed his attention once more and he headed toward the bright red wonder.

"Hold on," yelled a boy with light hair and lots of freckles. "We got a special one coming over."

The boy picked up the ball and looked at Noah with a smirk

on his face. "What's your name, dumbshit?"

The other kids giggled.

Noah, seeing only the red ball, reached for it.

"What're you doing?" the boy said. He backed away. "Oh, you want the ball?"

Noah reached his hands up.

"Then catch."

The ball hit Noah in the chest and bounced off before his hands could close around it. The force knocked him backward several steps. Noah let out an anguished cry. His hands began to flap.

Someone kicked the ball back to the freckle-faced boy, who picked it up again. "Ah. Poor baby. Too stupid to catch a ball?"

"Do it again, Tim," a different boy said.

"Okay, dummy," the boy named Tim said. "Get ready." He threw the ball once more and hit Noah in the head, knocking him to his knees.

Climbing back to his feet, Noah noticed many faces laughing at him. They were loud. Too loud. He moaned.

Noah clenched his right hand and, with another anguished cry, slammed it against the side of his face.

"Whoa, stupid," Tim said. "Don't beat yourself up. That's our job." He threw the ball again, hitting Noah squarely in the side of his head.

Stunned, Noah stumbled backward a few more steps. The noise of the laughter was too loud. Noah balled his fists once more and swung at Tim. The freckle-faced boy did not expect it because Noah's fist caught him squarely in the face and sent him to the ground in a heap.

Tim felt his nose, and pulled a bloody hand back. "You piece of shit. I'm gonna beat the crap out of you."

But Noah dropped on Tim and swung wildly.

Tim cried and covered his bloody face with his hands. The

crowd gathered around, even noisier now. Their screams and jeers were fuel for Noah's swinging fists.

"Stop that, this minute!" a man's voice said.

The following is an excerpt from the article "Special Needs + Special Rehab = Special Circumstances," written by Dr. Warren Q. Fitzpatrick, of Marmont State College, and published in "American Psychology Magazine," October 2019.

As I compile my reports on this highly divisive topic, I find myself in the unfamiliar and uncomfortable position of having to defend the legitimacy of undertaking the project in the first place.

The endeavor itself was born from the extraordinarily successful programs that use inmates to train guide dogs, now active in several correctional facilities around the country.

In these programs, the inmates are given the task of caring for and raising dogs, while running them through intensive preparation to become fully functional leader dogs, explosive detection dogs, and veteran assistant dogs. The fact that well-trained, highly effective canine workers and companions come out of these programs is impressive enough to call them successful, but what is even more remarkable is the effect the process has on the interred. It becomes a time of healing, and offers the prisoners the realization that they can make a difference for the better in this world.

The multi-level success of these programs is what made me want to "raise the bar" if you will, on what's possible with this kind of project, in this kind of environment. The idea was this: if training dogs in prisons can have such a remarkable impact on both the trained and the trainers, what would be possible if we introduced special needs children?

For the inmates the benefit would be the chance to develop knowledge and skills they could rely on post-incarceration. The program would ready them to test for specific accreditations such as Direct Support Professional, or Applied Behavioral Analysis certifications.

For the children, the benefit would be sole and concentrated care and attention for a specific period of time, a commodity that is rare indeed for special needs such as theirs.

My hope was that the benefits to both parties would be totally transforming. For better or worse, that continues to be the debate raging throughout the nation today.

Chapter One

Judith Higgins stared into the vast sea of numbers that flowed across her computer monitor. After a few hours of work they tended to drift together, becoming nothing more than a blob of digits. She shook her head, sat back in her chair and stared up at all the memos pinned to the light blue fabric of her cubicle. Among the pages of highlights and redactions was her favorite picture, snapped by her sister when she brought Noah home from the hospital for the first time. Noah looked almost as if he were smiling, and she was beaming. Her blond hair still had hints of the beautiful highlights and lowlights she used to be able to spend a fortune on.

Looking back down at the computer screen, Judith shook her head and sighed. There were moments when dealing with all the number-crunching became overwhelming. That was the signal that she needed another cup of coffee. She pulled open her personal drawer where she kept her purse, bags of pizza-flavored Combos, and the occasional bag of Kit Kat Minis. She grabbed a container of sugar-free mocha creamer and her coffee cup and headed to the break-room. Usually she took her coffee black, but she liked to treat herself by adding a little of the chocolaty-flavored powder when it felt like work was besting her.

As an entry-level business analyst for Filmore National Life, there wasn't a whole lot of diversity in the projects she worked on. Much different from her previous life as a creative director for Danser Advertising and Public Relations. She had her pick of the projects there, and every day was different with a brand new challenge to tackle. Here the only difference between projects was the black name on the white sticker on the header of the manila file folder.

"Uh oh." Simon Bensinger, a senior analyst, breezed past her. "The lady needs a little java juice."

Judith smiled at him. "Just a little. Fives and twos starting to look too much alike, and all that."

"Ah, drink up then," Simon said. "We can't have that."

Judith poured her coffee, added her creamer, stirred it in and reminisced about the days when she would be whisked off to New York, Minneapolis, or Las Vegas. She'd even been to London for work a few times.

She took a sip of her coffee to test the mocha-ness of it. Perfect the first time. She picked up her container and headed back.

The traveling days were long gone now. Her new world was contained in a 6x6, light blue square, and consisted of the numbers on her screen.

She put her creamer back in the drawer and slid her chair back up to her computer. In truth, it wasn't the job that got her down. She was good at numbers, easily better than any other entry-level analyst Filmore had. But she was also the longest-running entry-level analyst Filmore had. She had yet to be promoted. In fact, others had come after her and had been promoted ahead of her. And it wasn't because she was bad at her job. On the contrary. It was because….

Judith's phone buzzed and shook on her desk. She grabbed it to see Hanson Elementary on the screen. She tapped it and brought it to her ear. "Hello. This is Judith."

"Hello, Miss Higgins. This is Ellen VanAmburg at Hanson

Elementary School."

Judith rolled her eyes. Ellen VanAmburg must have called her a dozen times or more in the past seven months, but she always started her calls by explaining who she was in her nasally, drawling voice. "Yes, Ellen. Is something wrong with Noah?"

"Well, Principal Wilcox asked me to call you. It seems he caught Noah beating up another boy on the playground and..."

"Wait, what?" Judith slid her chair back. "I think you mean Noah was beatenvv up. Is he okay?"

"Well, uh, no. Noah beat up the other boy. Pretty soundly too. Nose bleeding and all. Sent him to the school nurse."

"That can't be. Noah doesn't like to be touched. There's no way he would touch someone else unless he was defending himself or something."

"Well, he's here in the office. Principal Wilcox brought him in in a pretty agitated state. Put him in the safe room awhile till he calmed down. He would like you to come in and talk."

Judith stood. "Of course. I'll be right in."

"Oh good. We'll see...."

Judith tapped the screen, opened her personal drawer and tossed it into her purse. She bent over her computer, saved her files, and shut it down. She grabbed her purse and jacket and headed out to talk to Bernie.

Bernie Herbstreit, supervisor over her team, was not what one could consider a gentle man. He had little patience for the types of issues she had to handle with Noah. And he was an obnoxious oaf on top of that. Not to mention the singular reason she hadn't been promoted.

True to form, he was racing out of his cubicle, constipated look on his face, eyes set squarely on her. He was bouncing his stomach in her direction as fast as he could waddle. "Did you think I didn't notice you log off? I get an alert when that happens, you know."

"No, Bernie," Judith said, biting her tongue lest she say more. One day she would, but there was no way she could afford to lose this job now. "The school just called. Noah was in a fight, and I have to go pick him up."

"The kid again." Bernie put his hands on his hips. "So will you be back to grace us with a little more work today?"

Judith turned and headed to the elevators. "I'm not sure. I have to talk to the principal. See what's going on." An elevator opened and she stepped in, hit lobby and the door close button three times before the doors began to slide shut. She looked out and saw Bernie rushing to catch up.

"Well, the Raymor account is your responsibility and I need to go over it before it can be turned…."

The doors shut.

Judith sighed.

Chapter Two

"So how is your foster family?" Delton Hayes said to his little sister, Danna.

"Okay, I guess," she replied.

Hushed voices bounced off the cold cement block walls of the Visitors Center at Two Rivers Correctional Facility. Huddled around five other small round tables sat inmates talking to their visitors, and an armed guard stood in every corner of the room, with another at the door.

"Just okay?" Delton realized that Danna was growing fast now. No longer was she the skinny little hungry nine-year-old girl she had been when he was sentenced seven years ago. She had been kicked from foster home to foster home in that time. Some of those people were nice and some were downright cruel to her. But it appeared to Delton that this family was the best yet. Danna's dirty, crusty dreads were cut off and her hair was now short and looked professionally cut. "It looks to me like they're pretty good to you. They dress you up nice. Got your hair cut real good."

She wore new jeans, a shirt with little pink roses on it, a light pink sweater and white shoes, with her ankles crossed. Danna looked like a proper girl in an upstanding family—not the product of a drug-addicted mother, a father who split before

15

she'd entered the world, and a brother who was now in prison for armed robbery.

"Oh, we're just getting started on the hair." Danna ran her fingers through her short curls. "Once this grows a bit, Mama Rose says she's gonna get me a weave."

"And that's a good thing?" Delton asked.

"That's Beyoncé-style!" Danna dropped her hands and looked at him, wide-eyed. "And it ain't cheap."

Delton nodded. "That's a good thing then." He laughed when she rolled her eyes. "They's treating you all right then."

"They's good to me, I guess." Danna said with a one-shoulder shrug. "They's just a little weird."

"What do you mean weird?"

"Like I gotta be at the supper table at a specific time and all, or I get talked to."

"Do they yell at you?"

"No."

"They don't hit you, do they?" This was one of Delton's worst fears. Danna had a foster father once that hit her with a belt for sneaking out one night. Danna was removed from the house and they are out of the program now, but there's nothing guaranteeing that won't happen again, and there isn't anything Delton can do about it from the inside.

"No. Nothin' like that." Danna said, squirming in her chair. "They just say they's disappointed in me, they want me to feel like family, and like I'm at home with them."

Delton laughed out loud. A couple of the guards and the other visitors looked over.

"What you laughing for?" Danna asked him, smiling.

"Cuz you silly, girl." Delton said. "You complaining cuz they treating you proper. They dressing you all up nice and cutting your hair. How much more horrible can they be? Give you dessert at every meal?"

"Yeah, but," Danna sounded flustered but smiled back brightly. "No. You don't get it. Sometimes I don't wanna eat what they eat. They make weird stuff."

"Like what?"

"Like…." Danna thought for a moment. "Grilled cheese with Swiss cheese and tomatoes." She crinkled her face. "That's sick. Who ever heard of something stupid like using Swiss cheese for grilled cheese?"

Delton looked toward the ceiling for a moment, pretending to be thinking it over. Then he looked back at her with a confirming nod. "Okay, I'll grant you, that's a little weird."

"See?"

"But girl, you gotta be grateful," Delton said firmly.

Danna balled her hands in her lap and looked at them.

"When they give you something that you think is weird, you thank them with all your heart."

Danna still stared at her hands.

"Look at me," Delton said.

Danna looked up.

Delton leaned in and rested his elbows on his knees. "It wasn't all that long ago you was going to sleep hungry every night. I had to lie there and listen to you cry, and it broke my heart every time. So if someone is telling you they want you to join them for dinner, and they will fill that belly of yours with good food—even if it has Swiss cheese on it…."

Danna smiled.

"I'm grateful. You feel me?"

Danna nodded.

"And you need to be grateful too. And you need to be sayin' thank you to them, like a girl with proper manners would do. You got that?"

Danna nodded and looked back down at her hands.

Delton sat back and looked around the room. The guard at

the door had been watching him, but looked away when Delton caught his eye.

"Are you nervous?"

Delton looked back at his sister, concern etched on her face. She was asking about his parole board hearing later. He wanted to ease her mind but not give her too much hope. No saying what could happen. He could tell them the God's honest truth—that he was sorry every day of his life for what he did, that he was just desperate because his family was starving—but it might not be enough. He nodded. "I'm a little nervous. But I think I got a good shot at it. I ain't had no real trouble since I been in here."

Danna looked at her hands once more. "Then you can come be with me?"

"I can't be with you, girl," Delton said. "I'm too old for a foster family. They think you should be out on your own by the time you're twenty-four. But I will definitely be able to spend more time with you."

"Can I come live with you?"

Delton smiled. "You know there's nobody gonna let that happen. Not for a long while. And by then you won't be wanting to live with me anyway."

"Yes, I will," Danna said to her hands.

Delton studied her for a moment. "You ever hear from Mama?"

Danna shook her head.

"Okay, Hayes. That's time," a guard said, approaching.

Delton nodded at him and stood. Danna jumped out of her chair and threw her arms around his chest. "Good luck today."

He hugged her back. "Thanks, Sis."

The guard led Danna out a far door, the one that led to fresh air and sunshine. Delton turned and walked to his door that led back into the block that smelled like sweat and piss twenty-four hours a day.

Reaching the door the guard said, "Nice job, Hayes."

"Pardon me?" Delton said.

"I listen in to conversations sometimes, and I picked yours just now. You're a good brother, and I wanted you to know that."

Delton eyed the man suspiciously. "Thanks."

"Listen, we get asked all the time from members of the parole board, to give our input on certain inmates. I'm going to let them know I think you're a stand-up guy."

Delton crossed his arms. "And what's that gonna cost me?"

The guard chuckled and then nodded at him with a raised eyebrow. "Good question. But I don't play those games, son. It'll cost you never taking up a cage in here for the rest of your life. Do we have a deal?"

Delton smiled. "We have a deal." He walked out the door and two other inmates exited the visiting room right behind him.

Delton heard a low whistle followed by, "Damn, Hayes, that was one fine piece you had in there today."

Delton stopped and turned around to see Rick Simpson, a red-necked, freckle-faced inmate looking back at him through his thin eyes and his big yellow-toothed grin. He always wore a navy-blue stocking cap to cover up his greasy, stringy, red hair.

"Dude, that's my little sister."

"Oops," Simpson raised his hands in mock surrender. "My bad, dude. Well, she's not mine. Can I have her phone number?"

Delton lunged and slammed Simpson up against the hard cement wall with a low thump. The air whooshed from his lungs. "She's fifteen, you piece of…."

"Cut that shit out, Hayes!"

Delton could see a guard running at him from his left.

A hand reached across his chest. "Whoa, chief. Stop. He's not worth it." Hector Sanchez, easily Delton's best friend in the joint, grabbed his shoulder and pulled him off before the guards could use their clubs. "You have that little sister to think about, man. There's no need to give anybody a reason to keep you in here now."

Simpson bent over, gasping for breath. "What the fuck, Hayes. I was just jokin' around, asshole."

Delton glared at Simpson over Hector's shoulder. "Learning respect would do you some good, shithead."

"Shut up, Hayes, and walk away," the guard said, taking a position in front of Simpson and clutching his club tightly.

Delton shook off Hector's hands.

"C'mon, Delton. It ain't worth it, man," Hector said, both hands raised to calm his friend.

Delton took an angry breath, turned, and stomped off back to the block.

Chapter Three

Judith climbed from her yellow Kia and slammed the door. Entering the building, she breezed past the "Welcome to Hanson Elementary!" sign and headed straight for the main office. In one of the many rooms down the hall she heard several very off-key voices singing "Little Bunny Foo Foo," a song Judith always considered a bit violent for young grade schoolers. She remembered, a hundred years ago, feeling sorry for the field mice when she had to sing it.

Reaching the office she opened the glass door and walked in. The older woman behind the counter took off her glasses and let them hang from the cord around her neck. On the counter, a wooden veneer sign with white letters spelled out "Mrs. VanAmburg." Mrs. VanAmburg had on a sweater with multi-colored tulips in the pattern. "Hello, Miss Higgins." She pointed to the door to her left. "You can go right in."

"Thank you," Judith said.

Mrs. VanAmburg smiled. "Um hmm." She placed her glasses on her nose and looked back at the People magazine on her desk.

Judith sighed and opened the door.

"Miss Higgins, come in and have a seat." Principal David Wilkins, usually an extremely charming man, looked all business.

His dark hair was a bit messy and his smiling face was now cold and stony.

"What's happened?" Judith asked, taking her seat. "Someone hurt Noah? Where is he now?"

"Your son is in the safe room, and he's calm now," Principal Wilkins said, raising a hand to assure her. "But nobody hurt him. He beat up another student."

Judith shook her head. "That's not possible. There's no way Noah would attack anyone. Whatever kid said he did, has to be lying."

"Miss Higgins, I pulled your son off the boy myself. Noah had him on the ground and was punching him relentlessly. I sent the child to the nurse with blood covering his face."

"He had to have been goaded into it," she said, shaking her head. "Autistic kids don't like to be touched. Everybody knows that. There's no way he would just hit somebody for no reason at all. They pushed him too far. You know how kids are."

"Miss Higgins, I don't disagree with you. I have a feeling things went down out there that the kids aren't fessing up to. They all said Noah started it."

"We both know that's not true. Just tell them all to leave him alone, and there won't be any more trouble."

"I can't tell every child who goes to this school not to speak to another child for fear he may become violent."

"But he isn't violent," Judith said.

Principal Wilkins opened a file on his desk, lifted a piece of paper, and waved it. "Noah has a history of extreme meltdowns and generally only hits himself, but it is recorded that on a few occasions he has hit others, mostly teachers. In fact, just after returning from winter break, he hit Allison Engel, the student teacher, and gave her a black eye."

"What?" Judith gasped. "Why am I just hearing about this now?"

"I can't answer that. I think Miss Engel was embarrassed, but that's no excuse. What's important is that the parents of the student that Noah beat up today are furious. They want your son expelled and they're going to the school board to make their case."

"Then we'll have to be there to defend him."

Principal Wilkins sighed. "The problem is that we have a documented pattern of misconduct, including violent outbursts. And with Noah clearly growing stronger, and developing a tendency of hitting others...."

"So what are you saying?"

"I'm saying there is a chance that he won't be allowed to remain at this school." He paused to let that sink in. "I wanted you to know so that you might start thinking now about other arrangements for Noah's education. I'm sorry."

"You're sorry?" Judith leaned forward in her chair. "You think 'sorry' covers it? What's Noah supposed to do with your 'sorry'? Where is he going to go to school?"

"You can enroll him in another district, or you can send him to Keener School for Special Needs."

"He's been to Keener before. They didn't do him much good, and they were too expensive." Judith recalled the year she had sent Noah to Keener, a private school for special needs children. She was determined to pay whatever it took to get Noah the best education. But he saw very little progress there, nor did he seem to like it. Plus, the end of the school year was close and the cost for summer care at Keener was exorbitant. She would barely be able to afford that and rent too, let alone have anything left over to eat. A simple parking ticket would put her way over budget.

"I can speak to one of the schools over in Washtenaw County," Principal Wilkins said. "I can think of two that could be a good fit."

Judith closed her eyes tight. She didn't care to share her tears with this man. Taking a deep breath, she stood while letting it out. "Well, that's it then." She turned and walked toward the door.

"Miss Higgins," Principal Wilkins said.

"Save it. I don't need pity."

"It's not pity. It's just…well…I heard of another program that may be a benefit to Noah. And it's free."

Gripping the doorknob tightly, she stopped and turned. She stared at the principal a moment, trying to judge his sincerity. "For real?"

"For real," Mr. Wilkins said with a nod. "But you'd better sit down. It's a bit…unorthodox."

Chapter Four

Delton Hayes sat quietly. If he shifted his weight the slightest amount, the old wooden chair creaked loudly in the oppressive silence of the barren room.

Five strangers sat in folding chairs at an old portable pressed-board table, flipping through papers in file folders. Delton scanned the people who were going to judge him—who were going to decide the next five years of his life. Three men and two women. All of them white. Two of the men were dressed in gray suits and one in blue. The man in blue who sat in the center wore reading glasses. He had dark hair rimming a shiny pale bald head. The woman on the end, a brunette in a yellow dress with a white sweater and a silver necklace didn't look up much. She spent her time swiping the screen on her cell phone. The woman next to her was much older. Gray streamed through her dark hair. She also wore reading glasses and had on a blue woman's business suit.

Delton realized that he was about to be judged by people who had no idea what life could be like in a neighborhood like his. They looked like the kind of people who got a new cell phone every year, had country club memberships, and wallets full of credit cards. He doubted if any of them ever went to bed hungry even once in their lives.

"So, Mister Hayes," the man in the center said. He put down his papers and took off his reading glasses. "Would you like to make a statement?"

"Sir…ahhh…yes sir," Delton said. He swallowed hard and rubbed his moist palms on his knees. "I've had five years behind bars to think about what I've done. I know it was wrong. I now know I had other options, like the food bank and the shelter. I should have never taken matters into my own hands. I should have never been too proud to ask somebody else for help."

"Is that what you call robbing a convenience store with a gun? Pride?"

"The gun was broke," Delton said. "It didn't even have a trigger."

"You know by now that doesn't matter."

Delton cradled his hands in his lap and let his gaze drop to them. "Yes, sir. I know."

The man put his glasses back on, and picked up some of the papers again. "You have always claimed you just wanted to take care of your family. Do you still hold to that claim?"

Looking up, Delton nodded. "Yes, sir. My little sister, Danna. She was ten at the time. Very thin. Very hungry. One night she was lyin' in bed cryin', you know, cuz she was so hungry. Our mama was too busy doing drugs to get anything for her. I offered to go buy food, but Mama wouldn't give me no money, so…."

All five sets of eyes stared at him. They listened intently to every word he said. Delton thought he noticed the slightest, almost imperceptible nod from the gray-haired woman, like he'd made a connection.

The man broke his gaze and looked back to his papers flipping a page or two.

The gray-haired lady never took her eyes off him. "Mister Hayes, what would your plans be were you to walk out of here today?"

"I…" He hadn't expected this question. All he expected

them to want to hear was that he learned his lesson and he would never do it again. He realized he hadn't given any real thought to life after prison, other than somehow getting a job, and being with his sister. He shrugged. "I guess I get a job, and find a place to live."

"So, you have no plans in place for your life after leaving Two Rivers?" the woman said.

"Nothin' written in stone."

"You need to know this is concerning to us," the woman said as casually as a doctor discussing a throat culture. "Inmates such as yourself who walk out of prison without their high school diploma, and no real prospects at gainful employment, often find their way back behind these walls within two years." She let that comment sink in for a moment, and then added, "And usually for much more serious crimes the second time around."

His stomach lurched, like he'd swallowed a rock, and it just landed hard. The connection he thought he'd made was nothing more than a frail thread, which this woman just clipped with her golden scissors.

Delton didn't want to listen anymore. He couldn't take hearing them say he wasn't fit for society or safe to roam the streets. He stood up to leave. "Look, I understand you don't think I'm ready to go...."

"Mr. Hayes, sit down." the woman said. Her eyes, which carried so much warmth a moment ago, were now stern and cold.

He sat.

"We have a very important decision to make here," she said to him. "And we need your cooperation."

"Mr. Hayes," the man began again. "It says here, that in five years behind bars you have never been reprimanded for anything. Could this be true?"

"I guess so." Delton said.

"Considering the reasons behind the crime you committed, would you say that you see yourself as...oh, perhaps...a nurturing individual?"

Delton glanced at the other members sitting at the table trying to understand what the man was getting at. "Come again?"

"You have said your only thoughts that night were to get your sister food. Do you feel you have a calling to care for others?"

Shifting his weight slightly in the chair, Delton pondered the question a moment before responding. "I've never given it any thought. I just wanted to take care of my sister is all."

"I think you ought to know," the man said. "There is a guard in this prison who thinks very highly of you."

Delton fought the urge to smile. "Thank you, sir. That's nice to know." He didn't know why he was surprised the guard did what he said he would do.

The man folded his hands in front of him on the table. "I'm going to be frank with you, Mr. Hayes. We have concerns about letting you out of here today. It's clear you have been a model inmate, and you have a very good reputation with the guards. But we struggle at your lack of planning for your future. That being said, we've looked over your files very carefully, and we are considering you for a special program. Before we do that, we need to know that you are serious about your future." The man looked at the two women to his right. They both nodded. He glanced over to the two men to his left who also nodded. He looked back at Delton. "So, Mr. Hayes. Are you up for a challenge?"

Delton crossed his arms. Sighed. "What kinda challenge?"

The following is an excerpt from the article "Special Needs + Special Rehab = Special Circumstances," written by Dr. Warren Q. Fitzpatrick, of Marmont State College, and published in "American Psychology Magazine," October 2019.

I put a great deal of thought and care into determining the pairings. In truth I felt the success or failure of this whole program rested on the choices I made at this point.

My first consideration was the numbers. Too many would make the project unwieldy, and too few would not allow us the information we needed to make a determination on the success or failure of the program. I landed on ten pairs, believing that to be the perfect number to achieve our goals.

I needed a good control group for the special needs children. I'd entertained the idea of having all children with the same type of disability, i.e., all ten children with cerebral palsy. But I came to the conclusion that would not give my experiment the proper litmus test it needed. If I were to go with all children with cerebral palsy, and it were a success, one could only conclude that a program like this was successful with cerebral palsy, leading to questions such as, "But what about autism?"

I decided on five unique and distinct disabilities — cerebral palsy, Down syndrome, autism, intellectual disability, and physically limiting disabilities. The main groups would consist of two children of each disability. In each disability grouping I would have one child with a mild case and one child with a severe case, thus allowing degrees of severity to factor into final determinations of the outcomes of the project.

The name of now-famous Noah Higgins was forwarded to me by one of the principals of a nearby elementary school that has a number of students with special needs. Noah was on the autistic spectrum, had as yet, not spoken a word, and was prone to meltdowns, so I added him to my list as the more severe autism case.

On the inmates side there were givens. Obviously sex offenders and those convicted of violent crimes were off the list. Those who were considered troublemakers or malcontents while incarcerated were also not considered.

I poured over courtroom transcripts and parole board notes, I talked to the warden and the guards within the correctional facility, and I scoured the records to find workable candidates. There were many within the system who knew a prisoner and thought they would be perfect for my program. Such was the case with the controversial Delton Hayes. He was referred to me by a member of the parole board, who had been assured by a guard within the Two Rivers Correctional Facility that Mr. Hayes was a good prospect. It was because of this reference that I added him to my list.

Chapter Five

"What the hell do you mean they want to put Noah with a convict?" Darlene Longwood screeched over the small cellphone speaker.

Judith reached over and gave the volume-down button a couple of clicks. "Yes, like an inmate. It's this special experiment they're doing through Marmont State College."

Judith heard two claps from Noah. She looked up from her laptop screen and saw him still playing with the glasses of water she had put out for him. He would pick up one half full glass of water, pour all the water into the other glass, set them next to each other, and then clap twice. It was one of his most satisfying activities, and it was usually worth doing for at least an hour at a time.

"Sis, you're not going to do this, are you?"

Judith flipped her mouse wheel and scrolled through another page on her laptop screen. "Dar, I have to at least look into it."

"How can you even think of it?"

Judith looked down at her phone and talked to it as if it were a person. "What choice do I have? The principal at Hanson Elementary told me Noah is probably expelled, and Keener costs a fortune, especially during the summer. I can't afford it."

Darlene moaned. "Ugh. Judith. Why did you think a sperm-bank baby was a good idea again?"

"Why do you always go there when something comes up?" Judith snapped.

"I'm sorry. But if you had someone to help you with him…."

"I don't. I made my decision and I'm living with it."

"Well, if you'd let us help with Noah's costs, you wouldn't have to even consider this."

"You do this every time we talk." Judith picked up the phone and spoke into it. "For the last time, I'm not going to take any money from you. You and Jim have to save your money for your own kids someday. You're not going to fund my life. It would ruin our perfect sisterly relationship, you piece of shit."

Darlene laughed. "All right, bitch. Shut the hell up already."

Noah clapped twice, picked up the full glass, and started pouring.

Judith smiled, set the phone down, and looked back at her computer screen.

"So, what's the next step?"

Judith clicked on a link. "I'm trying to look up any information on this Dr. Fitzpatrick from Marmont. Apparently this whole thing is his grand idea. He's going to be here soon to discuss this with me and I'd like to know something about him before he shows up."

"Find anything?"

"Not a thing, other than his listing in the college directory. So at least I know for sure he works there as a professor of applied sociology."

The doorbell startled Judith. "I think he's here. I gotta go."

"Good luck, Sis."

"Thanks. Love you."

"Love…" Judith tapped off the call, shut her laptop and ran

to answer the door.

Noah clapped twice, picked up the full glass, and started pouring.

Opening the door, Judith was surprised to see two people standing there.

"Hello, Mrs. Higgins. I'm Dr. Warren Fitzpatrick." He was a tall man, at least six foot, with dark hair, graying on the sides, and a face, pockmarked from a long, obviously agonizing battle with acne throughout his teens. His dark, thick-framed glasses helped hide much of it. He held out his hand and Judith shook it.

"It's Miss Higgins. But you can call me Judith."

To his right stood what appeared to be a bottle-blond coed with perfect skin, remarkably bright red lipstick, short black skirt, and a white doctor's jacket over a blue cami. Basically, a nerd's dream girl.

"This is Rena Blossom," Dr. Fitzpatrick said.

Great. She even had a stripper name.

"She's one of the assistants on the project and has been assigned specifically to your case."

"Nice to meet you, Rena."

Shaking hands, Rena smiled with the brightest white, Colgate-commercial smile.

"Please come in," Judith said.

When Dr. Fitzpatrick entered, his foot squeaked. There was an issue with his left shoe, and one clearly knew when the big man stepped with his left. His size made Judith's small apartment seem tiny.

Noah clapped twice, picked up the full glass, and started pouring.

"Ah, there's the little guy," Dr. Fitzpatrick gestured, and looked down at Rena.

Rena slowly walked over, knelt down about 10 feet from Noah and spoke quietly. "Hello, Noah. My name is Rena."

The girl obviously understood autism. She walked slowly and spoke quietly so as not to overwhelm or over-stimulate him. "He doesn't speak," Judith said.

Rena nodded. "Principal Wilkins had mentioned that." She stood and walked back to Judith. "He seems to have good motor skills. He isn't spilling the water. How self-sufficient is he?"

Judith thought about it for a moment. "Well, he can feed himself. But he really can't do much more than that. He has trouble getting his clothes on—things like that."

"Do you ever try to force the issue?" Rena asked. "Leave one arm out so he has to finish putting the shirt on himself?"

"Yeah. I've tried that a few times. It takes a while, and I don't always have the time to follow through with it. You know. I have to get to work and all. Also, he can be prone to meltdowns."

"Oh. That can be difficult," Rena said.

Dr. Fitzpatrick looked at his watch. "Well, the main reason we stopped by is to see if there are any specific toys or items that Noah is particularly fond of. We're setting up the rooms and we'd like to have those things there to make him more comfortable in the environment."

Judith gestured to the couch. "Would you like to sit while we talk? Can I get you something to drink?"

"No, ma'am," Dr. Fitzpatrick tapped on his watch. "As you can imagine, I'm on a pretty tight schedule. I have a few more visits today before I have to get back for class."

"But I have questions," Judith said. "I thought we were going to discuss this."

Dr. Fitzpatrick frowned. "I don't understand. I was informed you had agreed to this."

"I had agreed to entertain the idea," Judith said. "But I need to know more about the project first."

Dr. Fitzpatrick crossed his arms. "What is it you need to know?"

"Well, for one," Judith put her hands on her hips, "why do we think it's a good idea to put little kids with criminals? How can you guarantee their safety?"

Dr. Fitzpatrick sighed. "Miss Higgins, this is a two-way rehabilitation project, in which the hope is, both sides can enjoy significant benefit. There is no room for implicit bias in a project of this scope."

Judith looked at Rena, then back at Dr. Fitzpatrick. "I don't understand what you mean by that."

"Of course you don't." Dr. Fitzpatrick shuffled his weight to his left, his shoe let out a low squawk. "Look, your boy will be fine. There will be plenty of guards there."

"Okay, let me come at this a little differently," Judith said. "My Noah, and any other special needs children, are not dogs that can just be trained to sit up and speak on cue. To infer that they are interchangeable with puppies is, quite frankly, insulting to the highest degree. So this whole inmate thing is giving me a great deal of pause. You're asking me to put my faith in a man who has committed a crime, to work with and care for my son. I want to know why I should consider something like this, and if you don't have the decency to give me a straight answer without looking down your nose at me, then you can leave my home and shove your special program up your ass. Now, does that have a little less implicit bias?"

"Well...uh," Dr. Fitzpatrick's shoulders drooped sharply, and his eyes darted over to Rena and around the room. "No, those are very important concerns, indeed." He shifted his weight and his left shoe squeaked again. "I never meant to infer that your son was like a dog. This is not like that program at all. There is a special building where the program will be taking place, and the men working with the children are all searching for a life change. This is a concentrated program where your son's teacher will be learning—studying if you will, under the watchful eye of Miss Blossom here—the intricacies of working with the special needs population. While your son will gain the benefits of

35

having someone concentrate solely on his needs, his teacher will be preparing to be tested for ABA certification. It truly should be a transforming experience for all involved." Dr. Fitzpatrick shrugged.

It took Judith a moment, but eventually she nodded. "Thank you. You've given me something to consider now."

Dr. Fitzpatrick took a breath. "It appears you still have some soul-searching to do on this." He turned to the door and opened it. "Miss Blossom will leave you her card. If you have any more questions, please feel free to contact her." And with that, Dr. Fitzpatrick squeak-stepped out.

Rena put a gentle hand on Judith's arm. "The number one complaint about Dr. Fitzpatrick is his people skills," she said. "But trust me, this is a good project, and I believe it will be a good experience for Noah." She reached into the pocket of her jacket, pulled out a card, and handed it to Judith. "If you want to discuss it further, please call me any time, night or day. Okay?"

Judith nodded.

Rena walked out, and Judith pushed the door, letting it swing shut with a clunk.

Noah clapped twice, picked up the full glass, and started pouring.

PRISONS

Excerpts from the transcript of the GINfo (Global Information Network) interview between Brooke Winthrop and Judith Higgins.

Brooke: Are we rolling?

Off Camera: Uh huh.

Brooke: How are you feeling?

Judith: I'm good, thanks.

Brooke: Ever done anything like this before?

Judith: Actually, I did a corporate video about seven or eight years ago. I was sort of in your role. I walked around a convention center and asked the convention goers a few questions. But that was a much smaller production. I just had a camera guy go with me. There weren't all these cameras and lights – certainly no make-up. (Laughs)

Brooke: Oh. I won't do any video without make-up. My career would be over. (chuckles) Okay, if you're ready we can begin. Let's talk a little bit about where you were when all this started. So you decided to become a single mother and have a baby on your own. Why did you decide to do that?

Judith: Ahhh…why do you want to ask that?

Brooke: I believe it's an important aspect to the story.

Judith: I don't think it is at all. A lot of women have babies on their own. That's not what's at issue here.

Brooke: What I'm trying to do is create the setting. I want the audience to understand the position you were in when all of this began.

Judith: My position was as a desperate mom. Noah was losing his school, and my choice was to either take him to other schools 30 minutes or more away, or pay for a private school that I couldn't afford. Don't get me wrong, I would have done that if not for the Marmont program. But the story really isn't about me or any woman who decides to have a baby on their own. The story is about Noah…a boy with ASD whose future is always in doubt, because he can't communicate like everyone else can. He became a guinea pig in a strange experiment to pair up with an inmate—someone behind bars. That's the real story. To look at a program like that and truly wonder if it's the best option.

Brooke: I'm sure it had to give you pause.

Judith: It kept me up at night. And now after everything that's happened…Noah has given up. (voice cracks) (pauses)

Brooke: It's all right.

Judith: He's not doing well. (wipes tear from edge of eye) He's worse now than when all this started.

Chapter Six

A guard led Delton down a narrow hallway with several green metal doors lining one side, scratched and dented from years of use. A handful of these doors had other guards standing outside them, forcing Delton to turn sideways and sidle past them. Halfway down the hall, his escort stopped, opened a door and nodded for him to enter.

Delton peered in to see a short African American woman sitting at a table. He stepped into the small cement block room and the guard closed the door behind him.

"Hello, Delton," the woman said with a pleasant smile. She stood up and held out her hand. "Taysha Williams. I'm the counselor assigned to you during your time with the project."

Delton accepted her handshake. "Hey."

She gestured to a chair. "Sit down and relax before Dr. Fitzpatrick arrives."

Delton stepped over and sat, arms folded.

"So what do you think?" Taysha asked, sitting across from him.

"Lady, you don't want to know what I think," Delton said.

Taysha sat up straight. "Hey, what's with the attitude? You

have a great opportunity here."

"This ain't no opportunity and you know it."

"Why you talkin' like that?" Her voice squealed.

"Because the parole board said a guy like me, without his high school degree, is doomed to fail on the outside." He leaned forward and tapped at the table for emphasis. "They want to set me up to fail. So they put me in this dumbass program to prove they right."

"Son, did you fall down and knock your fool head on somethin', or do you just have shit for brains?"

Delton sat back in his chair. "What kind of counselor are you?"

"I'm the kind of counselor who's about to come 'round there and knock some sense upside your tiny little head." She stood and looked down at him. "This is an opportunity and one that you best be taking serious too. You got a chance to actually do some good in the world with this project. You can change your life. Ain't that better than just sitting there all smelly in some stupid cell and then going off to do someone else's damn laundry? You say the parole board wants you to fail. So what you gonna do? You just gonna roll over 'cause poor little Delton feels he got a bad deal and prove them right? Or are you gonna do the right thing, outshine every other one of them rejects out there, who're also in this program?" She flicked a thumb at the door. "And prove them tight-ass, no-nothing, think-their-shit-don't-stink, parole board mother-fuckers wrong."

Delton realized his mouth was hanging open. He closed it and stared over at this short woman's tenacious look, like a bulldog on a scent. Then he burst out laughing. "You are my kind of counselor." He pushed out his fist. Taysha smiled and bumped his with hers.

"I'm a good counselor because I speak a language my clients can understand. It's called street." She emphasized her statement with a sharp nod.

"Did you learn that in college too?"

"No. Detroit."

Delton nodded. "Respect." The two fist-bumped again.

The door opened. A tall white man with glasses and bad skin walked in followed by the hottest white girl Delton had ever seen.

"Ah, good. You're both here," the man said. "I'm Dr. Warren Fitzpatrick, and this is my assistant on this case, Miss Rena Blossom."

Delton stood and shook both their hands. "I'm Delton," he said to Rena.

"Nice to meet you, Delton," Rena said back with a bright smile.

"And I'm Taysha Williams. I'm the counselor appointed to this project by the Two Rivers Correctional Facility."

"Very nice to meet you, Taysha." Dr. Fitzpatrick pulled out a chair next to Delton and sat down, thumping a thick manila file folder down on the table. Delton watched Rena sit down across from him.

He smiled as he took his seat and looked over at Taysha who glared back at him through thin eyes.

He stopped smiling.

"So I think it's important to inform you," Dr. Fitzpatrick began. "That earlier today we met with the mother of the child we were planning to pair you with, and she expressed some misgivings."

"What kind of misgivings?" Taysha asked.

"Why?" Delton looked at her. "You gonna go give her some counseling?"

Taysha nodded at him. "If I have to."

"I appreciate the effort, Miss Williams, I really do," Dr. Fitzpatrick said. "But I feel that Miss Blossom had an excellent idea on the way over here." He turned to face Delton. "Quite

41

often people become stressed and afraid of what and who they don't know. Miss Higgins is obviously nervous about this project. She feels anxious about putting her son into the same room with a gentleman who is currently being incarcerated. So what if we were to hold a special meeting between you two?"

"A meeting?" Delton asked.

"It would be an opportunity to break the ice," Rena Blossom said. "If Miss Higgins could meet you, I'm sure she would feel satisfied that you have the best intentions of her son at heart."

"Delton would be happy to do that," Taysha said. "Wouldn't you, Delton? You'd love to show this woman how excited you are to work with her kid."

Delton looked from Taysha to Rena. Shrugging, he said, "Sure."

"Excellent," Dr. Fitzpatrick said, with a relieved sigh.

"But I need y'all to know somethin'," Delton said. "I can tell her this niceness and everything, but then I have to do something with this kid, and I don't have a clue what I'm supposed to be doing."

Dr. Fitzpatrick slid the large manila folder across the table in front of him. "We have prepared an extensive study packet for you."

Rena reached over and tapped at the folder with her forefinger. "In here you will find an in-depth explanation of Autistic Spectrum Disorder and how children on the spectrum are affected. There is also a summarization of Noah Higgins who is dealing with a more profound diagnosis of ASD. You will discover what the challenges are that he faces in life, what challenges you may face in working with him, as well as several options for activities and games to try with him."

"This isn't everything though," Dr. Fitzpatrick added. "As you were told when you agreed to this project, one of the major outcomes we are looking for is for you to be able to test for, and excel at, Advanced Behavioral Analysis certification."

Delton flipped the top of the folder open. The small typewritten pages overwhelmed him at first glance. "Autism, huh?"

"Do you know what that is?" Rena asked.

"It's like..." Delton looked up at her. "How do I put this delicately? He ain't that smart?"

"That's actually a very common and unfortunate misconception," Rena said, scooting her chair closer to Delton.

Delton closed the cover of the folder, smiled, and gave Rena his undivided attention.

"The truth is that autism has nothing to do with intelligence. There are many, very brilliant people who suffer with the condition. Autism is a developmental disorder that affects an individual's ability to interact normally with others. Some, like in Noah Higgins' case, do not even have the ability to speak. Autistic children also have behaviors that are restricted and repetitive. They may not be able to run and jump well, but that doesn't matter to them because they want to spend their time doing things like stacking cans of food to a certain height, then dismantling the structure, and starting over again."

Delton's smile faded, and he pursed his lips. "How is it you think I can do anything for this boy?"

Rena tapped again on the folder. "I have put together a list of specific activities you can attempt, that will challenge him in positive ways."

Delton opened the folder and flipped through the top few pages.

"There isn't anything in here you can't try with him. The activities will increase in complexity as time passes, your studies continue, and you gain more experience and comfort with the subject."

"The subject?"

"The boy...uh...Noah." Rena said. She put her hand on the folder. Delton looked up. "I want to warn you though, this will take an enormous amount of patience and focus. You will be tested like you've never been tested before."

"That's no problem," Taysha chimed in. "He's up to any challenge. Aren't you, Delton?"

Delton looked back down at the papers; flipped through a few more pages. "I guess."

PRISONS

Transcript from phone conversation from Two Rivers Correctional Facility between HAYES, DELTON, B. (576684-GT) and Danna G. Hayes, sister of the incarcerated. May 25, 2019.

DBH: Hey, Dann. How ya doin'?

DGH: Hey. You was supposed to call me days ago. Let me know when you was getting out.

DBH: Yeah, well, I don't know just yet.

DGH: They are letting you out though, right?

DBH: There's a chance. But I gotta take care of some stuff first.

DGH: What?

DBH: I gotta do something first.

DGH: What you gotta do?

DBH: I gotta work with a kid who's got autism.

DGH: What kid?

DBH: There's this kid. And he has autism.

DGH: Since when do they have kids in jail?

DBH: No, they're not here. It's a program.

DGH: Delton, what's goin on? You was supposed to be getting out so we could hang out together.

DBH: I know. I will. It's just going to take a little longer is all.

DGH: How much longer? This is bullshit.

DBH: Danna. Listen to me. When I talked with the parole board they acted all concerned that I didn't have my high school diploma, I didn't have a place to live, or even a job lined up. They wanted me to get some experience doing something so I don't end up right back in here in a couple a months.

DGH: So they tell you you gotta babysit some stupid kid?

DBH: He ain't stupid. He's got autism.

DGH: I don't care what he got. They making you do a bunch of shit so you can't be out with me.

DBH: Well, maybe this could be a good opportunity for me.

DGH: Opportunity for what? Taking care of someone else's family instead of taking care of your own?

DBH: Danna, don't be like that. I'm doing what I gotta do to get out of here.

DGH: No. You rolling over like the dog they want you to be.

DBH: You're acting like I have a choice. It's not like I can just say, "Naw, I think I'll just skate instead."

DGH: No. But you just said it's a good opportunity for you.

DBH: It might be.

DGH: So you want to do it.

DBH: I'm willing to give it a shot. I'm gonna go meet the mom as soon as I'm done talking to you.

DGH: Fine. If you'd rather go hang with someone else's family rather than being with me, that's great.

DBH: I never said that.

DGH: You said you wanted to do this.

DBH: That's not what I meant.

DGH: Delton, kiss my ass! LINE DISCONNECTED

DBH: Stop acting.... Danna? Danna? Danna! Mother....
LINE DISCONNECTED

Chapter Seven

"I'm Judith Higgins," she said to the guard at the gate at Two Rivers Correctional Facility. "I'm supposed to meet Dr. Warren Fitzpatrick in Building E."

The guard turned to a computer monitor in his shack. "Yes, Miss Higgins, I have you right here." He handed her a lanyard with a neon green visitor tag hanging on it. "Put this around your neck, and please keep it visible the entire time you are within the walls." He leaned out the window of his guard house and pointed. "Stay on this road past two buildings, then make a right and you'll see Building E. It'll be the third building down on your left."

Judith draped the lanyard over her head. "Thank you."

"Yes, ma'am."

Following his directions to the letter she soon arrived at Building E. She parked next to Dr. Fitzpatrick's maroon Buick. Dr. Fitzpatrick burst out the door before she even got out of her car. "Mrs. Higgins, I'm glad you agreed to meet today." He held out his big hand.

"Miss Higgins." She shook it. "But please call me Judith."

"Okay, Judith." He walked her to the door and opened it for her. "Miss Blossom and I met yesterday with Mr. Hayes, and Mrs. Williams, his counselor assigned to this project by the prison system. And I have to say, we were both very impressed by the young man. I think you'll be pleasantly surprised when you sit down with him. He seems like such a sharp guy."

It seemed to Judith that the good doctor had changed his personality chip. He'd replaced the "arrogant asshole" chip with the "used car salesman" chip.

"Sharp, huh? That's good to hear."

The building was nothing more than a brick box on the outside with a large E over the door. Once inside the small foyer, they had to wait in front of a thick glass door, while someone peered at them through the video camera in the upper right corner. Satisfied they were no threat, the door buzzed and Dr. Fitzpatrick pulled it open with a loud clack.

Inside the tiny lobby, the building appeared much older than it had from the outside. Once white walls had long ago become a dingy gray. Streaks and scrapes marred the finish, and large dings and chips dotted the surface, highlighted by the bright white drywall underneath.

"Will Rena not be joining us?"

"Not today," Dr. Fitzpatrick said. "She had a family wedding something or other, and couldn't get out of it."

The squeak from Dr. Fitzpatrick's left shoe echoed off the walls of the spartan room. Judith could tell he was struggling to hide his irritation that Rena wasn't there. It made more sense now that he was going over the top to be nice, probably relying on his assistants to take on that role with people. Having to deal with this on his own today was probably eating him alive inside.

They walked down a hall, past a break area that was filled with the smell of fresh brewed, very strong coffee, turned a corner to another blank hallway with doors on the right, spaced every ten feet apart. He opened the first one for her, and she entered. This room was small, just enough space for a table in the center with two chairs on each side. The walls were clean, charcoal gray, and the room was lit with two long bright fluorescent tubes in the center of the ceiling. In one of the chairs sat a very young, African American man, arms crossed, looking none too happy.

Dr. Fitzpatrick made the introductions. "Miss Judith Higgins, let me introduce you to Mr. Delton Hayes."

"Hello, Delton," Judith said, doing her best to be upbeat.

"Hey," the man said with a curt nod.

An awkward silence followed, before Dr. Fitzpatrick tried to move the meeting forward. "Okay...ahhh...." He pulled out the chair across from Delton for her. "Why don't you sit here and we can all have a meaningful discussion."

Good Lord, this guy truly did not know how to deal with people. She took the seat and looked at the man across the table. Not a man. A boy. A boy in prison clothes. Sitting there, arms folded, waiting for her to do something. This was who Dr. Fitzpatrick and Rena decided was a good match for her son? Looking at him now, it didn't seem like a good idea. What could this man possibly teach Noah?

Dr. Fitzpatrick pulled a chair around to the end of the table. He sat down with a big, dumb smile and looked back and forth at them. "Well, this is nice."

There was an awkward silence. Judith looked at Dr. Fitzpatrick, who looked as uncomfortable in this role as a squid in a desert. And Delton sat quietly, staring intently at one of the many scratches on the table. Clearly he did not want to be here. If this was supposed to be the program that turned his life around, he didn't appear to be putting too much effort into it. Nor did he seem to care.

"Okay," Dr. Fitzpatrick said. "Shall we talk about Noah?"

"Yes. Let's," Judith said. "What do you know about autism, and why do you think you make a good candidate to work with him on this project?"

Delton sighed, leaned forward and put his elbows on the table. "I told the doc here and his girl that I didn't know nothin' about autism. They said it was okay and gave me a bunch of stuff to read and things to go through about your boy and all. Said it was easy so...."

"That's not exactly how the conversation went," Dr. Fitzpatrick said.

"Have you read any of the things they gave you?" Judith asked.

"I skimmed through some."

"Miss Blossom did say that you were capable of the activities given to you," Dr. Fitzpatrick cleared his throat and adjusted his glasses. "But it would also require a great deal of patience."

"Mr. Hayes," Judith said. "How interested are you in being a part of this program?"

Delton flattened his hand on the table in front of her. "Truth?"

Judith shrugged. "That's why we're here."

"I'm pissed about it." Delton leaned back and crossed his arms again.

Judith's mouthed dropped open. She looked over at Dr. Fitzpatrick, and shook her head.

Dr. Fitzpatrick avoided her glare and spoke to Delton. "What is upsetting you?"

"I'm pissed because I have to jump through hoops for everyone."

"What?" Dr. Fitzpatrick said.

"I'm in this program because the parole board can't trust a black man to learn from his mistakes and make something of himself outside the walls."

"Tell me you're kidding," Judith said.

"I ain't kidding," Delton snapped. "If I was white, I would have been let out."

"That is such bull," Judith said, scowling. "You're behind bars because of the stupid decisions that you made, not because you're black."

"You don't know why I'm in here," Delton said pointing at her. "You don't know nothin' about me, or my situation,"

"Okay," Dr. Fitzpatrick said, holding has hands up. "Let's relax and have a conver…."

"You're in here because you robbed a store with a gun," Judith said, pointing back. "I do know because I actually took the time to read the files I was given." She knew her voice was growing steadily louder, but she couldn't hold herself back. "I have a job and a special needs son to take care of—I'm not just sitting around in some jail cell—and I still found time to read your file. That's what you do when something is important."

"In Mr. Hayes' defense," Dr. Fitzpatrick, clearly rattled now, tried his best to speak calmly, "he just received his file yesterday."

"Man, this is bullshit." Delton jerked his chair away from the table with a loud screech across the cement floor, startling Judith and Dr. Fitzpatrick. "I didn't sign on to be lectured by some uppity white woman who don't know nothin' about nothin'."

A door opened in the other side of the room and a guard stepped in.

Judith fought back angry tears. There was no way she was going to let this little prick know he got to her. She glared at Dr. Fitzpatrick. "Oh, you're so right, Doc. I feel much better now." She jumped up, and her chair fell backward, clattering to the cement floor. She slammed open the door and rushed out.

Dr. Fitzpatrick was right on her heels. "Miss Higgins."

Judith stuck up her hand and shook her head. He stopped his pursuit. Tears streamed down her face by the time she reached the exterior doors. She slammed both open loudly and exited the building, bursting into a full-on cry when she reached her Kia. She sat in her car and wept hard for several minutes before turning the key and driving away.

Chapter Eight

The guard opened the door to the interrogation room, and nodded for Delton to enter. When he did, he was met with Taysha's scowl, jaw clenched tight as a vise. He dropped into a chair.

Taysha jumped up, reached over, and smacked him on the side of his head.

Delton rubbed his head and glared back at her.

"Oh no, you don't give me a look like that." Taysha walked around the table and smacked him again.

"What the hell you doing?" Delton rubbed his head again.

"I'm trying to knock some sense loose in a place where I don't think there is any to begin with."

Delton shook his head. "You wasn't there. You'd a probably hit her too."

"No, I wouldn't have, Delton Benjamin Hayes. Because I'm not plumb stupid." She raised her hand again, and Delton covered his head with his hand. "What in the whole great green world were you thinking?"

"I don't know." Delton shook his head and looked at the table. "I don't know."

"You was acting all excited, like you wanted to impress Miss Rosie Blossom. What happened after we all met?"

"I talked to my little sister."

"What does that have to do with anything?"

"She was upset."

Taysha walked back to her chair and sat down. "All right then. Let me hear it."

Delton looked up at her. "Where did you learn to be a counselor—the army?"

Taysha pointed a finger at him. "Don't give me anymore lip. Just tell me about your sister."

Delton sighed. "Well, when I told her about the parole board sending me into this program 'steada letting me out, she flipped. I tried to explain that it might be a good opportunity for me, and she took it to mean I was more excited to be with this kid than be with her. Then she hung up on me." Delton shook his head again and looked at the wall. "That was just before I met with Miss Higgins. By the time I got in there, I was so upset about Danna, I kinda lost it with the mom and the doc."

"Yes, you did." Taysha said. "Which means you blew it for your little sister too, because you won't be getting outta here anytime soon."

Delton slapped both hands on his forehead and sat back in his chair. "Fuck, I'm an idiot."

"Son, look at me."

Delton dropped his hands to the table and looked up at the woman across from him. "I'm glad you said that. It means I hit you up-side the head just in the nick of time."

Delton couldn't help but smile.

"As of right now, I have been informed that you have been dropped from this program. I don't know if I can straighten this out or not, but I'm gonna try my darndest."

"You think you can fix this?"

Taysha shrugged. "We'll see. But if I do, I want you to keep in the forefront of your mind who you are doing this for, so you never go off the nut again."

Delton nodded. "Got it. I'm doing it for Danna."

"That's a nice thought, but no."

"Oh, I get it. I have to put all my energies into the boy."

"Nope." Taysha leaned in. "You're doing this for me."

"What?"

Taysha sat back and threw her hands up. "Don't act like that. I get paid extra for being in this. If you get kicked out I lose a really good gig."

Delton smirked.

"It ain't funny, son. Christmas is seven months away and my grandkids always got a list as long as my arm."

Chapter Nine

Sipping on her favorite stress snack, a chocolate chip malt from Lance's Drive-In Burgers, Judith sat in her car in her usual spot, kitty-corner from Grant Park. She had spent a great deal of time at that spot, watching a man she knew from her days at Danser, bring his wife, who was stricken too early with multiple sclerosis. Over the years, Judith had tracked the progression of the woman's disease. She went from walking slowly, to walking with a cane, to using a walker. And in just the last few weeks, they'd shown up with her in a wheelchair. Judith knew the disease was debilitating and destructive. She also knew the man loved his wife very much. She'd heard him talk of her at work. He was the kind of man who would do anything for his wife and never complain, because he knew every day he had left with her was a gift.

It gave Judith some peace to know this kind of love existed in the world.

The credit union commercial ended on the radio and "Ironic," by Alanis Morrisette began with its subtle guitar strums. Judith sighed, and tapped the power button on the radio. Now was not the time to listen to that song. It was "ironic" that it even came on the radio just then. Shaking her head she sipped on the straw only to hear a deep gurgling sound. It was a horrible noise—the dying cry of one of the most delightful treats ever. She shook the cup. It was nothing more than a used shell now. She had sucked the sweet soul out of it and still felt crummy.

Tossing it into the bag, she knew who she needed to talk to right now. She picked up her phone, and tapped on Darlene's face in the favorites section.

"Hey, Jude. How'd it go?"

"Don't ask. Can you watch Noah for a little while longer, while I go see Dad?"

"Oh no. It didn't go well?"

"I'll tell you later. Are you good with Noah?"

"Sure thing. He's here being a regular Lego architect. We're good."

"Thanks, Sis," Judith flipped the phone closed and started the car.

Judith was told at the front desk of Pleasant Oaks Retirement Home that she could find her dad in the Reception Hall. They called it the Reception Hall even though it was the everything room, from event and meeting room, to the dining hall where they ate every meal. All other times it was used as a commons for the residents to just hang out. Entering the well-lit room, she searched for her father. There was a large group of men watching baseball on the big screen TV. There were foursomes scattered here and there playing euchre. And then she spied her dad at a small table over by a window, playing chess. Perhaps, with some unseen dad power, he could feel her presence, because he looked up, smiled his gentle smile, and waved her over. She walked to him and kissed him on the cheek.

Grabbing a chair from another table, Judith slid it over and took a seat. Her dad gestured to the man across from him. "Jude, this is Lee Dunham who's losing to me today."

Lee chuckled, "Yes, I am. It's nice to meet you."

"Nice to meet you, Lee." She shook his hand.

"So what brings you in today, honey?" Her father said, his voice now soft and frail. Judith could see how time had taken him down. He reached for a chess piece with a hand withering from years, skin bunching up around the knuckles. Skin drooped under his chin and around his eyes. But what Judith always keyed into the most was the voice—once strong, loud, and firm—now soft, quiet, and calm.

She thought about the other important voice in her life—her mother's sweet, tender voice; like a song when she spoke. Just the sound of it eased the all the tensions of life. Judith had kept a few voice mails on her old phone, after her mother had passed away, that she would listen to often. But when she switched phones they were lost. Judith went into a depression for another week. It was like losing her mother all over again.

"Eh?" her dad said.

Judith shook her head back to the moment. "What?"

"What brings you in today?"

"Oh, you know." Judith took a deep breath. "Sometimes a girl just wants to see her dad."

He smiled and patted her shoulder. "Well, a dad always wants to see his daughter."

She smiled.

"Everything okay?" He looked at the board to see Lee move his rook two spaces sideways.

"Just..." Judith sighed. "Life." She put her elbow on the table and leaned into her hand heavily.

"Darlene told me about the thing you got Noah into."

"Remind me to hit her later," Judith said. "But Noah isn't getting into it."

"Why's that?" her father asked.

"Because it turned out to be a very bad situation. And not

one I'm looking to expose Noah to."

Her father reached down, slid a bishop three spaces diagonally right, and left his finger on it, scanning the rest of the board. "What happened?"

"I met with the guy today. In fact I just came from there. He was a complete jerk who had this attitude against me for no reason at all."

Her father released his finger from the bishop and took off his glasses. He grabbed the corner of his shirt and wiped the lenses. "I guess that doesn't matter, does it?"

"What do you mean?"

"You're not the one who has to spend each day with him. He's Noah's guy. It probably should've been Noah who went to meet with him instead of you."

"Dad. What are you saying?" She pulled her head back from her hand and looked at her father, trying to see if he was joking with her. "Noah doesn't know any better. It's my job to protect him from things like this."

"Things like what? People that you don't like?"

"He had a real attitude. Like he was about to go off the rails kind of attitude. I'm not going to put Noah into that kind of environment."

Her father put his glasses back on and looked her straight in the eye for the first time this visit. "Jude, how much better is Noah getting just going to a regular school every day?"

"He has autism, Dad," Judith said. "He's not going to ever grow out of it."

"But is there a chance he could improve?"

"Yes, but...."

"Has he shown any signs of it in the last two years at his school?"

"Not yet. But it's a process."

Her father shook his head. "Doesn't sound like a very good

process to me."

"I can't believe I'm hearing you tell me it's a good idea to put Noah with a crazed prisoner."

"I don't believe he's crazed or they never would have picked this guy. What I do believe is that my grandson, who is facing so many challenges, should be able to get every opportunity available to him. There's a doctor at a very fine university who thinks this would be a good program for the boy. So much so, that he was selected, out of God knows how many other children, and assigned a person to work with him."

"It's an experiment, Dad," Judith pleaded.

"Sure it is," her dad said. "But life is an experiment." He looked back up from the board again. "Look, I know it's hard for a parent to let a child go out on his own, especially one with so many challenges, but I also know that you can't protect them from everything forever. Once in a while they have to bump their knees, skin their elbows, and even deal with people with attitudes."

"I'm not afraid of this guy giving Noah attitude. I'm afraid of him getting pissed off and hitting Noah...or worse."

Her father nodded his understanding while watching Lee move his rook across the board to take his bishop. "Well, if you're truly worried that it could be a violent situation, I get your unwillingness to move forward. But I have a hard time believing they would pick violent criminals for a project with kids." He moved his queen to take the rook. "Check."

Lee winced. "Crap. You led me right into that, you son of a gun."

Her father turned in his chair to look at her. "Jude, the biggest thing parents should worry about is not protecting their kids, but overprotecting them so much that they will never have the where-with-all to handle the world on their own when the parents aren't around anymore. And I think in Noah's case, that would concern you much more than putting him with a guy who may have an attitude. In fact, I would think it would scare the hell out of you."

Judith stared at her father. She remembered times as a teenager when he said things she disagreed with, and she was positive he was the most stupid person in the world. She realized she much preferred that to now, when she disagreed with him, but felt he was probably the smartest man she ever knew. She had nothing to say. No perfect words to counter his argument. And somehow saying, whatever, like she flippantly threw out when she was 16, wasn't going to cut it here. Judith leaned over, threw her arms around him, and buried her head in his shoulder. "Dad, I'm scared."

"Judith, I have news for you," he said. She felt his arm slowly reach around her shoulder. "I can't tell you how many nights I lost sleep because I was scared or hurting about something having to do with you and Dar. Being a parent takes a special kind of strength. It takes more gumption to let your kid fall flat on his face to learn a lesson, than it does to catch him before he ever gets a bruise." He leaned his head against hers. "Jude, you're a good mother. And if all your alarms are going off and telling you this is the wrong move for Noah, then don't do it. Just be sure."

Judith lifted her head and kissed his cheek. "Thanks for always being my dad. And just so you know, my alarms are going off like crazy about this. There's no way I'm sending Noah into this program."

He smiled. "I understand. And for the record, I don't think that fear ever goes away. If you knew how much I still worry about you and your sister every day…." his soft voice trailed off.

Judith looked up at him. "I'm sorry I still give you so much to worry about." Then her phone buzzed. She pulled it out of her coat pocket and saw Darlene was calling. "Hold on, Dad, it's Dar." She tapped it. "Hey, what's up?"

"There's a woman here from the Two Rivers Correctional Facility. She says she's Delton Hayes' counselor and she wants to talk to you."

"His counselor? What does she want?"

"Ahhh...I just said...to talk to you."

Judith rolled her eyes. "Okay. Tell her I'll be right there."

"All right. Tell Dad I..." Judith tapped off the call. "Gotta go, Dad. There's someone from the prison at my apartment to talk about this." She kissed his cheek one more time.

"Okay, hon. Tell Dar I said hi."

"I will." Judith stood, and set the chair back to the other table. "Nice to meet you, Lee."

"Yeah," Lee waved, but never took his scowling face off the chess board.

Outside, Judith noticed an envelope on her car windshield. As she got closer she realized it was a parking ticket. She looked at the space where she was parked, and to her horror she saw blue lines. "Oh no." She jerked the envelope from under the wiper and ripped it open. Her knees wobbled when she saw the $200 fine for parking in a handicapped space. Closing her eyes, Judith screamed to the sky. "Fuck!"

Chapter Ten

When she opened the door to her apartment, Judith saw a short African American woman sitting on her sofa talking to Darlene. She threw her purse, keys, and the damn ticket down on a stool next to the door and took off her jacket.

"There she is," Darlene said. "Hey, Jude, this is Taysha Williams. Taysha, this is my sister, Judith Higgins."

Taysha stood with a bright pleasant smile, and offered her hand. "It's so nice to meet you, Miss Higgins."

"Sure, what can I do for you, Miss Williams?" Still burning about the ticket, Judith plopped down into a chair next to Dar.

"Well, uh…" Taysha sat back down. "I wanted to take a moment and discuss your meeting with Delton."

"Yeah?" Judith scoffed. "What's there to discuss?"

"Well, Delton had just come from a disappointing phone call with his little sister, and he was a bit out of sorts."

"Out of sorts?" Judith sat forward. "Your boy went off the rails, Miss Williams. I was afraid he was going to jump me."

"Oh, Miss Higgins, there's no need to worry about that. Delton wouldn't hurt anybody."

Judith scowled. "Are you crazy? He's in prison. He's capable of anything."

"Judith," Darlene said, patting her sister's hand. "Calm down."

"Calm down?" Judith pulled her hand back, and turned on her sister. "Darlene, you weren't there. He had this crazed look in his eyes!"

"Kind of like you do now?" Darlene said. "Look, Sis, I know you want to protect Noah, but Taysha here just wanted to explain something. She's not here to argue with you."

Judith could sense her eyes filling with tears. Tilting her head to the ceiling, she took a deep breath, and blew it out slowly through her mouth.

"What's wrong, Jude? Did something go wrong at Dad's?"

Judith closed her eyes and shook her head. "No." A tear escaped from her right eye and she immediately wiped it away. "But when I came out, I saw that I hadn't been paying attention where I parked, and I had a ticket for parking in a handicapped spot."

"Ouch," Darlene said.

"Yeah, ouch." Judith sniffled. "Two hundred dollars that I can't afford to pay."

"Oh, I get it. That makes sense to me," Taysha said.

"What makes sense?" Judith asked.

"You had a troubling moment before you came here, and you were less than gracious at our first meeting." She looked over at Darlene. "I was about to walk out of this room thinking this white woman was off the rails."

Judith smiled. "I'm sorry, Miss Williams."

"It's Mrs. Williams, and let me ask you something. Do you know why Delton is in prison?"

"Yes," Judith nodded. "I read his file. He robbed a store at gunpoint."

"That's not the real story," Taysha said. "He wasn't robbing the store for money, he was robbing it for food. It wasn't even a working gun. It didn't have a trigger. He found it in a dumpster that he had climbed in, just to find food for his sister to eat. Their mother spent all the money on drugs, and they didn't have anything left for food. His sister was so hungry she was crying all night, so he tried to do something about it."

"Are you kidding me?" Darlene said.

"No, ma'am," Taysha said. "And they were sure the parole board was going to let him out. But that didn't happen. They put him in this program instead. And when he tried to explain it to his little sister, she was very upset, and hung up on him. So Delton came to your meeting, feeling like he let his little sister down again. All he wanted to do was make it all right with her. He was frustrated and couldn't think of anything else."

Judith took another deep breath.

"Jude?" Darlene said.

Judith nodded. "Okay, Mrs. Williams. Set up another meeting with Delton. We'll try this again."

"That's good news," Taysha said with a smile. She stood. "And please call me Taysha."

Judith stood and shook her hand. "Thank you, Taysha."

Chapter Eleven

Judith sat in the room alone, looking over at the mirror. The fact that there could be someone behind that glass watching her, creeped her out. Fortunately she didn't have to wait long before Taysha entered, with Delton following. When his eyes met Judith's, he looked down, sheepishly.

"How are you, Miss Higgins?" Taysha pointed to a chair and Delton sat in it. Taysha took the chair next to him. "Well," she said with an overly joyful breath. "Here we are again for Take Two."

There was a moment of awkward silence. Delton put his hands on the table and never took his eyes off them.

"Delton, do you have anything to say to Miss Higgins?" Taysha prodded.

"Yeah. Uh…" he said quietly. He put his hands in his lap and sat up straight. His eyes only met hers every now and then when he spoke. "I wanted to say that I'm sorry for my attitude last time we met. I was upset before I came into the room, and I took it out on you. I apologize."

"Thank you, Delton," Judith said. "Your apology is accepted. It takes maturity to own it when one screws up."

Delton gave her an appreciative smile and a nod.

Taysha nudged him with her elbow. "And how do you feel about the project?"

"I'm actually looking forward to working with your son. I think it will be a great opportunity for me. And I hope I can make a difference."

Judith crossed her arms on the table and leaned in close. "Okay, Mr. Hayes. Let's cut the bullshit."

Delton looked up at her.

And Taysha looked over, mouth open in surprise.

"I don't want you to sit there and talk to me like Mrs. Williams' trained parrot." She looked over at Taysha. "In fact it would be good if you just left."

Taysha and Delton looked at each other nervously.

Judith waved her out. "Go on. Get out." She nodded to the mirror. You can stand behind the glass with God knows who else is back there, and let me talk with Delton alone."

"Ah…Miss Higgins," Taysha said quietly. "Actually there's supposed to be a representative of the correctional facility in this room with you at all times when you're here with a prisoner."

"Okay." Judith nodded. "Let me put it like this. If I don't get some one-on-one time with Delton, I am out of this project for good. How clear is that for you?"

Taysha stood. "I'll just be right outside if either of you need anything." She walked over and opened the door. A guard stood there blocking her way. She smacked him in the chest. "Move! Give these two some time." She turned, smiled brightly, closing the door behind her.

Delton looked back at Judith. She thought she saw trepidation in his eyes.

"Now I want the truth," she said. "How do you feel about taking care of my son?"

"Oh." Delton shrugged nervously. "I think it'll be good."

"I'll tell you how I feel," Judith said. "I don't want you

anywhere near him." She could read in Delton's eyes that she'd struck a direct hit. "But it really isn't about me or how I feel. It's about my son, and how he feels."

Delton gave her a moment, then spoke. "Okay then. So you're going to go on with the program?"

"I will if you can be honest with me about how you feel about working with him."

"I'm looking forward to it." Delton said. "I think it'll be good."

"And I said cut the bullshit." Judith said.

Delton shook his head in frustration. "Look, lady. What do you want from me? I said I wanted to work with your child."

"And I don't believe you for a second."

"Why not?"

"Because I know you'd rather be with your sister than with my son."

Delton stopped. His eyes narrowed. "I don't think that part is any of your business."

"Mr. Hayes, let me explain this to you. I am about to trust you," she pointed at him, "you, with the single most precious thing I'll ever have in this life. I'm supposed to agree to hand over my very heart and soul to someone who has committed a crime, and is behind bars for it. Do you have any idea the stress that causes me?"

Delton looked at the table.

Judith continued. "There's no way you do, because you have yet to have a child of your own. But if I'm going to do this, everything needs to become my business. Because I've witnessed, from past experience with you, that other things in your life can affect your attitude. And that frightens me where my son is concerned."

Delton put up a hand. "Okay. I see where you're going with this, and I want to assure you…."

"No." Judith said. "Answer my fucking question. How do you feel about taking care of my son?"

Delton nodded, put his arms on the table and looked Judith straight in the eye. "The truth is, it would not be my first decision of things to do. I have a sister outside of here that I worry about every day, and I thought I was going to get a chance to be with her again. But I was told I have to prove myself in this program before I get a shot at life outside the walls. So it's not that I don't want to take care of your son, I just felt that I shouldn't have to jump through any more hoops. I've done my time for my crime."

Judith gave him a moment to see if he would say anything more. He stared sternly back at her, unflinching. She nodded. "Thank you for your honesty. Now let's talk about my son."

"Yes, let's talk about Noah Higgins," Delton said. "Six years old, but has never spoken a real word. He attended Keener School for Special Needs for one year and Hanson Elementary for the last two and has seen little to no progress. He spends his days doing particularly autistic child things like stacking cans and pouring water from glass to glass. Playing with Legos is a favorite pastime. He gets overwhelmed with loud noises, does not do well with human contact, and is prone to meltdowns."

Judith sat back in her chair and looked at the young man across the table. He was no longer the cowed little boy he had been when he entered the room.

Delton shrugged. "Yeah, I read the file. It's what you do when something is important."

Judith looked away for a moment and then back at Delton. "Delton Hayes, I don't like you. I think you are a cocky little prick."

Delton smiled. "Judith Higgins, I don't like you either. I think you're an up-tight control freak, who thinks she's the only one on the planet with the right answer for everything."

Judith's eyes narrowed and she fought the urge to smile back.

"So," Delton said. "Are you in, or are you out?"

Judith scratched the side of her head. "You going to do the best job you can?"

"My best is all I know how to do. I don't even know how to turn the dial back from that. Besides, it's just as important for me and my sister's future, as it is for you and your boy's future."

Judith extended her hand. "Okay, I'll let Dr. Fitzpatrick know we're going ahead with this."

Delton smiled and shook her hand. "It'll be good. I promise."

The door burst open and Taysha re-entered the room. "Thank God that's over." She put her hand on her heart and appeared out of breath. "Working with you two is going to kill me from all the stress."

Chapter Twelve

It felt odd not dressing in the usual orange jumpsuit. Delton was given a new uniform for the special needs program. He wore dark trousers, a bright blue long-sleeved t-shirt with the Marmont College logo on it, and a gray jacket for the bus ride over to the facility. Everybody looked up at Hector and him when they walked into the cafeteria. He was happy that Hector was a part of the program too. Hector had always been a stand-up guy, and deserved to be involved.

Delton felt proud in his new clothes, and wished he had the opportunity to show Danna what he looked like. He had not heard one word from her since she hung up on their phone call the previous week. She hadn't even shown up at her usual visit time. Delton decided he couldn't worry about it. She had to deal with it however she could. It was a disappointment to him as well, but he would show her how to deal with setbacks by standing up to the challenge, and not falling apart every time things didn't go his way. Challenges were a part of life, and his response to them was what mattered most.

Now that the cafeteria was clearing out and most of the inmates were headed off to their duties for the day, Delton could see who was in the program with him.

Dwight Lawson walked up and fist-bumped him and Hector. "Man, you two is in this?"

"Yeah, we are." Hector said.

Ken Miller, a white dude in his mid-thirties walked over and nodded at them. Delton knew him by name but never talked to him. The guy was always quiet and kept to himself pretty much.

"Dude! We're gettin' outta here for the day!" Delton turned and saw Rick Simpson walking up. He had no hat and his hair was washed and slicked back. His hand was raised waiting for a high five.

"How'd you get in this?" Delton asked him.

Rick stopped in front of him, hand still held high. "It has been said that I show great potential for caring for others."

"Damn, man." Delton said. "I didn't even know you could take care of yourself."

Rick still had his hand up. "Don't leave me hanging here, brother."

"I ain't your brother." But he slapped Rick's hand anyway, to get him to move on more than anything else. Delton turned to Hector. "How did a hayseed like that get picked?"

Hector shrugged. "Maybe they thought one of the kids could teach him something." They both laughed.

"So, what kind of kid you got?" Delton asked Hector.

"Down syndrome,"

"Nervous?"

Hector smiled and nodded. "I wish I could say no. But yeah. I am."

"No problem, man. Me too."

"All right. Listen up," a guard named Jones said, walking up. "All of you line up against the wall here. We're going to have a few words." He was one of two armed guards. The other stood back a few feet behind him and watched all the inmates line up against the wall. When they were all in position, the guard continued.

"You have all been given a golden opportunity here. You have the chance to make a difference in the life of a young person. It's a pretty special thing and I hope you don't fuck it up. I'm saying that to you, to keep you on track." He started pacing back and forth in front of the men. "Since this program deals with kids, you need to be aware that there will be a zero-tolerance policy. There is to be no hitting of the kids. There is to be no shaking of the kids. There is to be no harsh language used. I don't even want to hear that you raised your voice. Are we clear?"

All of the men nodded.

"Good. Because if I do hear of any of those behaviors, myself, or Officer Gardener behind me, will come in there, drag your ass out, and you will never go back again. That is what zero tolerance means. You don't get two chances to fuck up. Just one. Got it?"

Again all of the men nodded.

Officer Jones nodded back and continued in a much softer voice. "All right, I got the business portion out of the way, now let me tell you how proud of you guys I am. This is a big challenge, and it takes guts to step up like this. I want you all to know that we're really pulling for you here." He looked back and forth across the line, then walked to a door to their left. "Okay. Outside this door is the bus. It will be here every morning. Today, we're walking you through the process, but from now on after breakfast you have the go-ahead to just come out this door and get on the bus." He opened the door. "Follow me."

They filed out and Delton saw the large blue bus sitting there chugging loudly, with the words "Michigan Department of Corrections" written across the side. Climbing aboard, he saw that all the counselors were already seated and waiting for them. Each of the inmates located their counselor and sat next to them. Delton found Taysha sitting right up front. "You ready?" She asked.

"I think so?" He shrugged. "Are you gonna be on here every day too?"

"No way." Taysha said looking out. "I'm not interested in being bussed around. We just come today because it's the first day and we wanted to talk you fools off the ledge if you felt you was about ready to jump."

Delton chuckled and sat back. "I can see that happening on the way back maybe. But right now we're all too excited just to be going off the reservation."

Once everyone was seated, the doors closed, the driver shifted gears, and the bus lurched forward toward their new adventure.

Arriving at the facility, Officer Jones stood up in front. "Listen up. You are to proceed out of this bus and straight in through those double doors. Do not take one step off the sidewalk. Your counselors will show you which room is yours. That will be your room every day for the next three months. Student assistants are already inside the rooms and ready to answer any questions you may have before the kids arrive. Are you ready to begin?"

Delton gave a small nod and looked back at Hector who was doing the same.

"All right. Let's move, men." Officer Jones stepped off the bus, and took up his position on one side of the short sidewalk. Officer Gardener was already in position on the other side.

Delton stood and stepped aside, letting Taysha take the lead. He followed her off the bus and put his foot down on a civilian sidewalk for the first time in five years. He took a deep breath. The air was cool and crisp and the sunlight seemed brighter here.

"Keep it moving, Hayes," Officer Gardener said.

Delton walked the 15 feet from the bus to the building, his heart leaping with excitement. This was the path of a man with a job and he was going to do his damnedest to impress everyone involved. He followed Taysha through the steel double doors into the building. They went down a long carpeted hallway with numbered doors on either side. Next to each door was a clear plastic sign with a printed piece of paper slid into it with two last names. One on his left read, "Hall - Miller," and one on his right read, "Lawton - Sanchez." Taysha led him to the end of the hall, to room number five. She opened the door and walked in. The sign next to the door read, "Higgins - Hayes." Delton smiled and touched it.

"Delton, c'mon," Taysha said waving him in. They passed through a small dark room with a large window, and a counter in front of it with big cushy barstools. Taysha walked straight through, into the room where Rena Blossom stood, looking as beautiful as ever. She smiled when she saw him. "Hello Delton," she said, offering her hand. "Believe it or not, we made it here."

Delton shook her hand. "I know it. I'm happy to be here."

Then Rena went instantly into business mode. "Okay, as you can see we have stocked the room with a few things. Unfortunately, due to the nature of getting the subject involved, we really didn't have the chance to determine exactly what the favorite playthings were. So I had to make some calls here myself."

Delton quickly scanned the room. The walls were off-white, with two large beanbag chairs in one corner. In another corner was a small pile of stuffed animals. Along one wall was a low shelf with a various assortment of items including Legos, blocks, and cans of food. In the center of the room sat a table with two chairs on either side. Delton stared at it. That was his desk at this new job. He pulled out a chair and sat down. He swiveled back and forth while he listened to Rena speak.

"I did see that he had Legos in his house so I made sure you were well stocked with those. He was playing with glasses of water when we made our initial visit so I have a couple of plastic glasses there too. If you need water, we can get you some." Rena pointed to each of the items as she spoke. "There is a bin of blocks here and some Play-Doh. There are also some books if he will allow you to read to him." She gestured to the corner. "There are a few stuffed animals there as well. I didn't see those at his house but quite often they can be soothing to a child with autism." She turned back to Delton. "Do you have any questions for me before the subject arrives?"

"The subject?" Delton asked.

Rena smiled. "I mean, Noah."

Delton wondered how they referred to him when he wasn't there. He shook his head. "I don't think I know enough yet to have any questions. I'll probably have some before lunch though."

"Okay then," she pointed to the mirror in the wall. "Mrs. Williams, another guard, and I will be right behind that glass the entire day. If anything comes up we will be available immediately to help."

"Sounds good," Delton said.

"Right now I have to leave you and go meet Miss Higgins out front. Noah should be in shortly," she said with her bright white smile. She walked to the door and waited for Taysha.

Taysha nudged his knee with hers. "Good luck."

"Thanks," Delton said.

They both walked out of the room and closed the door. Then Delton heard the unmistakable sound of a lock clicking in the door. A stern reminder that this was not really a job.

Chapter Thirteen

She could hear the Darth Vader theme coming from her purse. Judith looked in the rear-view mirror to check on her son. His head was leaning against the side of his carseat, staring blankly out the window. She pulled the phone out and tapped on the call. "Morning, Bernie."

"I just saw the email that says you won't be in today." Bernie sounded like he had been gargling with tacks again.

"Right. The project with Marmont starts today, and they wanted the parents to be there on the first day."

"But you had canceled the time-off request last week."

"Well, I had another meeting this weekend and decided to go ahead with the program. That's why I sent the email."

"Sure you did," Bernie said. "It gives you an opportunity to blow off work."

"What was that?" Judith couldn't imagine someone being that snarky.

"Nothing."

Judith held the phone out in front of her face. "You caught me red handed, Bernie. There's nothing I like more than not coming in to work so I can take my autistic son to a special crazy-ass experimental program with guys from prison. Oh joy, the day I'll have." She put the phone back to her ear.

There was a long pause before, "So, you'll be in tomorrow then?"

"That's the plan."

"See you then." The call clicked dead.

Judith tossed her phone onto the seat next to her. She knew Bernie would never let this drop. Somehow, he would make her pay for being so lippy with him. She looked in the rearview again. "Noah, Mommy needs to know when to keep her mouth shut, or she's going to get herself in trouble." Noah had not changed position. She'd always wondered what was going on behind those eyes. She had spent the weekend discussing with him how today would be different. He tended not to deal with change very well, so she at least had to make him aware how vastly different this was going to be. She wanted him to be prepared, but she knew it was still going to be difficult.

She arrived at the address she was given. It was a long plain cement building in a well-established office park. The parking lot was full, and there was a good amount of activity outside. Pulling in, she noticed a large blue bus parked by the side of the building with the words, "Michigan Department of Corrections" on the side. Judith pointed at it. "Look, Noah. Your new friend is already here."

She saw a line of young people in white jackets along the front of the building. They were obviously the student assistants waiting for their children to arrive. One by one they made their way to the parking lot to greet the parents and the children. Judith saw a boy with a walker, another was holding his mother's and father's hands and shaking his head back and forth while they were trying to walk him inside. Picking out an open spot in the center of the small lot, Judith pulled in, turned off the car, opened the door, and stood up. She shaded her eyes from the sunlight while she looked for Rena Blossom. She didn't have to look long.

She caught sight of Rena's red lips, looking neon as they reflected the early morning sunshine.

Rena waved, and rushed over. "Good morning," she said, smiling. "Isn't this exciting?"

"Okay," Judith said. "I'll go with exciting." She closed her door, walked around to the other side, and opened the back door. "Here we are, Noah." She unlatched his car seat, took him by the hand, and he jumped down on his own.

Rena knelt in front of him. "Hello, Noah. I'm glad to see you."

Noah sidled in next to his mother and buried his face in her leg.

Rena stood up immediately and took a few steps back. "Sorry," she said in a whisper.

"Not a problem," Judith said, patting Noah's head. "He overwhelms easily." She jerked his hand gently. "Come, Noah. Let's go in."

Noah stayed close but walked with her until they reached the front of the car. Then he could see all the people and the activity of the busy parking lot. He jerked his hand free, scooted back to his car door and covered his face with his hands.

Judith looked at Rena and shrugged. "Maybe by the end of this thing he'll feel comfortable enough to walk."

"That's something to shoot for," Rena said.

"C'mon, boy." Judith reached down and lifted him up.

Noah moaned his disagreement, but then saw Rena and covered his face with his hands again.

When they reached the building, Rena opened the door. Judith stepped in and immediately recognized the smells of new carpeting and fresh paint. The place looked and smelled clean, which she had to admit, instilled a certain amount of confidence.

Dr. Fitzpatrick was in the lobby, talking to someone who looked like a reporter. He nodded and waved at her when she passed. Judith realized that was the most pleasant experience she'd had with the man since they met.

Rena led her down a hallway that had doors on both sides. "Right in here." She opened a door and stepped back so Judith could enter.

Judith caught sight of the sign next to the door that read "Higgins-Hayes." She stopped for a moment and stared at it. She was really doing this. She was going to offer the greatest treasure of her life up to this man she hardly knew and didn't care for.

"Delton is waiting right through there," Rena said, probably wondering what was taking Judith so long.

Judith stepped into a small room with a window and a counter. Through a large window she saw Delton, sitting at a table. She could tell he was nervous, and that gave her some comfort. If he was nervous that meant he was taking this seriously.

"This is where we will be observing everything that goes on in there." Rena stepped up to the next door and flipped the latch. Judith caught sight of Delton jerk straight, preparing for the inevitable.

The door opened and Judith walked through with Noah. She nodded to Delton and he nodded back. "Are you ready for this?"

He smiled. "Ready as I'm gonna be."

She sat Noah down in a chair at the table and knelt in front of him. "Okay, Noah honey, today is the big day we've been talking about." She brushed hair out of his face. "Today you get to make a new friend." Gently she swiveled his chair. "His name is Delton."

Noah looked at Delton, his eyes grew wide, and he froze.

"Delton is going to teach you things, and play with you." She stood and stepped back next to Rena.

Delton lowered his shoulders and looked at Noah with a big toothy smile. "Hello, Noah. My name is Delton," he said, in the softest voice he could. "I want to be friends, and play together."

Noah continued to stare at him.

"Okay, Noah honey, I'm going to be right outside," Judith said. "You stay here and play with Delton."

Noah continued to stare.

Delton looked from Noah to Judith. "Let me guess, he ain't never seen a black man before, right?"

"What?" Judith said, scowling. "Yes."

Delton looked back at Noah. "What, did you have the TV on or something?"

Judith rolled her eyes and walked out the door.

"Okay, Delton and Noah, your time together starts now. Enjoy." Rena closed the door and turned to Judith. "Your sheet said that a Darlene Longwood will be picking him up every day. But she hasn't come in and signed the forms yet."

Judith nodded. "She will be by this afternoon."

"Okay, good. We can't release Noah to her until we meet her and she signs the forms." Rena took a seat on the closest stool to the door, opened a notebook that was on the counter, looked at her watch, and began writing.

There were three small thuds on the hallway door. Judith opened it to see Taysha standing there balancing three cups of coffee in her hands. "Oh, I got caught by a reporter. Did I miss the opening bell?"

"You didn't miss a thing. We just got here." Judith took two of the cups of coffee from her. "Bless you." She handed one to Rena who thanked her and took a drink.

Judith and Taysha each grabbed a stool at the counter and watched Delton struggle.

"So do you have any favorite games or toys you like to play with?"

Noah just stared at him, as if in a trance.

The door clicked open and Dr. Fitzpatrick poked his head through the opening. He looked at Judith and waved. "Ah. Hi,

Miss Higgins. How is it going?"

"It just started," Judith said. "But Noah's not protesting, which is..." She held up two thumbs.

"Good. Good." Clearly anxious, Dr. Fitzpatrick stepped into the room and walked over to her, his left foot squeaking with each step. "I saw you in the lobby but couldn't get away." He held out his hand and she shook his limp grip. "I wanted to say that I was surprised to hear you were going to be a part of this. I mean after...the talk."

"You can thank Taysha for that," Judith nodded toward her. "She helped us work everything out."

"Oh. Certainly." He rubbed his hand on his jacket. "Thank you, Miss Williams."

"Umm hmm," Taysha said.

"Well, ah, good luck."

"Thanks."

He smiled, squeak-stepped out of the room, and closed the door.

The three women looked back and saw Delton placing toys on the table for Noah to pick.

Taysha spoke quietly. "Does anybody know if he's ever gonna fix that damn shoe?"

All three women laughed.

Chapter Fourteen

He was wishing he could tap out right about now. This kid was doing nothing but staring at him, like he had a worm hanging out of his nose or something. Delton had laid out some Legos, a can of Play-Doh, and a few blocks on the table, but Noah wasn't having any of it. He didn't even look down at them. He only stared straight at Delton.

He looked up at the mirror. He knew all three women were in there watching him. Were they all laughing at this point? He wondered if they would eventually come in with a suggestion—something to help him out. He thought that at least Taysha would give a brother a hand. But there had been nothing so far from any of them.

Finally, Delton crossed his arms on the table, bent down, rested his chin on his hands, and stared back at Noah.

Noah looked back at him for another minute, then, for the first time since he got into the room, looked away from Delton's eyes to his hands. He studied Delton's position, then crossed his arms on the table, and rested his chin on his hands too.

Surprised, Delton sat up straight.

Noah sat back, startled.

"Oh no, man, I'm sorry." Delton dropped his head back

down. "It's cool. Let's just sit here like this for a minute."

It took a moment for Noah to settle again, but Delton was patient. Eventually the boy resumed his position and the two stared at each other.

Delton smiled at Noah and held it, but the boy did not follow suit. Though he stared back, he was expressionless. So the two remained in that position for what seemed like an hour, but Delton surmised was probably about five minutes.

Tired of sitting, doing nothing, and seemingly out of options, Delton scanned the room. Noah didn't appear to be interested in toys; perhaps there was something else. Spying the stuffed animals in the corner he looked back at Noah. "So what's your favorite animal?" Avoiding any quick movements, he slid back off the table, crawled out of his chair, across the room, and over to the pile of stuffed animals.

Noah lifted his head, sat back, and looked over his shoulder at Delton.

"You like any of these?" Delton picked up a small green dragon with little floppy wings. "How about this dragon?" He made it fly in the air, mouthing a whooshing sound. Using his fingers he rustled them in front of the dragon's mouth and tried his best to sound like a stream of fire.

Noah sat there, looking over his shoulder in what, Delton thought, was a most uncomfortable position. He crawled over and slowly put a hand on Noah's chair, swiveling it around.

Noah looked down at his feet, then quickly on both sides of the chair.

"Sorry, Noah. I didn't mean to spook you. I was just turning you around so you could see better."

Noah jumped from his chair, turned around, and looked at it. He reached over and gave it a shove and it swiveled until the back hit the table. He grabbed the arm and pulled it farther away and gave it another shove. The chair turned all the way around.

"Do you want to sit in it, and I'll spin you?"

Noah positioned himself along one of the arms, and then walked it around and around.

Delton watched him for a few minutes. Noah continued to turn the chair in circles and walk around it. "I can spin you while you sit in it?" Noah acted as if he no longer existed. All that existed now was the chair. He continued to turn in circles with it.

Perhaps, Noah didn't understand what he meant. Standing, Delton stepped over and reached down to catch Noah and place him in the chair. "Here. Let me show you something fun." But as soon as his hands were around Noah, the boy made a sound that was half crying, half screaming. The volume of it startled Delton and he jumped back. "Sorry," Delton said. He turned to the mirror. "I'm sorry. I didn't hurt him. I swear." He could feel his own heart pounding for fear he would get thrown out of the program on the first day. "I'm sorry, Miss Higgins. I wasn't trying to do nothin' but spin him in the chair."

Three taps were heard on the glass. Nothing more. He assumed that meant everything was okay. At least there weren't any guards busting through the doors dragging him out to the bus. It appeared he was going to remain in the program.

Looking back at Noah, who was still turning the chair, Delton realized he was completely out of options. The boy was running this show and there was nothing he could do about it. He decided to nestle down into one of the bean bag chairs and relax while Noah got this out of his system.

One hour later the boy was still going at it. He didn't slow, didn't change directions, didn't stop for a breath. He just continued to spin the chair in circles. Delton had no idea how that could be fun, let alone how the boy continued without puking. "Aren't you getting tired of that yet?"

Noah continued.

Delton picked up a plush stuffed duck, surprised at how soft it was. Rolling it over in his hands he realized there was something inside the head. When he squeezed, it squeaked.

Noah stopped turning and looked at the duck.

Delton squeaked it two more times.

Noah looked from the duck to Delton and back to the duck.

Delton squeaked it again.

Noah started turning the chair once more.

Squeaking the duck a few more times, Delton was searching for even the slightest reaction, but Noah never slowed again. The duck squeak was nothing more than distant background noise to the boy, and of no concern. Delton realized he, too, was as useless to the boy as the squeak of the duck.

Chapter Fifteen

"I'm telling you right now, this day is pretty much done," Judith said. She'd seen her son discover new items or actions before and knew he could last for hours, or even all day doing the same thing. "This is new for him and he's found something to take the edge off. He's going to be turning that chair the rest of the day."

"That's okay," Rena said. "Noah is only half of the project. Now we have the opportunity to see how Mr. Hayes reacts to the situation." She continued to jot small sentences down in her notebook.

Judith looked out at Delton. He sat on the bean bag chair looking at the duck in his hands. She could read the frustration on his face, and she found herself almost feeling sorry for him. She knew he had not anticipated his morning running this way at all. But he would quickly learn what she had experienced; that there is no way to be sure you're making a difference with an autistic child until all of a sudden he decides to let you know.

"I'm going to get some air and stretch my legs." Judith stood and walked to the door. "Can I get anything for anybody while I'm out?"

Rena shook her head. "No, thank you." Taysha was leaning

on her hand, eyes closed.

Judith left the room and walked down the now silent hallway. Looking at the names on the walls by the doors, she wondered how things were going in each room—wondered what hurdles each of these parents had to jump on a daily basis.

When she reached the lobby, a man sprung from a chair. "Excuse me, are you a parent of one of the children?" It was the reporter that had been talking to Dr. Fitzpatrick when she walked in. He had on a blue windbreaker over a yellow sweater, and he was holding his phone out in front of him like a microphone.

"Yes, I am."

"Hi. I'm Jason Kitchener with Michigan-Online. Do you mind if I ask you a few questions?"

"I'm sorry, Jason," she said, shaking her head. "I'm really not the one to talk to about this." She turned and left him hanging there with his phone in the air.

"Okay," he said. "Have a good day."

She opened the outer doors and took a deep breath of fresh air. Except for the occasional car winding down the curvy road, it was quiet out here as well. It gave her a chance to be alone with her thoughts.

She had been impressed with Delton so far. Not that he'd made a big impact on Noah, but that he showed the patience necessary to handle a child with that deep a disability. He had real terror in his eyes after Noah's outburst. Judith had to let him off the hook by tapping on the glass. Rena had told her not to interfere in any way with the interaction between them, but Judith couldn't let him twist in the wind. She felt that in order for this experiment to be worth anything, he had to at least be aware of what was acceptable and what wasn't. If Delton felt afraid every time Noah squawked, he would be completely ineffectual—not willing to really try anything for fear of upsetting her son.

Looking to her right, Judith spied a woman leaning against the corner of the building, smoking a cigarette. Thinking this was probably another one of the mothers, she decided to go say hi to a fellow guinea pig parent. As she drew closer she saw the woman's long hair was unbrushed, and pulled back into a frizzy ponytail. The woman turned to her and nodded. Judith could see she wore a black t-shirt with a picture of skulls surrounded by lightning bolts with the words "Metallica, World Magnetic Tour."

The woman blew out a puff of smoke and said, "Hi."

Judith nodded. "How are you?"

"Eh," the woman shrugged. "Not used to getting up this early." She laughed. "But you gotta do what you gotta do. Right?"

"Yep." Judith instantly regretted walking down.

"I'm Sadie."

"Ju...dee. I'm Judy."

"I'm assuming you got a kid here?" Sadie said, and took another puff.

"Yes."

"What's wrong with him?"

"He's autistic," Judith said.

Sadie blew out her smoke. "Autism, man. That's some serious shit."

"Yes, it is," Judith said. "How about your child?"

"Intellectual development disorder. They say it's caused by fetal alcohol syndrome, but I think that's horse shit."

"Why is that? Did you not drink when you were pregnant?"

"Oh, I drank," the woman said. "But so have so many other mothers, since the dawn of time, and there's nothing wrong with any of us." The woman took another drag off her cigarette and blew out the smoke. "They are continually finding ways to make people feel guilty about enjoying their lives." She flicked the butt into the parking lot. "Well, I better get back in there. Catch ya later, Judy."

Judith nodded. "Yes."

The woman walked back into the building leaving Judith to

wonder how much Sadie's mother drank while being pregnant. She just couldn't understand that type of thinking. You are given a great responsibility when you're pregnant. All you have to do is go for nine months without succumbing to your little vices. Literally a human life depends on you. And you are so damn selfish that you can't even do that? You can't bother to do whatever it takes to give your defenseless unborn child every opportunity to thrive… to have a shot at being healthy?

She decided to get back. Walking to the door she saw Jason Kitchener coming out. He saw her, gave her a wave, and headed into the parking lot.

Judith walked back in and re-entered the hallway of doors. She scanned the name signs again, and thought about the parents one more time. Were they like Sadie? Were their kids victims of selfish parents whose abuses started while they were still in the womb?

She opened door number five and walked in. Through the window, she saw Noah still turning the chair.

The following is the article that appeared on michigan-online. com, June 3, 2019.

Unique Special-Needs Program Begins Today

Posted 11:32 a.m.

By Jason Kitchener jkitchener@michigan-online.com

The parents of 10 children with special needs such as autism, cerebral palsy, and muscular dystrophy are bringing their kids to Two Rivers today to be part of an ambitious sociological project coordinated by Marmont State College. Each child is to be paired with an inmate from Two Rivers Correctional Facility in a combined special needs/rehabilitation program. Dr. Warren Fitzpatrick, sociology professor at MSC, describes the project as "raising the bar" of what is capable in a rehab program. "It takes a much closer look at the extraordinary successes of programs like Puppies Behind Bars and hopes to build on those," Dr. Fitzpatrick said. "And at the end of the program, the inmates will be able to test for certification in the area of their child's disability."

A team of assistants and counselors are working on the project. "We have a graduate assistant for each child and they will be observing and recording every day," Dr. Fitzpatrick explained. "In each case, it is a student focusing primarily on that specific special need in their studies at the college."

Along with the student assistants, Two Rivers Correctional Facility has assigned each inmate with their own counselor. Taysha Williams, one of the counselors, explains her role. "It can often be frustrating to work with special needs children. We are there to guide the inmates, help them understand what is going through the mind of the child, and help them work through their own frustrations too." Mrs. Williams explains that it is not always the needs of the children the inmates have to concern themselves with. "This is a big step for the parents as well. The counselor may have to step in and handle any issues that may arise between the mother and the inmate."

Sadie Hanson, mother of one of the children is excited about the project. "It gives the mothers a break from the constant care we have to give."

"It is truly a unique collaboration between families and two state institutions," Dr. Fitzpatrick explained. "It's a great example of what is possible when everyone shares the same vision."

The program is scheduled to last for the next six months, but Dr. Fitzpatrick said it could take much longer to judge the value of the project. "It will take another year or two after that to sift through and organize all the data, to determine the level of success of the project."

COMMENTS:

Tigerfan25: Am I the only one who thinks this is a bad idea?

EWarner: Negative Tigerfan25. I can't imagine anyone putting there kids in a room with a prisoner. Seems like there asking fro trouble.

Guinesslover: WTF! Did this doctor just compare special needs kids with dogs?!?!

roseglass: Actually I know a Iraq War vet with terrible PTSD who has a stress dog from the Puppies Behind Bars program. The dog has been great and he has said many times that he would have probably put a bullet in his own head if it weren't for that dog. It has saved his life and that is because of the effort put in by an inmate. I'm excited to see what these guys are capable of when given the chance!

Chapter Sixteen

Noah turned the chair the remainder of the morning. There was nothing that would dissuade him—nothing else that interested him.

Delton checked all the stuffed animals to see if any of the others made noises. Only the duck squeaked. He lined them up neatly in the corner, the bigger, taller ones in back, and the shorter, smaller ones in front. He remembered hearing Rena say something about Noah having Legos at home, so that was where he headed next. He built buildings, bridges, little cars to drive over them, and set up the little Lego people along the edge of the table. Noah never looked up once, from his circle tour, to see what was happening. However, Delton had to admit, he enjoyed the time. As a kid he had heard of Legos, but his mother would never have spent the money on such things. This was the first time he had ever seen them, let alone touched and played with them. He could understand the draw. The bright clean colors, and the millions of ways they could go together and allow you to build anything you could think of. He wished he could get Noah involved. He was sure they could have fun together.

Eventually he lost interest with the Legos and put them all away. He disassembled everything and then swept his arm across the table, pushing all of the Legos back into the bucket, making a racket doing so. He looked over at Noah. The boy never slowed.

Returning the Legos to the shelf, Delton decided to get out the Play-Doh next. This was a toy that he'd had as a kid, and when he popped the lid off the blue, he caught a whiff of that unique smell. It instantly took him back 12 years. He raised the can in the air, tipped it and let the dough plop onto the table.

No response from Noah.

Delton opened the other jars and started rolling out logs, and flattening pancakes. He made little Play-Doh people, dogs, horses, and trees. Each time he finished another creation, he set it at the edge of the table in front of Noah, hoping it would spark his interest. Noah showed none.

Then Rena's voice came from a speaker in the ceiling. "Lunch in fifteen minutes."

Noah stopped, looked up, stood for a moment staring at the ceiling, then continued spinning the chair again.

"Little dude, I can't believe you can do that for so long," Delton said. "I can't do anything for that long except sleep." He got busy disassembling his dough people and putting the colors back in the correct cans.

On cue, fifteen minutes later, Rena opened the door and walked in with two trays. Each tray had a plate with macaroni and cheese, applesauce, and peas and carrots. Taysha followed her with two drinks.

Judith leaned against the door jamb.

Noah stopped and looked back at his mom.

"Time to eat, honey." Judith said.

Noah pushed the chair back to the table and sat down.

"Man," Delton looked up at Judith. "I've been trying to get him to do that all freaking morning long."

Judith smiled.

Rena set the trays on the table. "I hope you like mac and

cheese. Judith said that Noah liked it."

"Sounds good to me," Delton said. "If it ain't prison food, it's a gourmet meal as far as I'm concerned."

Noah took a bite of his mac and cheese and set down the spoon. With both hands he flapped his fingers back and forth against his palms.

Rena stepped back from the table. "Eventually you will probably feed him without us in here, but today, being the first day and all, we wanted to come in and give you a little company."

"I appreciate it."

Taysha set the small drink in front of Noah. "Here you go, honey." Then she set a large drink in front of Delton. "How you doing?"

"I feel about as useful as...," he shrugged, "as nothin'."

"You're doing well," Judith said.

Delton stopped chewing for a moment, surprised at her positive response.

"Patience is the name of the game here, and quite frankly," Judith shrugged, "I'm pleasantly surprised so far."

"I was sorry about getting him all upset."

Judith smiled. "That wasn't a problem. All kids get upset now and then. Autistic kids get upset even more than that."

"There will be times," Rena added, "that he will be very upset, either by something you did, said, or inferred. You can't let that stop you from trying."

Noah picked up his spoon and scooped up some applesauce. He continued his finger flapping with the other hand.

"What's he doing there?" Delton asked, nodding toward Noah. "That thing he's doing with his fingers like that."

"That's his stimming response," Rena said.

"His what?"

"It's a self-stimulating activity," Rena explained. "It helps him cope with his anxieties."

Delton must have looked completely confused, because Taysha continued with the explanation. "You know what it's like when you drop a bottle of soda pop? You have to twist the cap off slowly and let the fizz escape so it don't explode?"

Delton nodded.

"That's what he's doing when he flaps his fingers. He's letting his fizz out."

Delton watched Noah closer. The boy made no eye contact with anyone in the room. He looked only at the food in front of him, but when there was nothing in his hands his fingers flapped madly.

"So he's coping just fine," Taysha said. "How are you doing?"

"I'm all right," Delton took a drink and swallowed. "Just frustrated is all. I feel so useless. He don't even know I'm here." He pointed over at the stuffed animals with his burger. "Other than when he walked in here, he never looked at me again until I made that duck quack over there. He stopped for two seconds, and then," he swirled his finger in the air, "around he goes again, for the rest of the morning."

"A typical autistic response," Rena said. "Especially in an unfamiliar environment, to find a new activity like this that is safe, time consuming, and all encompassing."

"You think he's gonna do that all afternoon too?" Delton asked.

"I'd put money on it," Judith said.

Delton sat back and threw his hands in the air. "What good am I, then?"

"Easy, tiger," Taysha said.

"I don't want you to be frustrated," Rena said. "This is a long journey, and the first steps are the hardest ones to take. It's important that you're here, in the room with him. He will get used to you. This is his way of doing it."

"So what do I do the rest of the afternoon if he plays merry-go-round with the chair again?"

"Read to him," Judith said. Everyone looked back at her. "Let him hear your voice." She stepped forward. "It doesn't matter if he doesn't respond to it. He hears you. And the more he hears you, the more he will get used to you, and the more comfortable he will become around you. Eventually, there will be interaction between you two. I can't tell you how long that will take. It took months for him to get used to my own sister. But it happened."

Delton nodded to her, and ate a spoonful of mac and cheese.

The three women stayed with them until they finished eating, then they cleaned up the table while Delton and Noah took bathroom breaks.

As soon as lunch was over, they left the room for round two to begin.

It started promisingly enough. Noah sat at the table staring at Delton, hands flapping madly. The boy looked at him as if he were from another planet or something, but that was okay. If the boy was looking at him that meant he had his attention, even if for the briefest of moments. "Do you want to try the Legos now?" He reached over, grabbed the Legos bucket, and dumped it out on the table, letting the pieces rattle loudly across the fake wood surface.

At the sound, Noah sat back in his chair. Then he jumped down and turned it. The back of it hit the table again. He pulled it away and began to turn with it once more.

Delton crossed his arms and sighed. He looked up at the window, hoping for them to come back in and take him away now. Obviously, if this was all he was going to do today, what was the point in keeping it going? End the torture. But nobody came in.

He struggled to his feet, grabbed every book off the shelf, trudged over to the bean bag chair, and plopped down, sitting back as far as he could. He set the stack of books on the floor next to him and picked up the top one. "Red Fish Blue Fish, by Dr. Seuss," He looked over at Noah — nothing. Still turning. Delton read the whole book and picked up the next one, "Is Your Mama a Llama?" He'd never heard of that one, and to be honest, found it silly, but he read the whole thing nevertheless.

He would pick up a book from the pile on his left, read it, and drop it onto a pile on his right.

One book, Where the Wild Things Are, he read twice. He'd never heard of that book, but he liked it very much. He read it two more times before dropping it onto the completed pile. When he had finished the last book on his left, he reached around, flipped over the pile on his right and began all the books again.

Eventually he was too weary to read anymore. He settled back and closed his eyes for a moment.

"Delton, honey," Taysha called to him.

He could feel his shoulder being nudged.

"Come on, Delton. It's time to go."

Delton opened his eyes, saw Taysha staring down at him, took a second to remember where he was, then jumped upright and looked around the room. "Where's the boy?"

"You missed him. He just left with his mama and his aunt."

Delton slapped his hands over his face and sunk back into the bean bag. "Oh my God. How long have I been sleeping?"

"A couple hours now."

Delton looked up at her. "Am I out?"

"What?"

"Am I out of the project? Did I screw it up for myself?"

Taysha shook her head and walked to the door. "Hell, no. But you didn't impress anybody this afternoon either. Now get your butt out of that chair, and get on the bus before the guards come in here and drag you out."

Delton jumped up and scrambled out. The guards had them line up in the hall next to their doors, and then walked them all out and onto the bus. The counselors didn't ride back to the facility, so the inmates had the opportunity to sit where they wanted.

Delton saw Hector sitting alone staring out the window and took the seat next to him. "How was your day?"

Hector looked over at him, his eyes red. "It was one of the most amazing days I've ever had in my life."

"Really?"

Nodding, Hector gazed off into the distance. "Me and the little guy—his name is Sammie—me and Sammie connected right away. Like immediately after I walked into the room we were best friends. Sammie likes board games, so we played all kinds of board games most of the day. He has like this cerebral palsy thing, right? So I would have to help him move his pieces on the boards, and every single time I did, the kid said 'thank you.' Imagine that. A kid that polite." Hector shook his head. "It blows my mind how happy the kid was. He has so much going against him, but he was the happiest little guy I'd ever met. And then, when we decided to take a break from playing games, we both sat in these bean bag chairs—which I think is the most comfortable chair I've ever sat in in my whole life—anyway we sat in these chairs and talked. He has these dreams—not dreams, goals. He plans on being the very first astronaut with cerebral palsy. I told him, 'You can do it, little guy. I believe in you.' And you know what he did? He got out of his bean bag and he hugged me. Can you believe that? He hugged me." Hector's eyes were watering. "I don't have any kids of my own, but if I did, I don't think I could love them as much as I love Sammie. And after only one day too. What do you think of that?" Hector gulped in air and wiped his eyes. "I am going to hate it tonight. I have to wait all night long to see him again."

Delton looked forward. Would he admit to his friend that he had slept through most of the afternoon?

Rick Simpson sat to his left. "Damn, I'm glad that's over, aren't you?"

"My day was fine," Delton said.

"Oh shit, man. If I would have had to spend one more minute with that retard, I think I would slit my own throat. I guess I gotta settle in for the longest three months of my life." He slid down and put his knees on the back of the seat in front of him. "I'll tell you this though, the mother was a total babe. We kind of hit it off pretty good too. I'd sure like to bang her when I get out of this joint. Can't live with her though. Can't deal with living with that retard the rest of my life."

"Cut the shit, man," Delton said.

"What the fuck is your problem?" Simpson said.

"You don't call them retards for one thing. They kids with problems and issues. It ain't their fault they like that. If you don't want to be around them, then drop out of the program."

"Shit, Hayes. Take the stick out of your ass." Simpson said. "I'm just making conversation. And anyways, there ain't no way I'm dropping. This shit is going to get me out sooner, and if I get to spend the next three months on the outside of those walls, it's worth hanging with a kid, no matter how fucking stupid he is."

Delton glared at Rick. "Get outta my sight, you piece of shit."

Rick sat up. "Hayes, you are one high-strung mother-fucker." He stood and moved farther back in the bus.

Hector nudged Delton with his elbow. "Relax, man. Don't let that asshole get to you."

Delton sat back and sighed.

"You didn't say how your day went." Hector said.

"It went fine," he said. "I had a good day." But he couldn't help feeling disappointed—in himself—in his day—in the program. After listening to Hector, he felt cheated somehow. He knew he never expected to feel that deeply at the end of the day, but knowing that it was possible made him feel ripped off. It was the luck of the draw, and he got screwed one more time. Not only did he have the nightmare mother, he got the kid who can't communicate and lives in his own world, on his own planet. How would he be feeling right now if he'd had a kid like Sammie? He was sure he wouldn't have slept through it.

Chapter Seventeen

Taysha was not on the bus the next day. She and Rena met Delton once he got into the room. "Are you well rested?" she asked.

"Yeah, I guess so." Delton said.

"We've made a couple of changes," Rena said. "There are a whole new selection of books on the shelves."

"Thank you," Delton said. "I was scared I'd have to read that damn llama book one more time."

"You're welcome," Rena said. She walked over and put her hand on a chair. "And the chairs are different now."

Delton saw the swivel chairs had been replaced by chairs with four legs on the floor. "Oh, snap. That shit is gonna rock little dude's whole world."

"That's what we're afraid of," Taysha said. "We want to make sure you're up to it."

"Are you kidding me? This is great." Delton lifted the chair, and looked at the legs. "This is going to force him to deal with me."

"Well, he'll be here soon," Rena said. "We're going outside to bring him in."

They left and Delton took his seat at the table. They returned a few minutes later with Judith in tow, carrying Noah. Just like the day before, she stood him on the ground, spoke softly to him, and turned him around. And again, the boy looked at Delton wide-eyed. She led him by the hand to the chair, sat him down, and knelt next to him. "Okay, Noah. I have to go to work. I'm going to leave you with Delton again. He's your new friend, so you play nice with him, okay?" She stood, gave Delton a polite nod, and walked out of the room. Delton felt sure she regretted saying the nice things to him yesterday.

Rena's cheery voice cut the tension. "Have a fun time, Noah."

Taysha looked at Delton and mouthed, "Good luck." And both women left the room, quietly closing the door behind them.

Delton looked down at Noah, who stared back at him intently, hands flapping like baby chicken wings. He recalled the only time he felt like he had any sort of connection with the boy yesterday was this moment, when they sat at the table, and he put his head down. Once again, he folded his arms on the table and rested his chin on them. Noah watched him for several seconds, and then dropped his head down to his arms as well.

After a few minutes of staring at each other Delton spoke softly. "So, little dude, would you like to play with me?"

Noah stared.

A few more minutes went by and Delton slowly sat back. Noah watched his every move. Delton reached way over, grabbed the bucket of Legos, and slid it next to him. He dipped into it with both hands, pulled out a large selection, and, as quietly as he could, set them on the table in front of the boy.

Noah raised up, looked from the pile to Delton and back to the pile a few times. Then he slid out of his chair and tried to spin it. When it didn't spin at all, he dragged it away from the table and tried again.

"This chair don't turn like the one did yesterday, Noah,"

Delton said. "Let's play with Legos instead." He held two pieces in the air and clicked them together to demonstrate.

Noah cried out. He pulled the chair farther away from the table and tried to spin it again, to no avail.

Delton spoke as quietly and as calmly as he could. "It's all right, we have other toys to play with today."

Noah pulled the chair around in a circle, but it didn't turn easily for him like yesterday's chair. He gave a long sad moaning sound until the point he'd had enough. Then he screamed, knocked the chair over, balled up his hands, and began hitting himself in the face, back and forth with each hand.

"Don't do that!" Delton jumped from his chair, ran around the table, and grabbed Noah's hands, which made the boy scream louder.

Noah jerked free and hit himself more.

Not knowing what else to do, Delton covered Noah's face with his hands to protect the boy from his own fists.

Crying, Noah collapsed to the floor. He lay on his back and banged his head on the carpeted cement.

"A little help here!" Delton yelled at the window.

Rena's voice came over the speakers in the ceiling. "We've discussed this Delton. Noah is having a meltdown. You have to hold him. He can hurt himself if you don't."

Dropping to his knees, Delton scooted around to the boy's head, and slid his hands under to cushion it.

Rena's voice crackled over the speakers again. "We've called his mother, and she's on her way back."

Apparently with no more pain involved, Noah had no more interest in banging his head. The boy rolled over, sat up and screamed. Large tears rolled out of his eyes. That was fine. Though his screams were ear-splitting, Delton could deal with it. Screaming was safe. He sat back and said things like, "It'll be okay," and, "Your mama'll be here soon," but nothing soothed the boy. Delton was beginning to fear Noah would scream and cry as long today as he spun the chair yesterday.

Then Noah balled up his fists again, and slammed them into his face.

"Hey, stop that," Delton said.

Noah did it again, seemingly as hard as he could. His head rocked back with each blow.

Delton reached over and grabbed the boy's hands again. Noah screamed and tried to jerk them free, but Delton held them firmly this time.

Like an autistic arms race, it became Noah's turn to increase the stakes. He began kicking violently, catching Delton in the chin. More by surprise than pain, Delton released the boy's hands, freeing him to again beat on his face. "Oh no," Delton said. "This ain't gonna turn into you against me. And there ain't nothin' bad gonna happen to you on my watch." Delton laid the boy down flat on his back and held each hand to the floor, positioning himself over the stomach so the boy couldn't kick him anymore.

Noah strained against Delton. When he realized he couldn't move, he screamed so loud, and with so much force that his face turned red. He kicked his feet wildly, but they were behind Delton now and completely harmless.

The door burst open and the guard named Johnson stepped in with his gun drawn. "Get off him now!"

Terrified he was going to be shot, Delton sat back and threw his hands in the air. This freed Noah to begin beating his face again.

Taysha shoved her way through the door and stood in front of the guard. "I said no! And when I say no, you need to listen to me." She waved her finger in his face. "You are not the authority in this room. I am. Now get the hell out of here."

Noah was still beating his face, and Delton had his hands in the air, when Judith Higgins rushed into the room. She looked at the guard with his gun drawn. "What the fuck is going on here?!"

She rushed to Noah, smacking Delton's shoulder with the back of her hand. "Get off him."

Delton jumped up and backed to the wall, leaving Noah to flail his legs, and hit his face with his fists.

Judith sat on the floor at Noah's head and dragged him up to her. She reached around and grabbed his left hand with her right, and his right with her left and pulled them close, straight jacket style. Then she crossed her legs around his legs, trapping them, making him unable to kick. Noah screamed and tried to beat his head on hers. She was prepared for this and dodged the blow. She waited until he slammed back again, and she clenched his head between her chin and her shoulder. Noah was now completely incapacitated. He screamed, tried to wriggle free, but there was no give.

"Lady, this is messed up," Delton said.

Judith whispered calmly into Noah's ear.

Rena walked in followed by Dr. Fitzpatrick. The big man scanned the situation. He looked at Judith holding down a still upset Noah, the armed guard, and Delton standing back in the far corner. For several minutes, everyone stood still while Noah's rage subsided, and his screams devolved into quiet whimpers.

Watching Judith, Delton had a new respect for this woman. It was true she had an edge to her, but that was because she fought a battle every day—a battle she had no hope of winning. He stepped forward, knelt down and spoke quietly to her. "I been sayin' this too much lately, but I'm sorry. I've never seen anything like that, ever."

Judith rubbed her cheek against Noah's head. "You know, this is the only time I really get to hold him."

Delton saw another side to her for the first time. He realized that all she wanted to do was be a mother. She rocked her son slowly back and forth, and whispered in his ear. Another five minutes and the boy was quiet. The horrible angst that had completely consumed him, had gone.

Dr. Fitzpatrick stepped forward. "I thank you for coming back in, Miss Higgins. I'm sure we can take it from here."

"Not today you can't," Judith said.

"Pardon?"

"I'm not leaving him here today." She released her son and he sat upright, wobbling a bit. His face was puffy from the crying and red from the beating. Getting her legs under her she stood and lifted him into her arms.

"Miss Higgins, your son will be perfectly...."

"Look around you, Doctor." Judith cut him off. "Does anything look perfect to you? How many other rooms have the armed guards had to enter? Look at my son." She turned Noah around so the doctor could see. "I'm sure he will be bruised. Today your little experiment is over." She walked toward the door, stopped, and turned back. "I have to think long and hard on whether he is ever coming back again." She walked out, leaving a room full of stunned observers.

Officer Johnson turned to Delton. "With no kid, you have no reason to be here. Get to the bus and we'll take you back."

Excerpts from the transcript of the GINfo (Global Information Network) interview between Brooke Winthrop and Judith Higgins.

Brooke: Explain a meltdown.

Judith: Oh…you saw the video too?

Brooke: Yes, and I have to be honest. When I see someone's kid in the mall behaving like that, and unloading with earsplitting screams, I look at the parents and say to myself 'why aren't you doing something about your kid.' But from what I'm learning, there's not much a parent of an autistic child can do in this situation. So please explain. What's the difference between a meltdown and a tantrum? Why doesn't someone just give an autistic child a timeout when they're acting so unacceptably?

Judith: Okay well, they're completely different. An autistic person doesn't understand how to process their emotions, and quite often, they can't process outside stimuli either. Things like loud noises, or…they don't even have to be that loud actually. Large crowds, lots of flashing lights, and lots of movement…those kinds of things, can take an autistic child over the edge. It's like taking a bottle of soda and shaking and shaking it. All that pressure builds up and there's no rational way to release it. And just like a plastic bottle can't keep the top from blowing off, an autistic child can't keep from blowing either. It's not like a tantrum, where they're whining because they didn't get what they want. An autistic child has no control over the explosion. And they lose the control until all the pressure is released. And if you're a parent, and the top has blown off the soda bottle, you can't hold your hand over it and try to keep it in. All you can do is hold it until it's done spilling over, and try to minimize the damage to everything else. An autistic child is the same way, except they will often hurt themselves, so you have to hold them until they're done.

Brooke: I had no idea. That must be terribly hard on the parent.

Judith: Well...yeah, it is. But think about it. It's hard enough to deal with at this age, but an autistic child grows. And boys are autistic at a higher percentage than girls, so when they get older, they need to be able to learn coping skills somehow, or they'll not only hurt themselves, they can really injure someone who is just trying to help them out. That's my big fear with Noah. What am I going to do in seven, eight years, when he'll be stronger than I am?

Chapter Eighteen

Judith strapped Noah into his car seat. After such a long, sustained meltdown, he was little more than a rag doll, and she was able to get him into the car with no fuss. She quickly slid into her seat, started the car, and drove away—wanting to get out of there before anybody ran after her and tried to talk her into having Noah stay.

Reaching into her purse, she grabbed her phone, and tried to hit her sister's number. Her hands were trembling so much, she missed the first time, calling her dad's retirement home instead. "Shit." She tapped off the call and had better luck the next time.

"What's up?" Darlene said when she answered.

"Dar, I need your help. By any chance can you hang with Noah today?"

"Uh oh."

"Yeah. Uh oh. I can't even freaking talk about it right now."

"I'm there. I just gotta throw some clothes on and I'll meet you at your place."

"Thank you, so much."

"No prob..."

Judith tapped off the call and tossed the phone into the seat next to her. She checked Noah in the rearview mirror. His eyes were already shut, and he was sleeping soundly.

True to her word, Darlene was waiting when she pulled into the driveway. Opening the door she waved to her sister. "Thank you, Sis. It was a major cluster there today."

Darlene came down and opened Noah's door. "Hey, come on, champ," she said, shaking his shoulder. His eyes opened and his head lifted slightly and then he fell back asleep. "Boy. He is out of it." She unbuckled him from his seat and stepped back to let Judith in to pick him up.

Judith lifted him out of the car. "He's had a hell of a morning."

Darlene closed the car door for her. "Already?"

Trying to get hold of the correct key while carrying Noah was a struggle. Thankfully Darlene grabbed her keys and unlocked the door. "You have to tell me what happened."

Judith lay Noah down on the sofa and he crumpled into the fetal position. She brushed her hand through her hair. "I had dropped Noah off, and it looked like everything was going to be cool like yesterday. I was hoping Delton dumbass could stay awake the whole day, but at least Noah was fine with everything. You know? Anyway, I'm out of the parking lot, like five minutes and my phone starts ringing. Noah is in full meltdown. So I turn around. And when I get back there, there's this guard in the room holding a gun on Delton. Delton's got his hands up, but he's sitting on Noah on the floor, and Noah's beating the shit out of his face."

"You've got to be kidding me." Darlene said. She leaned down and pushed Noah's hair back. "Poor little guy."

"Thank you so much, Dar." Judith looked at her watch and headed to the door. "I'm so late for work. Bernie's going to kill me." Before closing the door she turned back to her sister. "Please don't let him sleep too long or he won't sleep tonight."

"Got it," Darlene said.

Scurrying into her cubicle, she flicked her computer on first before taking off her jacket and sitting in her chair. Then she sat down and breathed deeply while her computer booted up.

"Looks like you've had a day already,"

Looking up, Judith saw Simon Bensinger, her cubicle neighbor, leaning over the wall. Simon was a loving husband, remarkable father, and one of the kindest work associates she knew. "Morning, Simon. Yes. It's been a little bit horrible." She nodded toward Bernie's office. "Any word from him?"

Simon shook his head. "Nah. But you haven't logged in yet."

"True." Just then her login screen came up. She typed in her username and password and hit return. "Here we go."

Simon chuckled. "Best of luck." He sat back down, disappearing behind the cubicle wall.

Thirty seconds later—she could have used him as an egg timer—Bernie appeared in her cubicle entryway, belly hanging over his belt. He still hadn't cut down on the three custard-filled long johns for breakfast. "Nice of you to join us, Higgins."

"Sorry, Bernie," She didn't look up at him. "It got crazy with Noah and the Marmont Project this morning. I had to take him back home and have my sister come over to take care of him." She opened up her email and scanned it for any high priority alerts.

"Again with the kid," Bernie stepped into her cubicle. "Look, Judith…."

"Bernie, before you get started," Judith spun around in her chair to face him, "This morning was off the grid out there. It's not the type of thing that will ever be repeated."

"Well, what did you expect? You put the kid in an 'off the grid' situation," he made air quotes to be a bigger dick, "and 'off the grid' types of things are gonna happen."

"Hey, Bernie, leave her alone, will ya?" Simon Bensinger was now in her cubicle entryway.

"Mind your own, Simon. This doesn't concern you."

"It does concern me," Simon said. "She's a member of my team."

Bernie put his thumb to his chest, like an ape. "I run the team, and I'm saying let me handle this."

"Why don't we handle it?" Shelly Walker slid past Simon into the cubicle, followed by Evelyn Reese, two older ladies on the analyst team. Judith's cubicle was full now. "We are the team."

Bernie put his hands out. "What? You're all going to stick your neck out for one of your team members who isn't pulling her own weight?"

"When she struggles, we pick up the slack," Shelly said. "We got this."

"Why would you do that?" Bernie asked.

"Because, it takes a village, Bernie," Simon said. "Have you never heard that?"

The last thing Judith wanted to do was lose it at work, but after the morning she'd had, Simon's statement flipped a switch — the one that caused her to burst into tears. She leaned forward and buried her face in her hands.

"Oh, geez," Bernie said. "Here we go."

Evelyn's sweet voice spoke next. "Hush, Bernie. You've done enough already." Judith felt Evelyn's hand rub her back. "I'm sorry, honey. You cry if you need to."

"My God." Bernie said. "You people deserve each other. Higgins, if you could grace us with some effort at some point today, I would be ever so grateful." She heard him walk out.

A moment later she heard Simon's voice whisper, "What a dick." Then he spoke louder. "Let me know if you need any help with anything, Judith."

"That goes for all of us," Shelley said.

Judith had always thought that the majority of her teammates felt the same way Bernie did, and were just relying on him to handle things. She was touched that they understood her predicament, and were willing to help her out. She took a moment to collect herself before pulling her hands from her face. "Thank y…" Her cubicle was empty. They had left her to do exactly what they said they were going to do…pick up the slack. She spun around, pulled a tissue, blew her nose and wiped it. "Okay." She clicked on an email that looked important. "Time to grace that shithead with some effort."

Chapter Nineteen

By ten o'clock, Delton was back at the prison. He was given his overalls, told to change, and report to the yard. He did as he was ordered. He sat and watched guys play basketball, while he replayed the day's earlier events in his mind. Noah Higgins' file said he was "prone to meltdowns." It didn't go into great detail about what actually happened during the meltdowns. Some of the other materials mentioned the kids hitting themselves, and even Rena discussed it with him, but he hadn't taken it seriously. He wasn't prepared for it when it happened.

A basketball bounced out of bounds. He reached over, caught it, and tossed it back.

"Hayes, you playing?" One of the guys asked.

"Nah, man," Delton said. "I'm good."

Delton wanted to blame Rena, or Dr. Fitzpatrick, for not preparing him as completely as they should have. But that was a cop-out. He was really angry with himself. They can only spoon-feed him so much. If he agreed to take part in something like this, then he needed to step up and learn what he needed to know, so things like that morning never took place.

He pictured the notebook in the room behind the mirror, and next to his name was the word, "failed." Thinking about it was making him crazy. It was proving the parole board right. For all he knew that was part of the experiment. Put an inmate into a situation he isn't truly prepared for, and watch him sink like a stone. Make sure everyone knew they were right to lock him up in the first place.

Taysha's words started ringing in his ears again. "So what you gonna do? You just gonna roll over 'cause poor little Delton feels he got a bad deal, and by doing that, prove them right? Or are you gonna do the right thing: outshine every other one of them rejects out there who's also in this program, and prove the parole board wrong?" Delton smiled remembering she used language that was a bit more foul.

He jumped from his seat in the yard and headed to a part of the prison he'd never been before—the library. Now that the shock of the morning had worn off, Delton was seriously pissed. He felt like that kid got the better of him today. But it wasn't the kid, it was the issue the kid was a victim to. And he let the kid down by being unprepared. Delton wasn't sure if he was still a part of this project or not, but he did have the power to make sure things like this didn't happen again if he was.

He walked into the prison library and an older gray-haired white man looked up at him. "How are you doing, sir? Can I help you find something?"

"I need whatever you got on autism."

"Autism?" The older man said. "Nobody's ever asked for anything on autism before." He typed away at a keyboard next to him. Delton watched as the man reached for the mouse and began scrolling it with his forefinger. "I don't have anything here, but I can get it delivered by tomorrow."

"How can you do that?"

"The county library shares their collection with us," the old man sat back and cracked his knuckles. "They'll make a delivery for something we need within a day."

"But I don't know what to ask for."

The old man jumped up. "Take a seat," he said, patting the back of the chair. "I have everything that's available right here."

Delton walked around the desk and sat down. The older man showed him how to scroll through the selections and gave him a piece of paper to write his choices down, then left him alone to do his research. Skimming through the lists, Delton found there were a number of books on the topic, many of which he was afraid he wouldn't understand. They seemed to have been written by doctors for doctors. In the end he picked three books: A Beginner's Guide to Autism Spectrum Disorder by Paul G. Taylor, Children and Autism: Stories of Triumph and Hope by Ennio Cipani, and 101 Games and Activities for Children with Autism by Tara Delany.

Delton waved the man back, and gave him the list. Then the man showed him how to look up videos on YouTube to get information on topics he was interested in. Delton was amazed to find literally hundreds of videos regarding autism spectrum disorder. He settled in and began clicking on them. The first video was called "Five Things to Know about Autism." It was pretty much the same thing as was written in the paperwork he was given by Rena Blossom.

Next he watched a video showing an autistic kid having a meltdown. Having just experienced the situation first-hand, Delton found himself riveted to the screen as the scenario played out. The little girl began a sad moaning as she worked at some type of craft on a table. Then, completely upset with it, she took her arm, brushed it away and screamed. She stood and began hitting her face. The hairs stood up on Delton's arms. It was as if Noah and this girl were playing the same role as little actors. The actions and movements were exactly the same. A woman came into view, took the little girl and put her into the same straight-jacket position that Miss Higgins had used, wrapping her legs around to completely incapacitate the girl until she calmed down. The video cut, and text at the bottom of the screen said "35 minutes later," which was longer than Noah took to calm down.

But Noah had been in full meltdown mode longer than this girl, before Judith had gotten him wrapped up. The girl was now calm and acted as if nothing had happened.

Another video showed a kid going off the rails at a mall. From the videos, Delton learned that the kids weren't actually acting out, they were compensating for emotions they didn't know how to control. It was useless to get mad at them, they didn't even realize they were behaving badly.

Delton stood and called to the old man. "When will those books be here?"

"Tomorrow," the man said, looking up from a book he was reading.

"All right," Delton waved. "See ya then."

The old man smiled and waved back. "See ya then, son."

Delton headed back to his cell to grab the materials he'd already been given. He would reread them while he waited for the new books. Perhaps the benefit of experience would give him a new perspective on what they said.

Chapter Twenty

Noah sipped quietly on his vanilla shake while he looked blankly out the window through his bruised and puffy eyes. His fingers on his left hand slowly opened and closed.

Judith looked back and forth from Noah to the park across the street where the man was helping his stricken wife into her wheelchair. When she was seated, he leaned the wheelchair back, and pushed it through the grass onto the asphalt. Then he relaxed and casually rolled her down the path, soon lost from view in the small stand of trees on the far side of the park.

A small chocolate chip traveled up her straw and she chewed the sweet little treasure. After the day she'd had, she earned it.

She thought about how grateful she was for places like Lance's Drive-in Burgers. Lance probably had not realized what a service he provided for mothers with special needs children when he initially had the idea for his restaurant. She was sure he just wanted to create a throw-back experience for his customers. But to be able to take her son out for a dinner after a hard day, and never even have to get out of the car was an absolute treat. If Noah had issues, or even another meltdown, she didn't have to drag him out of a crowded restaurant. All she had to do was turn the key and drive away.

Her phone buzzed in her purse. Pulling it out, she looked at the screen, saw it was Rena, and dropped it onto the seat next to her. Rena wasn't Dr. Fitzpatrick, in fact she was a very sweet girl, but Judith still did not want to talk to anyone from Marmont anymore today…perhaps ever again. She had already called Keener at lunch, and informed them that Noah would be attending from now on. Though the costs were exorbitant, she would just have to figure it out. She could no longer put Noah into a situation like he was this morning.

The voicemail alarm dinged on her phone. She decided to listen to it. After punching in her code she put the phone on speaker. "Hello Miss Higgins, this is Rena Blossom. I was calling to check on Noah. But…I wanted to check on you too. I'm sure this morning was a traumatic experience for you as well, coming in the way you did. I wanted you to know that Delton was actually doing well with the situation before the guard came in and it got out of hand. Anyway, I was checking on Noah's status for tomor…" Judith hit the delete button. She quickly texted, "Noah won't be in tomorrow." and hit send.

It was all bullshit. If Delton had been doing well, the situation wouldn't have ever gotten out of hand. It was so disappointing. Though she couldn't say she was a big fan of Delton, there seemed to be something there the first day—a connection she sensed. And even though he fell asleep like a dumb shit, she thought there was something unique there. But then when she saw the total chaos, it was clear she'd been wrong.

Judith looked at her son—at the bruise around his left eye. She had half a mind to drive over to her father's, drag Noah in, and say "See, I was right." But she knew her father would casually look over and softly say, "Is he dead?" He had always been one to subscribe to the "Whatever doesn't kill you…" philosophy, and that would just make her more angry.

Noah stopped sipping, leaned his head against his car seat, and watched a squirrel run around outside. He was so calm and serene now, but he was capable of so much rage. Somehow she could understand it. Without the ability to communicate, feelings of frustration can overwhelm and turn into something much worse.

And that's what her father would say, "The boy needs to communicate, and those fancy schools aren't helping him do that."

There's a part of Judith that agreed with him. Though Keener had been successful in getting him to do things like eat, drink, and put away toys, they hadn't figured out how to help him communicate. He could understand words and orders but not give them back. There was no real way to determine what he wanted, until he was frustrated that he didn't have it.

A large part of it was an ideological difference. The Keener School philosophy was that autism was not necessarily a disability to be overcome, as it was a genetic gift that made a person unique, like red hair or something. So instead of trying to overcome it, embrace it, and be the special person you were born to be. And though there was a certain amount of logic to that, the fact was, that without the ability to communicate properly, one could not thrive in the world.

Her phone buzzed again. She knew it was Rena calling back to discuss the text, and she didn't want to go into it right now. But when she picked up the phone she saw it was Darlene. She tapped it, "Hey, Dar. What's up?"

"Okay, Jim has a great idea."

"Idea for what?"

"Judith, I want you to think about this and let it sink in, okay?"

"Oh, great," Judith said, turning back around in her seat. "That's a great way to start a conversation. I can feel a 'no' forming in my belly now."

"Just hear me out."

"I'm listening." Judith took a long drink from her shake and looked back at the man with his wife in the park coming around the far side of the path.

"Jim says there's this new guy where he works who would be perfect for you."

"Mmmm." Judith shook her head and swallowed her shake. "You have got to be kidding me. I am in no way ready to date anybody. Nor am I in that frame of mind."

"Jude, listen. The guy is from Pennsylvania, and he doesn't know anybody around here. Jim told him about you and he was interested in meeting you."

"Sure he was. Until he finds out I have an autistic son, and then he forgets to call…for the rest of his life."

"Nope. Jim told him all about Noah too. It didn't faze the guy a bit. He said he wanted to meet you after he found out about Noah's autism."

Judith pulled the phone away and looked at it, if for no other reason than to make sure it was on and working right. She put it back to her ear. "Are you sure he knows about Noah?"

"Jim told him all about Noah. Jude, Jim's not going to set you up for a fall. He's gonna have your back."

Judith took a breath. "I don't even know if I'm ready to be in a relationship yet. But let me think about it."

"Relationship. I don't give a shit about a relationship. I just want you to get laid. You've been so damn cranky lately." Darlene laughed.

"Oh, blow it out your butt," Judith said, smiling.

"See what I mean?" Darlene said.

Judith laughed. "Thanks, Dar. I needed to smile."

"You're welcome. I got your back too, Sis."

"You really do. Thanks again for today."

"No problem."

"Listen," Jude said, setting her cup down in the holder. "Tell Jim I'm not saying no, I just have to figure out my next move with Noah right now."

"Yes," Darlene squeaked.

"That's not a yes," Judith said. "It's just not a no."

"I get it. I'll tell him."

"Thanks, Sis."

"You're wel…"

Judith tapped the call off and tossed it onto the seat next to her. She looked over at the man and his wife. Their walk was finished and he was helping her back into the car. "Let's go home, Noah." She turned the key, threw the car into gear and drove away.

Chapter Twenty-One

Delton had been informed the night before not to report to the bus. Noah was taking the day off. So after breakfast he grabbed his books from the library, took them to a table in the yard and spent the day pouring over them. Since he was technically still part of the program—there had been no official cancellation of Noah's involvement—he was not given a work detail within the prison. He could spend the day studying.

Reading about the anti-social behaviors, the meltdowns, and the repeated movements, he realized that having gone through all of this with an autistic child in a short span of time, did give him perspective. He knew that if he had read this without ever meeting Noah, or spending any time with the boy, the books would have been nothing more than words on a page that he was required to get through, much like the materials he'd already been supplied. There would have been no real understanding of the actual challenges involved.

"Hayes." A guard waved him over from across the yard. "Your appointment is here."

He dog-eared the page, gathered his books and ran over to the guard. Danna was supposed to stop by after school. Perhaps she got out early and decided to come in. It was lucky he had not been over with Noah.

But the guard did not take him to the visitation room; he took him to the interrogation hallway and into a room where Taysha Williams was waiting for him.

He took a seat across from her. "What's the word, Taysha?"

"No word yet," she said. "I just thought, since I'm still getting paid, I ought to do something to earn it. So I stopped by to see how you was doing and if you wanted to talk."

Delton shook his head. "I'm fine." He spread out the three books he had checked out from the library. "I spent some time yesterday watching videos on the computer about autistic kids , and today these books came in for me to read."

Taysha picked up one of the books and flipped through it. "Are they helping?"

"They're giving me a few ideas." Delton opened the book he was just reading to a few pages before the dog-ear flap. "Check this out." He spun it around, and pointed to it. "This is all about Applied Behavior Analysis—you know, what they want me to test for when this is done."

"What about it?" Taysha asked, sliding the book closer.

"It says here that some people hate it."

"Does it work?"

"Seems to," Delton said.

Taysha pulled out a pair of readers, put them on, and looked at the book more closely. "Well, if it works, why would people hate it?"

"A couple of reasons," Delton said. "One is that they feel it treats autistic kids like they were dogs or something. Training them to sit up and shake and all that. But others say that autism is this way of being a special person and that it's cruel to try to make an autistic person into a normal person because they aren't naturally wired that way."

Taysha took off her readers and looked at him. "And just

what does Delton believe?"

Delton sat back. "Looking at Noah these last two days, I have to admit he's wired a different way and all, but I can't say that his life is some great gift or something. I mean, a kid that screams that loud and beats himself silly...that is some messed up shit."

"I gotta say, my man," Taysha said. "I am mighty impressed with all you're doing. Aren't you concerned that you're doing it for no reason?"

Delton shrugged. "I may be. But if I do get to go back there, and I'm no more prepared than I was in the first place, I'm sure not gonna do no better. And if I never go back there again...well then, at least I know something I didn't know before."

"That's a good way of looking at it." Taysha said with a nod. "I know Miss Blossom and Dr. Fitzpatrick are going to go over and talk to Miss Higgins after the program closes for the day. They told me to give you the heads up that they may have her call and talk to you about how things are going to go moving forward. I think if you tell her about all the studying you've been doing, all will be well."

The door opened and the guard stuck his head in. "Hayes, you've got a visitor."

Delton stood. "That's Danna. She finally got over her hissy-fit and decided she wanted to see me again."

Taysha stood and walked out with him. "I'll go get some coffee while you two talk. I'd like to be around if Miss Higgins makes the phone call."

Delton followed the guard out of the room, down several corridors, and into the visitation room. Scanning the area, Delton looked at every table but did not see his sister.

"That guy over there." The guard pointed to a table to the right. There was a middle-aged black man with glasses sitting there. He wore a Detroit Tigers jacket and had his arms folded in front of him. "He's the one who came to see you."

Delton walked over to the table. The man looked up at him, smiled, and stood when he got closer. "You must be Delton. I'm Reggie Fountain." He held out his hand. "It's good to meet you."

Delton shook. "Likewise."

Reggie waved at the seat. "Please, have a seat and let's talk."

Delton sat down, slowly. He was unsure of this man and was waiting for some unseen shoe to drop.

"I am Danna's foster father," Reggie said.

"Oh. Okay," Delton said, looking around the room. "So where's Danna?"

"Well," Reggie said, his hands up. "Unfortunately Danna couldn't make it today because she's grounded. She was…"

"Grounded?" Delton said. "What you talkin' about?"

"Yes, grounded," Reggie said. "Since your last phone call with her she's been very agitated, and even quite disrespectful to Rosalind, my wife, so we grounded her."

"But don't ground her from seeing me. I'm her brother. I'll talk to her. Tell her to be more respectful."

Reggie rested his elbows on the table and folded his hands. "It's like this. As her foster father I am completely responsible for her. Nobody else is."

Delton sat back and crossed his arms. This was starting to seem like that unseen shoe he had been expecting, was getting ready to drop.

Reggie said, holding up a finger to make his point, "And as I mentioned, it was after her last phone call with you that things started to go bad. When we asked her about it she refused to tell us anything. She just became belligerent. So I came to meet you and assess the situation. If I leave here feeling that you are a bad influence on her, then we'll have to end this relationship."

"End this relationship?" Delton said. "You can't make me not her brother."

Reggie shook his head. "No. I can't do that. But I can and

will end these visits and keep you out of her life."

Delton jumped to his feet. Reggie jumped up as well and the two men stood face to face, noses nearly touching. Two guards rushed over.

"You know why she became agitated?" Delton said. "Because she found out I was going to be in here at least another three months and she couldn't be with me. That's what got her so upset."

"C'mon, Hayes," one of the guards said. "Let's go before you do or say something you'll regret."

"So by you grounding her, and threatening to keep her from me, you're just making matters worse for yourself."

The guards grabbed his arms and pulled him back.

"She's my sister and I'm her brother. Ain't you, or anybody else ever going to break that bond." Delton pointed at him. "Shame on you for wanting to break a family apart."

"Let's go, Hayes." The guards dragged him back.

"Shame on you." Delton cried out. "Shame on you." He was dragged from the room.

Chapter Twenty-Two

"Come, Noah. It's dinner time." She placed a plate of macaroni and cheese with cut-up hot dogs mixed in, along with a big scoop of apple sauce, on the table next to his glass of milk.

Noah had been watching Spider-Man on TV. He came into the kitchen, quietly slid into his chair, picked up his fork and started eating. Judith sat down with her plate when the doorbell rang.

She opened the door to see Rena and Dr. Fitzpatrick standing on her front porch. "We didn't hear a word from you today," Dr. Fitzpatrick said. "So we thought we should come and check in on you two."

"We're fine," Judith said.

"Miss Higgins, can we talk for a minute?" Rena said.

Judith could see the concern in the young girl's eyes. She stepped aside and let them in. Rena mouthed "Thank you," as she passed.

They saw Noah sitting at the table, eating. He did not acknowledge them; he never took looked up from his plate. Rena noticed the bruises around both eyes. "The poor little guy." She turned to Judith.

"Is he all right?" Dr. Fitzpatrick asked. "I mean, aside from the black eyes?"

Rena clutched at Dr. Fitzpatrick's arm. "Doctor, if you don't mind, I'd like to say some things."

Dr. Fitzpatrick nodded and stepped back with a squeak.

Rena turned to Judith. "I understand what it looked like when you walked back in there yesterday, but I want you to try to do something for me. I want you to picture the same room without the guard holding his gun. What I want you to picture is Noah not beating at his face, because he is being held firmly and safely by Delton. It's true, Delton was out of his element. He'd never witnessed an autistic meltdown before, and it caught him by surprise. I won't deny that. But if you saw how well he handled it, you wouldn't be scared of having Noah in his presence. You'd be proud of Delton, and you would feel secure that Noah was safe, and well cared for."

"Well cared for?" Judith pointed toward Noah. "Does he look well cared for? What you don't see is the bump on the back of his head, from beating it against the floor so hard. How am I to ever take Noah back there, and feel like he's well cared for?"

"In all fairness, Miss Higgins..." Dr. Fitzpatrick said.

"Doctor, please." Rena stepped in front of him. "Do you believe in your program?"

"Why, yes. I do," he said, standing tall.

"Then you've just said all you could possibly say to help out the situation," Rena said. "Please let me take it from here." Dr. Fitzpatrick did not hide his hurt ego very well, but Rena didn't care. She turned back to Judith. "Miss Higgins, I get that. Those bruises can't be explained away, or excused either. They happened because an overzealous guard took it upon himself to intervene in something he clearly didn't understand. But the fault doesn't lie with him. It lies with those of us who helped set up this program. We made sure all the participants had all the information necessary, but not those in charge of running the facility. In his defense, he thought he was trying to keep your son safe from harm. He did not know his actions would harm him more."

Judith looked at her son, and back at Rena. "Are these dumbass guards aware now?"

"They are," Rena said. "We all spent last night making information packets about our children, their special needs, and what guards could expect to see. This way they won't be caught by surprise again."

Judith sighed. She stepped over to her son, and ran her fingers through his hair. He made a grunting noise and pushed her hand away. Judith looked at Rena. "My gut is telling me not to take the chance again."

"Can you do one more thing before you make your decision?" Rena asked. "Can you call Delton, and talk to him about it. I think once you realize that he knows what he's doing, you'll feel better about things." She pulled her phone out of her purse and held it up.

"You really think he can pull this off?" Judith said.

"You said yourself that you felt like there was something there."

"That was before he fell asleep for the rest of the afternoon." Judith walked around the table and back to Rena. "Those feelings pretty much faded away when that happened."

"Well, I think we can rekindle those feelings again." She held her phone out to Judith. "Just press redial. They already know to get Delton when you ask for him. Taysha is with him now so he's ready for your phone call."

"Oh, you were pretty confident I'd do this, eh?"

Rena smiled. "Just a hunch."

Judith smiled back. She took the phone and hit the dial icon on the screen. The phone rang once and then was picked up. "Two Rivers Correctional Facility,"

"Hi. My name is Judith Higgins, and I'm calling an inmate

there by the name of Delton Hayes."

"Yes, Miss Higgins," the woman's voice on the other end said. "We were told to expect your call. Please hold."

Judith looked at Rena. "Very nice. They were expecting my call."

Rena smiled and shrugged.

Chapter Twenty-Three

Fuming, Delton was led back to the room where Taysha was waiting. She recognized the anger in him the moment he set foot in the room. "Oh son, what happened?"

Delton paced back and forth. "Danna didn't show. It was her foster father. He grounded her, and told me that I shouldn't see her because I may be a bad influence on her."

"Oh, Delton," Taysha said. "I'm sorry."

"I don't want sorry," Delton snarled. "I want out of here." He picked up the folding chair and with a scream, threw it against the wall. It clanged loudly to the floor.

The door burst open and two guards rushed in, guns drawn. "That's enough, Hayes. On the floor."

"Oh, did you think that was him?" Taysha stood and rushed over to stand in front of the guards, chuckling. "That wasn't him. That was me showing him what I'd do to his head if he stepped out of line with me. I'm so sorry I startled you all." She shooed at them. "Go ahead and put those guns away, and get out of here, and let me put the fear of God in him."

"Lady, what do you take us for?" One of the guards said.

"What do I take you for?" Taysha stepped in front of him. "I'll tell you what I take you for. I take you for a man who truly loves his family. In fact he loves his family so much he would probably lay down his own life for them. So a man like that could completely understand exactly how frustrating it would be if something bad happened to one of them, and he was somewhere else knowing there wasn't a damn thing he could do about it."

The guard looked from Taysha to Delton, and back to Taysha. He nodded, and holstered his gun. The other guard did likewise. "I feel you, Hayes. Could you do this nice lady a favor, and pick up that chair she flung across the room."

"Thank you, gentlemen." Taysha said, smiling. "I'll try to keep the furniture on the floor from now on."

They turned and walked out, closing the door behind them. Taysha walked over to Delton, grabbed both his arms and looked up into his eyes. "My boy, I need you to look at me, and listen very closely. You can help Danna. You can help her by not losing your head. You can help her by keeping calm, staying steady, and getting out of here. I know you don't like hearing this, but it don't matter if you don't talk to her one more minute before you get out. But once you're free of this place, ain't nobody can keep you from your family. Do you understand me?"

Delton looked from the floor to her. He nodded, almost imperceptibly.

The door opened again. "Hayes, you got a phone call."

"Oh God," Taysha said. "Delton, the last time you spoke, after you were upset about your sister, it was a complete disaster. I need you to pull yourself together and be the best Delton you can be right this very moment. Can you do that? Can you think about how it will help Danna to keep your head on your shoulders right now?"

Delton looked at her and narrowed his eyes. "I got this." He turned and let the guard lead him out of the room.

Transcript from phone conversation from Two Rivers Correctional Facility between HAYES, DELTON, B. (576684-GT) and Judith C. Higgins, mother of one of the children from the Marmont State College cooperative project. June 5, 2019.

DBH: Hello?

JCH: Delton. It's Judith.

DBH: Hey, Miss Higgins.

JCH: So, I have Rena and the doc here. They're telling me that you were actually doing a good job yesterday before I got there, and it was the guard who screwed everything up for you. — Hello?

DBH: I'm here.

JCH: Did you hear what I said.

DBH: Yeah. That was nice of them.

JCH: Do you agree with them?

DBH: I don't know.

JCH: So, you don't think you were doing a good job with Noah?

DBH: Well, I didn't handle it as well as you did.

JCH: That's not what I asked.

DBH: Look Miss Higgins, I'm gonna be straight with you. I was totally not prepared for your son to go completely off the nut like he did. I did my best at the time. Did I do a good job? Well, if you're saying 'he did a good job for someone who didn't know what the hell he was doing' then I guess, yeah, you could say I did a good job. But if you're saying, 'did he do everything right?' Then, no. I can't say that.

JCH: Wow. I appreciate your honesty.

DBH: Right now, honesty is about the only thing we got between you and me, because I think I screwed up your trust in me.

JCH: If I'm being honest....

DBH: I know.

JCH: Rena and the doc are telling me you're ready to have another shot at this.

DBH: Tell them they're wrong.

JCH: What?

DBH: I ain't ready yet. But I'm getting there. See, I read the file on Noah before I started the project, and a bit of the stuff they gave me, but I didn't realize all I needed to know about autism. So I went to the library and got some more books, and I'm doing a lot of reading on it now. So, Miss Higgins, if you and them can give me till Monday, I'd like to finish my studying, and come in with a real game plan next week, so I'm prepared for any more crazy shit that comes up.

JCH: You continue to surprise me, Delton Hayes.

DBH: Thank you, but I seen something in you yesterday, and I have an even more important job now.

JCH: Did you say you saw something in me?

DBH: Yes ma'am. After watching you yesterday, handling Noah and all, I realized that what you really want is just to be a mom, and because of this thing your boy has, you can't. Take it from someone who really didn't have a mother who gave a shit, it's nice to see one who does. I think you'd be a great mom. And in the short amount of time I have with you and your son, I'll do what I can to help you out.— Hello?

JCH: I heard you. I...uh...Thank you, Delton.

DBH: Don't thank me yet, Miss Higgins. I ain't done shit yet. But do you think we could have till Monday?

JCH: Yes. You'll have till Monday. I'll let them know.

DBH: Thank you. And does Noah like things like M&M's?

JCH: Ummm...Skittles. Noah's not really a chocolate

lover.

DBH: Skittles it is then.

JCH: Good luck with your studies, and I'll see you Monday. LINE DISCONNECTED

DBH: Thank you, Miss….Hello? LINE DISCONNECTED

Chapter Twenty-Four

Monday morning, Judith pulled into the parking lot with Noah. It no longer seemed as busy as it had the previous Monday. By now, people knew where they were going, what they were supposed to be doing, and what to expect.

The only assistant waiting outside when she pulled up was Rena. Just like she had the week before, she walked to the car and greeted them. "I'm so glad to see you both again."

Judith unbuckled Noah, took him by the hand and helped him down. As they walked into the building, Rena gave her an update. "It appears Delton has a complete strategy mapped out today. He has asked for a few specific things, including two glasses, one filled with water, a big bag of Skittles, and a large beach blanket."

"What's the beach blanket for?"

"I didn't ask," Rena said. "He seems so determined, I'm just trusting he's prepared and giving him the encouragement."

"I'm not sure I'm as trusting," Judith said. "At the risk of pissing off my boss even more, I took today off to observe once again. You know, for peace of mind."

Rena opened the front door and held it. "I completely understand. That's probably a good idea."

Dr. Fitzpatrick was in the lobby, talking to a couple of assistants. He smiled and waved as Judith passed through. She walked Noah straight to their room. Delton jumped to his feet when they entered, rushed over to Noah, and knelt down. He took Noah's hand, curled it into a fist, and before Noah had a chance to pull it back, performed a fist bump. "Hello, my man," he said, and let go.

Noah put his hand behind his back and turned his head to his mother's leg.

"So what's the plan here?" Judith asked.

Delton stood smiling. "The plan is that I'm going to insert myself into Noah's life."

"You're going to what?"

"I am going to be a part of Noah's every move. He is going to have to get used to doing something with someone all day, every day."

Judith eyed him suspiciously. "You told me you knew what you were doing."

"I know exactly what I'm doing,"

"He won't like that."

"Not at first," Delton said, smiling. "But he'll get used to me." He knelt back down. "Noah and Delton are going to have lots of fun together."

Judith sighed and shook her head. "Just so you know, I took the day off work. I'll be here to see this."

"That's excellent," Delton said. "I told you I'd be ready today, and I am."

Walking Noah over to the chair, she took his jacket from him. "Okay, Noah honey. Mommy's going to go now and you're going to be here with your new friend, Delton."

Noah turned and moaned, reaching for his mother, but she walked out with Rena and closed the door.

"All right, let's start with something really fun to do,"

Delton said. He sat two glasses on the table. One was nearly full of water. "Okay, Noah, you start."

Noah looked at him, then at the glasses. He stared at them for a moment, then reached for the full glass, lifted it, and poured it into the other glass. He set the empty glass down and clapped twice.

"Excellent," Delton said and slid the glasses over in front of himself. "Now it's my turn."

Noah cried out, but Delton poured the water, set down the glass, and clapped twice. Then he slid them over to Noah. "Okay, now it's your turn."

Noah quieted, waited a moment, then poured the water again and clapped.

"Delton's turn." When he slid the water glasses back in front of him, Noah cried out even louder. Delton reached down, grabbed two Skittles from a bag and set them in front of Noah. "Thanks for sharing your water glasses with me, Noah."

Noah stopped crying. He looked at the Skittles and back up to Delton.

Delton poured the water, clapped, and slid the glasses back in front of Noah. "Noah's turn again."

Looking at the choices in front of him, Noah took a moment to decide in what order he would do things. He picked up one Skittle and put it in his mouth. Then he poured a glass of water and clapped.

"Very good. Now it's Delton's turn again." He pulled the water glasses back to him again, and Noah screamed loudly. Delton smiled and put two more Skittles in front of Noah. "Thank you for being so kind and sharing," he said. He poured the water, clapped twice, and slid the glasses back.

The boy whimpered and put his arms around both glasses to prevent them from being pulled away again.

"It's your turn," Delton said smiling. "Go ahead and pour the water."

Noah looked up at him and scowled, throwing his bottom lip out. He hugged the glasses closer.

"Did you want to rest for a minute?" Delton said. "That's okay. I will wait until you go before I try it again."

Noah sat there, untrusting, wary of Delton. Then the bright colors of the Skittles caught his eye. He reached for another one and put it in his mouth. It was like a pill that calmed him down. His mood eased a bit, he sat up, then slowly poured one glass into the other, set it down and clapped twice.

"Great job," Delton said. "My turn again." He pulled the glasses back to his side of the table.

Noah screamed and slammed his hands on the table repeatedly.

"I like it when you share with me, Noah." Delton set down two more Skittles.

Noah wiped his arm across the table and sent the Skittles flying. Then he jumped from his chair, swung at the glasses and flipped them too, spilling the water across the table. Noah stood back and, with a horrified look, watched the water run from the table and onto the floor.

"Oops," Delton said. "The water spilled. That's okay."

But to Noah it was definitely not okay. He screamed, stomped around, and then came the fists to the head.

This time Delton was ready. He scooped up Noah with one arm, pinning the boy's arms to his side. Noah started kicking and banging his head, but neither action had any damaging affect. "It's gonna be just fine, Noah. Your friend, Delton, is here. Everything's going to be okay." Using his free hand, Delton unfolded the beach blanket and spread it out flat on the floor. He laid Noah down on his side and then folded him up in it. With Noah wrapped tightly, Delton lifted the blanket and swayed it back and forth. After several long minutes of screaming and crying Noah's rage subsided. Quiet whimpers were heard from the makeshift hammock-swing. Delton rocked him for a while longer, while Noah collected himself.

Delton looked to the window and smiled. "We got the meltdown behind us quick enough."

When Noah was quiet, Delton set him down on one of the beanbag chairs. He unwrapped him and knelt down to look into Noah's puffy, tired, and sad eyes. "I'm your friend, Noah. I will always have your back. That means I won't let anything bad happen to you anymore." Noah looked up at him, the corners of his mouth turned down. "I don't want you to be sad. Not when there's so much fun we can have together." Delton climbed into the other beanbag and wiggled his behind down into it. Then he over-exaggerated a happy face. "Oh, these chairs are so comfortable." Reaching over to a stack of books, he picked one off the top. "Now that you're all tired, I was thinking we might do some story time." He looked up at the window. "Hey, if I'm going to do a bunch of reading, it might be a good idea to get me some coffee."

Opening the book, Delton began to read. He selected Where the Wild Things Are because that was his favorite, and if he had to end up reading any of these twice, he wanted to be sure that was one of them. He realized that the reading this time was much different than the reading last week. This time Noah had already expended an enormous amount of energy on a meltdown. He was worn out, and even though he didn't look over at Delton, he sat quietly and listened.

Delton would read a page slowly and then hold the book up and show it to Noah. At first Noah didn't look over, but Delton continued to show him anyway. On page five, Noah glanced at the picture. He did again on page six, and page seven. By the time page eight came around, Noah decided to snuggle into the bean bag. He turned to his side to face Delton, folded his hands under his cheek, and stared at the man. When Delton read a line, he put the book down in front of Noah's face to show him the picture. He could see the boy's eyes scanning the page, taking in the details. If his blank expression didn't give any indication that he was interested in the story, his eyes told Delton everything he needed to know.

Just when he had finished the book, the door opened, and Taysha entered with a paper cup of coffee and a plastic top on it. She walked over and set it on the floor next to Delton, and whispered. "Son, I am so proud of you."

Delton smiled. "Thank you, Miss Taysha, for the coffee." He looked over at Noah. "Miss Taysha is a nice lady."

Taysha walked back to the door, paused, and looked back. She smiled, kissed two fingers, and flicked them in Delton's direction. Then she walked out, and closed the door.

Delton set the book down and picked up another. "Oh my goodness, Noah," he said, holding up the book so the boy could see it. "This one is called The Giving Tree. I've never read this book before. This is exciting to me."

He read The Giving Tree, Green Eggs and Ham, and If You Give a Mouse a Cookie. Noah lay there, seemingly content, listening to every word, looking at each page he was shown. But near the end of the mouse book, his tired eyes closed. Delton noticed and stopped reading. "Noah," he said, in a half whisper. The little boy did not move. Delton stared at him, and listened while his breathing became rhythmic and heavy. Noah had drifted off to sleep, and Delton couldn't help but take that as a victory. For a brief moment anyway, he had tamed the rage in the boy's soul, and made him feel comfortable enough to fall asleep.

Whether it was a win or not, Delton felt he'd accomplished something. He climbed out of the beanbag, picked up his coffee, and cheered toward the window.

Delton had cleaned up the water and put the glasses away before Noah awoke to avoid upsetting the boy. He had Legos and blocks out on the table, offering Noah whichever one he wanted to play with. Noah began to play with the Legos, and Delton set two Skittles out on the table. "That's the way to make a decision." He held out his fist but Noah just looked at it and then back at the Legos. "No boy, you can't leave me hanging. You gotta bump me." He took Noah's hand, and bumped his fist with the back of the boy's knuckles. Noah pulled his hand back and hid it under his other arm. Delton laughed. "That's how you do a fist bump."

The door opened shortly afterward, and Rena walked in with a tray of food. "Lunch time." She placed a chicken breast and dish of macaroni and cheese in front of both of them along with a Coke and plastic sporks. "Here you go, honey." She rubbed the back of Noah's head and smiled. When she stood back up Delton saw Judith, standing in the doorway. "I'll be right back, buddy." He jumped up and walked over. She was smiling, so that was a good sign.

"Well done," she said.

"So you're not upset with me for setting off a meltdown?"

She shook her head. "I'll be honest, I don't like to watch it, but I was very impressed that you were ready to handle it."

"Thanks." Delton smiled. "I saw something like that on YouTube. It was a gamble, and I'm glad it worked."

"My dad would be very proud of you."

"Think so?"

"Oh, yeah," she said. "I could hear his voice in my head. 'The boy isn't dying is he?'"

Delton laughed. "No. That's not part of my grand plan."

"So tell me about your..." Judith made air quotes, "'grand plan.' And how do the Skittles fit into that?"

Delton shrugged. "So, I did a lot of reading about this applied behavior analysis. It uses treats to get autistic kids to do what you want them to do."

"I've heard of it," Judith said. "I know they hate it at Keener."

"Well, it does make sense to me," Delton said. "Positive reinforcement for good behavior is not a bad thing. So when I took the glasses from him and thanked him for sharing, he'd get the idea that sharing was a good thing."

Judith nodded. "I like that. But it's going to be hard, because you're going to get push back like you did today. Can you keep it up?"

Delton smiled. "Believe me, I got nothin' better to do. I'm all in."

Judith shook his hand. "Keep up the good work."

"Thanks. I will. But we're gonna be pretty chill this afternoon."

She closed the door and went back into the room. Taking her seat in front of the window, she picked up her turkey sandwich and took a bite. Taysha reached over and rubbed her back. "What do you think, honey?"

Judith chewed and sipped her Coke, then swallowed. "I can't believe the change a week makes. When I left here last Monday, I thought he was probably the biggest dumbass, and I was an idiot signing on for this. But today, now that he's had time to process, study, and understand, I'm thinking that this is going to be a pretty okay experience for Noah."

Taysha smiled. "Pretty okay is exactly what he was shooting for."

For the remainder of the afternoon, Judith sat patiently watching while Noah played with the Legos, and Delton played with the blocks. But Delton continued to talk about anything and everything, so the boy could get used to his voice, and thereby, his presence. His voice sounded tinny over the speakers. "You know what, Noah? You and I have something in common. When I was a kid I didn't have a daddy neither. I mean, I had a daddy. You have to have a daddy or you can't be here. But my daddy took off when I was little, right after my sister was born, so he wasn't around."

Delton knocked over his stack of blocks with a loud crash. Noah looked over and then back at his own Lego...thing. "I'll tell you something else though," Delton continued. "You are luckier than me and my sister. You've got a really great mommy."

Judith's breath stuck in her throat.

"My mommy never really gave a...didn't care much about my sister and me. She had other things to worry about." Delton continued. "You though, you have a mommy who really loves you. She would do anything for you." He smiled and looked over at Noah. "I think she would fight all the Wild Things for you."

Judith looked over to see both Taysha and Rena smiling at her. She smiled back embarrassed, grabbed her Coke, and took a long drink.

Delton tried a couple of other things with Noah, such as walking backward, and trying to get Noah interested in throwing the stuffed animals across the room into a waste basket. But Noah would have none of it. He quietly played with his Legos. It seemed to give Delton more of a break than it did anything for Noah. But Judith thought that was all right. Delton had been engaged all day and he was probably losing his sanity.

When the time came for the kids to leave, Judith could tell Delton was spent. His eyes were red and weary. "Great job today," she said to him, while she put on Noah's jacket.

"Thanks," Delton said. He knelt down to Noah and held out his fist again. "Have a good night, my man."

Noah did not look at him. Delton grabbed his hand again and hit the boy's knuckles with his fist. Noah squeaked resentment at this, and Delton chuckled. "We'll work on that, little guy." He stood. "See you tomorrow."

"See you tomorrow." Judith noticed that this was the first time since she was involved in this program that she actually felt good saying that.

Chapter Twenty-Five

The rest of the week went pretty much the same way as Monday. Judith dropped Noah off on her way to work and Darlene picked him up at the end of the schoolday. When Judith would bring Noah in, Delton would attempt an awkward fist bump. Judith wondered when he'd give up on that, but he started each day by saying, "My man," and then grabbing Noah's hand and bumping his own. Then Delton would take Noah over to the table and try the water sharing. The first couple of days, he had Noah in total meltdown mode before she even left for work. Judith would say goodbye to Rena and Taysha as Delton was swinging Noah in the beach blanket hammock. From what they reported to her when she dropped him off Friday morning is that Thursday was a double meltdown day. Darlene had told her that when she picked up Noah that day, Delton looked extremely tired.

But, eventually, the meltdowns became delayed — coming after she'd left. It looked as if Noah was acclimating to the situation, and to Delton. By Friday of the following week, when Delton knelt down and held out his fist, Noah half-heartedly hit it with the back of his hand. Delton thanked him kindly, and stood. When Judith walked Noah to the table, Delton quietly pumped his fist in the air.

It seemed that every day, when Judith dropped off Noah, Rena and Taysha were more excited than the day before. They would often show Judith specific segments of the video recordings for the previous day.

As time went on, Delton became adept at getting Noah interested in whatever he was doing. One day the recording showed Delton placing a ping-pong ball on the table and blowing it off into a bucket. Noah watched him several times, then picked it out of the bucket before Delton could get to it. "Wanna try?" Delton asked him. But Noah didn't need to be asked. He ran to the other end of the table, placed the ball on it and blew. It went off to the side and Noah screeched angrily at it.

"Nice try," Delton said, and he put two Skittles on the table. Noah snatched them both up instantly and tossed them into his mouth. Delton picked up the ball and set it down on the table. "Are you ready?" Noah put his face down by the ball and blew. Delton let go of the ball and it went off to the side again. Delton put his arm along the table so the ball couldn't fall off. Noah climbed up onto the table and kept blowing. "Blow, blow, blow!" Delton yelled. Noah blew until Delton steered the ball off the table into the bucket. "Nicely done," Delton said and held his fist out. Noah bumped his fist with his own.

Delton was single-handedly surpassing everything that the teachers at Keener had ever done. Each day, as he had more success, and as Noah became more responsive, Judith found herself growing more depressed. One day Darlene was busy and Judith had to leave work early to get Noah. When she pulled into the parking lot, Taysha was at the door waving her in excitedly. Delton had already been removed with the other inmates and taken back to Two Rivers, but Rena had a video recording cued and ready to show her. Judith watched her son playing with Delton. They stood at one side of the room and heaved each of the stuffed animals across, and into the waste basket against the far wall. Whenever one went in, Noah laughed. It started out as an awkward little giggle, but as the play went on, and Noah would throw an animal, have it slam into the wall and drop into the bucket, Noah's little giggles grew into loud cackles of laughter. To Judith it was the most beautiful sound she'd ever heard, and she broke down in tears.

She thanked them, took Noah out into the car, and strapped him into his car seat. She drove down the road about a mile, pulled into a Kroger parking lot, put the car in park and cried. Her body shook, and tears streamed down her face. She put her hands on the top of the steering wheel and laid her head on them. She was happy that Noah was responding, showing signs of improving, but she didn't want to just witness it from the sidelines, she wanted to be a part of it. This was like reliving his first steps, his first words, all over again, and she wasn't there by his side where a mother should be. She was stuck 20 miles away in an office building, with a boss who didn't give a shit about either of them.

A knock at the window startled her. She looked up, "Is everything okay, miss?" It was an older gentleman with a single sack of groceries in his hand.

Judith wiped her eyes and nodded. "Fine."

He nodded back, and walked off.

Judith decided it was a great night for Lance's. "Are you hungry, buddy?"

Forty-five minutes later, they were sitting across from the park once again, sipping on their shakes. She watched the man helping his wife back into the car. When he also got back in and drove away, Judith turned in her seat and looked at her son. He sipped slowly at his shake and looked out the window, as if there weren't a care in the world. She had seen him express happiness today. He had experienced elation. This was something she thought he would never do. All his emotions seemed buried under a mountain of bland, the only one able to reach the surface had been rage. She thought rage was the only thing he would ever feel. But now that happiness had found its way out, what else might come through—jealousy?...Pride?...Perhaps love?

"Did you have a good time today, honey?"

Noah said nothing. He didn't even look at her. He took another sip from his cup and reached the empty, sucking gurgle at the bottom. Dropping the cup on the floor, Noah laid his head back on the car seat, turned, and stared blankly into her eyes.

"What is going on in there?" Judith whispered to him. "What are you thinking about after a day like today?"

Noah still said nothing. He continued to stare back at her.

Her phone buzzed in her purse. Judith pulled it out to see Darlene's name on the screen. She tapped on the call. "Hi, Dar."

"Uh oh. What's wrong?"

"Absolutely nothing. Noah laughed out loud today."

"He did what?"

"Yep. He and Delton were playing this game where they throw stuffed animals into a bucket, and Noah had so much fun he laughed really loud. Right from his belly."

"But that's great, isn't it?"

"Yeah. It's so great I cried all the way home."

"Why are you crying about that?"

"Because I'm not there, Dar." Judith's voice cracked. "I'm not the one he's laughing with. It's this other guy who relates to him better than his own mom." She wiped tears out of her eyes with the used Lance's napkin.

"Jude, I get it. But this is why you signed the little guy up for this crazy-ass thing. Because there was an outside chance that the miracle could happen. Now that it's happened you need to rejoice a little bit. You, as his mom, made an excellent choice and you should celebrate. In fact, I know this guy that Jim works with who you should celebrate with."

"Oh my God, did you just do that?" Judith couldn't help but smile. "Did you just take my angst and try to spin it into a reason to date?"

"How'd I do?"

"It was awful, and unfeeling."

"Damn. I thought I was really clever. But what about it?"

Judith sighed. "I'm sorry. I'm not in the mood to talk about that right now. I'll catch you later."

"Okay, I'll talk to…."

Judith tapped off the call and threw it onto the seat next to her. She looked back at Noah who was still staring at her. "Will you laugh like that with me someday?" She put her right arm on the back of the seat and set her chin on it. "I'd really love to hear it."

Excerpts from the transcript of the GINfo (Global Information Network) interview between Brooke Winthrop and Rena Blossom.

Brooke: So, Rena is a unique name. Is it short for anything?

Rena: No, it's just Rena. It's like an old family name from my mother's side. Like before they even came over on the boat kind of old.

Off Camera: Rolling.

Brooke: Okay Rena, I don't want you to be nervous. All these people around us are just here to make sure you look and sound great. Think of this as just a conversation between you and me. Okay?

Rena: Okay. But I'm not nervous. I'm more sad that it's all come to this.

Brooke: I understand. Well, let's take a moment and talk about an incident that happened early on in the project. Noah Higgins was having a meltdown, Delton was trying to restrain him and a guard felt he needed to come in, with his gun drawn, to save the boy.

Rena: Who told you about that?

Brooke: It's been confirmed from a couple of sources.

Rena: Well that has nothing to do with any of this. And if anybody told you it did, they were either mistaken or lying.

Brooke: I was informed that Judith Higgins was so concerned by it, that she had pulled Noah from the program.

Rena: Okay, stop rolling. I'm pissed. All of this is being taken way out of context to make things look worse than they really were. And you're ambushing me with all of this right now, to see if I'll say something to incriminate someone.

Brooke: All right, let's start over. I truly wasn't trying to ambush you. We've invited you here as a content expert as to what went on inside the Marmont Project Building. You were there every minute of every day. It has been represented that Judith Higgins, Delton Hayes, and Noah Higgins hit it off from the very first time they met. That was our assumption when we started this story. We have since been informed that wasn't the case.

Rena: No. That was not the case at all.

Brooke: And then one of our researchers discovered this incident where a guard came into the room. I'm coming to you for clarity on this.

Rena: Okay, I'll give you clarity. It literally happened on the second day of the program. Noah had a meltdown. It wasn't because he was mistreated or anything. Delton had nothing to do with that. Noah had spun a chair all day the day before. We replaced the chair with one that didn't spin and he got upset. Noah started screaming and hitting himself. When this happens, it's important to restrain the child or they can hurt themselves. Taysha had called Miss Higgins and asked her to come back. A guard heard the noise, looked in and thought Delton was hurting Noah. We tried to tell him that everything was fine but he didn't listen, he went in and pulled his gun. That was right when Miss Higgins showed up. So you could understand how a mother could be a little bit freaked out about the situation. But up until that point, Delton was doing everything right. And it has nothing to do with the reason you came here in the first place. You shouldn't even bring it up in your story.

Brooke: You're sounding like a champion for Delton—ready to fight me tooth and nail for his honor.

Rena: Because you guys just want to tear him down. And after everything that's happened it's easy to do that. But Delton was good to Noah, and he was good in the program. When he wasn't with him, he studied hard on his own to be the best guide…companion…teacher, that Noah needed him to be. He connected with Noah, and it wasn't just some miracle connection. Delton worked hard at it. And I think that's why they were so good together. Delton wasn't just putting in his time every day. He put Noah first every single minute. He was definitely the right person for Noah, and even after all of this, I am glad I had him with me.

Brooke: I wish I had the chance to meet him.

Rena: So do I. All of this is so heartbreaking.

Chapter Twenty-Six

On the bus ride back to the prison, Delton could not stop smiling. The results of that afternoon played over in his mind. This boy who could not communicate, could not, or would not show any kind of emotion toward anybody or anything, had just laughed, and smiled, and played. He knew that Rena, Taysha, and Doctor F. were very pleased with the progress, and they would study the video all night long. But Delton felt as if he had just done the impossible. He took a deep breath and felt like he wanted to jump up and do a victory lap.

He remembered how his friend Hector had teared up the very first day, when he'd had a remarkable fulfilling time with his kid. He wished Hector were still in the program, but his special kid moved to another state, so Hector had to drop out. But Delton's feelings were different than Hector's. He had no sense that he wanted to cry. He was ready to climb the ladder and cut down the nets.

Rick Simpson moved up a few seats and sat across the aisle from Delton. "Place was buzzing this afternoon 'bout you. Heard them all saying you and your boy had a breakthrough."

Delton grinned. "Yeah, I guess we did. I got my kid to laugh."

"A laugh is a breakthrough?" Rick Simpson snorted.

"It is when your kid is as autistic as my boy is. He hasn't ever laughed."

"Well, that's great I guess," Simpson said. He sat back in his seat, then looked back over to Delton. "The only breakthrough I'm concerned about with my kid, is breaking through his mom's panties." He laughed and looked out the window. "Damn, she's a hot thing."

Delton discovered his smile was gone. He wanted to tell this hick that the rest of the crew was taking this thing seriously, and if he didn't want to, then get out and stop wasting everyone's time. Perhaps Hector could take over for his kid. Hector had been putting effort into it. Simpson clearly wasn't.

That is what affected Delton the most. He studied, learned, and planned what to do with Noah. This wasn't just a way to get out from behind the walls for a day. It was a mission, a responsibility he signed up for, and he was going to give his best to it. He resented the fact that someone else was just coasting along, giving minimum effort.

When they reached the prison and got off the bus, one of the guards called to him. "Hayes, you got a phone call."

He wasn't surprised. Judith was clearly happy about the news and they had arranged a phone call for her. When he got to the phone, a guard spoke into the receiver. "Here he is now, honey." The guard handed the receiver to Delton, "She sounds upset." Then he left the room.

Delton put the receiver to his ear. "Hello?"

"Delton, it's Danna,"

It was good to hear her voice, and he smiled. "Hey girl. How's it…"

"Delton, I don't want to be here no more."

His smile faded. "What's wrong?"

"They's awful."

"Are they hurting you?"

"No. They just won't let me do anything. They won't even let me come see you no more. They say you're a bad guy, and that I need to forget about you. They only want me around good people from now on."

Delton ground his teeth. "Put Reggie on the phone."

"Oh my God. No. They'd kill me if they knew I was talking to you. I snuck Jamie's phone in here, and I'm using that to call you because they got the prison number blocked on my phone."

Delton could feel his heartbeat in his throat. It kept him from speaking.

"If I say anything back to them about being unfair, they ground me and make me do all these chores and shit like that."

Delton took a breath to calm himself, and tried to think up the best thing to say to pacify his sister. "Danna, there's…."

A distant voice yelled on the phone line. "Who are you talking to?" Some rustling was heard, and Danna's muffled voice replied, "Nobody."

"Give me that phone,"

"No."

More rustling could be heard, and Danna's voice cried out, "No! Stop that."

Then a man's voice came on the phone. "Who is this?"

Delton was in so much rage he could hardly utter a word, but he collected himself and said in the most stable voice he could pull together, "This is Delton Hayes. Who is this?"

"Delton, we talked about you having no more contact with Danna."

In the background Delton could hear Danna crying. "Give me back that phone. You've got no right to keep me from my brother."

"But I'm her brother. Can't you see she wants to talk to me?"

"That doesn't matter. We're her family now. It is our

responsibility to see that she is surrounded by a respectable group of people, not those who make poor decisions and get themselves thrown into jail. Now I'd appreciate it if you'd stop trying to talk to her, and let her move on with her life. We can give her much more than anything you could ever offer her." Then the line went dead.

Delton stood holding the phone to his ear, trying to process both the words and the feelings that were now coursing through him like a raging evil drug. He wanted to rip the phone off the wall, and smash it on the floor. He remembered Taysha saying that by helping Noah, he would be helping Danna.

Delton was squeezing the receiver in his hand so tightly he thought the plastic might break.

Eventually he hung up the phone, closed his eyes, leaned his head against it, and concentrated on breathing. He told himself that Danna was going to be fine. She just didn't like the people, and one day he would be able to help her with that, but today was not the day.

He stood straight, took one deep breath and nodded to the guard to let him out of the phone room. He walked back to the cafeteria realizing just how quickly his feelings of winning could come crashing down into helplessness and rage.

The roller coaster of life was going full speed.

Chapter Twenty-Seven

"Woof, woof, woof," barked the basset hound alarm clock. "Woof, woof, woof,"

Noah blinked his eyes open, stared for a moment at the little plastic basset hound lying on the digital clock, then sat up in bed.

"Woof, woof, woof."

"Noah, honey," Judith said as she rushed into his room. "It's time to get up." She reached down and tapped the dog on the top of his head.

"Woof, wo...."

Noah jumped from his bed and ran into the bathroom. Such quick movement surprised Judith. Normally her son slogged through the morning routine. She would have to continually prod him to keep moving forward. The toilet flushed and out he ran, back into his room and threw on his pants, and t-shirt that she'd laid out for him the night before.

Trying to stay ahead of him, Judith filled his bowl with Captain Crunch and was pouring the milk when Noah rushed into the kitchen. Judith smiled. "Slow down, Speed Racer. We can't be the first ones there today." She brushed his hair with her fingers while he ate. "When you're done eating, go in and brush your teeth."

She poured herself a cup of coffee and headed back to her bathroom to paint her face. She picked up the eyeliner and looked into the mirror, admitting to herself that seeing this reaction from Noah helped calm her struggle from the day before. Even though it hurt to be away from her son when he was seeing so much growth, watching him appear excited to go back was a great validation that she had made the right decision.

Judith pulled the top on her mascara and slowly began to apply it to her lashes.

Noah's success was also the perfect ammunition to use for everyone who reacted with disbelief and disdain that she had ever put her son in a program like this in the first place. He had gone farther in less than a month than he had in the last three years at school.

Judith twirled up the Peach Passion lipstick.

She wondered what Delton's secret was. Was it the location? The room? The other people involved? Perhaps it was all the factors combined. She knew she signed up for a sociological experiment, and Noah's success thus far had to be one of the highlights of the project. She was sure they would study his outcomes and determine what the factors were. In the meantime, she was happy with the gains.

She put away her lipstick just as Noah walked in to brush his teeth. "You made quick work of that bowl of cereal, buddy. You must really be in a hurry."

The parking lot at the project building was starting to look a little thinner. Four of the children had dropped out of the program—one because his inmate became aggressive and shook the child, two of them because their inmates refused to stop swearing, and the last because the father got another job, and moved out of state. That meant at least eight parking spaces were free, so she pulled up very near the front door. "Look buddy. We got a close spot today."

Walking around and opening the door, Judith unlocked Noah's seat belt. He jumped down, grabbed her hand and dragged her into the building. "Oh my goodness," she said, giggling as she followed along. "Noah, I can't keep up with you."

Noah went as fast as he could down the hall to his room. He even knew which door was his by this point. The outer door was open, and Rena and Taysha were surprised to see them so early. Judith could see Delton through the glass, sitting at the table reading something.

Noah walked up to the door and moaned for her to open it.

"My goodness, we're excited to begin today, aren't we?" Rena said.

Judith laughed. "I guess so." She opened the door for Noah, and he ran inside.

Delton looked up. "Hey there." He put his fist down, like every day before.

Noah ran around the table to him, bumped his fist and cried out, "Hey, me min!"

Delton stood up, throwing his hands to his head in utter disbelief. "What the f...." He said no more. He looked over at Judith with wide disbelieving eyes.

Judith thought her heart stopped. A dizziness hit her, and her knees wobbled slightly. Her hand was on her mouth, she didn't know why, perhaps so she wouldn't say anything in case Noah would speak more.

That voice. That beautiful little voice that had been kept silent by the autism monster. It had been liberated to be shared with the rest of the world.

Rena and Taysha both entered the room slowly, their mouths wide open with no sound coming out. It was as if once Noah found his voice, everyone else in the room lost theirs.

Judith's blouse was damp before she realized tears were

running down her face. She looked at Delton, and discovered small tears running from his red eyes as well. She tried to say thank you, and laughed when it came out as an incoherent babble. She stumbled over and wrapped her arms around him, holding on tight, lest her knees give out completely.

"Wow." Delton whispered in her ear. "I needed to hear that today, more than you'll ever know."

Rena and Taysha joined them, and all four adults shared a group hug. They heard a muffled thunk and then a happy giggle. Looking over, they saw Noah picking up where they'd left off the day before, tossing stuffed animals into the waste basket. He threw two more that bounced off to either side, then grabbed a monkey and threw it. It hit the wall and dropped in. Noah raised his arms and laughed.

Looking at his face, filled with so much joy, Judith felt his smile was so brilliant and bright, it lit up the whole room.

"We need to leave so these two can get on with their day," Rena said.

Taysha put a hand on Delton's cheek and smiled proudly. "You're not only proving it to yourself, you're proving it to the whole world, the kind of man you are. Keep it up."

Delton wiped his eye, and leaned down for a hug from her.

Judith dropped to her knees in front of Noah. Trying her best not to cry, she spoke to him. "Honey, mommy has to go now. You have a fun day, okay?"

Noah picked up a stuffed flamingo and spoke again. "Bye." He stepped to the side and tossed the bird, missing his target.

Tears flooded Judith's eyes once more. She rubbed them and tried to stand. Rena grabbed her arm and helped her up. Still rubbing away tears, they walked out of the room and Judith spun around to look through the window. Her breath fogged the glass, she clung so close to it.

Taysha came in last, and closed the door behind her.

Delton still stood over by the table. He crossed his arms,

stared at the floor, smiling and shaking his head. Then he rubbed his eyes once more, took a deep breath and blew it out.

Noah ran to the waste basket, tipped it over, dragged the stuffed animals out of it, and across the room.

Delton walked over to him. "So, you decided to talk today, huh?"

Noah ignored the question. He went back for more animals. Delton sat on the floor and watched him work. When Noah passed by, Delton put a hand out to stop him. "Hey buddy, let's try this again." He held out his fist one more time.

Noah looked down and once more, hit it with his own. "Hey, me min." Then he rushed off to get the last of the animals.

Judith watched Delton crawl to a beanbag and sit in it. He looked exhausted, as if the effort of coaxing three words out of Noah sapped his strength, but she tried to understand it from his point of view. He truly had given effort in this. He studied to understand Noah's issues, and made a plan of action that he could follow, to try and help Noah succeed. He had battled through Noah's meltdowns and continued on, day after day, even when it looked like there was going to be no progress. Judith was so proud of him. As Noah began with his next round of animal tossing, Judith turned away from the window to Rena and Taysha. "Thank you," she said.

"For what?" Taysha said. "For sitting here on our rumps, while we watched Delton do all of the work?" She shook her head. "No, darling. I'm not taking any of the credit here."

Rena smiled. "I agree with her. Delton has worked very hard at this, and he deserves all the credit."

"Thank you for sitting on your rumps, and being here with Delton." She smiled at them and walked out the door. As she walked down the hall, she heard a squeak-step, behind her. She spun around to see Dr. Fitzpatrick heading in her direction. He smiled when he saw her, "Ah. Good morning, Miss Higgins."

Judith ran to him, and wrapped her arms around his chest.

"Good morning, Dr. Fitzpatrick. And thank you."

"Oh my goodness." After a short pause, Dr. Fitzpatrick patted her shoulders awkwardly. "Thank me for what?"

She pulled back and looked up at him. "Go in and check on Noah and Delton. You'll see." She turned and walked out. "Have a great day, Doctor."

As soon as Judith pulled the car out of the parking lot, she hit Darlene on speed dial.

"Hey, Jude. What's up?"

"Noah spoke, Dar!" Judith screamed the news, surprising herself for being so loud.

"Are you f-ing kidding me?"

"No. He fist-bumped Delton and said, 'Hey, me mon,' or something like that. And when I said goodbye to him, he said 'bye' back to me."

"Oh, Jude," Judith could hear a quiver in her sister's voice, and it made her tear up once again. "I'm so happy for you."

"I am so excited, I can't even see straight."

"Well then, you need a man who can make you breakfast and drive you to work. Hey, I know of one."

Judith laughed. "You did not just turn my little victory into an attempt at a booty call."

Darlene laughed. "Not a booty call, girl. Just a blind date call."

"Not going there right now, Sister, but thanks. Love you."

"Just think about...." Judith tapped off the call and tossed the phone onto the seat next to her. The sun was shining brightly this morning, but to her it wouldn't have mattered if it was pouring down rain. Today was already one of the brightest in her life.

Once at work, she flipped on her computer and logged in.

"Just letting you know, Bernie's been asking about you."

Judith spun her chair around to see Simon peeking his head

into her cubicle. "Bring him in," she said. "I'll give him a hug too." She jumped up, yanked Simon in, and hugged him tight. "Noah spoke this morning,"

Simon pulled back, excited. "You're shitting me."

"No. I'm not," she said with a squeak.

"Nice of you to join us, Higgins," Bernie's gruff voice came from the door of her cubicle. "We got a party going on in here now?"

"Yes, we do, you big beautiful Bernie, you." She wrapped her arms around his neck and squeezed hard.

"What the hell?" Bernie said.

Judith jumped back. "Noah spoke this morning."

"Oh, that's wonderful," Evelyn pushed past Bernie, and hugged Judith. "I know how worried you've been about this whole prison project thing, but it looks like it's working out."

"Oh my God, Evelyn. It's working out so well." She pulled back and told all three of them about Noah's laughter the day before, and then the fist bump this morning, and how he said "bye" to his mommy. Shelly came in for her hug too, and they all seemed happy for her. Even Bernie had quit his bitching for the time being. But he was the one who ended the festivities.

"Okay, we have clients that depend on us too. It's not just a feel good for ourselves, party time all day thing." They each shook Judith's hand and congratulated her once again before heading back to their own cubicles. "I was looking for you earlier, Judith. I need the Rothchild Expenditure Report by noon. Harrington's been asking for it for two days now and I've been covering for you, but I can't hold him off anymore. He's really getting pissed at me."

Judith looked at him wide-eyed. "You've been covering for me? Why?"

Bernie scowled, and walked out the door. "Because I heard it takes a village, or some shit like that."

Judith chased after him. "Bernie Herbstreit."

Bernie stopped and turned around.

"Thank you. I appreciate you."

She could tell he was doing everything he could to fight off a smile. "Just get me the damn report by noon."

"You got it." She rushed back into her cubicle and opened the file on her computer. Grabbing her keys, she unlocked her cabinet and grabbed the bulging folder she had on the Rothchild account. She sat it down on her desk and was beginning to organize it when her phone rang. She picked up the receiver, pinched it into the crook of her neck, and continued to work. "Filmore National; this is Judith."

"Oh hello, Miss Higgins," a woman's voice spoke hesitantly. "This is Emily Deluca, a nurse here at Pleasant Oaks, and I'm calling about your father."

Judith felt her face flush. She tried to speak but her throat didn't seem to want to release the words. She practically had to cough out, "What's wrong?"

"Well, we hate to have to say these things over the phone, but he just left for the hospital in an ambulance. The doctors here think he's suffered a stroke."

Chapter Twenty-Eight

Taking the corner too fast, the tires screeched. "Settle down, Judith," she said aloud to herself. "You don't need a ticket, and you want to get there in one piece."

She picked the phone out of her purse and awkwardly hit Darlene on speed dial.

"Hey, Jude,"

"Dar. Dad's in the hospital. He's had a stroke." She felt bad for just blurting it out like that, but there really wasn't any sense for small talk.

"He what?"

"He had a stroke. Pleasant Ridge called an ambulance for him."

"Is he going to be okay?" Darlene's voice cracked.

"Right now you know everything I know. Can you come down?"

"Yes. What hospital?"

"Cardinal, West."

"I'll be there in twenty minutes." The phone clicked dead.

"Dar?" When there was no answer, Judith tossed the phone onto the seat next to her. "Fine. Just hang up on me." She was easily agitated right now—sharp contrast to the complete elation she felt a mere five minutes ago. One phone call changed her whole outlook. She felt horrible telling Bernie she had to leave. He had actually been trying to be good to her, and she let him down again. Thankfully, Evelyn went into her office and took over the report. But she didn't look happy about it, and Judith couldn't stop the nagging feeling that the whole office was beginning to think she was more of a burden than an asset.

Judith parked the car, and sprinted into the emergency room.

After explaining that her father was brought in, they ran her through the metal detector, and a hostess led her down to her father's room. He was lying in the bed, unconscious, a tube running into his nose, and an IV into his wrist. An African American nurse named Edna was there taking his blood pressure.

"Do we know how he is?" Judith asked her.

She finished listening through the stethoscope, then pulled them from her ears, and pulled the blood pressure cuff off with its standard Velcro rip. She looked up at Judith and offered a friendly smile. "Are you family?"

Judith nodded. "Daughter."

"Doctor Russo was looking him over. He should be back in a minute to talk with you." Edna grabbed her father's wrist, and held it while she looked at her watch. Then she set it down and pulled his sheet back up. "If I see him I'll let him know you're here."

"Thank you," Judith said. She pulled a chair next to her father's bed, sat down and gripped his hand. She realized she was crying again. Rubbing her eyes, she didn't know there could be any more tears left in them. She probably should start drinking something before she completely dehydrated. She reached over, grabbed a tissue from the box on the bed stand, dabbed at her eyes, and blew her nose.

Darlene breezed through the door. "Any word?" She had

on jeans with a ripped knee, a stained t-shirt and an Under Armor sweat jacket on over it, but not zipped up in front.

"Darlene," Judith said. "Why did you come here looking like that?"

Darlene looked down at her clothes and back up at Judith. "Nobody gives a shit what you look like in the emergency room. They just want you here so they can get your permission to run the damn tests."

"Don't you give a shit?"

"When my father's lying unconscious in a bed?" She shook her head. "No."

The doctor scooted through the doorway behind Darlene. "Hello, I'm Doctor Russo. I take it you're his family?"

"Hi, Doctor." Judith stood and shook his hand. "We're his daughters. I'm Judith Higgins and this is Darlene Longwood."

Dr. Russo shook both their hands. "I'm glad you're here. I wanted to get your permission to treat him." He went to the sink and washed his hands.

Darlene sneered at Judith when his back was turned.

"Your father had symptoms of a very serious stroke," Dr. Russo said. "From what I understand, he was playing chess, when all of a sudden he couldn't lift his arm to move a piece on the board. According to the man he was playing against, his eyes grew distant, he tried to speak, but it all came out as a garbled murmur, and he slumped in his chair."

"Oh my God," Darlene said. "He must have been terrified."

"I'm sure it shook him up," Dr. Russo said. "We gave him something to help him rest, but we're going to go ahead and do a CT scan as quickly as possible, to see what exactly is going on. The hope is that we can stop whatever is causing this."

"If you can stop it, will he be better?" Judith asked.

"There's no guarantee that he will be better. The hope is that he will get better over time. But we want to keep whatever it is from getting worse."

"Go ahead and do whatever you need to do," Darlene said.

"Someone will be in to get him very soon."

"Thank you, Doctor," Judith said.

He smiled at her. "You bet." Then he walked out.

Judith went over, sat down, and reached for her father's hand once again.

"Wow, he sure smiled at you." Darlene kicked the doctor's stool over and sat down.

"What do you mean? No, he didn't."

"He sure as hell did," Darlene said. She used her feet to slide the stool back and forth across the floor. "And he had no ring on."

"Darlene, stop with the whole man thing," Judith said. She was irritated that her sister continued to push the subject at the most inappropriate times. "I'm not ready for something like that right now," she pointed at their dad. "And our father is lying here unconscious right in front of us. My love life isn't even on the radar of topics to be discussed right now."

An orderly walked in to take their father away. Judith was thankful for his perfect timing. She was sure her sister had some snappy rebuttal, and she just didn't want to deal with it. He rolled the bed out of the room, and told them it should only be a half hour or so and they would bring him right back.

Judith's phone buzzed and she checked her text. It was from Rena. "Dr. F. would like to sit with you and Delton to discuss next steps, when you pick up Noah, if you have time." Judith quickly thumbed out, "Sure."

It was quiet for a few minutes while Darlene checked Facebook on her phone. Then she shoved it back into her pocket and looked at Judith. "So tell me all about talking Noah."

Judith had to stop and think. That whole incident seemed so long ago and so unimportant now. "He just walked right up to

Delton, fist-bumped him and said, 'My man,' as if they had been saying it to each other every day for weeks."

Darlene waved her hands in the air. "Hold on, you have to back way up." She pulled a chair over and sat it down facing Judith. "I want it from the start. Why would Noah say 'my man?'"

She couldn't help but smile now, recalling all the events leading up to Noah's first words. She told about Delton studying and having plans for things to do each day. She talked about Noah giggling with joy at throwing the stuffed animals. And she explained how Delton started every day with a fist-bump with Noah, because he knew Noah didn't like to be touched all that much and a fist-bump was the least intrusive greeting he could think of.

It all seemed so impossible when she said it out loud, but she had witnessed it actually happen. Otherwise, Judith thought she might be having the same disbelieving look as her sister. But then anger crept into her heart. On the most brilliant day of her young son's life, Judith's father had to fight for his. And Judith realized that, even though she loved telling her sister the whole story, she really wanted to tell her father. After all, if it weren't for him, Noah wouldn't be in the program, and there wouldn't ever have been a breakthrough.

Somehow, fathers really did know best after all.

The bed rolled back in, and their father was put back in place, still unconscious. "The doctor will be right in to talk to you," the orderly said.

"In fact, I'm right here," Dr. Russo said, coming in right behind him. He walked over and leaned against the sink with his arms crossed. Judith and Darlene turned their chairs to face him. "Okay, we know exactly what's going on now and we know what to do. Your father has had an ischemic stroke on the left side of his brain due to plaque buildup in the artery. I would say there's about 75% occlusion in the carotid and it needs to be taken care of soon."

"Taken care of…like…surgery?" Darlene asked.

"Yes. It's called an endarterectomy. It's not a terribly complicated procedure but we need to do it fairly quickly."

"Fine. Where do we sign?" Judith said. "Let's get it going."

They spent the next four hours in the surgical waiting lounge watching a "Fix That House" marathon on the Home Channel. Judith and Darlene disagreed with every single make-over that was done. Considering that they were sisters, their decorating styles were incredibly different.

Finally Dr. Russo, dressed in scrubs, came through the post-op door and walked over. "It went well. He's in recovery now and you'll be able to see him in another hour or so."

"Will there be lasting effects with this?" Judith asked.

"There could be. The left brain was affected so that can mean some very specific things, the scariest for him being paralysis on the right side of the body, and speech issues. This makes sense with the story that he couldn't move a chess piece and his speech was slurred."

"Will he recover his speech?" Darlene asked.

"It's tough to predict," Dr. Russo said. "He should recover a good amount. Perhaps not completely, but you should also know that it will take some time, and some patience." Dr. Russo told them that they would admit their father to the hospital and watch him for the next few days to make sure he was on the road to recovery. Then, with his bright smile, he shook both their hands and went on to help someone else's shattered lives.

The rest of the day was spent flanking their father while he lay unconscious in the bed.

Eventually Judith looked at the clock, and realized she was about five minutes past the time she should have left.

"Go," Darlene said. "I got this."

Judith grabbed her purse and rushed to the car. She was going to have to speed in order to make it there on time. She hoped the prison bus could stay a little longer so she had a chance to meet with Delton too.

Chapter Twenty-Nine

Noah was sleeping in his beanbag chair when Dr. Fitzpatrick came in and joined Rena, Taysha, and Delton at the table. He smiled. "The little guy had a big day."

"Yes, he did," Taysha said.

Judith ran in, acting like she was late. "I'm sorry," she said. She looked at Noah, and sat down at the table breathing heavily. Delton thought she appeared flustered. Rena asked her about it before Delton had a chance to. "Is everything all right?"

Judith sighed, and shook her head. "My father isn't doing well."

Everyone, including Delton, gave some voice of support and condolence.

"Thank you," she said, doing her best not to cry.

What struck Delton was the similarity of it all. Somehow it didn't matter what side of the bars you were on, your family could be in trouble and there wasn't a damn thing you could do about it. She couldn't fix her father, no more than he could fix his sister's predicament. Even if he were on the outside, there wouldn't be anything he could do. In fact, he felt that if he were out, and he tried to do something, Reggie would have him arrested and he'd be right back in again for another who knows how many years. At least he had Noah to concentrate on, and keep his head straight. And now Judith did too.

"So what did you want to talk to me about?" she said.

Dr. Fitzpatrick was about to speak when a guard called from the doorway. "Hayes, you need to get on the bus."

"Oh, ahhh…" Dr. Fitzpatrick stood up and turned to the guard. "We really need him in this meeting. He's had an incredible breakthrough here today, and we need to discuss next steps. Can I drive him back when the meeting's over?"

"Are you kidding me?" The guard guffawed. "Doc, I don't care if he's freaking Helen Keller's miracle worker. He's still an inmate at Two Rivers Correctional Facility and property of the State of Michigan. He rides the bus. Period."

"Oh, ahhh…" Dr. Fitzpatrick was obviously intimidated. He looked back and forth between Delton and the guard.

"Look, Doc, it won't be a problem for the bus to be a little late if this meeting is that important. Can we keep it to ten minutes or less?"

Dr. Fitzpatrick smiled. "Yes sir. I think we can do that."

The guard looked back to Delton. "I'll be right outside the door, Hayes."

"Yes sir," Delton said, and the guard left the room.

"Okay, Judith, there was a bit more success today after you left." Dr. Fitzpatrick sat back down. "Noah managed several more words," he looked over to Rena. "What were they again, Rena?"

Rena flipped a couple of pages back in her notebook. "He said 'Yeah,' 'Fun,' 'Boom,'" She turned the page. "'I'm hungry,' 'Yum,' 'No,' 'Legos,' 'Blue,' 'Green,' 'Yellow,'" She turned another page. "'Delton,' and 'I'm tired.'"

Delton looked at Judith. Her hand was over her mouth and her eyes were watering again.

"That is a very comprehensive list, Rena. Thank you." Dr. Fitzpatrick looked at Delton. "And you, young man, are to be commended for the brilliant amount of work and dedication you have put into this project. The fruits of your labors have blossomed today."

Delton smiled. "So this is what proud feels like."

"Thank you." Judith said. She looked at him with sweet, kind, caring eyes. He almost didn't recognize her.

Delton recalled when those eyes were cold, the voice was harsh, there was no warmth at all. But then there was no warmth in him either. Noah had changed him as well. "You don't have to thank me. This is probably one of the best days of my life."

She turned to Dr. Fitzpatrick. "Can you tell me why now? Why this project? Why Delton could get him to talk, when nobody else could?"

"Rena has some thoughts on that," Dr. Fitzpatrick said.

"We all know that children with autism respond to the world differently than children without autism." Rena said. "There are everyday things that can easily overwhelm them, such as loud noises, crowds in a mall or on the street, even fast-moving clouds in the sky can sometimes be hard for them to relate to." She looked around the room. "So the environment created in here is safe for Noah. The walls are bland, there are no windows, so there's no outside noise. Also, I'm guessing he's never been given the amount of time, one-on-one, in any other setting than he's been shown here."

Judith shook her head. "No. You're right. He hasn't."

"That's what I thought," Rena said. "And lastly, I think his race actually plays a part in it."

"What?" Delton said. "You're saying that Noah is speaking to me because I'm black?"

"No. That's not what I'm saying," Rena said. "Noah is speaking with you, because you have found a way to connect with him. But if you'll recall, I said that children with autism view and experience the world differently. It was clear, based on interaction between you and Miss Higgins, that to this point, Noah has been racially sheltered. So you don't represent the typical adult in the world. You don't carry the intimidation factor that any other white adult would. Because of your race, Noah has had no preconceived notions about you. You have had the opportunity to create your own persona inside his head. And because you were calm, caring, encouraging, and remarkably persistent, you have built a relationship where Noah feels safe. And when an individual feels safe, they have the opportunity to open up, to be themselves. Thus, Noah has found his voice."

Delton thought long and hard on her explanation. He smiled, not so much at her kind words to him, but more at the irony of the fact that this was the first time he ever remembered having a leg up on anybody because he was black.

"Are you saying he doesn't feel safe with me?" Judith looked hurt.

Rena shook her head. "He clearly feels safe with you. When you take his hand he follows along without question. And when something arises that causes him stress, he buries his face in your leg. But there are things outside this room that are overwhelming to him, and make him feel vulnerable."

Dr. Fitzpatrick spoke up. "So before Delton leaves, I would like to discuss the next steps."

"I'd like to talk about that too." Judith said. "Where do we go from here?"

"How about the zoo?" Dr. Fitzpatrick said. "As Rena stated, Noah feels safe in here. We expect his vocabulary to grow exponentially each day from this point. But it won't do any good if he will only speak in this room. He needs an opportunity to open up outside these walls. And since we have also had some good experiences with the other kids, I'm looking into the possibility of taking a field trip to the zoo. But I'd like to have the parents along as well. In Noah's case I think it would be very beneficial for him to see Mother and Delton together in a fun and relaxed atmosphere."

"You want to take me to the zoo?" Delton said.

Dr. Fitzpatrick nodded. "We're working with Two Rivers now to get it cleared and manned. And we've discussed it with Sterling Park Zoo. They are talking about closing down for a day so we can have sole access to it."

"But don't you think that will freak out Noah, with all of those people?" Judith said. "He'll shut down again."

"If the zoo is closed, there will only be us," Dr. Fitzpatrick said. "And this will give us an opportunity to see how Noah responds to Delton outside this haven of a room."

Delton shrugged. "I'm in. I've never been to the zoo."

"Okay, Hayes. Time's up." The guard walked back into the room. "On the bus."

Chapter Thirty

When Judith got home with Noah, before starting on dinner, she made big changes in the apartment. All artwork came off the walls. All knick-knacks were put in a box in the closet. She removed as much clutter as possible, making the place a calm and empty environment where Noah could feel safe.

The remainder of the week was full of extremes for Judith. She would drop Noah off, rush to work, and visit her dad at lunch. After work, she'd rush home to get Noah from Darlene, then take him to see his grandpa in the hospital.

Noah's vocabulary grew exponentially. With each day came a handful of new words, which he eventually managed to weave into sentences. He even started talking at home; his first words there were "I'm hungry." But the most beautiful word Judith heard him say was "Mommy." It was a word she had actually given up hope of ever hearing.

When they went to see her father, Noah called him "Gompa." It made him smile. Even though her father couldn't talk, Judith sat next to him and regaled him with all of the things Noah was able to do now, each day thanking him for talking her into going through with the project. It had been one of the smartest moves she had made, and it wouldn't have happened without his listening and calmly talking through her fears with her.

In that time Delton was obsessed with reading about autism activities, and trying them out with Noah. He had sent Rena to the store for something else nearly every day after they were done. He felt like he was wearing her out, but she never seemed to be low on enthusiasm.

She had purchased flash cards and he drilled Noah on animals, not only making him say the names, but having him make the sounds as well.

Another day, he had Rena bring in a can of shaving cream. Delton spread it all over the table, and they drew pictures in it. Noah seemed to enjoy that. He didn't laugh, like he had with the stuffed animal toss, but he smiled the whole time they were playing in the white foamy mess.

One thing he'd done that didn't work out so well was the floating balloon game. He started with one balloon and bounced it in the air to Noah, who was supposed to bounce it back to him. The object, of course, was not to let the balloon hit the ground. Noah handled one balloon fine, so Delton introduced a second balloon. Noah seemed to enjoy dealing with two balloons even more. But when Delton added a third balloon, Noah became agitated. So agitated in fact, that Delton should have known better than to throw up a fourth balloon. Noah couldn't handle all four. The frenetic pace got him all worked up. He fell on a balloon and it burst loudly, scaring him. Then the other balloons hit the ground and Noah went into major meltdown mode. Delton had to rock him in the blanket for nearly forty-five minutes. His arms were ready to fall out of their sockets onto the floor, by the time Noah calmed down.

In truth, Delton felt that Noah was helping him, by getting his mind off of Danna, from whom he hadn't heard since the frantic phone call that was interrupted and cut off.

The zoo visit was on a Tuesday. Dr. Fitzpatrick said they'd worked it out with the zoo to close for a half day to allow the children, their families and the inmates in. The folks at the zoo chose a Tuesday because that was usually their slowest morning of the week.

The bus took Delton, the inmates, and the guards directly to the zoo. The guards now rode the bus routinely. They were getting to know the inmates pretty well and vice versa. It was becoming a strange little family group, rather than the typical prison guard/prisoner thing. Many of the guards knew each of the inmates well, and listened to stories of their families, along with sharing a few stories of their own. Delton noticed though, as friendly as the guards were, when talking about their family, they never mentioned anyone by name—instead calling them "my son," or "my wife."

Once they arrived at the zoo, they waited on the bus until all the children and their parents arrived.

Judith and Noah were the second-to-last family to make it. Dr. Fitzpatrick had them all wait inside the zoo gate. When every child and parent was accounted for, Dr. Fitzpatrick gave a signal to Johnson, the head guard. He stood and ushered everyone off the bus.

When they weren't on the bus and all relaxed, the guards went into their usual intimidating asshole mode. They stood in a line, on either side of the inmates, one hand on a gun at their side, the other on a club hanging from their belt on the other side. The inmates walked in a direct line from the door of the bus, into the gate of the zoo. Delton looked over at the old white woman who was sitting inside the ticket booth. She looked terrified that they were walking in under armed guard. He smiled at her, wanted to say something like, "It's all part of the procedure, ma'am." She looked away as soon as he caught her eye.

The inmates walked through the floor-to-ceiling barred turnstile to enter. It was then Delton realized why the zoo was such a good choice for an outing like this. He scanned the perimeter. A ten-foot wire fence, ringed with barbed wire at the top, surrounded the whole zoo. It was designed to keep all these wild animals in. There wasn't any way one of these inmates was going to make it out of here either.

Delton saw that the whole Marmont Program army was here in full force. Rena and Taysha had arrived earlier and were standing off to the side holding cups of coffee with the rest of the counselors and assistants. There was zoo staff off to one side, and the prison guards walked in and stood in perimeter positions. The entrance area to the zoo was crowded.

Delton saw Judith standing behind everybody. Noah had his face buried in her leg, looking none too happy, the large number of people stressing him out. When he walked toward them, Rena rushed over and pulled Delton's surprise for Noah out of her purse. Delton had made it when he learned of the trip to the zoo. It was a circle cut out of cardboard from a cereal box, taped to a paint stir stick, so it looked like a big floppy magnifying glass. She handed it to Delton. He knelt in front of Noah and held up his fist. They both said, "My man," together and bumped. Delton then showed him the cardboard. "Okay buddy, this is what you call a zoo viewfinder." He spun it around for Noah to see. "When we're going through the zoo, I will call out an animal. You have to look through the hole in this circle and find the animal. Got it?"

Noah nodded. "Yeah."

"Okay, let's test it out." He handed Noah the viewfinder. Noah grabbed the handle and looked through the circle. "Now, find a mommy."

Noah smiled, and looked up at Judith.

"Nicely done, Noah," she said, with a giggle.

"I think you got the hang of it, champ," Delton said, and stood. He smiled at Judith. "How're you doing?"

Her head bobbed a little. "I'm doing okay, thanks."

"All right you guys, look this way." Rena was holding her phone out in front of her. "I want a picture of this momentous event."

"Oh. Noah. Look up at Miss Rena," Judith said. Noah looked up at her, then turned into his mother's leg again.

Rena clicked the picture. "Noah, you looked great."

Noah grunted and turned away a little more.

"Okay, everybody. Can you listen to me, over here?" Dr. Fitzpatrick stood in the center of the crowd and waved his hand in the air. He waited an awkward moment for people to quiet down. He was dressed casually today, with khaki pants, docksiders, and a light blue polo shirt. The sunlight did his complexion no favors, however. Delton noticed it made the pockmarks on his face seem darker. When he had everyone's attention he continued. "I want to thank the staff at Sterling Park Zoo for altering their schedules and making this day possible."

All of Dr. Fitzpatrick's assistants clapped. Everyone else in the crowd followed suit. The zoo workers smiled and waved.

"Now, aside from having nobody else in the entire zoo but us, and being trailed by student assistants and security guards all morning long, I want this to be a casual day at the zoo." There were a few chuckles from the crowd. "The object is to have as relaxing a morning as possible." He took a deep breath, and rubbed his hands together excitedly. "Okay, let's go."

Judith took hold of Noah's hand. "Let's go see the animals, Noah."

They walked into the zoo proper and the crowd began to disperse. Delton looked around. "Is there a map somewhere?"

"I'm sure there is," Judith said. "But we shouldn't need one. The place isn't that big." She looked over at him. "Haven't you ever been here before?"

Delton shook his head. "No. We didn't make it out this way."

Judith pointed to a building. "Let's start over there. I want to get Noah away from all these people so he can relax."

Getting closer, Delton read the inscription above the door of the large stone building. It read, "Cat House." He opened one of the double doors for them and they entered. Inside, the building was all stone as well. The cement floor was uneven and textured to look like dirt on the plains of Africa or something. There were several enclosures fronted with thick glass. Each enclosure had a chest high stone wall surrounding it, with planters along the top, with large green leaves streaming out in all directions. From the entryway, Delton could see the signs above all the enclosures so one could tell where each animal was, without having to look at them all. Off to the right he found the one that read, "African Lion." It had a smaller name underneath it, "Panthera Leo," which, he assumed, was what the scientists were supposed to call it, but he was sure nobody did when the word "lion" was quicker and easier to say.

The door opened behind them and in walked Rena, Taysha, and Officer Engels, an African American prison guard who was apparently their designated escort for the day.

"Okay, Noah," Delton said. "Your first mission is to find a lion."

Noah let go of his mother's hand and ran around the wall to the left.

"Be careful, Noah," Judith called after him.

"C,mon," Delton said. "Let's watch him."

They slipped behind the wall and found Noah, standing still as a statue, looking through the hole in his viewfinder, totally entranced by a tiger that was at least twice as big as he was, pacing back and forth in its enclosure. Another tiger lay off in the corner nestled between two rocks. It lifted its head and yawned, its big tongue hanging out between two massive white fangs. Then it licked its lips and laid its head back down.

Delton whispered to Judith. "Has he never been here

either?"

"He has, several years ago," Judith whispered back, "but I'm sure he doesn't remember it."

Delton gave Noah a few more seconds to watch the tiger before telling him it was not a lion. Noah moved on down to see the American mountain lions. "Nope," Delton said. In the last enclosure on that side of the building were three cheetahs. "Still not a lion."

Noah ran to the other side, where he found a female lion lying on a high rock in the enclosure. He looked through his viewfinder, and Delton raised his arms in triumph. "Yes. You did it, boy. That's a lion." He put his fist down and Noah bumped it, smiling proudly. "But it's only the mama lion, we need to find the papa lion too."

"I'm sure he's outside," Judith said. "Let's go check him out."

Judith took Noah's hand and Delton opened the back door to the cat house to let them out. Standing in the doorway were Rick Simpson, the boy he was caring for, and the mother. She had her stringy hair pulled back in a ponytail and wore an orange down vest over a black t-shirt. She was in the process of handing Rick a small plastic bag of white powder, very casually, with the hand that was facing the building, so the guards and assistants on the other side of them couldn't see what was going on. They were in mid-hand-off when Delton opened the door.

The mother looked up at him, clearly rattled. Simpson snatched the bag from her hand and slipped it into his pocket. "What the hell you doin', Hayes?" He looked at Delton with a scowl. "You got nothin' better to do than go snoopin' on other people's business?"

"Just going to check out the papa lion," Delton said. Judith and Noah slipped by him. Judith patted the mother's shoulder as she passed. "How's it going, Sadie?"

"It's goin' good." Sadie said, and stepped aside to give them room to pass.

Judith and Noah stepped out onto the walkway, followed by Taysha, and then Rena.

"Go ahead, Hayes," Officer Engels said, and held the door.

Delton walked out to Noah and Judith, Rick Simpson staring malevolently at him with every step. "Let's go find papa lion," Delton pointed toward the outside viewing area. "This way, Noah."

Noah dragged at his mother's hand.

"No, Noah," Delton said. He reached for their hands and pulled them apart. "You walk on your own here."

Noah reached for his mother's hand once more, but Delton took his hand and knelt down to look him in the eye. "Buddy, listen to me. This place is filled with people whose only job is to keep you safe. There isn't anything or anybody that is going to hurt you here. And if there were, they'd have to hurt me real bad before I ever let them get to you. So you can walk on your own, without holding your mom's hand all day, okay?"

Noah looked at the ground and nodded. "Okay."

"That's my man. Now go find papa lion."

Delton stood and glanced at Judith, who looked concerned. He smiled at her. "I'm sorry, I probably should've talked to you first before I did that."

"Uh....ya think?" She said.

"But you know he's going to be all right...right?"

She nodded, begrudgingly.

Noah turned and walked a few steps, stopping every now and then to look back and make sure that Mom was following along. Delton chuckled. "We're right behind you, buddy. Lead the way."

Making their way around the front of the enclosure, they saw a structure created to look like a rocky outcropping on a mountain. Up at the top was the male lion, lying in all his glory, sunning himself and looking down on the world below, as if it were his kingdom. Noah brought up the viewfinder and looked through it.

"Nice job," Delton said.

They took Noah around other areas of the zoo and had him locate penguins and peacocks, monkeys and meerkats.

They walked into the bird house for about a minute. As soon as they entered, Noah dropped his viewfinder and covered his ears with his hands. The place was very noisy and Noah couldn't handle it. He started his pre-meltdown whining and they rushed him out the door quickly. Delton realized then that he didn't have his blanket with him, and Noah would have to be totally restrained in order to stop his meltdown. Delton would hate to see that have to happen.

After a couple hours of walking around the zoo, they decided to stop for a snack. The hot dog vendors were open for business, so Delton turned to Rena to get them some hot dogs and drinks. Rena pulled an envelope out of her purse and grabbed a twenty. She started to walk to the hot dog stand when Taysha grabbed the twenty out of her hand. "If a man is taking a mom and her son out for the day, he needs to feel like he is the one taking care of them. That means he pays for the food, and serves it to them." Taysha walked over and handed the twenty-dollar bill to Delton. "You take care of them, young man."

Delton smiled at her. "Thank you." He turned back to Judith and pointed at a table. "Go have a seat, and I'll bring everything to you."

Judith smiled back. "Mustard only."

"Of course," Delton said, and walked to the hot dog stand.

"Get a receipt," Rena called to him.

Delton purchased the food, and brought the tray over to the table. "Since I had my own money, I got everyone a chocolate chip cookie for dessert."

Rena stepped up and held her fingers in the air pinched

together. "Receipt?"

"Oh, I forgot that," Delton said. "I'm sorry."

Rena spun around and ran back to the hot dog stand.

Delton unwrapped Noah's hot dog for him, and put a straw in his orange drink.

Judith smiled. "You look pretty natural at that."

"At what?" Delton asked, and took a bite of his hot dog.

"Taking care of a kid. You do it very well."

Delton shrugged and took a drink of his Coke. "I tried to take care of my little sister and failed at that. I think your boy is the first person I've ever had an impact on."

"Tell me about your little sister," Judith said, washing her hot dog down with a sip of Coke.

"Truth. I don't think I could love a kid more if she were my own daughter. She's eight years younger than me and she's had it rough every day of her life. Our mom was strung out most of the time, and didn't really take care of her. I dropped out of high school to make money in a gang, but when my best friend got capped right in front of me, I decided that wasn't gonna be my future."

"Oh my God," Judith said. "That's awful."

"It was." Delton crunched a chip to give himself a moment before continuing. "I got a job at Vinnie G's Italian Restaurant doing dishes, but it didn't pay much, and mom usually stole the money from me anyway."

"Is that what led to the robbery?" Judith asked. Delton visibly winced, looking as if he'd been struck with something. "I'm sorry," Judith said. "I shouldn't even have brought that up."

"Naw, man." Delton shook his head. "It ain't you. It was just a plain stupid decision." He crunched on a chip and looked away.

Judith looked down at Noah, who would take a bite from his hot dog, then set it down gently and stare at it while he chewed, as if the thing might run away if he didn't keep his eye on it.

"One night, mom was there but not there, you know what I'm saying, cuz of the drugs and all," Delton said, looking off at a peacock that was roaming the grounds. "Danna had just turned ten, and she hadn't had nothin' for dinner. I'd given mom everything I had to get food that day, but she came back wasted instead. So Danna was lying in bed so hungry she was crying."

"Oh Delton, I'm so sorry." Judith put her hand over her mouth.

"Well, I was pissed, and decided to do somethin' about it. I went out and started going through a dumpster by our building. I didn't find anything to eat, but I did find an old gun that was broken. It was empty and it didn't have a trigger but I thought I could at least scare somebody with it. So I went a couple blocks over to a quick store that I never go into and loaded up the pocket of my hoodie with soda, SpaghettiOs, packages of cookies…crap like that. Then I started to walk out. The guy behind the counter started yelling at me so I pulled the gun out of my pants pocket. Only problem was, a cop was walking in right at that moment."

Judith's hand went from her mouth to her eyes. "You're kidding me."

Delton chuckled under his breath. "Stupid, right?"

Judith shook her head. "No. Tragic." She moved her hand and looked at him. "So what happened to Danna?"

"Well, mom got busted for drug use, and neither me or Danna heard from her again. Danna got taken by social services and has had a couple of foster families so far. She used to come see me every week, but the latest family won't let me even talk to her on the phone."

"What? Why not? You're her brother."

"But they consider me a bad influence."

Judith looked like she was ready to jump out of her seat. "That pisses me off."

Delton looked away. Just talking about it, he could feel

his heart beating faster. "Nothing I can do about it." He sighed. "Thank God for Taysha. She has kept me focused on what I can do… and that's work with Noah." He patted Noah on the back. "And thank God for you, little guy, because you have given me a goal in life."

"Delton, I feel like such an idiot," Judith said. "All those times you were distracted and moody, I never thought you were actually going through something too."

Delton shrugged. "S'okay. All those times you were distracted and moody I never thought that you were dealing with stuff too." He took a drink and watched Noah concentrate intently on picking up his hot dog and taking a bite of it. "So what's up with Noah's dad?" He looked at Judith. "Why's he making you do all this alone?"

Judith stopped chewing, surprised at the question.

"Oh, sorry," Delton said. "I get it's none of my business."

"No," Judith said, holding her hand over her mouth and swallowing. "It's just that nobody ever asks me that." She took a drink and then whispered. "I decided to have a baby on my own. Noah came as a withdrawal from a certain kind of bank."

Delton nodded and let the matter drop. He actually had a great many questions, like 'did they give her bad sperm?' and 'why they aren't being held responsible for Noah's autism?' but he assumed there was some no-money-back clause, and she'd probably already looked into all that. He'd probably just end up upsetting her.

They finished their hot dogs and cookies in silence, mulling over what they had learned about each other. Delton felt that a new understanding had been established between them—and perhaps they'd reached a level of mutual respect.

Finishing their morning at the zoo, they passed by the other six groups at least once. In each case everybody smiled and was friendly. In the case of Rick Simpson and Sadie Hanson, there was an awkward silence. Judith smiled and waved at them, but they said nothing back. Rick gave Delton an angry stare all the way past.

"That was weird," Judith said, when they had cleared them by a good distance. "Something must've happened between them."

They had Noah find foxes, buffalo, otters, and even a rhino, before Engels told them it was time to head back to the entrance.

Once the entire group had congregated, Dr. Fitzpatrick thanked the zoo again, and the officers for their support with the outing. He alluded to the fact that since it went so smoothly, it opened the door to other opportunities for outings. The inmates clapped the loudest at this news, then they got back on the bus and everyone drove off.

Simpson sat in the seat directly behind Delton. The bus pulled out and was en route for five minutes before Delton heard Rick's voice talking quietly in his ear. "I'm thinking you're smart enough to mind your own fucking business, if you know what's good for you."

Delton spun around so quickly, it startled Simpson and he jerked back in his seat. "If you know what's good for you, you won't do anything like that again, and take a chance at screwing up this program. It's important to everyone but you. And if you ever threaten me again, I will bust you up, fast."

"Hayes," Officer Johnson barked. "Everything all right?"

Delton turned back around. "Copacetic."

"Keep your eyes forward," he said, pointing to his eyes with two fingers. "Simpson, shut your damn mouth."

There was not another word from Simpson the rest of the way back. And one thing was made clear, the camaraderie the officers and inmates felt this morning had just been ended. Nobody spoke another word for the duration of the drive.

Chapter Thirty-One

Judith walked Noah into the room, watched him bump fists with Delton, waved and closed the door. Rena and Taysha were back in their usual positions at the window.

"Did the zoo tire him out yesterday?" Taysha said.

"Yes, it did, but I need to talk to you." Judith took a chair at the counter next to Taysha. "Delton opened up to me a little bit about his sister."

Taysha's jaw dropped open. "He did?"

"Yes. And I want to do something."

Taysha shook her head. "Honey, it is truly something that boy said anything to you about this. And I love the fact that you want to help. But you would have to go through Social Services, and that is the proverbial brick wall. They ain't going to tell you anything about his sister. You can't just go in there and say, 'I'd like you to give me the location of a child under your care,' and them say, 'Oh, hold on a minute while I look up the address.'"

"But Delton told me they think he's a bad influence on his sister." She looked through the window and saw Delton handing Noah stuffed animals to throw. Her son was laughing again. She pointed to him. "Look at that. Nothing could be further from the truth."

Taysha put a hand on Judith's shoulder. "Sweety, you are a good person, and you have an open mind. Others don't. They don't bother to look at a situation and try to find any facts in it. They make snap judgments based on something they think they know and go with those decisions, believing they are doing the right thing."

"I know," Judith said. She threw her purse down on the counter and folded her arms. "I was that person you're talking about. This program has been as good for me as it has for them."

"Then you have to understand that people need to be able to come to their own conclusions." She nodded toward Delton. "He's had some real struggles with all of this. Wanted to put a chair through a cement wall one day. But I told him to calm down and concentrate on what he could do. So he's done that, and your son has blossomed since."

Judith looked over at Taysha, "Thank you for being there for him."

"It's been my privilege to be a part of this whole thing." Taysha said with a smile. "What you need to understand is that it's the storms in life that make things bloom the brightest. Often they aren't the things we want to bloom at the time, but if you can get part of your garden going great, then there's a good chance that green thumb will bleed into the area that you've been having trouble with. You know, get a new perspective on how to deal with things."

Judith thought for a moment. She looked back at Taysha and smiled. "My God, you've got your head on straight."

Taysha sat back. "Besides, what would you even say to Reginald Fountain if you had the chance?"

"What?"

Taysha looked back at her. "What."

"Did you say Reginald Fountain?"

Taysha put her hand to her chin. "Reginald Fountain? Why does that name sound familiar?" She shrugged. "Hmph." Then she sat back in her chair.

Judith laughed, leaned over and kissed her cheek. "You are the strangest counselor I've ever met. And that probably makes you the best." She grabbed her purse, said bye to Rena, and rushed out.

Once she was in her car driving down the road she called Darlene.

"Hey, Jude, what's..."

"Dar, I need a favor."

"What do you need?"

"Can you Google Reginald Fountain and see if you can come up with an address around here?"

"Sure, give me a sec." Judith heard shuffling on the other end of the line. After a few seconds she heard the familiar click of a keyboard. "Got a White Pages address for Reginald Fountain."

"Great. What is it?"

"752 Lenore Lane, over in Whitewater."

"Ugh," Judith said. "That's thirty minutes the other way."

"Who is this guy?" Darlene asked.

"He's kind of holding Delton's sister hostage."

"And what are you going to do?"

"I'm going to talk to him."

"Jude, are you doing something you shouldn't?"

"No. I'm doing exactly what I should be doing. But it will have to wait until after work. Can you stay with Noah for just a little longer today?"

"Sure. If you promise not to get into trouble."

Judith chuckled. "I'll do my best. Now I know I'm asking a lot, but I need one more thing from you."

"Okay. What now?"

"Set it up," Judith said. "It's time."

"What's time?"

"Dar, I had a great day at the zoo with Noah and Delton, yesterday. Things are going great. It's time for me to work on a different area of my garden."

"Jude, what the hell are you....holy shit, are you talking about going on a date?"

"I am." Judith heard screams and then a large clunking sound.

"Shit, I dropped the phone. Are you still there?"

Judith laughed. "Yes. Set it up."

"I will. I'm gonna call Jim right...." Judith tapped off the call and tossed the phone onto the seat next to her.

Turning down Lenore Lane, Judith checked the address numbers on the houses on both sides of the street. Creeping her car slowly along, she realized that all the even numbers were on the right side of the road. Eventually reaching 752, she stopped out front and put the car in park. Getting out of the car, she walked up the driveway and was impressed with the exterior of the house—a two-story, craftsman style, with charcoal-colored siding and white trim. Flowerpots hung from the porch, with lush white and red petunias streaming down. Judith had to admit it was a beautiful place.

The front door was open. Through the screen door Judith could hear commotion from inside the house. Music was on, rumbles and zaps from a video game were coming from the room off to the left, and a woman, whom Judith assumed was the mother, was barking orders to anyone who would listen. "I need someone to open a can of baked beans and get them in the microwave."

Judith reached up and rang the doorbell. The mother reacted to the new interruption. "Someone tell whoever it is that suppertime is not the time to be coming around asking for anything."

A young African American girl wearing blue shorts and a gray t-shirt with the word "Pink" written across it in big white letters, appeared. She spoke through the screen door. "Can I help you?"

Judith smiled at her. "By any chance are you Danna?"

The girl paused for a moment and then asked, "Who wants to know?"

Judith chuckled, embarrassed. "Right. I'm a stranger. Good for you. My name is Judith Higgins and I have a very good friend named Delton Hayes, who is very concerned about his little sister, Danna."

At the mention of Delton's name the little girl stepped closer. "You know Delton?"

"Who is it, Danna?" The mother called from the distant kitchen.

Danna looked back toward the kitchen and then back to Judith. She looked nervous.

"Go ahead," Judith said. "Tell her who I am. The reason I came was to talk to your foster parents."

Danna looked reluctant, but turned back and called to her foster mother. "It's a lady who knows my brother."

"What?" A man's voice boomed. The video game sounds abruptly stopped, and a young boy complained. "Hold on. I have to take this."

An African American man appeared in the doorway. He pushed open the screen door and burst onto the porch. Judith had to scurry backward down the steps to avoid him running into her. "You can leave right now. We are not interested in hearing about criminals in this house."

"Sir, if you'll just listen…" Judith tried.

"I said leave," Mr. Fountain pointed to the road.

Judith turned but stopped herself. "No." She turned back. "I'll leave once you've listened to me, and stop acting like a bully."

"Bully?" Reginald stepped off the porch. "All I'm doing is protecting my family."

Judith backed a couple more steps. "No. All you're doing is breaking up a family by being bull-headed."

The mother came out the door rubbing her hands on a towel. Danna and a younger boy followed.

Reginald put his hands on his hips and stuck out his chest. "And just how am I doing that?" His head bounced as he spoke.

Judith put her hands on her hips and stepped toward him. "By keeping Danna and Delton separated."

Reginald pointed his finger at her. "I don't know who you are, lady. But I'm doing what's best for Danna. Delton Hayes is a violent criminal, and I don't want him around her, or my family. I met the man, and it almost came to blows within mere minutes. So don't come around here and tell me what a great guy Delton Hayes is."

"You don't know shit," Judith said. "I'll tell you who I am." She pulled out her phone, and brought up a picture of Noah. "I'm Judith Higgins," she held out the phone so Reginald could see it. "And this is my son, Noah. He has autism spectrum disorder. Hasn't uttered a single word in all seven years of his life. He has worked with professionals and gotten nowhere. But he's in a special program now, and working with someone who gives him patience, respect, and unconditional love. And now my son has found his voice. He's spoken his first words ever, thanks to Delton Hayes."

Reginald was quiet. The mother came down the steps and stood next to him.

"That's right," Judith said. "The violent criminal you're protecting your whole family from, has been the best person in the world my baby boy has ever met."

Danna stepped up and stood next to the mother. "Why did you come here?"

Judith looked down at her. "Because, honey, Delton loves

you, and the fact that he can't see you is breaking his heart. And since he has done so much for Noah and me, I wanted to see if there was something I could do for him." She looked back at Reginald. "I understand your first meeting didn't go well with him. I should tell you about mine." She chuckled and looked at Danna. "Your brother isn't the best at first impressions." Looking back up at Reginald she added, "But if you'll just give him the opportunity to prove himself...."

Reginald glanced down at Danna and then back to his wife. She smiled at him and nodded. He looked back at Judith. "He's been good to you and your boy?"

"There hasn't been anybody better for Noah," Judith said.

Reginald paused a moment and then nodded. "All right. We'll go see him again."

Danna ran to Judith and hugged her tightly around the waist. "Thank you."

The mother stepped over, smiled, and touched her arm. "I'm Rosalind. Would you like to come in for a bit?"

"No, but thank you." Judith said. "I have to get back to my son."

Chapter Thirty-Two

When Delton saw Judith the next morning, she wore a smirk on her face like she had just pasted a "kick me" sign on his back. "What?" he asked her, but she just smiled and shook her head.

She knelt down and kissed Noah on the top of the head. "Have a good day, honey." She stood up and winked at him. You have a good weekend." Then she walked out the door, closing it behind her.

Delton frowned suspiciously. "Thanks." He looked down at Noah. "What's up with Ma?"

Noah held out his fist. Delton bumped it and they both yelled, "My man!"

Ushering the boy over to the table, Delton slid some coloring books in front of his chair. "Miss Blossom got you some animal coloring books for today, since we went to the zoo yesterday."

"What we do?" Noah asked.

"Well," Delton flipped through a couple of pages in the book. "We decide what animals we liked at the zoo." He pointed at a few of the line drawings of lions, ferrets, and rhinos. "And when we see one we like, we color it with these crayons." He went over and sat down, leaving the book with Noah.

Noah slowly and awkwardly turned the next page, tearing it slightly. He moaned his distress.

"Ain't no thing," Delton said. "The pages can be torn right out if you want. It makes them easier to frame if you're really happy with the job you done."

Noah turned the next page slowly and carefully. A drawing of two foxes were on the page, one lying down, and the other standing behind it looking off into the distance. "Doggies!" Noah cried out, and he started to clap.

"Them's foxes," Delton said. He opened the box of crayons and turned it to face the boy. "Now you pick out the crayons you want to use and color them in."

Noah picked out a bright green crayon, and awkwardly scrawled across the page. When a bright green line went outside the closed lines of the foxes, Noah whined and pointed at it.

"It's all good, Noah," Delton said. "You can't go wrong here. Nothing has to be inside the lines. Mommies love it when you go outside the lines. Trust me."

Noah calmed instantly, and seemed to take Delton's words to heart. He sat in the chair, concentrated harder and scribbled in and around the fox that was standing.

Delton watched him work. The boy was remarkably intent on what he was doing, but at the same time, had a distance to him—like his mind was working hard on the project at hand, but also drifting off into another time zone too. Often wondering what was going through his head, Delton thought about the fact that he'd never tried to converse with the boy. He'd gotten him to speak, to share a quick feeling, or verbalize a desire, but nothing more. Delton wanted to know about Noah's heart. What did a boy like that wish for? Did he have dreams, goals, aspirations?" "Did you like going to the zoo yesterday, Noah?" He asked.

"Uh huh." Noah said, not taking an ounce of concentration off the fox.

"Why's that?"

"Like animals." Noah said. He lifted his head and stared off to the wall. "Don't laugh at me, or yell at me." Then he started coloring again.

"What?" Delton asked. "Who yells at you and laughs at you?"

"Kids,"

"What kids?"

"School," Noah said. "They're not fun." He set the green crayon aside and selected a blue crayon from the box. Then he set to work on the fox lying down.

"Why would they do that?"

But Noah didn't answer. He pulled out a blue crayon, sniffed it, then began to color the grass.

Delton could feel his face flush. He knew why the kids did it. Because Noah was different. And they always tear down someone who's different—kids and adults. "Do you like people at all?"

"Uh huh," Noah said. "Love Mommy, Aunt Darlene, and Dellon."

Sitting back in his chair, Delton was astonished the boy expressed love for him. Had he truly made that much of an impact? He searched his own feelings and had to admit. "Delton loves you too."

Noah looked over at the opposite wall. "But, I make mommy sad."

"What?" Delton said. "Who told you that?"

"See her sad all the time."

Delton shook his head. "Noah, you got it all wrong."

Noah looked back down and scribbled blue onto the fox again.

"Mommy isn't sad because you make her sad." Delton wanted to get down, force the boy to look into his eyes so he was sure the message would sink in. But he knew that wouldn't work.

The boy would react to being touched like that. He decided to just speak plainly and hope it sunk in. "Mommy is sad because she thinks you're sad. She wants you to be happy. She wants that more than anything in the whole world."

Noah continued to scribble for the next moment before acknowledging. "Okay."

Delton sat back and watched Noah color, stunned at how he perceived people's feelings. People either didn't like him or he made them sad. In either case he was the impetus of it all. He didn't have an understanding of the world beyond his involvement in it. He couldn't relate to the fact that his mother worried, and kids could be just plain assholes. Delton wondered if he should let Judith know about the conversation he'd just had. He decided not to. There wasn't anything she would be able to do about it, and it would just give her more to stress over. All he could do was take care of things on this end, and reassure the boy. "Noah, Mommy loves you very much."

Noah finished with the blue fox. "Okay," he said, dropping the crayon. He picked out a purple crayon and went to work on the grass.

"I love you too, Noah," Delton said.

Noah scribbled away at the grass. After several seconds, he said, "Okay."

Chapter Thirty-Three

Judith stopped walking before she reached the large front window of Francisco's. She looked up at the glowing red neon sign. It was by far the best Italian restaurant for 50 miles in any direction, and she remembered the last time she was here. It was a business lunch with her team at Danser, and it was a time in her past she has since tried to forget. Now she was headed in to meet her blind date, and she couldn't help but wonder if it was a bad omen to try and start a new relationship here or not.

She gulped in a breath. Her breathing wasn't coming as easily as it should. In fact, she felt that her breathing hadn't been coming easily since the moment her brother-in-law called her and said the date was all set up. It had been years since she'd been involved with a man; it didn't go so well then. She didn't even know if she had what it took to carry on a real conversation with someone other than her sister and her father. But her father's voice rang in her ears now. "Will it kill you?" she could hear him say as clearly as if he were standing right next to her. Admitting to herself that she would indeed survive the night, that was if her heavily beating heart didn't give out before then. She gritted her teeth and walked into the restaurant.

The hostess at the front counter who looked like she wasn't

old enough to be home without a babysitter, flashed her a bright smile. "May I help you?"

"I'm meeting Neil Keating," Judith said.

"Oh, sure," the hostess, who's name badge read Mikayla, said. "Mr. Keating is waiting for you. Follow me."

A huge lump formed in Judith's stomach. This was really happening. A distant voice told her it would be a good idea to head out the door and keep on walking, but Judith didn't listen to that voice anymore. Though her feet felt heavy all of a sudden, she followed young Mikayla into the dining room and right up to the table of her date.

Neil Keating stood to greet her. A handsome man, with charcoal-colored hair graying at the temples, he stood tall and straight, with a bit of a belly, but not so much that he was overweight. He had a warm pleasant smile, and all of his teeth. So far this was going well. "Hi, Judith," he said, holding out his hand as if they were getting ready to conduct a business meeting. "I'm Neil Keating. It's nice to finally meet you."

Judith took the hand and shook it firmly. "Hi, Neil. It's nice to meet you too."

They took a seat and Mikayla let them know that their server, Dezi, would be with them soon.

"I was going to order us a bottle of wine," Neil said. "But then I realized I don't know what kind of wine you like, or even if you drink at all."

"Oh, I drink," Judith said. "But I am very picky about my wine. It has to be made with grapes or I'm not going to touch it."

Neil looked confused for a moment, but then seemed to realize it was a joke and laughed politely.

Another extremely young woman stepped up with a small dish of olive oil and a basket of warm bread. "Hi, I'm Dezi. May I get you started with anything to drink?" She had a pepper grinder under her arm and gave a few turns of fresh ground pepper into the oil.

"I think we'll have a bottle of the house red." Neil said.

"Okay, I'll be right back with that."

"Neil, I need to tell you something," Judith said when Dezi had left. "I have a son who's autistic."

Neil nodded. "I know. Jim mentioned that. I have a niece who's on the spectrum too."

"You do?"

Neil nodded. "Yes. She's in a special school, and she's delightful."

"Okay," Judith realized he didn't have the real story. "My son, Noah, is profoundly autistic."

Neil picked up the basket of bread and offered it to her. "Yes. Jim said that he hasn't been able to speak until very recently."

Judith waved off the bread. He set the basket back down and took a piece for himself. She watched him, trying her best to gauge his intent. Was he really okay with this, or was this night out just a quick fling for him—something to do to get him out of the house? How could he, in his right mind, plan to develop a relationship with a woman who brought in so much…baggage?

Dezi came with two wine glasses and poured a small amount in Neil's glass. He made the proper show of tasting it and nodding. She then poured glasses for them both. She asked about their order but Neil told her to come back in a bit. When she left he held up his glass. "To new beginnings."

That was a tasteful, politically correct toast. She smiled and clinked his glass and then took a probably-too-large, drink of the wine. When she swallowed, she decided to ask the "elephant in the room" question. "So what made you decide to go on a blind date?"

Neil smiled, like he knew the question would eventually be asked and he was glad to have it over. "It was time. I've been divorced for over four years now from a woman who loved her pain meds more than she ever loved me. It was a terrible divorce and I was gun-shy for a long time. I moved here from Pittsburgh to get a fresh start. I really like Jim, so I trusted him when he said he had someone great for me to meet." He smiled at her and raised his glass again. "So far he's been proven to be spot on."

Judith felt herself blush.

Neil took a drink and set his glass down. "Okay. Your turn."

"I don't know," Judith said. "I guess I'm growing up."

Neil snickered. "From what I understand, you are a great mother who handles the challenges of raising an autistic boy well. It sounds to me like you're all grown up already."

"Except I think I was hiding behind my son," Judith said. "Yes, he can be a challenge, but it's a known commodity. I know what my responsibilities are each and every day, and that doesn't change. It can be hard work at times but it's safe." She looked down at her wine glass and twirled it on the table by its stem. "My father always said that nobody can live free in a comfort zone. Once they've become comfortable they've stopped growing, and that was like creating their own prison cell to live in for their remaining days."

"Your father sounds like a wise man," Neil said.

Judith smiled. "He's very wise. But it took my son to prove it to me. I've got Noah involved in this crazy program."

"Jim's been telling me about it. An inmate care-taking program through Marmont State."

"Yes," Judith took a small drink. "It sounds insane when you say it out loud, and it has definitely been outside the comfort zone. But Noah has thrived in this program beyond anyone's wildest imaginings. And Delton, the young man who's working with Noah, he was way outside his comfort zone too. And I've sat back and watched him become capable and confident. It's been an amazing journey to witness."

Neil raised his glass. "Here's to Noah and Delton."

Judith smiled and clinked her glass and they took another drink.

"So how does that explain you being here tonight?" Neil asked.

Judith set her glass down and twirled it some more, thinking on the question. "I don't know if it's jealously or obligation, but I realized I couldn't be the only one who isn't growing. I needed to get out of the cell I had crawled into and start living life again."

Neil nodded and smiled. "You've honored me with a great responsibility. I need to be the cloud."

"The cloud?" Judith asked.

"Yes. You see I'm very much enjoying this evening with you, and the last thing I want is for you to see your shadow and climb back into your hole for who-knows-how-long."

Judith laughed. Neil chuckled. "So, I'm happy to be the cloud."

They clinked glasses and drank again. The remainder of the evening was less intense. It was light conversation about good books to read, movies and music they liked, and concerts they had been to in their youth. Before either of them realized it, two and a half hours had gone by. They were finally interrupted by Judith's phone ringing.

"I'm so sorry," Darlene said. "But I don't know what to do. Noah won't go to bed. He just keeps calling for Dellon over and over again."

"No problem," Judith said. "I'll be home soon."

When she flipped her phone closed, Neil smiled at her. "Duty calls?"

"Yes. I'm sorry."

Neil reached over and touched her hand. "Don't be sorry. I don't remember an evening, in the last ten or more years, that I've enjoyed this much."

"You said you've only been divorced for four years."

"I have," Neil said with a big smile.

Judith caught herself blushing again.

Neil paid for the check and walked her out to her car. "Do you remember the scene in Annie Hall where Woody Allen asked to get the kiss out of the way first thing?"

"I do," Judith said. She had been wondering how this night was going to end.

"Well, I'm not Woody Allen," he said. "And I'm taking the kiss off the table. I like you, Judith, and more than that, I respect you and your feelings. This is the first night out of your hole, and I very much want there to be a second one. But I'm giving notice right now, I will be kissing you then."

Judith stopped him, spun him around and kissed him long and deeply. When she pulled back, he looked down at her and took a deep breath. She smiled up at him. "Now you'll have to figure out something else to do on the second date."

Chapter Thirty-Four

Delton was tired of the powdered eggs, and the bacon-like product they put on each man's plate every morning. On a good day it was hard to swallow, but this morning it seemed even worse. It wasn't that it was improperly prepared. As powdered eggs go, he was sure it was exceptional fare. He surmised it was the company with whom he was sharing his morning meal. For whatever reason, Rick Simpson felt he needed to shadow Delton as much as he possibly could.

"And so's I told that son of a bitch," Simpson said, pieces of egg dropping from his mouth. "Mister, if you think I'm gonna pay that much, then I expect you're gonna at least lick my balls too." Rick burst into loud throaty laughter, along with the other four assholes sitting around him, who seemed to hang on every word he said.

Either Rick thought they had the chance to be real good friends, and Delton couldn't imagine how he could have ever gotten that signal, or he felt he needed to keep an eye on Delton after he saw the drug exchange at the zoo. It didn't matter which, Delton couldn't take his brand of humor, and his smell, that of wet dog, made it hard for him to breathe, let alone digest his food.

Rick picked up his toast and took a bite. He looked over at

Delton. "I don't know what's wrong with you all the time, Hayes. It's like you got a permanent stick up your ass or something."

Delton said nothing, he simply tried to continue to chew. When he reached for his coffee, Rick nudged him hard, and he spilled it.

"Come on, Hayes. Show some sign of life."

Delton looked down at the plate of eggs, now floating in coffee. "Dammit, man!" He whirled on Rick.

"Hayes!" a guard called.

Delton looked over.

"You got visitors," the guard said. "Come on. They're waiting."

Delton glared at Rick, then stood and walked away.

"Hey, Hayes," Rick called after him. "If it's your sister again, tell her I'm very interested." He heard the gang of assholes laugh again. He gritted his teeth and walked to the guard.

"Do not let him get under your skin," the guard said.

"Who's here?" Delton asked.

The guard shrugged. "Don't know. They just called and said to get you."

When they let Delton into the visitor's room, he looked around, and his eye caught Danna as she stood up from a table full of people. She smiled shyly when she saw him. "Danna," he whispered and took a step toward her.

A man at the table, who had his back to him, turned and Delton recognized Reggie Fountain. He stopped, but Reginald smiled, stood, and held out his hand. "I want to apologize to you, Delton. I judged you harshly and you didn't deserve it."

Delton looked over to Danna. When she smiled and nodded, he shook the man's hand. "Thanks."

Reginald chuckled, smacked him on the shoulder and gestured to his sister. "There's someone here who really wants to see you."

Danna threw her arms around Delton. "I missed you so much."

"Me too," Delton said, and held her tightly for several moments…like they were afraid to let go in case they didn't get this chance again.

Reginald tapped Delton on the shoulder. "Delton, I'd like to introduce my wife, Rosalind."

Delton released his sister, and turned to see an attractive woman with a bright, pleasant smile. "It's good to finally meet you, Delton."

Delton shook her hand and gave her an awkward smile back. "Likewise."

"Come on over, Isaiah," Reginald said, waving over a boy, still sitting at the table. The boy slowly slid out of his chair and walked around. "This is Danna's foster brother, Isaiah."

"Good to meet you, man," Delton said, and fist-pumped the boy.

"Let's all sit down," Reginald said. "We can talk a bit."

They took their seats. Delton sat next to Danna and Reginald sat on her other side. "I'm happy to see you all," Delton said. "But…." He didn't know how to ask the simple question.

"What the hell are we doing here?" Reginald laughed. Rosalind smiled sheepishly. "Mr. Hayes," Reginald continued. "You have a very good lobbyist."

"A what?"

"The other day, we were getting ready for dinner and the doorbell rang," Reginald explained. "It was a white woman who started talking about you."

"Me?" Delton asked, wondering for a moment who it could be.

"Yes, you." Reginald said, as if he were telling the most hard-to-believe thing in history. "I asked her to leave, but she pulled out her phone and brought up pictures of her son. Said he couldn't speak until he met Delton Hayes. And that Delton Hayes was the reason the sun rises over Two Rivers, and on and on...." Reginald laughed.

"You're kidding me," Delton said. He looked over at Danna.

She smiled and nodded. "It's true. I heard it. And I was so proud of you."

"Of course, we were very surprised by this," Rosalind said. "But she was tenacious and persistent. And we all agreed at dinner that night, that we would come down here as a family and meet you, and tell you how sorry we were for how we've acted."

All eyes were on Delton as he tried to sort out his feelings as quickly as he could. There was a strain of anger running through him, like a rope being dragged up through a pool of mud. It was grinding at him. He had harsh things to say to the man who judged him, and ripped his sister from his life. How dare that man just sit and smile at him now.

But somehow, Delton could feel Taysha's hand smack him on the side of his head again. Her voice, all high pitched and screechy like it does when she's pissed off, was ripping through his ears. "Delton Hayes, don't you dare say a bad word to this man who came to you with his tail between his legs. You show him how tall you can stand, and be forgiving. Let him see exactly how wrong he was."

"It's okay," Delton said. "I'm glad you're here now, and I appreciate being able to see my sister again."

Everyone at the table smiled. Delton made a note to thank Taysha for the words she never said.

From that moment, the awkwardness was over. The Fountains treated Delton as one of their own. They asked him all about the experiment and his time with Noah. He told them of his first two disastrous days, but he left out the part about arguing so mush with Judith that they were almost out of the program. They wanted to hear about how Noah started speaking, and Delton described the moment, and all the studying he had done on his own up to that point. Reginald seemed particularly proud of him about that.

Then it was Delton's turn to ask questions. Reginald was a technical engineer at a software company, and Danna was now going to a decent school. She admitted that she wasn't as interested in it as she should be, but she had been seeing a tutor twice a week, and her grades were getting better as the semester went on.

The visitation period was over far too quickly. They all hugged Delton and promised they would be back each week until he was out. With promises to keep him in their prayers, they left.

The following Monday, Judith brought Noah in.

"My man," Noah said with his usual fist bump. Then Delton walked over to Judith and hugged her tight. She hugged back.

"Nobody has ever done anything like that for me," he said. "Ever."

"It's not even close to what you deserve for what you've done for Noah." She pulled back. "When you told me about how they thought you weren't fit to be around your own sister, I felt it was my duty to tell them how wrong they were."

They both heard Dr. Fitzpatrick's shoe squeaking before he entered the room. "Ah, Miss Higgins," he said. "I didn't miss you. I'm glad I have you both here." He squeak-stepped over. "I wanted to let you both know that this coming Thursday, I have all the clearances set for the pairs to go to a Two Rivers Pirates baseball game."

"You do?" Delton was sure he sounded too excited.

"Yes," Dr. Fitzpatrick said. He turned to Judith. "But this time we are only having the pairs go. We want them to have the responsibility of being in charge of the little ones in a public venue."

Judith turned to Delton. "Are you up for that?"

"Hell yeah," Delton said. He threw his hand over his mouth and glanced over at Noah. "I mean, heck yeah," he said through his fingers.

Excerpts from the transcript of the GINfo (Global Information Network) interview between Brooke Winthrop and Dr. Warren Fitzpatrick.

Dr. F: I'd like to make it clear right from the start, I'm not at all happy to be here. And the only reason I'm with you today is because the board ordered me here.

Off Camera: I'm rolling, Brooke.

Brooke: I'm sorry you feel that way, Doctor. Can you tell me why?

Dr. F: Certainly. It's because I have no interest in being placed in the position of having to defend my research projects...especially to the media. The board has also asked me to write a journal article discussing the fallout, months before I have even sifted through all the data, for no other reason than to defend my work, and save the college a black eye.

Brooke: Well, Dr. Fitzpatrick, let me put your mind at ease. I have no intention of putting you in such a position. You are here simply as a content expert. We want to report on the Delton Hayes, and Noah and Judith Higgins situation, and we're talking to you because it was your project they were involved in. Is that correct?

Dr. F: Yes. That is correct.

Brooke: And correct me if I'm wrong— the project was to put special needs children into the care of convicted criminals.

Dr. F: Very clever. You say you're not going to put me on the defensive, and then you start in on me right away.

Brooke: Doctor, I asked you to correct me if I'm wrong. Please do so.

Dr. F: It doesn't really matter what I say does it? You are going to portray it however you want anyway. You'll just say he threw helpless kids in with dangerous criminals just to sensationalize it, and that will be that.

Brooke: I apologize, Doctor. I'm truly not trying to mock you or your work in any way. But you have to admit, when you say it out loud, it does sound...reckless.

Dr. F: Well, the idea didn't just come to me when I was drinking heavily one night. It has an actual established precedent in reality, and a very successful reality at that. Just look at the Puppies Behind Bars program, and the remarkable results from that project. There are a great many success stories that have come from it, both in terms of well-trained helpful animals, and interred men who have had the chance to do something positive with their life. But you don't see PETA running around campaigning for the poor puppies, do you?

Brooke: You make a great point. So here's what I would like to do. Rather than me paraphrasing what your project is all about, what if you were to describe it for the viewers, in your own words. That will keep me from misconstruing any of the facts.

Dr. F: Thank you very much. I can both embrace and appreciate that strategy. Well...it's quite simple, really. The idea was to pair a special needs child with a person in a correctional facility, with the hope of having positive responses on both sides of the equation. The children would get special attention like they've never had before, and the inmates would be able to make a substantial difference for good in someone's life, and have the ability to test for certification in the areas in which they garnered the expertise. The hope was that positive gains would be measured on both sides of the table.

Brooke: That's it?

Dr. F: That's it. Succinct and to the point. I want to leave as little room for interpretation as possible.

Brooke: Okay, then. May I ask you a few questions regarding Delton Hayes?

Chapter Thirty-Five

The bus arrived at the stadium long before the game was supposed to start. Delton noticed the guards were agitated about this trip. Obviously, they weren't excited about having to deal with security in a crowd as large as that at a baseball game. The zoo was easy, since they were the only people allowed in. But it wasn't possible to tell the rest of the fans they couldn't come into a baseball stadium and cheer on the team because six convicts had decided to be there.

The guards ushered them off the bus, single file into the stadium. Delton looked at his tickets and saw they had assigned seats dispersed in one section, along the third base line. Each of the inmate's seats was positioned at least five seats down a row, which would prohibit them from getting up and running anywhere quickly. And they had an armed guard positioned directly behind each of them. There were also armed guards positioned at the top of the stands and the bottom in case support was needed. Two rows behind Delton was Ken Miller, and three rows and to the right in front of Delton, sat Rick Simpson.

Delton was impressed by the strategic placement, but he didn't know how they managed to swing getting ten armed men into the stadium.

Once they were seated, the gates opened. The rest of the crowd filed in, and the atmosphere was upbeat. The Two Rivers Pirates were two games behind first and coming off a three-win road trip.

Delton watched the families stroll in. He saw two boys smacking each other on the back of the head until the father said, "You'll stop that now, unless you want me to play that game too." They stopped and sat down.

Another mother was dealing with her little girl, who was crying because she spilled her popcorn. The mother was obviously losing her patience, and Delton couldn't help but chuckle at this. After dealing with Noah's meltdowns, this woman didn't know how bad things could really be. The mother looked up and caught him. "What are you looking at?" she yelled.

Delton smiled and waved to her. "Nothing ma'am. Just happy to be here."

It was only about five minutes more and Judith showed up, leading Noah through the crowd by the hand. She had taken precautions and gotten a comically large sound-deadening ear protection headset for him, which wobbled back and forth on his head with each step. He didn't act like the sound bothered him, but his right hand flapped furiously. He was obviously shaken by the large number of people. She led Noah down the aisle to sit next to Delton. Once he reached his seat, Noah buried his face in Delton's arm—another first. He had never done this with anyone but Judith before.

"Good luck," she said. "I know we aren't supposed to be here today, but I got myself a ticket anyway. If he gets overwhelmed, I don't want you to have to deal with a meltdown in the middle of all this. I'll swoop in and get him out of here."

Delton nodded. "That's a great idea. Thank you."

"No problem. Have fun." She reached down and pushed Noah's face up, and waved. He pulled his head back and buried it in Delton's arm again.

She waved at Delton and scooted back out the row and off into the next section over to the left. Delton let Noah hide his face for a while. He didn't want to move, gratified by the fact that he had created a bond and a trust with the boy. The fact that Noah felt comfortable in this position was a testament to everything Delton had worked for. He sat back and watched all the other Marmont kids delivered to their caretakers. Sadie Hanson brought young Eddie and let him walk down the row himself. Eddie was excited to be there and put one arm around Rick in a quick hug, but Simpson pushed him off and pointed to the seat. Rick waved to Sadie and she winked back before wandering off.

Delton scooted down in his seat to be more eye to eye with Noah. He reached over and lifted one of the headphones off his ear. "Is this your first baseball game?"

Noah, hands flapping madly, nodded.

"Mine too. Want me to tell you about it?"

Noah shook his head.

Gently, Delton leaned Noah back into the seat. The boy's head never raised, and his brow was tightly knotted with anxiety. Delton lifted the headset off one ear slightly, and spoke quietly into it. "I know this all makes you nervous, but if you can trust me, you might enjoy this." He pointed to the field. "See that mound of dirt out there in the middle of the field?"

Noah didn't move.

"You have to look up to see it."

Noah quickly glanced up, and then back down again. He nodded.

"Okay. That was good," Delton said, trying to be encouraging. "A man is going to stand on that pile of dirt and throw a little ball as fast as he can," Delton cupped his hand to show the size of the ball. "And another guy is going to stand back by the fence with a wooden stick and try to hit it."

The announcer came on the loudspeaker, welcoming everyone to the game and naming the players on both teams.

Graphics blazed across the big screen at the back of the park but Noah didn't lift his head for any of it. When the National Anthem played, everyone stood, but Noah remained seated and buried his head into Delton's leg. Once the anthem was over, everyone applauded and cheered. Noah crouched down into his seat and began to moan.

Delton dropped back into the seat and began to rub his back. Leaning in close, he spoke softly in Noah's ear. "It's okay, boy. Everything is going to be all right."

Noah flapped his hands, and rocked back and forth while he moaned anxiously.

After a few moments, Delton was able to calm him down, but it was clear that Noah was not going to enjoy this outing one bit. Delton realized, there would be no teaching moment. The big thing would be that Noah managed to survive in a crowd of this size, with this much activity and noise. That would be the win for the day.

The first three innings were relatively uneventful. Three up, three down for each team, except the top of the second when the visiting team got a base hit.

Noah remained calm during playtime. It was in between the innings where the boy had issues. After the first inning, music boomed through the stadium, and the camera took shots of people dancing and projected them on the big screen at the back of the field. Noah wasn't fazed by this. His headset kept him fairly well protected from the loud noises, and nobody near him danced.

After the second inning it got a little wilder. A group of young workers drove a golf cart around the warning track, and shot t-shirts out of a big pneumatic gun. One of the t-shirts was headed in Noah's direction. Two guys caught it over the boy's head and fought for it briefly. Noah cried out, and cowered down. "Take it easy," Delton said. The man who ended up with the t-shirt pointed it at Delton. "Relax, man." Then he turned and held his t-shirt up. His buddies cheered.

Delton gently straightened Noah back up, into his seat. "It's all good, Noah. It's over now."

Noah sat back, hands flapping wildly, brow furrowed and eyes staring at his own shoes. He shook his head. "Don't like this."

"I understand, buddy. I'm glad you used your words and told me how you're feeling." Delton was trying sound upbeat and encouraging. "It won't always be that crazy. It's over now." He looked up to see Judith at the end of the row. She put her hands out in a questioning gesture. He put his thumb up to let her know that everything was okay. He didn't want to give up on it now. The boy had gone this far outside of his comfort zone; Delton wanted to see how far Noah could stretch himself.

At the bottom of the third inning, the Pirates got two men on base, which caused a good amount of excitement. The clean-up hitter nailed the first pitch and sent it over the big screen, out of the park. The crowd jumped up screaming and high-fiving each other. That, along with the loud sound effects and music, was the breaking point for Noah. He rocked again, and he skipped the uncomfortable moaning signal, opting instead for open screaming. He hit his face with both his hands, and Delton grabbed his wrists and pulled him in tight.

Noah screamed and writhed in his grasp, but Delton held him firmly. He glanced back at the guard behind him. "He's going into meltdown mode. I need to get him out of here."

It was Johnson, the same guard who had pulled his gun the month before, so he understood what this meant now. Jumping to his feet, Johnson called to the people along the row. "Excuse us, please. We have a disabled child who needs attention immediately."

To Delton's surprise, everyone stood. Lifting a struggling Noah, he tried to make his way out, but there was little room, and with Noah wiggling and screaming, maneuvering through was nearly impossible.

He saw Judith coming down the row toward him. She

raised her hands, signaling him to lift Noah up to her. Delton did as instructed and Noah started to kick in every direction.

"Please watch yourselves," Johnson cried out. People covered their faces, while Delton rushed him down and handed him off to Judith. He had to deal with several "What the fucks," along the way.

Judith took Noah with a quick, "Thanks," and quickly whisked the screaming boy away. Noah's screams faded with the distance.

Looking back at Johnson, Delton wondered what his next move was. Johnson smiled, and nodded back toward his seat. "Nice job. Enjoy the rest of the game."

When Delton sat back down, the man who had caught the t-shirt gave him another "What the fuck," then pointed at him and said, "Next time, leave Special Ed at home."

Delton looked back at Johnson, who pursed his lips and shook his head. Delton plopped into his seat, gave the man a scowl, and avoided his stare after that. The man, apparently now more courageous after downing a beer every inning, finally turned away and sat back down.

The Pirates ended the inning, up three runs. During the intermission, the announcer gave a welcome to all of the special groups in attendance. Right after Boy Scout Troupe #403, he gave a welcome to the six inmates of Two Rivers Correctional Facility who were caring for, and escorting, six special needs children in a program with Marmont State College. The crowd applauded. The drunk asshole who gave him shit earlier, looked cautiously back over his shoulder at Delton. Delton glared back at the dude, who looked away.

The next few innings were over quickly, and Delton was thinking the game was dragging on a little long. Without Noah here to share it with, it was boring to sit in a baseball stadium by yourself and watch two teams you really couldn't care less about. He found himself watching the back of Rick Simpson's head—his greasy, stringy red hair looking like copper wire, sprawling out from under his filthy University of Michigan baseball cap.

Rick had little patience for Eddie. Anytime Eddie talked to him, Rick would wave him off. When Eddie held up the program to show him a picture, Rick would push the boy's hand back down. He clearly did not want to have anything to do with his charge. Delton on the other hand, found himself missing Noah. He had looked forward to this opportunity since the moment Dr. Fitzpatrick had brought it up. It was the first baseball game for both of them, and a chance to create a lasting memory together.

Unlike Simpson, Delton found he liked spending time with Noah. Once they got used to each other, they had grown to know each other, accept each other, like and, even love each other. He knew Noah liked being with him, because Judith had told him that on many occasions, Noah would speak of wanting to see him while at home. What surprised Delton was that he shared those feelings. He enjoyed his time with the boy so much that he hated the weekends because he would have to wait two days to see him again.

At the top of the eighth inning, Sadie Hanson walked over to the end of the row with a large bag of popcorn and two small sodas. She got Rick's attention and winked at him. Then she handed the sodas to the woman sitting on the end. They were passed on down the row to Rick, who sat one in a holder for Eddie and one for himself. The popcorn followed. When Rick got the bag he looked into it carefully, then looked up at Sadie and nodded. She gave him the thumbs up and walked away. Delton wondered what this exchange was about, and he watched Rick carefully after that.

Simpson held up the popcorn for Eddie to take some, but kept his thumb around the edge of the bag in an awkward manner. Watching this carefully, Rick never took his hand off the edge of the bag. It wasn't until the bottom of the eighth, when a Pirates batter hit a double into left field, that Simpson made his move. When everybody stood to see if the ball would clear the fence,

Simpson slid out a small bag of powder from inside the popcorn, and quickly stuffed it into his pocket. By the time the runner had made it to second base, Simpson had given the rest of the popcorn to Eddie and everybody, including the guard assigned to watch him, had missed Rick's little maneuver.

Delton clenched the arm rests of his seat. The more he thought about the opportunity that Simpson had, and how he wasted it, the angrier he became. Simpson only used this whole program as a way to get outside the walls of the prison, and a chance to score some drugs.

Delton decided this farce had to end. He reached back and tapped Johnson on the knee. When the guard leaned forward, Delton spoke quietly in his ear. "When we get back, you need to check Simpson. He's got drugs on him."

Johnson sat back, then leaned forward again a moment later. "How do you know that?"

"I just watched the kid's mom sneak them to him in a bag of popcorn," Delton said.

Johnson leaned back. A moment later leaned back in. "His mom? Are you sure?"

Delton said no more. Just nodded.

Johnson patted his shoulder. "Thanks. We'll check them both out."

Chapter Thirty-Six

When the bus arrived back at the penitentiary, all six inmates got off. As soon as Rick Simpson's feet touched the pavement, Officer Jones yelled, "Simpson. Come with me."

Rick looked over and smiled. "Why's that?"

"Need to talk to you for a minute."

Rick glanced nervously at Delton, who looked away and marched inside with the others.

Before he entered the prison, he looked back over his shoulder. Rick was being marched away in the other direction with three guards.

Simpson didn't show up at dinner that evening. His six redneck friends all ate quietly together without their "life of the party" stirring them up.

"You're kind of quiet tonight," Hector said to Delton. "Everything go okay today?"

Delton looked up and then back down at his bowl of wallpaper paste that they had said was macaroni and cheese. "Yeah. I mean, not actually. Noah flipped out in the fourth inning and had to be taken out by his mother."

"Sorry, man," Hector said. "Wasn't nothin' you did though? Right?"

"Naw, man," Delton said. "He just can't do the crowd thing yet." He pushed his bowl away, turned to Hector, leaned in and spoke quietly. "But I saw Simpson take drugs from his kid's mom, and I told Johnson."

"You did what, man?"

"I know," Delton said.

"Are you fucking crazy?" Hector said. "You know you don't rat on nobody in here."

"Dude, I couldn't help it," Delton said. "These kids got nobody to fight for them—especially that kid. If his own mom don't give a shit, then the next man has got to step up. Today, I was the next man."

"That kid ain't here now to fight for you," Hector said. "What're you gonna do when the shitstorm comes?"

"I'll just have to handle it," Delton said.

It only took until the following morning for the shitstorm to arrive. Delton and Hector were headed into the showers when Simpson's scratchy voice cawed behind them. "There you are, Hayes, you piece of shit."

Delton turned to see Simpson strolling in, followed by his band of hillbillies.

Hector grabbed at his arm and tried to pull him. "C'mon, man. Let's keep going."

"Naw, man," Delton shook loose. "You go ahead. I'll handle this."

Simpson walked up to Delton and looked him straight in the eye. "The guards and the cops found some coke on me after the baseball game. Any idea how they got wind of it?"

Delton shrugged. "No, man. Tough luck."

"Tough luck, my ass." Simpson shoved him in the chest and Delton slipped a few steps back.

"Easy," Hector said, and took a step forward.

Simpson pointed at him. "You keep out of this, beaner." Two of Simpson's thugs walked over and stood by Hector.

"Simpson, why you gotta be such a fucking asshole?" Delton said.

"Oh, I'm the asshole?" Simpson said, smacking his chest with his hands. "Because of you, I'm out of the fucking Marmont program, and Eddie's mom is now in jail for drugs. And somehow I'm the asshole."

"Dude, there was drugs in the popcorn," Delton said.

Simpson walked back up to him. "So it was you."

"What would have happened if Eddie would have swallowed some of those drugs? Do you ever think of shit like that?" Delton said.

Simpson slapped his forehead. "He's a fucking retard. Nobody would have noticed, and nobody would have cared!"

Delton shook his head. He looked back at a man who had no grip on real life, nor how the decisions he made affected it. He only cared about how he could benefit from any given situation, everybody else be damned. "If you truly think like that, then it's good you're out of the program."

"Oh yeah?" Simpson reached back and pulled something out from behind him. "Well, if I'm out, you're out."

"Delton, watch out!" Hector yelled. He took an elbow to the side of his head and fell hard on the cement floor of the shower.

Simpson swung wildly, but Delton stepped back and a flash of metal whisked by his neck. Simpson bent his knees, as if he were ready to pounce. The piece of metal he waved back and forth appeared to be the back end of a cafeteria spoon, filed down to a sharp edge. He thrust it twice, and Delton dodged easily each time. The third thrust went deep into Delton's right shoulder. Blood poured out and Delton clutched at it, gritting his teeth against the pain.

"That hurt, Hayes?" Simpson and his thugs laughed. Simpson swung again.

Delton threw his right hand up instinctively, to block the blow, and the blade sliced through his palm. Delton cried out in pain.

His cry was met with more laughter. "Now you're sounding like that fine little sister of yours," Simpson said.

Delton could take being laughed at all day. He could even take being stabbed and slashed. But hearing this piece of shit even refer to his sister was too much. It was over now. Blood ran freely out of Delton's shoulder, down his arm and out his hand. When Rick swung again, Delton flicked his hand, sending a spray of blood across Simpson's face.

Simpson gagged, spit, and wiped at his face.

This was the opening Delton needed, he cocked his left arm back and brought his fist crashing against Simpson's jaw.

Simpson stumbled back, but Delton didn't slow. He followed with his bleeding right hand. The connection sent a spray of blood across the face of three of Simpson's allies. They all turned away and wiped their sleeves across their faces. They missed what came next.

Rick was clearly rocked by the hits, and he turned to get away. Delton charged, and tackled him to the ground. Simpson cried out quickly and then went limp. Delton stood and stepped back. Simpson lay there face down, unmoving, on the wet cement floor of the shower.

All was silent except for the running water in the next room. Delton assumed he'd knocked the piece of shit out when his head hit the floor. Perhaps a concussion would do the hayseed some good. Using his foot, he kicked Simpson over, only to find a large patch of wet blood soaking the man's shirt. A red puddle continued to grow around him. The spoon end of the makeshift knife was sticking out from under the left ribcage.

Chapter Thirty-Seven

"So he had to leave the game early. Didn't you, buddy?" Judith said, patting her son on the back.

Noah nodded. "Yeah," he said, without looking up, and continued to play a matching game on Darlene's smartphone.

Judith, Noah, and Darlene were sitting around their father's bed at Pleasant Oaks. When Noah spoke, the weary old man let his tired eyes fall on the boy, and he smiled. Then he looked up at Judith with a little twinkle.

Judith chuckled. "I know," she said, smiling and rolling her eyes at the ceiling. "Father knows best. You came through again."

Their father had been back at the retirement home for a few weeks now. He was given permission to move around the facility but mainly kept to his room. Though he could speak, his words came out sluggishly and he was embarrassed by how he sounded, so he rarely spoke at all anymore. He could walk with a walker but it took great concentration, and by the time he reached his destination, he was too tired to enjoy himself. A few times, Lee Dunham had gotten him out to play chess, but that was all that could entice him anymore.

"Did Judith tell you she has a boyfriend?" Darlene said.

Their father looked back at Judith with his eyebrows raised.

"Not a boyfriend." She forced a smile and glared at Darlene with her eyes. "Just a date."

"Sister, we're up to three dates now," Darlene said, hands on her hips. "That constitutes a relationship of some sort."

Judith looked over at her dad who smiled back at her. "He's a very nice man, Dad. And he treats me well." She nodded her head at Darlene. "He works with Jim. He hasn't met Noah yet, but he's familiar with autism so that's going to happen pretty soon." Judith leaned forward and rubbed her father's arm. "Then, I'd like to bring him in to meet you. I'd like to get my father's approval before I get serious with a guy."

Her father's smile faded and he looked away.

Judith's phone buzzed before she had the chance to tell him that she was proud to have a guy she liked meet her father. She reached for her phone to check the message. It was a group text from Dr. Fitzpatrick. "The Marmont project has ended. Please do not bring your children to the facility any longer. Thank you for your participation."

"What the hell?" Judith said.

"What is it?" Darlene asked.

Judith looked up from her phone. "It's a text from Dr. Fitzpatrick. It says the project is over, and not to bring our kids in anymore."

"Just like that?" Darlene said. "They just say it's over, with no warning?"

Judith looked down at Noah. "What's he going to do when he realizes he can't see Delton anymore?" She jumped from her seat. "Dar, stay here. I've got to call Dr. Fitzpatrick about this."

"No problem."

"Excuse me, Dad," Judith said, walking from the room. She pushed Dr. Fitzpatrick's number on her speed dial and walked down the hall. The phone rang four times and went to generic voice mail. "Dr. Fitzpatrick, this is Judith Higgins. Please call me. Noah has become very dependent upon this program. Is there a way he can still see Delton, even if the project is over?" She dialed Rena next.

Rena answered, but her voice sounded shaky. "Hi, Judith."

"Rena, what's going on?"

"I don't know the whole story...but the project is over."

"Rena, Noah needs this project," Judith said. "Is there any possible way he can still see Delton?"

"Judith...." Rena paused.

"What is it?" Judith said, her heart in her throat. "Did something happen to Delton?"

"All I know is that there was an altercation," Rena's voice shook. "And Delton is hurt."

Judith had to lean against the wall to steady herself. "What happened?"

"I don't know all the details. All I know is that Delton is hurt, and the project is over." Rena's breath quivered. "I'm sorry. I hope Noah..."

Judith tapped off the call. She walked out the front door and paced in the shade of the overhang. She was stressed about the well-being of this young man who she had so much contempt for when they first met. Delton had made himself one of the most important people in her son's life, and her life. If he was hurt, she had to know what was going on and see if there was anything she could do.

She called Taysha.

"Hello," Taysha said, quietly.

"Taysha, it's Judith. Please tell me you know what's going on with Delton."

"I do, honey," Taysha said. "I'm at Two Rivers now, but they won't let me see him."

"Rena said he's hurt. Is that true?"

"It is. He's in the infirmary getting fixed up."

"But the project is canceled." Judith's own voice cracked.

"Do you think it's possible that Delton can still see Noah on his own?"

"I'm sorry, honey, but that won't be possible. It doesn't sound like Delton will be seeing anybody for quite a while," Taysha said. "He killed a man this morning."

The following is the article that appeared on michigan-online. com, July 27, 2019.

A Death Ends Marmont/Two Rivers Program

Posted 8:35 p.m.

By Jason Kitchener jkitchener@michigan-online.com

The unorthodox rehabilitation project contrived between Marmont State College and Two Rivers Correctional Facility has ended. According to information received from a source at the Michigan Department of Corrections, one of the inmates involved in the program killed another inmate, who was also involved in the program.

The project consisted of a select group of inmates from Two Rivers Correctional Facility, giving care to special needs children. Spokespersons from both institutions have declined to make any official statements while an investigation is in process. However, Sheriff Kevin Gossinger of the Two Rivers Police Department has indicated that drugs were involved.

Although names are currently being withheld, Sheriff Gossinger, said the inmate who was killed had received drugs from the mother of one of the special needs children. She has since been taken into custody and charged with drug trafficking and child endangerment, and the child has been delivered into the care of a relative.

Dr. Warren Q. Fitzpatrick, professor at Marmont State and the man behind the project, has let the parents know the project is over, with no plans to continue.

Michigan-online will remain on top of this story, and update as the facts become available.

COMMENTS:

TammyG381: I wondered what kind of parents would

put their kids in with criminals. Now I know. The kind of parents who are criminals themselves!

EWarner: some things sound so much like a bad idea you should avoid em at all costs. This was one of those from the start.

Tigerfan25: Stupid, stupid, and stupid. They're in prison for a reason.

Blexxk: Everyone involved in this program was asking for trouble. It was only a matter of time before these guys showed their true colors.

RStandish: I actually knew Fitzpatrick in high school. He was a complete bonehead back then, and it don't seem like he's changed much.

SusanQ: Thank God only the inmates were hurt and no children were hurt.

EWArner: As far as we now no children were hurt. still don't have all the facts.

Chapter Thirty-Eight

Pain throbbed in his shoulder, down his arm, and through the palm of his hand. It was clear to Delton his meds were wearing off. As he lay on the bunk in his new cell, he looked around, realizing he could hold out his left hand and almost touch the far wall.

A guard had overheard Rick Simpson's buddies promise that Delton would pay for their friend's death, so after he was given stitches and drugs in the infirmary, he was whisked down into solitary, or "protective custody," as the guards described it.

The cell consisted of a sink and toilet at the end of his bunk, and a small desk jutting out from the wall, with a stool bolted to the floor. He was definitely in the "no frills" suite in the prison.

Keys rattled in the solid metal door and Delton sat up gingerly. Hopefully, they were bringing food because he was hungry.

The door opened with a creak, and in walked Johnson with one of the doctors from the infirmary. Delton was happy to see Johnson. Ever since the guard had screwed up and pulled his gun on Delton during Noah's meltdown, he had sort of been watching out for Delton.

"How ya doin', bud?" Johnson said.

"It's really starting to hurt."

The doctor sat on the bunk next to him and peeled back the bandage on Delton's shoulder.

"Well, sit tight. The doc here'll get you all set."

"How long I gotta be in here?" Delton said.

"Until we're sure you're gonna be safe," Johnson said.

The doctor replaced the bandage on his shoulder, then unwrapped his hand.

"But what're we gonna do about getting me to the Marmont program? Is somebody going to come get me?"

Johnson sighed. "Listen, Delton. I'm sorry to have to be the one to tell you this, but the program's been shut down."

"What?" Delton pulled his hand from the doctor and stood shakily. "No. It can't be. What about Noah?"

Johnson put up his hands. "Hey, sit down."

Delton leaned back and dropped on the bunk, shaking his head. "Who canceled it?"

"The warden," Johnson said. "It is becoming a media shitstorm out there, with two guys, who are supposed to be taking care of kids, fighting and killing each other."

"But the guy who started it is dead. Everyone is safe now."

Johnson shook his head. "It doesn't work that way and you know it."

Delton stared at a scratch on the wall. "But what about Noah? He needs me."

"Noah and Miss Higgins are just going to have to figure it out."

There was now a searing pain right through his heart, to match those of his shoulder and hand. But the doc couldn't help with this one. Not seeing Noah again, hearing his little giggles, seeing his joy when they fist-bumped, hurt right through the center of his chest. Delton saw his vision blur with tears. He closed his eyes and tried not to in front of these men.

"But you helped that little guy," Johnson said. "You gave him a great footing to build on in life. You should feel real proud of that, Delton. You made a real difference."

"Okay, things still look fine here," the doctor said. He reached into his pocket and pulled out a small packet of pills and set it on the desk. Take these with your food when it arrives. I'll check on you again in a couple of days."

Delton nodded and the doctor walked out.

"Dinner should be here real soon, bud," Johnson said. "I'm sorry again." He walked out, closed the heavy door, and locked it.

Delton stood, picked up the packet of pills, tore it open and popped them in his mouth. He didn't care to wait for the food. He was suddenly not hungry at all. He lay down on his bunk, resting his head on the ridiculously small pillow they supplied and stared at the ceiling. Tears ran from his eyes and soaked the little pillow until the drugs did their work, and dragged him off to sleep.

Chapter Thirty-Nine

As Judith had feared, Noah had trouble adjusting. She explained to him Sunday night that they wouldn't be seeing Delton the next day. He had said, "Okay," and acted as if he'd understood, but when Monday morning came around, Noah was upset they weren't going to see Delton. When she took Noah into Keener to get him enrolled, he had a meltdown, and she was late to work again.

Judith called Dr. Fitzpatrick to try to get more information. He answered, but had very little to say. "All I know is that there was a fight between two of the participants," Dr. Fitzpatrick said. "Delton came out of it quite severely injured, but Rick Simpson didn't come out of it at all." That's all Dr. Fitzpatrick said. He didn't mention that drugs were involved. She learned that from the news Monday night.

The story was run on all three news stations. The experiment that not one station had cared about when it began, were now all over it once blood was shed. Like vultures, they were circling, descending, ready to tear apart the carcass. Delton was made out to be a crazed violent criminal, who should never have been included in such a program after being locked up for armed robbery. The entire thing was portrayed as a huge boondoggle, with Dr. Fitzpatrick the idiot-in-charge.

Tuesday morning was a repeat of Monday morning. Noah struggled with going to Keener and not going to see Delton.

Tuesday night Noah was agitated at every little thing. Either his spoon for his chili was too big, or the chili was too spicy, or he was too hot. Each little thing seemed to require a great amount of screaming, and each time he made it clear he wanted to see Delton.

The reception at work throughout the week was cold. Her teammates spoke to her only when required, and then only about specific work topics. They did not engage her in any conversation regarding her son or the end of the program. On Wednesday, Judith couldn't take it any longer. When Simon walked past her cubicle she called out to him. He poked his head back in and she asked point blank. "Why is everybody treating me this way?"

Simon leaned on the cubicle door jam. "What way?"

"You know what way. Like I have shit in my hair, or something."

Simon flipped through the papers in his hand anxiously.

"What is it?" Judith asked. "Are you blaming me for what happened with the Marmont project? I had nothing to do with what happened."

Simon sighed. "We know, Judith. We are trying very hard not to judge, but you willingly put your son in a dangerous situation and some of us struggle with that."

Judith nearly choked on Simon's verbal Heimlich. "Are you kidding me? I would never have put Noah in any danger. This didn't even happen at the center. It happened at the prison."

"But it was the same men in both places," Simon said.

Judith stood. She didn't want to look up at him any longer. She wanted to look him in the eye. "You don't judge me, but you do judge Delton. And I'm guilty by association. Is that it?"

Simon raised his hands in a calming manner. "I'm sorry,

Judith. I don't want to get you upset."

"Too late," Judith said.

"Well, next time don't ask me anything, if you're just going to get angry with my answer." Simon stepped out of the cubicle but turned to give his parting shot. "If you'll remember, I tried to be supportive through the whole thing, even though I had misgivings with the program from the start. I couldn't understand how a mother could put her son in such an environment, but you did. And now you want everyone to feel sorry for you because a really bad decision blew up in your face." He opened his mouth to say more, but obviously thought the better of it. He shook his head and walked off.

Judith drove over to the Fountain's after work, to see if they had heard anything. But before she had put the car in park, Reggie Fountain burst out the door and descended on her. "I don't want you coming over here. Just get the hell out of my driveway."

Judith rolled down her window. "I just wanted to know if you've spoken to Delton."

"Oh, you mean that great guy you told us about?" Reggie said. "That terrific guy that I let the whole family meet? Well, in fact, no, we haven't talked to him. Because he's a murderer!" Reggie stood back and pointed toward the street. "Now back your car out of my driveway and stay the hell away from my house and my family."

Judith rolled her window up and drove off.

By Thursday evening, Noah stopped speaking completely. It was as if he'd never started the program. After two months of steady progress with Delton, he had regressed in less than a week's time to his pre-program status.

Judith felt like there was a growing hole in her stomach—like her anger was eating her from the inside out. She wanted to stand in front of Delton, scream at him, let him know that when you take on a responsibility with someone else, your selfishness has to be put aside. You can't just go off and do whatever the hell you want to do, because you have someone very fragile depending on you. She mulled over how little she had trusted Delton when this thing began, and how much he had come through since. It's true Noah had been lifted to heights he had never reached before, but her son had crashed now. And, although Delton had been the hand that lifted Noah out of the darkness, he was also the hand that freely let go, and let her son tumble back into the abyss.

And Judith wasn't sure she could forgive.

Her phone buzzed. It was Neil. Another hurdle to get over. She let it ring a couple more times while she thought of how she would say this. When nothing specifically came to mind, she hit the button. "Hello," she said, trying to sound as "matter-of-fact" as possible.

"Hey, Judith," Neil said. His voice was pleasant as always. "How's the boy?" And, as always, concerned about the right things.

"He's not doing well. Still not speaking."

"You sound stressed," Neil said. "Perhaps a nice dinner will help. Some wine…and maybe dancing?"

Why did he have to be so kind and supportive? It made the whole thing much harder. "I can't do this right now," she said.

"Oh, I'm sorry. Should I call back later?"

"No. I can't do us." Judith's voice cracked. "With Noah the way he is, I can't go ahead and have a relationship, and pretend that everything is okay."

"What are you saying?" Neil said, slowly, carefully, cautiously. "Are you breaking up with me?"

"There's no break-up," Judith said, a little too irritated. "This isn't high school. I'm not wearing your damn letterman jacket. What I'm saying is that I have to concentrate on Noah right now, and I can't have anybody else getting in the way of that."

"Judith, I don't want to get in your way. But you need support too."

"Neil, don't make this harder than it has to be. Can't you just listen to what I'm saying and not argue?"

There was a long silence on the other end of the phone. Judith was afraid to say anything, lest she apologize and tell him she wanted to see him, wanted him to hold her, and tell her everything would be fine. "I understand," Neil finally said. "Goodbye, Judith." Then the call beeped off.

Judith slowly placed her phone on the table in front of her, sat back, and cried uncontrollably.

"You ended it?" Dar said as soon as Judith opened the door.

"Dar, not now." Judith walked back into the kitchen and continued to work on the spaghetti.

"Not now?" Dar said, closing the door behind her and following, in step, right into the kitchen. "You had something, Judith. He accepted you and Noah. And he liked you both. Why are you turning your back on all that?"

"I have to concentrate on Noah right now. I have to figure this out."

"Figure what out?" Dar said. "That Noah has autism, and he struggles with things?"

Judith raised her hand. "Don't, Dar."

"Look, Judith, Noah responded to Delton—a man. Neil is a man. Perhaps Neil is just what Noah needs."

Judith glared at her sister. "Don't tell me what Noah needs. I'm his mother. I know what he needs."

"Right. You're his mother." Dar said. "But because of the choice you made, that's all he has."

"What are you saying?"

"I'm saying that perhaps it would be a good idea if there were a man in his life, and since you have no clue who his father is..."

Judith slammed the spaghetti spoon down on the counter, spraying sauce all over the wall. Dar closed her mouth and stepped back.

"Get in the car," Judith said.

"What?"

"I'll get Noah. You, get in the car."

"Where are we going?"

"Just get in my damn car."

Twenty minutes later, they were sitting in the car across from Grant Park. The man was there with his wife, pushing her wheelchair onto the paved walkway for their evening stroll. "See that man over there?" Judith pointed at him. "That's Noah's father."

Dar looked over at the man. She could tell he was middle-aged, and attractive. It was the slightly bent walk he had because he was tending to his afflicted wife that made him look older. "How do you know that? I thought they weren't allowed to tell at a sperm bank."

"Dar, don't be thick." Judith said. "I know he's the father because...."

Dar looked at her. It took several moments for her to catch on—her brain slow to process the fact that she'd been lied to all these years. She pointed at the man. "You and him?"

Judith nodded.

"What the hell are you saying here, Jude?"

Judith looked back over at the man, thinking on those days, years ago, when she had actually been in love. "His name is Jack Brody. I worked with him at Danser. We were part of the same strategy team, and I was so hung up on him." She looked back at Dar. "Let's face it, I was living pretty fast and loose in those days. All the traveling I did, I had a guy at pretty much every stop, and

I enjoyed my time with each and every one of them." She looked back at the man and his wife. "But none of them were like Jack. He was stable, emotionally strong, smart, funny, and he knew what a relationship should really be. I knew this because he would always talk about his wife, and all the little things he would do for her… and I loved him. It's not that I wanted a guy like him. I wanted him. Then, one day he was out of sorts, you know…just not with it. We were on a consulting trip to Baltimore, and he looked as if he couldn't even think straight. When our work was done, I asked him if he wanted to have a drink in the hotel lobby and discuss what was bothering him. When we met, he told me that they had found out his wife had been diagnosed with multiple sclerosis. It was all he could do to hold it together, so I whisked him back to his room so he could be free from prying eyes in case he needed to cry. When we were in his room, he cried hard." Judith paused. She noticed a tear rolling down her cheek and wiped it away. "And I was there to make everything all better. I completely took advantage of this guy for my own selfish desires."

"Ummm, you're kidding, right?" Dar said. "He was there too. He had a hand in it."

Judith shook her head. "No, that's just it. He wasn't there. He was so lost in his own desperation for his wife, that I just kept pouring him drinks. He'd cry, and I would fill his glass one more time. Then, when there weren't any more brain cells left, I moved in and did the only real thing I knew to make a guy feel good. In the morning, when he realized what happened, he cried even worse, and I knew I had completely destroyed this man's world."

"Jude, you can't take responsibility for this."

"Dar, I take complete responsibility for this," Judith said. "I had planned it out. When I saw him vulnerable, I did everything I could to move in on that. I just wanted to know what it felt like to be with someone who was that good a person. And so now I have Noah to let me know, every single day, what can happen when you do what you want, instead of what's right."

"Oh my God," Darlene said. "Are you telling me that you

believe Noah has autism because you behaved badly?"

Judith covered her face and broke down. She felt Darlene's hand grab her shoulder, pull her in, and hold her tight.

"Sister, that's crazy. But then again, you've always been my crazy-ass sister." Darlene held her for several minutes until Judith could control her tears. "So that's why you left Danser?"

Judith nodded.

"And you never told him you were pregnant."

Judith shook her head.

"And you were too ashamed at the whole ordeal to let anybody know about it, including me. So you made up the whole thing about quitting your job, and going to the sperm bank because you wanted a life change."

Judith nodded.

"Jude, you've put yourself in your own prison because of one stupid mistake you made. And for some reason you think it needs to be a life sentence."

Judith wiped at the tears on her cheeks.

Darlene kissed her sister's head. "This is breaking my freaking heart."

Judith sat back and looked at her. "Why? These are my mistakes, not yours."

"Yes," Darlene said. "But cold-blooded killers are treated better than you've been treating yourself."

Another week passed and Noah's voice did not return, nor were there any signs that it might. In fact, his mood seemed depressed, without hope. Everything he did was sluggish, with no happiness or childlike curiosity in his heart. The "Delton episode" as Judith referred to that period, had left Noah broken.

Sunday afternoon came around. Judith was on the couch watching as Noah sat on the floor, staring at two glasses on the coffee table. Not even this simple activity held joy in it anymore. The doorbell rang, and she dragged herself off the couch to answer it.

A young Hispanic man nodded at her. "Miss Judith Higgins," he said.

"Yes."

"I'm Hector Sanchez. I'm a friend of Delton Hayes' from Two Rivers, and there's something that I think you should know."

Chapter Forty

Delton recognized the hallway. He'd been here plenty of times to talk with Taysha and Miss Higgins. He wasn't sure why he was here this time though, until the door opened.

A short, balding white man in a wrinkled gray suit stood and smiled. "Hello, Delton. I'm Ray Bauer, and I've been asked to represent you for the death of Richard Simpson."

"Hey." Delton waved with his cuffed hands.

Ray gestured to the other side of the table. "Please take a seat and let us discuss it."

Delton shuffled over and plunked down.

Ray Bauer opened a file, spun it around, and slid it over. "First things first. I want to get your signature on this form giving Two Rivers Correctional Facility permission to keep you in protective custody for an extended period of time."

"Protective custody?" Delton said. "It ain't protective custody. It's solitary confinement."

"Maybe so. But you are safe because of it. From what I understand, Mr. Simpson had a great many friends who now want to do you harm."

"They ain't nothing but Simpson's hillbilly jug band. They

don't scare me."

"Simpson didn't scare you either, did he?" Ray tapped the form. "Please sign so we can get on with the rest of the meeting."

Delton scoffed, picked up the pen and signed the form. "I don't know why they don't put all of them in solitary. I'm the one who was attacked and I'm treated like the bad guy here."

Ray pulled the folder back, closed it and set it aside. "Right, well I've looked over the case and the statements of the witnesses and I think it would be in your best interest to plead out to voluntary manslaughter. With good behavior you could get out in four to six years."

"What?" Delton said. "I thought you were here to represent me?"

"I am," Bauer said. "And after looking everything over, I think this is the best possible option for you."

"I'm not pleading guilty to something I'm not guilty of. He tried to kill me. I was trying not to die."

"There are several eye-witness reports stating that you attacked him, and only one saying it was the other way around. I don't see how you would have a chance of winning by trying to plead self-defense."

Delton shook his head. "I'm not pleading guilty. It's not happening."

Ray sighed, shook his head, and gathered his papers together. "Then I guess we're done here for right now. I'll contact you when we get closer to a hearing on this." He stood, walked over to the door and knocked twice.

"How long you think this is gonna take?" Delton asked.

The door opened and Ray turned back. "I have no reasonable idea. Things like this can take weeks, months, or years. Have a good day." Then he walked out.

The guard looked at Delton and nodded to the door. "C'mon, Hayes. Let's get you back."

Delton let out a long breath, struggled to his feet, and headed back, feeling like he just signed away his chance to ever leave his tiny, lonely cell.

Chapter Forty-One

"It was self-defense!" Judith screamed.

All 200 students in the auditorium attending Dr. Fitzpatrick's sociology class turned to look at her. Dr. Fitzpatrick stopped writing on the white board and looked up to the top of the stairs. When he saw Judith, he capped the dry erase marker he had in his hand and placed it on the tray. "Students, will you excuse us for just a moment?"

Judith scurried down the stairs. A flurry of chatter erupted with every step she took. Dr. Fitzpatrick stepped over to a door at the side of the stage and opened it for Judith.

As soon as she breezed through the doorway into the small office, she spun around. "Delton killed that man in self-defense."

Dr. Fitzpatrick closed the door quietly. "Unfortunately, that doesn't change anything."

"Wait," Judith held up a hand. "You knew?"

Dr. Fitzpatrick shuffled nervously. "I found out the other day."

"And you didn't let me know?"

"Miss Higgins, my reaction was just the same as yours," Dr. Fitzpatrick said, rubbing his hands together. "And I petitioned to

253

have the project reinstated on the basis of this new revelation. But I was completely shut down. So I didn't feel there was any reason to bring it to your attention and have you get upset again."

"Who was it?"

"Pardon?"

"Who was it who shut you down? The board?"

"No. It was the warden at Two Rivers. He had not been a fan of the project from the start, and after the incident, he felt it better to not let it begin again."

Judith could feel her heart beat faster. "He felt it better?"

"You see, the public outcry has been quite severe and…."

"Oh, he hasn't seen severe yet," Judith said. She walked toward the door and threw it open. Nearly every student in the auditorium jumped in their seats and their chatter stopped abruptly.

Dr. Fitzpatrick followed her out of the room. "Miss Higgins, I don't think…."

But Judith didn't slow. She stomped up the steps and out the door, leaving a bewildered professor to deal with his stunned class.

"Mr. Luzynski can see you now," the elderly secretary of the Two Rivers Correctional Facility Warden said, with a pleasant smile.

Judith stood from the hard plastic orange chair in the lobby and walked through the thick metal door of the warden's office.

The office was hardly elaborate—cement block walls with thin fake wooden trim around the tile floor and the doorway. There was a very high, and very small window above and to the right of the warden's desk.

Warden Luzynski stood behind his large metal desk and gestured to a chair when Judith walked in. "Have a seat," he said, in a no-nonsense sort of way. What he left unspoken were the words, "so we can get this shit over with." He was a short, bulbous man with a large nose and a head of thick black and white hair that looked like it had been combed very well, two days ago.

Once Judith had taken her seat, he took his, in polite fashion. "So, Miss Higgins, I'm aware you were part of the Marmont project...."

"Yes, Warden, an integral part," Judith said.

"Eh...how do you mean?"

"My son, Noah, was cared for by Delton Hayes."

"Yes. Yes, I know that," the warden said. "So what is it you want from me?"

"I just learned that Delton's actions were in self-defense. I would like him reinstated into the program."

Warden Luzynski shook his head. "That ain't happening. The program is dead. Over."

"Well, perhaps you could allow Delton to see Noah on a one-on-one basis here."

Luzynski waved his hand. "I'm sorry, Miss Higgins, that can't happen."

Judith leaned in. "But why are you punishing Delton for something he didn't do?" She hated that she sounded like she was pleading.

"But he did do it," Luzynski said. "Have you not read the papers or seen the news? I'll clue you in if you haven't. The story is very clear—Delton Hayes killed Rick Simpson in a drug related incident in my prison. It's an incident that would not have happened if it weren't for that damn program."

"But that's not the whole story, and you know it," Judith said.

"Look, Miss Higgins, public opinion is a very fickle thing. The stories that people tell are beyond my control. I can only try my damnedest to not give them anything more to talk about. Now what do you think would happen if I were to allow that project to start up again? Do you think the news reporters would say, 'good for them for giving those guys a second chance?' No. They'd vilify me, and they'd vilify you for being a part of it."

"But what about letting Delton see Noah alone?"

"If I did that, the entire state would be holding their breath waiting for something to go wrong. And the minute your son stubbed his toe, they'd all call for the crucifixion of Delton Hayes. Not to mention all the investigations into child endangerment I would have to deal with, and probably lose, since the man had already killed somebody before I put him in a room with your son. Look what they're saying now. I have Delton locked away for his own safety, and the media is spinning it that he's kept by himself because he's so dangerous to everyone else."

Judith fought back tears. "But my son needs him."

"I feel for you, Miss Higgins. I really do," Luzynski said, trying and failing at sounding sympathetic. "But until something big changes, there isn't a thing I can do even if I wanted to."

Girding her strength, Judith stood. "Well then, I guess it's up to me to make big changes," she said.

"What do you mean?"

"Wait and see." She nodded at him. "Thank you for your time, Warden." Then she turned and walked out, not knowing what she would do—just knowing that, for Noah's sake, she couldn't stop here.

Chapter Forty-Two

"You can't be nervous," Darlene said. "You just have to be natural."

Judith fixed her hair in the reflection of the coffee table. "That's easy for you to say, you're not in front of the camera."

After obsessing over her conversation with Warden Luzynski for several days, as much as she hated to admit it, she understood his position, and would probably make the same decision if she were sitting in his chair. He talked about the media, and public opinion, and she knew those were extremely strong powers at work, and if they were ever lined up against you, that meant you were royally screwed. Judith knew this very well. When she worked at the PR firm, she did everything she could to help individuals and companies leverage the strength of public opinion.

So that is what she had decided to do now.

With Darlene's help, Judith was going to put out a video explaining everything that happened with Noah and Delton, explain Delton's plight, and attempt to steer the train that is public opinion and media bias.

"Okay, are you ready?" Darlene asked, pointing her phone at Judith.

"I'm ready," Judith said.

"I'm rolling…action."

"Hello there, I'm Judith Higgins. And this is my son, Noah." Judith quickly described Noah's ASD, his involvement in the Marmont program, and how, after working with Delton Hayes for two months, he had seen amazing progress and began to speak words for the first time in his life. And she discussed how Noah had regressed since the end of the program. "He's been depressed that Delton, his one true friend, is no longer in his life. He has had several meltdowns, and those of you who know anything about autism can understand how bad that is. But what is even more distressing is that Noah no longer tries to speak." Judith's voice cracked and she took a moment to regain herself. "And now, even small tasks and activities that used to bring him contentment, if not joy, hold no interest for him. He is a shell of what he used to be." Judith started crying. "Shut it off."

"I'm gonna keep rolling," Darlene said. "But we'll cut out everything we can't use. You're just doing so well I don't want to stop your momentum."

Judith gave herself the moment to cry, letting her tears flow until she felt soothed. Then she wiped her eyes and blew her nose, sat up, and looked into the camera again. "Now, I'm sure you're thinking, why would I want to put my son back with a man who killed another man over drugs? Well, the truth is, that is not the truth. The stories you have seen on the news and read about, are not what actually happened. I have talked to people who were there. What happened is that Delton turned another man in, who was in the program and was doing drugs. Delton feared for the child's safety and wanted to put a stop to it. The other man was thrown out of the program, and tried to get his revenge in prison. In trying to protect himself, Delton was hurt very badly, but the other man fell on and stabbed himself with his own makeshift knife. Delton did not kill the man. He acted solely in self-defense. But that doesn't matter in cases like this. If you're involved in a violent act, how can you possibly be around children? It doesn't matter if you were trying to help the children or not."

The doorbell rang. Darlene stopped the video recorder. "Damn, that was going well."

"This is good," Judith said. "We need them now anyway." She let in Rena and Taysha. They had both agreed to assist Judith with this public relations video to help Delton and Noah get back together again.

"With all the work we have to do today, I thought it might be good if we could add a little enjoyment," Taysha said, and she held up a jug of sangria.

"Well, now we know who's got the brains in this outfit," Darlene said, clapping. "I'll get the glasses."

The four women set to work on the video. Using what was already recorded as the foundation, Judith recorded more narration to be used as a voice over. Taysha, had brought the file on Delton she was given when she started the program. There were three pictures of Delton, which Darlene laid out on a table, shot and edited them in, using video-editing software she and Jim had purchased to edit their vacation videos.

"I've never put one damn video together," Darlene said. "So I'm kinda learning as I go."

"I put a small video together last year for a class project," Rena said. "I can do that if you want me to."

"Girl, take the wheel," Darlene said, and she relinquished her computer to Rena, who set to work like a pro.

Rena plugged in a small hard drive she'd brought with her that had all the recordings of Delton and Noah together in the room. She had already tagged the important days, such as Noah's first words, Noah laughing, and the conversations they had.

Drinking their sangria, and eating pizza they had delivered, the four women deliberated over what clips to show, wanting to keep the video from being too long for anybody to watch.

They made their decisions, and Judith recorded a bit more narration to introduce each segment. Rena finished the editing, leaving in the part where Judith broke down and asked for the camera to be turned off.

"Sweetie, you can't get more genuine than that," Taysha said, when Judith protested. "That is the money shot right there. That has to stay in."

By the time they were done they had finished two large pizzas, the whole jug of sangria, and had a four-and-a-half-minute video to show for their efforts.

Darlene set Judith up with a YouTube channel, and uploaded the video. "It begins now," she said.

The next morning Judith checked her channel before she went to work, and to her dismay, saw that her video had only logged 12 views. And she knew that four of them were Darlene, Rena, Taysha, and her. They had all agreed to check it on their computers when they got home to make sure it was playing correctly.

She called Darlene from work to share the sad news.

"Actually, it's worse than that," Darlene said. "I watched it twice myself, and then showed the thing to Jim. So three out of the 12 views were just me."

"Ugh," Judith groaned. "This is a disaster."

"No, not really. Jim thought the video was great."

"It doesn't matter how great it is, if nobody watches it."

"I have an idea," Darlene said. "I'll share it on Facebook. I'm sure it will get a little more play that way."

That evening, after Judith had gotten Noah's dinner, she sat down to rest and checked her views again. It was up to 985. By the end of the week the count had reached 37,056.

Judith was working alone in her cubicle on Friday, when

she heard a knock on the metal frame of her doorway. She turned to see Simon, Shelley, and Evelyn. "We came to give you a group apology," Simon said. "But I need to give you one just from me as well."

Judith said nothing. She couldn't. She knew if she opened her mouth, she would probably cry and that would completely destroy the moment. She pinched her left hand with her right one and listened.

"Well….eh…" Simon began, "we judged you, and we judged this Delton fellow, and we had no right to."

"We saw the video you made," Shelley said. "We realized we had no idea what was really going on."

"We only listened to what they said on the news," Evelyn said in her tired voice. "We never took into consideration there was another side to the story."

"I feel like a fool," Simon said, "after how I acted, and all the stupid things I said. I apologize."

There was no way Judith could pinch hard enough to keep the tears from coming now. She brought her hands to her face and cried.

Her team descended on her, gave her hugs and reassurances that everything would be all right, and they would stand by her completely from this moment forward.

Bernie strolled by carrying a large folder, saw what was taking place, and rolled his eyes. "My God, I'm like running a commune here." Then he shuffled away.

Not feeling much like cooking after work, Judith picked up Noah from Keener's and had Lance's Burgers by the park. She watched her son eat, stoically. There was something lost inside him. He went through the motions of life, but there was no engagement. Behind his eyes, where curiosity and giddiness bloomed just three short weeks ago, there was nothing. The light was extinguished. His movements now were made just to sustain breath. Nothing more.

Judith watched Jack Brody put his wife in the car and drive away. She finished her diet Coke and drove home as well. When she pulled into the driveway, she saw Neil sitting on her doorstep and sighed. This was certainly not something she needed to deal with right now. He walked over. "Hey, Judith. Can we talk?"

Judith got out and went around to the other side to let Noah out. "This is not a good time, Neil."

"There's no time like the present when you're fighting for something you care about," Neil said.

Judith unbuckled Noah and helped him down. "I don't just mean a good time to talk. I mean this is not a good time for a relationship."

Neil followed her to the door. "Judith, I've given you your space, but I still don't understand what from. If I did something wrong I wish you'd let me know so I have a chance to fix it."

Judith fumbled for her apartment key. "No. You didn't do anything wrong. I just have to focus on Noah right now with everything that's happened."

"Well, that's what has me confused," Neil said. "How is it I have to be out of the picture while you focus on Noah? Why can't I help you with that?"

"Because, you can't." The door opened and Judith pushed Noah through. "I have to do this myself." She walked in and Neil followed right behind her. "Oh, come on in. Make yourself at home."

"Why, Judith? Why do you have to do it by yourself?"

Judith threw her keys on the table and closed the door. "Neil, what do you want from me?"

"I want you to let me help. I want to be a part of the solution."

"There's no part for you to play." Judith was getting frustrated and started talking with her hands. "Noah has autism.

He has been through a traumatic experience. He needs me. I can't just go off and do whatever I want, whenever I want, when my son is hurting. I have to fix this. You can't fix this. I have to."

"I understand that. I care about Noah too, and I can help."

"How is it you think you can help?"

Neil shifted his weight and looked at her. She knew he was suppressing his bruised feelings. "I saw your video on Facebook."

Judith crossed her arms. "I'm glad you are one of the 38,000."

"I could have helped you put that together," Neil said. "I had video production classes all through high school. I would have loved to have worked on that with you."

"Oh really?" Judith blurted out.

"Yeah," Neil smirked, that damn cute, yet cocky little smirk that she always thought was attractive, but really irritated the hell out of her right at this moment. "It would have turned out a hell of a lot better too."

Judith pursed her lips. "Oh really?" She finally said.

Neil nodded. They stared at each other for a moment. Then his smirk faded. "Judith, I just want to spend time with you."

Judith's eyes watered, blurring her vision. "Neil, you don't even know me."

"Let me get to know you better."

"I'm not worth the trouble."

Neil stepped closer, and grasped her shoulders firmly. "I strongly doubt that."

The doorbell rang.

Judith moaned loudly. Neil stepped back and chuckled. "Timing is everything."

Judith raised a finger. "Give me one moment." She turned and opened the door.

Jack Brody stood on her doorstep. "Hello, Judith. I'm sorry to bother you, but I have to know. Do I have a son?"

Chapter Forty-Three

Jack Brody had the same look—handsome carved face, hair looking like he brushed it with his fingers, though always remaining perfectly in place—yet now it had wisps of gray that hadn't been there before. His stance was the same too. His waist was still trim, and shoulders broad, most of his weight on one leg, with his hands in his pockets and head bowed slightly, with an heir of James Dean cool. But what was different on Jack were his eyes. They now bore a few more lines; they looked tired. Years of caring for his beloved, failing wife had dimmed the light within them. Yet now those tired eyes were fixed sternly on her. "Well?"

"Uh…Jack." Judith stammered. "What are you doing here?"

"I saw your video. Your son, Noah, seemed…the right age," Jack said. "I had to come over to find out."

Neil stepped to the doorway. "Who is it, Judith?"

Jack held out his hand. "Name's Jack Brody. I'm sorry to interrupt, but I need a moment of Judith's time."

Neil shook his hand. "Neil Keating. It has to be okay with Judith."

Both men looked at her. She wished a trap door to hell would open and swallow her whole. That would be more comfortable. "Uh…sure, Jack. Come in."

She stepped back from the door and Jack entered. His eyes landed on Noah sitting on the couch. The boy acted unaware of anybody else in the room. He lay back, zipping and unzipping his jacket continuously. Jack slowly walked over. "Hello, Noah. I'm Jack."

There was no acknowledgment from Noah. He continued with the zipper on his jacket.

Jack looked up at Judith. "I have to know Judith. Is this my son?"

Ice coursed through her veins. She wanted to say yes, but was terrified to.

"What?" Neil said. "Your son?" He looked over at Judith. "I think you're mistaken. She said this was in vitro fertilization."

"Is that what you're telling everybody?" Jack said to Judith. "That you just decided to quit the firm and have a baby on your own?"

Neil looked at her. "Judith? What's the story here? Is this man Noah's father?"

Judith looked up at him, still unable to speak. Not knowing exactly what words should come out even if she were to try.

Neil nodded, and sighed sadly. "I see. Well, I'm sure you two have a great deal to discuss, so I'll get out of your way." He nodded toward Jack. "Nice to meet you, Jack."

"Neil, wait," Judith cried, but he did not slow. He bolted out the door and let it close behind him.

"Judith, I have to know," Jack said, from behind her.

She whirled on him, angry now. "What are you doing here, Jack?"

He looked shocked at her outburst. Gesturing toward Noah, he opened his mouth to speak but she cut him off. "What if he is your son? There's nothing you're going to do for him now anyway."

"If he's my son, I'll get involved," Jack said.

"I don't want you to get involved," Judith said. "I have everything under control. I don't need you."

"Oh, is that so?" Jack snickered. It was irritating. "Is that why there's a video out on YouTube discussing how screwed up things are?"

"Jack, I can't have you involved."

"He's my son, isn't he?" Jack said.

"Jack, you have too much going...."

"He's my son, isn't he?"

"It's okay, Jack...."

"He's my son, isn't he?" Jack yelled.

Then the only sound was Noah's zipper traveling up and down his jacket.

Judith looked at the floor, and nodded.

Jack ran his fingers through his hair, sat down in a chair across from the couch, and looked at Noah.

"Jack, I didn't want you to know about this," Judith said. She walked over and sat next to Noah. "You have so much going on with your wife, and that is exactly where your attention needs to be."

Jack looked from Noah to her. His tired eyes now glaring with anger, and perhaps hatred. After a moment he spoke. "I need to help my son."

Judith shook her head. "Jack, your wife's sick. She needs you now. Go be with her."

"Why did you put out that video?" Jack asked, ignoring her statement.

"I need to turn public opinion around," Judith said. "Noah needs Delton, more than he needs anybody else in the whole world. And Delton isn't getting out, because the whole world thinks he's a drug-crazed murderer who's better off behind bars. And that simply isn't the truth."

Jack nodded and looked back at Noah. His eyes calm now,

yet resolute. "That's how I can help my son."

"Jack, it's not…."

"I'll help get my son's most important person back into his life," Jack said.

"What do you mean?"

Jack looked over at her. "Turning public opinion is what I do for a living. I'll help you with that."

"And just how do you plan to do that?"

"I need to think on that for a bit. But you've gotten the ball rolling with your video already. Let's see what happens from here." He stood, and looked down at Noah. "Goodbye, son. Nice to finally meet you." He looked over at Judith. "I am still trying to figure out how I'm feeling about you right now. But I am going to help you with this." Then he walked slowly to the door, opened it and paused. "I'll be in touch, when I have something." He walked out and closed the door quietly behind him.

Noah continued with his jacket zipper, oblivious of the tempest of complex emotions that had been swirling around him the last several minutes.

Her phone buzzed. She ran over to her purse and pulled it out. Without recognizing the number she answered it anyway in case it had something to do with Noah.

"Miss Higgins?"

"Yes."

"I'm Jason Kitchener, from Michigan-Online. I'd like to set up a time to talk with you about your video that's on the verge of going viral."

The following is the article that appeared on michigan-online. com, August 25, 2019.

Mother of Marmont/Two Rivers Program Son, Speaks Out

Posted 10:10 p.m.

By Jason Kitchener jkitchener@michigan-online.com

What began as an unconventional rehab program for special needs children, disintegrated into a murderous drug ring scandal. But now one mother is speaking out against all the furor, and telling a much different tale.

And why does her voice mean anything? Because her son was at ground zero of the scandal. He was the one being cared for by the alleged "murderous drug lord."

A week ago a video appeared among the vast ocean of videos on the internet. What was different about this video was that it was narrated with a mother's desperate voice. A voice pleading for her son.

It was the voice of Judith Higgins, mother of Noah Higgins, a boy with autism spectrum disorder. Seven-year-old Noah had not spoken a word in his life until entering into the Marmont program, with direct thanks going to the man everyone thinks is the crazed drug lord inside Two Rivers Correctional Facility.

"He is not a murderer," Judith Higgins said. "He's actually a kind, gentle young man who has worked very hard in this program, and is now locked away for doing nothing more than defending himself."

Miss Higgins said she was visited by an inmate, weeks after the news broke about the murder, and the program being dissolved. "He was there the moment Rick Simpson was killed. He told me that there was a whole gang of men surrounding Delton. The rest of them held him back, while Rick Simpson attacked Delton with a shank (term for a knife crafted within a prison). Delton was slashed and stabbed several times, but in the end, Simpson slipped and fell on his own knife, and died."

This had not been the story that had flooded news outlets the past several weeks. "The news has been completely wrong about this," Higgins explained. "It was Rick Simpson who was into drugs. He was getting them from Sadie Hanson (the mother of the boy Simpson was assigned to), and Delton thought that was wrong. Delton told authorities about Rick, which resulted in Rick's removal from the program. Rick was retaliating when he died."

This is new information that, if true, spins this story in a whole new direction. But also brings up the question, why is Judith Higgins speaking out now?

"For several reasons," Higgins said. "Delton Hayes is being treated unfairly, unjustly, and if no one will speak out for him, then nothing will be done about this and he will be punished for something that was beyond his control. He has a little sister who loves him very much, and has been depending on him getting out soon." But Higgins' reasons weren't completely altruistic. "My son needs him. Noah began to speak after spending time with Delton. And now that Delton isn't in his life, Noah has lost his voice again. In fact he's worse off than he was before he started the program, because his heart is now broken too."

And so, amid the shouts of condemnation, comes one single voice of reason. But it is a voice powered by a mother's love.

COMMENTS:

TammyG381: Here's a stupid question. where's the boy's father?

EWarner: True whys the only man in this kids life some dude behind bars.

Tigerfan25: The saying is that it's time to cut bait. This guy may have helped her son but hes in prison for a reason. Hes always going to get messed up in this sort of thing. I can't imagine she wants her son around that as he grows up.

Blexxk: She wants it now because it's easier than taking responsibility herself. Why do any of the work of raising and helping your kid when somebody else can do it for you? Doesn't matter who they are or where they come from.

rjohnson875: Self defense is as overused as That's not mine, and I don't know how that got there. Keep him locked up and keep the kid safe.

roseglass: Have any of you actually watched the video they're talking about here? They have video of him working with the kid. He's really good with him.

Chapter Forty-Four

Francisco's neon sign looked a lot less flashy in the daytime. In fact, everything about the place was different; the street was busier and more noisy, the sun shone down hot, instead of the cool moonlight, which killed the atmosphere, and the pit in her stomach seemed like a deep crevasse.

Judith found it strangely ironic somehow that Jack wanted to meet her at the same place where Neil had set up the blind date just one month earlier. Two Rivers was a small town, but there were more places to eat than Francisco's.

For the second time in a month, Judith took a deep breath, girded her inner strength, and walked through the doors of the family-owned Italian eatery. She saw Jack immediately, sitting three booths down from where she and Neil had sat. He looked polished and handsome, wearing his finest business suit and a silver tie. He waved her over. They said their polite hellos, and she took her seat. "It didn't take you long to put together a plan."

"Have you seen the michigan-online article?" Jack said, holding up his smartphone.

"Yes. I thought it was good."

Jack nodded curtly. "Sure, it was good. But it didn't do much to sway public opinion."

"How do you mean?"

"Did you read the comments?"

Judith nodded, though she wished he hadn't seen the comments.

"The very first one…." Jack held up a finger for emphasis. "Where's the father?" He threw his hands up. "Little do they know that the father had no clue he was even a father."

Judith winced. "Jack, I'm…."

A waitress dropped off menus, and two glasses of water. "Our lunch special today is homemade spinach ravioli. Would you like a second before you order?"

"Yeah, give us a minute, and two cups of coffee, please," Jack said.

"Okay, I'll be right back with those." The waitress smiled brightly, and scurried off.

Judith tried again. "Jack, I'm…."

Jack held up his hand and cut her off. "I can't hear it right now." He pointed to his phone. "You don't fare any better. They say you'd rather put your son in the hands of a criminal than have to deal with him yourself." He leaned in. "How does that make you feel?"

Judith shrugged. "They don't understand."

"Judith," Jack shook his head. "This is the public opinion you're trying to turn around. You can't just shrug it off. And I," he put his phone in his breast pocket and tapped his finger on the table, "as the boy's father, am going to make sure this shit turns around right now."

Judith leaned in. "Jack, I think we need to discuss all of this before we move forward with any plans."

"Here's your coffee," the waitress said, setting two cups in front of them. "Are you ready to order?"

Neither looked up at the waitress. They stared uncomfortably at each other. At this point, even though the poor

272

young lady was just doing her job, she was a nuisance. They both choose the ravioli just to get rid of her as soon as possible. The waitress tapped her pen on her pad, said she'd get that order right in, and rushed away.

Judith sighed. "I knew you had your hands full with Kate. You were devastated at the time. And I only made things worse by...."

"Look," Jack said. He pulled his coffee closer and poured cream into it. "I was out of my head then, and I made the greatest mistake of my life. But I made it, and I owned it. So let's not go into too much detail about the 'good old days.'" He stirred his coffee. "I also understand I'm the interloper here right now. You've made it clear you don't want my support, or you would have come to me. But now that I know that I have a son, I am going to help. I want to help. I guess I feel that rather than sit around and act like Noah is a big mistake that we both should regret, I actually want to do something proactive to help him." Setting his spoon down he took a quick sip to test the temperature.

Judith nodded. "No, I agree. I...."

"Here you go," the waitress said, and dropped off two plates of spinach ravioli, with roasted asparagus. Judith and Jack were silent as she ground fresh Parmesan over both plates. "Is there anything else I can get you right now?"

"I think we're all set, thanks." Judith said.

"All right. Enjoy." The waitress gave them both a bright smile and walked away.

Jack leaned in and spoke quietly. "Can we agree that all talk of the past is over, and let's start planning Noah's future together?"

Judith nodded and looked at her plate. The food smelled great, but right now she felt if she were to take a bite, it wouldn't stay down.

Jack pulled out a yellow legal pad from his briefcase on the seat next to him, and threw it on the table. "I've thought a great deal about this, and I've jotted down some notes. I wanted to go over them with you, and get your thoughts."

Jack ate voraciously while he spoke. For some reason guys seemed to be hungry even when the world was in turmoil around them. He had written a great many ideas, and described them in detail to Judith.

For her part, she liked them. She even had ideas to improve upon a few of his strategies. He took out his pen, crossed out lines, and wrote updates in the margins. Judith found the whole thing exhilarating. It was like she fell right back into that role again. This was where she was comfortable, where she had something to add to the world. And she remembered what a great team she and Jack had made. They did the whole pitch-and-catch thing very well. Each new idea building from the last one, making the overall strategy incredibly well organized.

"But here's the kicker," Jack said with a proud smile. "I know it's a long shot, but there's a woman who works at Danser now, who has connections with a couple of the journalists at GINfo. I'm going to run your flag up their flagpole and see if the wind catches it."

"Do you really think there's a chance?"

Jack shrugged. "It's always a no, unless you ask. But I think with an autistic boy and an oppressed inmate, this has crazy-human-interest-story written all over it. In all honesty, I can't see them turning it down."

Judith had to take a deep breath in order to keep from tearing up again—a habit she'd started lately that was becoming annoying, especially to her. "Jack, I can't thank you enough for all your work on this."

Jack waved it off. "Don't thank me yet. We haven't seen if any of it will work."

The waitress stepped up to the table. "May I get you anything else?"

Jack pointed at Judith's untouched plate. "I think we need a box for her, and one bill please." The waitress nodded and walked away.

"You don't have to get my lunch, Jack."

He pulled out a business credit card, and set it on the table. "Not to worry. You are now an official pro-bono account of Danser."

Judith's phone buzzed, and she pulled it out of her purse. The screen read Pleasant Oaks. She flipped it open. "Hello?"

"Judith Higgins?"

"Yes."

"This is Maddy White, a nurse from Pleasant Oaks. I'm sorry to have to say this, but your father has had another stroke. An ambulance is on its way to take him to the hospital."

Chapter Forty-Five

When Judith pulled into the hospital parking lot, Darlene was just getting out of her car. She gave her horn a quick honk, and Darlene turned. Her sister looked exactly how Judith felt—stressed beyond reason.

She jumped out and caught up with Darlene. Darlene's hair was pulled back and she wore a baggy sweatshirt and leggings. When Judith closed for a hug, she said, "I'm sorry for the way I look. I was working out when I got the call." Judith took her hand and they walked into the emergency entrance together.

"We're here for Ben Higgins," Judith said, to the gray-haired woman behind the desk. "He was brought in by ambulance."

The woman spun in her chair and looked behind at an EMT standing off to the side reading something on his phone. "Ray." The man looked up and she nodded her head toward Judith and Darlene.

The EMT named Ray slid his phone in his pocket and walked over, clasping his hands in front of him. "Are you related to Ben Higgins?"

"We're his daughters," Darlene said.

"Follow me." He waved them forward and guided them through the crowded waiting room, down a hallway into a smaller room, and gestured for them to sit on an uncomfortable couch. Once they were seated, he closed the door and leaned against it. "I'm sorry to say that your father passed away on the ride here from Pleasant Oaks."

Judith's vision narrowed and her head swirled. She heard Darlene crying loudly. But Judith couldn't cry, probably because there was no breath. She wasn't breathing, couldn't breathe. The breath had just been knocked out of her.

Her sister reached over, grabbed her, pulled her in tight, buried her face in Judith's shoulder, and cried.

Judith brought her arms around Darlene. That is what it took to bring the air back to her lungs. It flooded in, and like an ocean wave, flooded out again with wails of grief.

The two sisters clung to each other for several minutes, not speaking; just drifting in and out of long moments of uncontrolled tears. To his credit, Ray let them have a few moments. Then stepped over and knelt. "I'm so sorry for your loss. I can tell he was a very special man. He is still on our ambulance. We're waiting for the medical examiner to see him, but then we would be happy to deliver him to a funeral home for you."

Judith and Darlene both nodded, and blew their noses in concert. They looked at each other, still holding the tissues to their noses, and to their surprise, they giggled. Judith pulled Darlene in close, and touched forehead to forehead. "I love you, Sister."

Darlene reached up and rubbed her shoulder. "I love you too, Sister."

Then they both sat back and pulled their phones out. "I'll call Jim and let him know. He may have an idea of a funeral home, if that's okay with you."

"That would be fine," Judith said. "I have to call work and let them know I'm not coming back in today."

Judith was happy that Bernie missed her call, and she could just leave a message. She didn't need his attitude right now. She was sure she would say something he would regret.

The rest of the afternoon was spent at Riley Spence Funeral Home, picking out the urn, writing the obituary, and making arrangements for the funeral.

That evening, after bringing Noah home from Keener, she sat in the chair across from the couch, and watched her son eat from a bowl of dry Cheerios while he watched Cartoon Network. He seemed more interested in the Cheerios, however. He would pick them out of the bowl one at a time, hold it up to his eye, look through it, and then pop it into his mouth and chew it. There were a few that were either not completely circular, or broken. Those he would carefully set on a coaster on the coffee table. The coaster became the island of unwanted Cheerios.

"Grandpa died today," Judith said to him. "We won't be able to see him anymore."

Noah continued on, not noticing that she spoke. She wished, at the very least, he could look up at her and say, "Sorry, mama," with that sweet little voice of his.

She thought about her dad's voice, and more tears ran from her eyes. When she was just a girl, his voice was strong and authoritative. When she grew older, his voice was tired but wise. After his stroke, it was muffled, but still sweet to her ears. And now it was gone, never to be heard again. She began to cry once more. She pulled the small pillow from behind her back, and buried her face in it, so as not to upset Noah.

The doorbell rang.

Judith dropped the pillow and grabbed a tissue. She dabbed her eyes and blew her nose, and the doorbell rang again. Judith stood, and shambled to the door. The bell rang again before she reached it, and she was about to say something snarly to the person on the other side but when she opened it, Jack was standing there, gleaming in his business attire. "Hey," he said. "Your dad?"

Judith felt her lip quiver. She couldn't speak. She shook her head.

Jack sighed, threw his hands in his pockets, and looked at

his shiny black shoes. "I'm sorry. I know how bad that hurts." He raised a thumb to his car. "I'll come back. We can do this another time."

"No," Judith said, surprised at how frantic she sounded. "Let's do it now. It's exactly what I need."

"Are you sure?"

She nodded, and stepped aside to let him enter.

Jack walked in, headed directly to the couch, and stopped. He stared while Noah performed his Cheerio ritual. "Why is he doing that?"

Judith shook her head. "Why does he do anything that he does?" She sat next to her son. "The world of an autistic person is vastly different than that of yours and mine. That is the biggest thing you have to get past. Once you realize that sounds are different to them than they are to you and I, lights are different, textures are different, communication is different, then you can begin to cope with the large amount of work you have ahead of you. You can try to do things based on their world view. You have to. They don't have the capacity to do them in your world view. If they did, they wouldn't be autistic."

"That's a very strong way to handle it." Jack sat in the chair across from them.

Judith smiled at the compliment. "It is what it is. Strength isn't the issue here. Learning how to make it through a day is."

Jack reached into his pocket and pulled out an over-sized smartphone. "This is for you." He held it up. "This is now Operation Noah-Delton Central, right here."

Judith's mouth fell open. "Jack. What are you doing? You aren't required to supply me with a phone."

"I'm not paying for this," Jack said. "Danser is covering the whole thing."

"Why would they pay for it?"

Jack sat back in the chair. "I told you, you're an official pro-bono client now. You have friends in high places over there. I showed Al your video and told him what we were trying to do, and he told me to do whatever it took, and to bill everything to the company."

"Did you tell him that...?"

"That Noah is my son?"

Judith nodded.

"No," Jack said. "Only you, me, and Kate know, and whoever you've told."

Judith took a breath. "Kate knows?"

"Kate is the one who saw your video and showed it to me." Jack sat the phone down on the table next to him. "Don't get me wrong, she's not home thinking this is the cutest thing ever but...."

"You told her...about...?"

"I had to. It was killing me from the inside out, just to look at her."

Judith stared at him, incredulous. "When?"

"I told her just before you quit." Jack picked up the phone and started fumbling with it. "Believe me when I tell you that it didn't go over well. We spent several months in separate bedrooms, and a great deal of counseling. I was glad that you left the agency when you did. You wouldn't have wanted to be around me then, trust me."

Judith clasped her hands in front of her and looked down at them.

"I'm sure that if she didn't have MS she would have left me. And she should have." His voice cracked. He coughed to cover it, waited a moment and spoke again. "But over time, she realized I was committed to her. We both worked very hard to put our marriage back together. So believe me when I tell you that I'm not all that happy to see you."

Judith looked him in the eye. "Then why are you helping

me? Why don't you just leave me alone? I'll figure this out on my own."

"The number one reason is because I'm accountable for this too," Jack said. He put the phone down again. "I was there that night. And even as drunk as I was, I should have stopped it... but I didn't. It would be incredibly small of me to blame you for everything. I won't do that. Number two, is that Noah is my son. I haven't been here through any of his life, and he's a boy who has very special needs. But his biggest need right now is to get another man into his life who appears to be able to help him be all he can be. And if that's my current role as his father, then you can be damned sure I'm going to do everything I can to make that happen."

"And Kate?"

"Kate is totally on board with this," Jack said. "I can say with certainty that she never wants to meet you, but she's... pleased, for lack of a better word, to know about Noah."

"She is?"

Jack nodded. "She's glad that I will have someone in my life to care for after she...." He looked down at his shiny shoes again.

Judith wanted to run to him, hold him, let him know she would be there for him. But that was what had gotten them into this predicament to begin with. And even though she wanted to tell him that she had never stopped loving him, she would forever bury those feelings.

Jack picked up the phone once more. "Okay, let's go over this." He acted very upbeat. "I have it all set up. There is a Noah-Delton Facebook account, Twitter account, and Pinterest account. You need to be active on these accounts. Something has to go up on each one every day." He waved her and Noah together. Go ahead and hug Noah, I want to get your picture."

"Jack. No." She wiped at her eyes. "I've been crying."

"That will only help us," Jack said. "Hug him, close, and give us just a hint of a smile."

"Okay, but he doesn't like to be touched, so when I hug him, you need to snap it fast."

"Understood," Jack said. He held up the camera. "Now."

Judith wrapped her arms around Noah and pulled him in tight. The light flashed, and Noah moaned and struggled. Judith released him.

"Oh, that's perfect," Jack said. "Now let me upload this to all three accounts."

Jack spent the next several minutes going over the accounts and the intricacies of the camera. The deep dive into business mode helped them get through the uneasiness of their previous conversation. Once she made it clear she understood how everything worked, Jack left as quickly as he could. He didn't linger to allow any uncomfortable goodbyes. This was a business arrangement only, and his actions were going to make that completely clear.

Once he had walked out the door, Judith sat next to Noah, who was still chewing his Cheerios, one by one. She thought about her dad again, and the fight she had to go through without him. More than anything she wished she had someone to lean on. She hated having to be the strong one every single day. "Hey, Noah. Mommy is very sad," she said to him.

Noah reached into his bowl, pulled out a Cheerio, and looked through it. Then he dropped it into her hand.

Chapter Forty-Six

A fly buzzed and thumped against the window. It was the only sound in Judith's tiny apartment, so it came across incredibly loud.

The TV was on, but the sound was down. Judith had the remote next to her in case a story about Delton came on. But other than that she wasn't watching it. She stared in disbelief at her father's urn, which sat on the stand next to her TV. She and Dar had chosen a brushed metal one, with Celtic-style markings around the rim, and a Celtic cross on the front of it. Their father would have loved it.

The funeral of Ben Higgins had been a somber, but proud affair. As is the case with most funerals, Judith saw aunts, uncles, and cousins she hadn't seen, or even thought of in over a decade. And she knew that when she said goodbye to them at the end of the day, she wouldn't see them again until the next funeral, when they would all leave and promise not to be strangers once again.

Seven soldiers from the Army Color Guard had stood by her father's urn during the three hours of visitation. After the service, everyone followed them outside, where they performed a twenty-one-gun salute in the parking lot. Judith knew her father would have been embarrassed by that. He never talked about his military service to anyone, because, in all four years he was in the service, he never spent one single second in any kind of danger. His first three years were spent at a base in Kansas, and the last year was at a base in upstate New York. Judith remembered an episode when she was in ninth grade, and her teacher asked her dad if he was ever in the armed services. "Nope, never served," he had said. When Judith asked him why he lied about his army days to her teacher, he shrugged. "When you tell someone you were in the Army, they always say thank you, like you put your life on the line or something. The guys who did put their lives on the line are true heroes, and I respect every damn one of them. But I can't take credit for anything they did. I don't feel it would be right. So it's just easier to say I didn't even do it." Integrity was probably one of her father's greatest assets.

Jack had called her in the morning to remind her to post pictures from her dad's funeral. She hadn't wanted to, thinking it to be a cheap way to get people's sympathy. "If you mean cheap as in inexpensive, I know funeral's don't come cheap. If you mean cheap as in tasteless, you couldn't be more wrong. People throw their support where they have an emotional connection. I know you're in a rough state right now, and I'm so sorry for the hurt you're feeling. But let your father help you get that emotional connection. It's the last thing he will be able to do for Noah."

So she took his advice and posted a single picture, on all three pages, of Noah and her standing in front of her father's urn, and a large picture of him that was on an easel.

Judith picked up her new phone and checked the different accounts. Her video was now up to 92,000 views. True to their words, most, if not all, of her relatives liked, and joined the pages that were created for Operation Noah-Delton. And they all said they would help spread the word. But none were more encouraging to her than her Aunt Edna, her mother's older sister, who always talked liked a mob hit man. She pulled Judith aside and told her not to give up. "Don't you let up, girl. You keep the heat on those sons of bitches," she had said, wagging her finger.

"They all think they're so damn smart and they know what's best for everybody. But they don't. They all have a hitch in their step, because they all have their heads stuck up their asses. Not because they're stupid, but because they think their farts smell like perfume. They can't get over themselves." She patted Judith on the shoulder. "You keep giving them hell, dear."

But, easily the most uncomfortable moment of the day was when Neil walked into the visitation. He had greeted Dar and Jim first, giving them both hugs, nods, and solemn expressions. Then he'd walked over to her, and gave her an uneasy hug. "I'm so sorry," he'd said when he pulled her close. And then the hug was over...too quickly. Like he'd just hugged his grandmother. "I just wanted to come by, and pay my respects to you and Jim." He'd said, acting like he needed an excuse to be there. He put his hands in his pockets and looked around. Judith had so much to say to him, but no room to say it. As is the case with visitations, six other people lined up behind Neil, and waited their turn to speak to her. Neil reached over and gave her shoulder a reassuring squeeze. He smiled, said, "Take care of yourself. I'll catch you another time." Then he walked out the door.

Judith watched him walk away. She wanted to run after him, explain to him about Jack, what had happened between them, and let him know there was no longer anything there. Ask him to hold her and help her through this difficult time in her life. Instead she watched from the dimness of the funeral home as Neil disappeared into the bright blaze of the doorway.

Looking at her father's urn, Judith felt contentment. When the funeral and the luncheon were over, and she and her sister were deciding on what to take, all Judith wanted was her father's urn. She didn't want the flowers and plants. To her that only represented more responsibility. They were just more things she would have to take care of. Right now all she wanted to take care of was herself and Noah. "I need Dad with me right now," she had said to Dar.

Darlene just nodded and said, "I agree." Again, her sister

got her.

Judith took a deep breath, and exhaled through pursed lips. Things were going to get intense now. They needed to get intense. She stared at her father's urn, and could hear his loving voice in the distance. "Noah needs you now, Judith. Fight like you've never fought before. I love you, and I'm so proud of you."

"Thank you, Dad," she whispered. "I miss you."

"I'll always be with you," she heard him say.

Judith picked up the remote and clicked the TV off. There hadn't been anything about Delton. That troubled her. He was old news. Somehow, she would have to figure out how to get it to become new news again. But she could talk to Jack about that tomorrow.

She brushed her teeth, popped a Xanax her sister had given her, and called it a day.

Chapter Forty-Seven

Almost ten minutes had passed since Judith signed into her account at work. Simon, Evelyn, and Shelly had already popped in and given her their condolences, told her to let them know if there was anything they could do to help, and generally made her feel welcomed.

Then Bernie sauntered in. "I see Miss Higgins has joined us again. Welcome back."

"Thanks, Bernie," she said, while flipping through her email.

"So are you sticking with us today, or is another major crisis going to pull you away?"

Judith felt like she had just been smacked on the back of the head. She looked over her shoulder to see Bernie, hands on his hips, with a shit-eating smirk across his face. "Bernie, you are aware that I've been on bereavement leave, right? My father's funeral was yesterday."

"Yeah, I know," Bernie said, shrugging it off. "But you have to admit, you have more life crisis moments than everyone else on my whole team combined. You come and go more than everybody, and that needs to stop."

Judith turned in her chair. "Bernie, whether or not you have a legitimate point to make, your message is not well-timed. Again, my father's funeral was yesterday."

"Right, and I said I'm sorry about that. But I'm talking about today, and tomorrow, and the day after that. This is a business, it's not a club. And you have a habit of breezing in and out when you want to. I'm just trying to make a point that it's not okay anymore. I'm putting you on notice."

"I don't breeze in and out when I want to. I have a son with a disability. When he needs me I have to go to him."

"No. You have a responsibility to your job, to your team, and ultimately to me. If your son has issues, you need to make other arrangements. But you can't continue here and not pull your weight anymore."

Now it felt like she had just taken a fist to the stomach. She grasped at the desk and struggled to her feet. "You don't think I pull my weight around here?"

Bernie stepped back. His smirk was gone. The bully was now on his heels. "I didn't say that exactly…."

"You just said I can't continue not pulling my weight."

"Well, your team has been complaining about all the extra work…."

Her aunt's words reverberated in her ears. "You keep the heat on those sons-of-bitches." And there was no bigger son of a bitch in her life right now than Bernie.

"Don't be a fucking coward, Bernie," she said. "Don't put this on the team. It was you who made the accusation. Own it."

Bernie shifted his weight nervously. "Higgins, you're trying to make this personal. You can't do that. I came in here to talk to you about your work habits."

"No, you didn't," Judith said. She felt her heart beating hard, and her face flush hot. "You came in her to be the fat-ass bully you've always been. You don't give a damn about what anybody else is going through, you just say what you think will make Bernie sound big in Bernie's own pea-sized brain. And you assume that if you say it, Mr. High-and-Mighty Associate Manager, that everybody else will just quake from your authoritative greatness." She took a step forward and Bernie backed up. "Well, I'm putting you on notice. I'm not taking your shit anymore. If you want to speak to me, you will do it with respect, or you won't speak to me at all. Do we have an understanding?"

She saw Bernie's neck redden. He glared at her. "Now who's being the bully?"

"Do we have an understanding?" Judith made sure she kept the heat on, just like her Aunt Edna had instructed.

Bernie brought his hands up to his hips. "Well, if you're so unhappy here, perhaps it's time for you to look for someplace else to work."

Judith opened her mouth to shout, but sense caught the better of it. He was certainly not of a mind to back down. And if he couldn't be the overbearing jerk to her, then he didn't even want her around. She calmly asked, "You're firing me?"

"Well…" Bernie stuttered. "I…er…I'm…suggesting."

She whirled around, grabbed her purse from the drawer, and grabbed pictures of Noah from her desk.

"What are doing?" Bernie said.

Judith threw her purse over her shoulder, and bolted from the cubicle.

"Where are you going now?" Bernie called after her. "You have a report due by the end of the day."

Judith picked up the pace, sped through the lobby, and onto an elevator that was just opening. Shelly stepped off carrying two cups of coffee. "Hey, Judith, where are you going? I got you some coffee."

"Goodbye, Shelly," Judith said.

Just before the doors closed, she heard Shelly. "What?"

She didn't know what had gotten into her, but as Judith sped out of the parking lot of Fillmore National, she felt invigorated.

She knew she should feel scared, terrified even, over what to do for money now. And she knew she would be hit by a huge wave of regret later. She would probably call Bernie tomorrow and beg him for forgiveness, but there was no time for that now. It was time to follow Aunt Edna's advice. "Don't let up on those sons of bitches," and she knew exactly what to do next.

She breezed into the hardware store and bought three mop handles, six large pieces of poster board, a staple gun, a pack of markers, and some white duct tape. Then she went home, threw on a nice running suit, and proceeded to create a picket sign. She took the markers and wrote "FREE DELTON HAYES" on one piece of poster board. On the other she wrote, "SELF DEFENSE IS NOT ILLEGAL." Then she stapled them to one of the mop handles and lined them neatly with the white duct tape.

She weaved the long sign through her little Kia, and headed to the prison.

Checking her smartphone, she saw that Jack had added his names to the contacts. "Call Jack Brody." A moment later the phone was ringing.

"Good morning, Judith."

"Good morning, Jack. I wanted to let you know that I'm on my way to the prison."

"Uh…what for?"

"I watched the news last night and there was nothing on about Delton. I think it's falling off the radar. I'm going to bring it back on again."

"So, what are you going to do?"

"Exercise my free speech. I'm going to picket the prison."

"Nice," Jack said. "I'll meet you there."

Twenty minutes later, Judith pulled into the parking lot of the Two Rivers State Correctional Facility. She parked near the road, removed the sign from the car, and walked across the long parking lot to the entrance of the compound. She stopped long enough to take a selfie, holding the sign with the Two Rivers entrance behind her. She posted it on all three sites with the words, "Trying to be heard." Then she paced back and forth in front of the building, yelling, "Free Delton Hayes!" as loud as she could every thirty seconds or so.

Five minutes later a security guard emerged and walked over to her. "I'm afraid I'm going to have to ask you to leave."

"I'm not causing any disturbance," Judith said. "I have a right to free speech in a free country."

"Yes ma'am. But you're on government property."

"Exactly, which means I have every right to be here. I pay taxes, and I'm not trying to do it inside where there could be trouble, so I'm fine right where I am."

A midnight blue Buick Acadia, pulled up in front and came to a quick stop. Jack jumped out of the car. "Hey, Judith. What's going on?"

"This man is telling me I have to leave."

Jack walked up. "Hi there. Jack Brody." He handed the guard his card. "I'm with Danser Advertising and Public Relations. Given the state of public opinion on this facility, I'm not so sure you want to make things worse by throwing a distraught mother off the property."

The guard looked up at Jack. "Sir, I don't want trouble here."

"You're the only one here who has the power to make trouble." He took a few steps back and held up his phone, ready to take pictures. "So, make a choice. What're you going to do?"

The guard pursed his lips, spun on his heels, and walked back into the facility.

Jack put the phone back in his breast pocket. "He made a good choice."

"Thank you," Judith said.

"Happy to help," Jack said, smiling. It was the first smile Judith had seen on him since they reconnected. "I've put in a couple of calls to contacts at channels 3 and 12. One of them should be able to come down for the story. In the meantime I'll hang around and make sure I get pictures of anyone who tries to bother you."

It was a cloudy, breezy day, but Jack was true to his word. He hung in with Judith throughout the morning. They paced back and forth together in front of the entrance to Two Rivers, and yelled, "Free Delton Hayes!" to anyone who walked in or out of the facility. And no guards bothered them anymore. Jack wanted to know what prompted Judith to come out and picket today and she told him of her Aunt Edna, and the debacle that became her last morning at Fillmore National Life.

Judith was concerned that Jack could be in trouble, spending so much time away from the office.

"I told you," Jack said, shaking his head. "Al told me to support you in every way possible. I had three meetings today with clients. When I told him about you being down here, he told me to "pitch a tent," Jack used finger quotes, and spoke with a husky voice to simulate his boss, "right there, and stay all day if you need to."

Judith chuckled. "That's so nice of him."

"No. It's typical," Jack said. "You were always his favorite."

They continued to pace while they argued about who was Al Danser's favorite employee. Then conversation moved on to how Noah was doing. Jack wanted to hear stories about his son—particularly those having to do with the Marmont/Two Rivers project and Delton Hayes.

After another hour Jack looked at his watch. "It's nearly 1:00, and I'm hungry. How about you? Fancy a Big Mac attack?"

"Actually, I'm starving. The exhilaration of the morning is wearing off, and I'm starting to freak out about what I've done." She lowered the sign and banged the stick on the sidewalk nervously. "I think I need to go bury my fears in French fries."

Jack held up his hands. "You can't go anywhere. You have

to be here doing the freedom march, if and when the news folks show up. I'll go get food." He walked to his car. "I'll be right back. There are places right up the road."

Judith watched him drive out one side of the parking lot, just as a Channel 12 car pulled in the other side. They parked a few spaces down from where she stood and two men got out. One, a scruffy young man in a Star Wars t-shirt and a baseball cap, went straight to the trunk and pulled out a camera and a tripod. The other, dressed in khakis, sports jacket and tie, looked like he had Middle Eastern ancestry. He carried a microphone in one hand and a small notebook in the other.

He walked over with a big smile. "Judith Higgins?"

"Yes?"

He threw his notebook under his arm and held out his hand. "I'm Muki Matek, from Channel 12. Let's talk about what you're doing out here today."

Chapter Forty-Eight

Waking early the next day, Judith made a second sign. If Jack showed up again she was prepared to give him real work to do.

She dropped Noah off at Keener, and headed to the prison in good spirits. The segment on Channel 12 had done her social media accounts a world of good. The followers had nearly doubled on all three accounts overnight. And people were now leaving comments like, "You go girl!" and, "Give 'em HELL!"

But what surprised her most, was the fact that there were already three people in front of the prison marching when she got there. There was an elderly man and woman in windbreakers and Hawaiian shirts, and Jennifer Hall, one of the other parents from the program. They had made their own signs as well. Jennifer had made one similar to Judith's that read "Free Delton Hayes," but the older couple were a little more creative; theirs read, "Hayes'd and Confused," and, "Blue Hayes."

They all cheered for Judith when she got out of her car, and she hugged and thanked each of them for being there.

"My son didn't do as well as yours did," Jennifer said to her. "But he did fairly well. And when you have the successes that your son had, it's worth the fight to try to get it going again."

Judith hugged her once more, touched by the kindred spirit she had found.

"I know how hard it is to try to raise a special needs child. It seems like the whole world is against you," Jennifer said. "So, I just felt we needed to stick together."

"Thank you so much," Judith said.

"It's my pleasure," Jennifer waved her sign and yelled, "Free Delton Hayes!"

Judith turned to see what appeared to be a husband and wife, walking past them toward the entrance to the building. The man looked at them and shook his head.

"Once this is over, we should get our kids together for play dates."

Judith couldn't help but smile. "I would like that very much."

"Excuse me," came a meek voice from behind her. "Miss Higgins?"

Judith turned to see Danna Hayes standing there, hands clasped nervously behind her. "Danna? How did you get here?"

"The bus stop's a couple miles up the road," Danna said, pointing. "I just walked from there."

"What are you doing here, and not in school?"

"I saw you on TV last night and...." Danna looked at the other people walking with their signs, then back up to Judith. "I gotta help with this."

Judith was running through her mind all the things wrong with encouraging a young girl to skip school. "Danna, I know this is important to you, but I can't have you stay here. You need to be in school."

"Miss Higgins, this is my brother we're talkin' 'bout here." Her eyes teared up and she wiped them quickly.

"Let me ask you something," Judith said. "What do you think Delton would say to me right now if I were to tell you it's okay to be here and not in school?"

Danna looked at the ground.

"You know the answer, don't you?"

Danna nodded, begrudgingly.

"Then you have to promise me that you will catch the noon bus back to school."

Danna's head snapped up excitedly.

Judith smiled down at her and handed over her sign. "Do we have a deal?"

"Deal." Danna grabbed the sign from Judith and waved it in the air. "Free Delton Hayes! Free Delton Hayes!"

An SUV pulled up and two middle-aged women got out, holding Starbucks cups. They sauntered around to the back and grabbed a "Free Delton" sign each. Then they walked up to the sidewalk, toasted Judith, and sipped on their coffees. "We got caramel mochas today," one woman said. "Looks like we'll need to walk them off."

Judith ran to her car and grabbed the other sign she'd made. She ran back, grabbed Danna and took a selfie with her to post later.

"Miss Higgins. A word?"

Judith looked up to see Warden Luzynski standing near the doorway, looking less than pleased.

When she walked over to him, he shook his head. "Miss Higgins, this simply can't go on."

"That's exactly what I was thinking," Judith replied.

The warden looked relieved. "So we're on the same page then?"

"Yes. Just as soon as the injustice is taken care of."

"What are you talking about?"

"You just said it, Warden." Judith said. "Delton's unfair incarceration simply can't go on. Once he's released, we'll stop picketing."

The warden scowled. "That's not what I meant, and you know it."

"Warden, all I'm doing is making your job easier."

"And just how are you going to spin that?"

"You said you couldn't let Delton work with Noah because of public opinion." She gestured toward the picketers. I'm changing public opinion for you so you won't have to worry about that anymore." She smiled at him.

Warden Luzynski did not smile back. He held up a finger to her. "I want you all out of here within one hour, or I will have you forcibly removed. Do you understand?"

"Oh, so you're willing to help us out?" Judith said, still smiling brightly. "Because if you do that, you will turn public opinion a whole lot faster for us all. I thank you very much, sir."

Warden Luzynski's face grew red. He scoffed, spun on his heels, slammed open the door and stormed back in the building.

Judith turned back to see a white GMC van with the words, Channel 3 News Now, pull into the parking lot. "This is really getting fun."

Chapter Forty-Nine

The following morning, when she pulled into the Keener School parking lot, Principal Phil Bria met Judith as she stepped out of her car.

"Miss Higgins, I wanted to let you know…the teachers had a meeting last night and we've decided that it's probably best that you find a different school for Noah."

"What do you mean, a different school?" Judith stammered. "Why?"

"Why?" Principal Bria gave her a smug smile. "Do you really have to ask? You go on the news, two nights in a row, and slam our school and the work they've done with your son. You put it out over and over again on all your social media sites that we have done nothing good for your son. Is it really that difficult to believe the teachers might have some hard feelings?"

Judith looked past the principal to the school. Several teachers were watching the interaction, either from the front entrance or a window. She fought the urge to scream at them. To tell them to grow up. Why was it whenever she took one small step forward, everyone else in the world tried to push her back three steps? Was Noah ever going to be a priority to anyone but her? But logic got the better of her, and she spoke calmly. "Principal

Bria, I wasn't trying to put your school, or your teachers down. I was fighting for my son. Surely you and your teachers can understand that."

Principal Bria shrugged. "All the same…it still would be a good idea to take Noah someplace else."

Judith took a deep breath. It was important to breathe when your instincts were telling you to reach up and choke somebody. "Well, then I guess I can leave here grateful," she said, as coldly as she could make it sound. "I was beginning to sound like a broken record on the news and my social media pages. But you've just given me a whole new rant, now that you're the latest to turn your back on Noah. And just when he needed you the most."

She opened her car door to get in, but Principal Bria stepped up to stop her. "Now, hold on. There's no need to be like that."

"Are you kidding me?" Judith snapped at him. "What do you expect? You and all of your poor little teachers. Crying, because I didn't make them sound magnificent." Judith wagged her knuckles by her eyes. "You're just the next names on the ever-growing list of people who have let Noah down." She jumped into her car and sped out of the parking lot, leaving Principal Bria, hands on his hips, growing smaller in her rearview mirror.

Her phone buzzed. She picked it out of her purse to see "Dr. F." lit on the screen. "All right. Be good news," she said, and tapped on the call, "Hello, Dr. Fitzpatrick."

"Miss Higgins, I'm so glad I got hold of you."

"What's going on?"

"I'm afraid I'm calling to ask you to put an end to your crusade. It's creating a bit of an untenable situation here at the college."

"Untenable?" Judith's blood had just been starting to cool, when the utterance of that word brought the heat back.

"Yes. The president, our board members, and I, have all been getting a great deal of email and phone calls regarding your situation."

"Oh my goodness," Judith feigned sympathy. "That must me terrible for you all."

"Well, it is a bit uncomfortable, as you might imagine. Thank you for understanding."

"Dr. Fitzpatrick, I owe you a debt of gratitude for getting Noah into your program," Judith said. "So I'm going to use proper language, and not the string of expletives that really want to fly out of my mouth right now." She took a breath. "I am in a fight, Doctor, literally for my son's future. Your program showed me what was possible. And now that it's ended, Noah has slipped away from me. That doesn't make me uncomfortable, Doctor. That terrifies me. So I am going to fight for my son. I am going to fight as hard as it takes. Do you understand? And I don't care if it's uncomfortable for you, your president, or your fucking board."

There was silence on the other end.

"Sorry about that 'fucking board' part. Have a nice day, Dr. Fitzpatrick."

"Miss Higgins...."

Judith tapped off the call and tossed the phone onto the seat next to her. She looked at her son in the rearview mirror. He was in rider-mode and stared blankly at the farmland as it passed by the window. "All our friends are turning against us, Noah. But don't worry, Mommy's just begun to fight."

Pulling into the Two Rivers parking lot, Judith noticed many more parked cars than there had been either of the two previous days. When her little yellow Kia rounded the long line of SUVs, she realized it was because there were close to 50 people already picketing. She parked one row from the front so Noah could stay in the car but never be out of her eyesight. And this way he wouldn't be so close that all the noise would get him upset. "Look at this, Noah. All of these people are here for you." She reached into the glove box and pulled out a deck of barnyard flashcards, took the rubber band off and handed them to her son. "No school today, Noah. We're just going to sit here for a little while. But mommy's gotta go be with all these people." Noah reached up and grabbed the cards, set them down in his lap, then leaned his head against the car door, and watched the people walking back and forth, waving their signs. Judith threw the rubber band onto the seat next to her and then looked at it. It was a nice thick rubber band. She picked it up. "Hey, Noah, look." He glanced her way and she stretched the rubber band with her hands. Noah reached for it and she let him have it. He stretched it over and over again while looking out the window. It could work well as a stimming tool while he waited. Judith carefully extracted her sign out of the car without clunking her son in the head. "I'll be right out there if you need me, Noah."

As soon as she stepped out of the car, the picketers cheered. Danna ran out of the crowd and gave her a hug. "You're here again?" Judith said.

"Uh huh," Danna said. She let go of Judith and walked to the car, looking through the side window. "Is that him?"

"Yes. Come with me." She took Danna's hand and ran around to Noah's side of the car and knelt outside the door. "Hey, Noah, I want you to meet someone special." Noah looked down at the rubber band he was stretching. "This is Danna. She's Delton's sister." Noah looked up at the mention of Delton's name. He glanced at Danna briefly, then looked back at his hands. Then he uttered, in a whisper. "Hi."

Judith caught her breath. She put her hand on her heart to make sure it was still beating.

Danna smiled. "Hi, Noah. It's nice to meet you."

Noah said no more, nor did he look up. "Let's leave him alone," Judith said. She and Danna backed away and walked toward the picketers. When they reached the sidewalk, many of the people hugged and high-fived Judith, shouting things like, "Give 'em hell, Judith," and, "We're with you, girl."

Judith couldn't stop smiling. With the morning she'd had, she thought everyone was bailing on her. But now there was hope Noah would make a comeback, and she had a small army of complete strangers standing with her in this fight. She quickly got in step with her new foxhole buddies. They had new signs too. One read, "Delton's been hazed," and another read, "Noah needs Delton!"

The group walked back and forth in front of the building, once in a while shouting chants of "Free Delton!" Whenever someone parked and walked into the facility, they were fed an earful of "Free Delton."

Thirty minutes into the morning, two police cars pulled into the parking lot. Judith stopped in her tracks, and watched them as they slowly circled around and parked, not too far from her car. Two officers from each car got out, each holding a Starbucks cup. They walked to the front of their cruisers and leaned against them while they sipped their coffee. Judith sighed, relieved. It appeared they were there to just monitor the situation.

She turned to get back in line when she noticed the front doors of the facility open up. Three men in suits walked out, followed by Taysha Williams. They spoke to Taysha, pointing in Judith's direction, and then angrily gestured, as if shooing Taysha toward Judith. Taysha nodded and walked over. "Hey, Judith. Can I have a word with you over here?" She pointed to the grass area next to the sidewalk.

"What now?" Judith said under her breath, and she walked over to meet Taysha.

Taysha stood with her back to the men and spoke softly. "Those men behind me sent me out to have a conversation with you to end this whole thing."

Judith shook her head. "Taysha. I'm...."

But Taysha held up her hand to cut her off. "No, no, not to worry, girl. I have no intention of asking you to stop. I just need you to help me."

"What do you need me to do?"

"Well, you see, I still work for the prison system. They sign my checks. So I have to at least give the appearance that I'm trying to do what they ask." She gestured toward the picketers. "So I'm going to point this way and that, to make it look like I'm working really hard to get you to change your mind on this." She touched Judith's arm lightly. "But honestly, dear, I am so happy you're out here sticking up for what's right. I'd be out here myself if they weren't paying my bills. I hope you understand."

Judith smiled and nodded. "I do."

"Oh, please don't look so agreeable," Taysha said. "You'll give the men behind me hope that I don't want them to have."

"Oh," Judith looked stern. "How's this?"

"Much better," Taysha said. "Don't ever let anyone know what I really said to you, and don't let them know that my husband is out here picketing with you today."

"He is?"

"Yes, he is. He's the big strapping, handsome thing, with the 'Free Delton' sign written in bold purple letters."

Judith looked up and saw the man coming in their direction. He was working at not looking at them.

"Now here's the part where you look angry, tell me off, and send me on my way," Taysha said.

"Oh, yes. Okay." Judith rested her sign on the ground and leaned on it. She furrowed her brows and pointed heatedly at the picketers. "Tell your husband thank you for me. I appreciate you coming out here and talking to me." She wagged her finger at Taysha. "Thank you for all you've done. And thanks for believing in Delton." She pointed back to the door of the facility. "Good luck with selling this inside."

Taysha nodded. "That was excellent. Keep up the fight, girl." She turned and walked back to the men, shaking her head as she walked. Their shoulders slumped and they stormed back inside. Taysha disappeared through the doors after them.

"Miss Higgins."

Judith turned to see one of the police officers walking toward her. He pointed to her car. "Is that the boy that we've all been hearing so much about, sitting all alone in your car?"

"Yes, sir. It is," Judith said, clearing her heart out of her throat. "His school kicked him out today, so I brought him here with me."

"And you're just leaving him in the car? The mother who cares so much for her child is leaving him abandoned in a car?"

"He's not abandoned," Judith said. "Thirty feet from me. I can see him the entire time I'm here."

The officer pointed to the building. "Ma'am, I just saw you in a conversation with a woman from this facility. You did not have your eye on your boy at any time during that conversation. There was plenty of time for anyone to grab your son and be off before you could take three steps."

Judith stammered. He had her on that one. "But…I felt safe, I guess…because there were four police officers standing fifteen feet from the car."

The officer frowned. "Ma'am, we are here to keep the peace, not to babysit your son."

Danna walked up. "Miss Higgins, if you go get him, I'll sit with him in the grass."

Judith nodded to the officer. "Okay." She handed Danna her sign and ran over to the car. "Come, Noah. We're going to spend some time outside." She unbuckled him, took him by the hand, and helped him out of the car. Noah dropped the rubber band and began to moan. Judith quickly snatched it up and handed it back. She walked him toward the sidewalk around the police cars, to avoid the loud crowd of boisterous people. Then she set him down on the grass with his rubber band, and Danna sat down next to him.

"Not too close," Judith said. "He could get upset by that."

Danna scooted a few feet away and sat, knees under her chin, looking at Noah with a big smile on her face.

Judith, trembling at the bullet she felt she just dodged, rejoined her army of picketers. She would walk back and forth, each time eyes nailed to Noah, trying not to let him out of her sight.

Not ten more minutes had gone by when a news van from Lansing drove in and parked. One sole cameraman got out and began setting up his gear.

Then a blue Buick SUV came squealing into the parking lot. The four police officers, instinctively put their hands to their guns.

"What now," Judith said.

The Buick wheeled around near the building and screeched to a halt. The crowd of picketers grew silent, and stepped back on the grass off the sidewalk.

Out of the car jumped Reginald Fountain, slamming his door. "Danna Hayes, you get your ass in this car right now!"

Danna, eyes wide with fright, jumped up from the grass and ran to the passenger side door.

Judith looked over at Noah, who brought his knees to his chest and buried his face in them. He dropped his rubber band and flapped his hands furiously. She turned and ran to Reginald. "Mr. Fountain, go easy on her. She's just trying to stick up for her brother."

Reginald looked at her, venom in his eyes. "I told you once before, woman—stay the hell away from my family. And you didn't listen. You lured Danna out here, against my wishes. And now she'll have to pay the price for it." He opened the door for her. "Get in there now." Danna scampered up into the seat, and Reginald slammed the door.

"Family?" Judith could feel her face get hot. Reginald Fountain was nothing more than a bully, and she hated to see Danna scurry around, afraid of him. "You're not her family. Her family is in the building behind me. That's why she's out here trying to fight for him. You're her foster-father."

Reginald put his nose two inches from hers. "Yes. And that

means I'm responsible for her. Not you, and not that murdering piece of shit in there. Now stay out of our business."

"Sir. I'm going to have to ask you to step back from the lady and calm down." Judith just noticed one of the police officers had moved into position ten feet behind Reginald.

"Oh, I'm calm." Reginald sneered at her one last time, and then turned away. He held his hands up. "Now that I know my family is safe, I'm calm. And I'm leaving." He started walking back to his car.

Judith was seething. There was no way she was going to let him have the last word on this. "The only family she has, you're trying to destroy." She followed him step for step back to his car. The officer put his arm up and stopped her. "Let him go, ma'am."

"Why is that, Fountain? What are you afraid of?"

He turned back and screamed, "Stay away from my family."

"She's not your family." Judith screamed.

"Ma'am, stop." The officer said. Another officer ran over to help her back.

Reggie jumped in, slammed his door, and sped out of the parking lot.

Judith could see Danna's face wet with tears when the car sped off. "Asshole!" she screamed.

"Ma'am, if you don't calm down right this minute, I will put you in cuffs and take you in to the station." the officer said.

A familiar scream was heard. Judith spun her head around to see Noah, lying on the ground, hitting himself in the face.

"Let me go," Judith said. "I need to get to him."

"Are you going to be calm?" the officer said.

"He's having a meltdown," Judith cried. "I need to get to him."

"Not until I know you're calm."

"Let her go!" Taysha Williams said, running out from the front doors of the building. "She needs to get to her son before he hurts himself."

When the officers saw Taysha run out, they released Judith. She sprang free and dropped to the ground next to her son. Noah was in full meltdown, screaming as if he'd just lost a limb, and hitting himself with both fists in his face. Judith pulled him up to her chest, wrapped her legs around his legs and grabbed his hands, restraining them across his body. She caught his head in her shoulder, rocked him, and whispered in his ear while he continued to scream and struggle. "It's all good, Noah. Mommy's all right." Soon Judith noticed all the picketers standing around, watching the spectacle; some were crying, some gaping, others looking on in pity. Twenty minutes went by before he became soothed and calm. Judith decided this was the last place she wanted to be.

She slowly released Noah and stood. "Thank you for being here," she said to the others. "I think we should go home now." She walked him out to the car, helped Noah get in, then climbed in herself. She started the car and pulled out of the driveway. A couple of miles down the road was a gas station. She pulled into the parking lot, put the car in park, rested her head on the steering wheel, and wept.

Chapter Fifty

Keys in the lock echoed through the quiet of the dark room, ripping Delton from a sound sleep. The door burst open, and the bright light of the hallway blinded him. Silhouettes of two guards appeared in the doorway. "Get your shit together, Hayes. We're heading out."

"Heading out?" Delton said, rubbing his eyes. "Where we heading to?"

"That's above my pay grade. I've just been told to get you out of here and on the bus," the guard said. "So I'm giving you five minutes to get your clothes on, and your shit together, or we're just gonna drag you out of here in your skivvies. Got it?"

Chapter Fifty-One

Thick clouds darkened the morning sky, souring Judith's mood even more. The news from the night before had not been kind. The cameraman from Lansing had recorded Noah's meltdown, and it was the top story on all of their newscasts. Other picketers who were there had recorded it vertically on their cell phones, and offered it up to the newscasts, who went on to portray Judith as an abusive mother.

Channel 12 had brought in a child development professor from Marmont, who described what a meltdown for an autistic child was like, but instead of getting some credit for dealing with the situation properly, they went on to say that Noah shouldn't have been there in the first place. And, of course, the expert agreed with everything they said.

Judith did her best to stop the bleeding by tweeting out that Keener had kicked Noah out of school. But nobody was visiting the pages now.

Her phone rang and she pulled it out of her purse. It was Neil. She thought about answering it, remembering him walking out of her father's funeral, and wanting nothing more than to run to him—have him hold her, and tell her it would all be fine. But she couldn't talk to him now. She let it ring until it stopped and went to voicemail. Then she set the phone down gently on the seat next to her and continued to drive.

A few minutes later the phone dinged, alerting her to a voicemail.

She would save it for later. Now she had to get herself ready for the fight. She breathed deeply. With Noah now in the care of Darlene, Judith was ready to continue the struggle, and handle all reporters' questions. "Bring it on," she said, pulling into the Two Rivers parking lot. But it was empty of picketers. She hoped that the cloudy day had slowed down her fellow warriors; made them too tired to get out of bed. Grabbing her "Free Delton," sign, she slogged up to the sidewalk and began her pacing.

For over a half hour she walked, back and forth, under dark clouds which crept by overhead, threatening rain at any moment. But something was different today. When people stepped out of their cars, and she yelled, "Free Delton!" they walked by, not even glancing in her direction.

An hour went by and not one person drove in to join her. The steady increase in support she had seen each day had completely eroded away. She wasn't even making a dent with the Two Rivers workers either. She had not been visited, or even gawked at by anyone from inside the building. The sidewalk was her island, and she was now marooned. A feeling of desperation seeped through her. Had everything been lost with Noah's meltdown the previous day? Was she seriously back to square one? Or worse yet, square minus ten?

A car drove in and she recognized it. Jack Brody pulled up to the sidewalk, and stepped out of the car. "I somehow had a feeling you'd be here."

"Where else would I be?"

Jack gave a sad smile and closed the car door. He walked around to the front of the car, put his hands in his pocket and leaned against the hood. "The big question is why?"

"What do you mean?" Judith asked. "It isn't raining. And I

don't think that would stop me anyway."

"It's not the rain I'm worried about," Jack said. "It's the lack of support. After the news reports last night, your fight is pretty much over."

"It's not over," Judith said. "It will never be over."

"Judith, you're no longer the loving courageous mother that you were at the start of the week. Now you're the crazy lady who really doesn't care about her kid. That's why she put him with a criminal in the first place."

Judith scowled at Jack. "That's not the truth."

"The truth has nothing to do with it," Jack said. "It's the message that counts. And right now your message has been drowned out."

"Then it's just going to take me a little longer to change the message again."

"There is another way to help Noah."

"How's that?"

Jack stood, and grabbed her shoulders. "Teach me what I need to know, so I can help you, and be a part of his life."

"What?" Judith stepped back. "No. What are you trying to pull?"

"I'm not trying to pull anything," Jack said. "I have a son. Therefore I have a right to see him, to know him. I've been doing some research on ASD. I just need to know how to reach him. I was hoping we could get Delton out so I could learn from him, but after yesterday it doesn't look like that's going to happen now. So I need your help."

"So you weren't helping out of the goodness of your heart. You had an agenda," Judith took another step back. "You bastard."

"I don't understand why you're getting so upset. Why is it so wrong for a man to want to spend time with his own son?"

"What's wrong is, that you weren't up front with me to begin with. How can I trust you now?"

"Trust?" Jack took a step forward. "That's rich. You're actually speaking of trust. If not for this crazy situation you've gotten yourself into, I would have never known I had a son. And now you dare to stand there and lecture me on trust."

Judith felt the sting of his words—words she could not refute. "What is it you want, Jack?"

"I want, what any man would want in my situation. I want to get to know my son. To be part of his life."

Judith looked in his eyes and saw something familiar. That small gleam of desperation. He was being honest with his feelings right now, and she couldn't turn down his request, not only because he was the boy's father, but also because he had done so much to further her cause. She nodded at him. "Fine. Help me get Delton out, and we'll discuss it."

"And if we can't get Delton out?" Jack said. "Yesterday pretty much ended that."

Judith shrugged, and looked away, afraid to acknowledge that thought just now. "We'll discuss it later."

"Thank you, Judith." He walked back to his car and opened the door. "I'll go back to the office and see what I can come up with."

Judith knew that line. She had worked with him too much in the past. When he said that to clients it was because he was clueless on what to do next, but he didn't want to tell them to their face. He truly did think it was over, and now he would just wait until she realized it and gave up. Then he would come in and take Noah away from her, every other weekend at first, and then for every other week. That was until summers, when Noah would go away for two weeks…or even a month.

She watched him slowly drive away, and found herself dealing with a swirling mixture of rage, and despair. "Keep walking, Judith," she said quietly to herself. "One step at a time. That's how we'll deal with it all."

She turned to the building to continue her march and saw

Warden Luzynski coming out of the front entrance.

He walked up to her. "It's over, Miss Higgins."

Judith walked past him. "No, Warden. It's not. I'm not giving up until Delton is free."

"Delton's gone, Miss Higgins."

She stopped. Turned to him. "What are you talking about?"

"He was transferred last night, to the El Dorado Correctional Facility in Kansas."

The dark clouds that had threatened all morning long, finally began to release a light rain. Droplets ran down their faces, and made spots on the sidewalk.

When she spoke her voice was weak and trembling. "Why did you do that?"

"It's standard procedure. When an inmate is threatened or attacked, they tend to get transferred to other facilities to keep them safe."

The rain started coming down harder.

"Or to keep your job safe." Judith said.

Warden Luzynski looked up and then back to her. "You should probably get out of the rain and go home, Miss Higgins. There's nothing more to do here, and you don't want to get yourself sick." He turned and rushed back into the building.

Judith stood in the rain, watching the door slowly swing closed behind the warden. It closed on all her hopes as well. Looking up, she saw that the ink from the words 'Free Delton,' was now running down the sign, and staining her gray Marmont sweatshirt. She lowered the sign, letting it clunk onto the sidewalk.

That was the end of it. All hopes for Delton being free—of Noah speaking again, were down the drain. Soaked, she dragged herself toward her car, sloshing through the small puddles in the parking lot, threw her sign on the passenger seat floor and slammed the car door. She noticed the voicemail icon on her phone, and remembered Neil had called earlier. She thought about what it could possibly say. Was it a message professing his love and devotion? Or perhaps he saw the news last night and wanted to tell her he thought she was as awful as the rest of the town apparently did. In either case this was not something she could deal with right now.

She threw the car in drive, and sped out of her parking spot. Before she reached the exit, she knew she needed to hear his voice, bad or good. She pulled to the side of the driveway, and put the car in park. A quick dial to voicemail, and she leaned her head back and closed her eyes to listen.

"Hey, Judith, it's Neil. Though your phone probably told you that. Anyway...I watched the news tonight...saw Noah's meltdown in living color. I'm sorry. That sounded glib. I just...I wanted to say I'm sorry. Sorry for Noah having his meltdown. Sorry that you had to take care of it by yourself. And sorry I got so judgmental with you. I know you're going through a very difficult time right now, especially just after losing your dad and all. And I also know that your life is complicated. I think it's so complicated that you find yourself overwhelmed by it all. I guess I just called to say that I don't care about your circumstances, or how you got there, other than to let you know I'm willing to help you with your complicated life, when you're ready to let someone in. That's all...Good luck with everything, Judith."

"If you'd like to save this message...." Judith tapped off the phone, and when she set it down on the seat next to her she saw her hand was trembling. She put her car in drive again, and slowly pulled out of the parking lot, feeling numb.

Seven years ago she was a different person. She was respected and well known in the business world. She knew how to walk in business circles and she was good at it. But now she seemed to be good at nothing. She was a horrible mother, sister, girlfriend...person. How did she end up such a dismal disappointment to everyone she knew?

She made it home, took a long hot shower, dried off, and sat on her couch with her legs pulled up tight to her chest, arms wrapped around them. She could feel the dull thud of her heart. Next to the TV sat her father's urn. Seeing it made her sad that he wasn't there to lean on. "What do I do now, Dad?" she said to the urn. "You had me take all of these risks and chances, and they've all fallen through. And now you're not here to help. What am I supposed to do now? What's your next big idea?"

Her phone buzzed on the end table next to her. Picking it up, Judith saw it was from New York. She almost set it back down, but she looked back at the urn and something told her she needed to answer this one. "Yeah?"

"Is this Miss Judith Higgins?"

"Yes, it is."

"Hi, Judith. I'm Brooke Winthrop, from Global Information Network."

The following is the audio transcript for the Global Information Network story that appeared on the news magazine series "Deep Dive with Brooke Winthrop" October 2, 2019.

BROOKE Voice Over: Tucked neatly into the middle of rural, lower Michigan, lies the small town of Two Rivers. It's a bedroom community, with the majority of its citizens working at the many business and tech companies 30 minutes to the east, and Marmont State College 15 minutes to the south. And then, of course, there is the State Correctional Facility, 12 miles down the road, which shares the same name.

But right now, the biggest claim to fame for Two Rivers are these two.

HIGGINS ONLINE VIDEO: Hello there, I'm Judith Higgins. And this is my son, Noah.

BROOKE Voice Over: This video has been seen by nearly one million people on the internet. It tells the plight of Judith Higgins, her son, Noah, and the man who is now at the center of the controversy here in Two Rivers—an inmate at the penitentiary, Delton Hayes. But as Judith will tell you, the story isn't about Delton, or her—it all starts with her son.

JUDITH HIGGINS: The story is about Noah...a boy with ASD who was facing dwindling options. Whose future is always in doubt, because he can't communicate like everyone else can.

BROOKE On Camera: Noah Higgins was going to

school. He attended The Keener School for Special Needs Children, in nearby Algonquin Township for one year, and here at Hanson Elementary in Two Rivers for the last two years. He had been learning. Noah can eat and drink by himself, he can dress himself, clean up after himself, and handle personal hygiene like brushing his teeth, and going to the bathroom. But what Noah couldn't do was speak.

BROOKE Voice Over: That's when this man entered the picture—Dr. Warren Fitzpatrick of Marmont State College. He selected Noah for a radical social experiment.

DR. WARREN FITZPATRICK: It's quite simple really. The idea was to pair a special needs child, with a person in a correctional facility, with the hope of having positive responses on both sides of the equation. The children would get special attention like they've never had before and the inmates would be able to make a substantial difference for good in someone's life, and have the ability to test for certification in the areas in which they garnered the expertise.

BROOKE On Camera: Dr. Fitzpatrick's idea was to bring convicted criminals out from behind the walls of this prison, and place them in rooms with other people's children. It was an idea that many in the community found crazy.

MAN-ON-STREET 1: I remember first reading about it. I told Carla, "Mark my words, this is going to lead to trouble. And I just hope nobody gets hurt."

MAN-ON-STREET 2: It was crazy. And look what's

happened.

MAN-ON-STREET 3: I couldn't believe they even had parents agree to that sort of thing.

DR. WARREN FITZPATRICK: Well the idea didn't just come to me when I was drinking heavily one night. It has an actual established precedent in reality, and a very successful reality at that. Just look at the Puppies Behind Bars program, and the remarkable results from that project.

BROOKE Voice Over: The program Dr. Fitzpatrick is talking about has been a success. It has literally been responsible for training hundreds of canine companions and leader dogs. And it has also been a very uplifting program for the inmates who have cared for and trained them as well. But dogs are one thing— children are quite another.

Darren and Susan Hall are parents to Billy, a nine-year-old with Down syndrome. They signed Billy into the program without hesitation.

DARREN HALL: We were on board right from the start. We loved everything about the program, and thought it was a good idea.

BROOKE: You weren't afraid Billy was going to be mistreated or hurt?

DARREN HALL: I guess I had confidence in Dr. Fitzpatrick— that he was in control of the situation, and that there wasn't going to be any real danger of anything happening to the kids.

BROOKE: And what are your feelings about the program now?

SUSAN HALL: We're actually sad it's over. Billy loved going to spend the day with Ken. And Ken really liked Billy too.

DARREN HALL: Yeah, Ken was good to Billy. They always had special activities for them to do together, and Billy got a lot out of it. He misses Ken now.

SUSAN HALL: But we'll see him again. We're making plans to have Ken over a lot after he gets out.

BROOKE Voice Over: As the Halls attest, they and Ken Miller were on the same page from the start. And even though that is the picture that has been portrayed about Judith Higgins and Delton Hayes, that is not entirely the truth.

Taysha Williams was the counselor hired by Two Rivers to oversee Hayes throughout the Marmont Program. She was with him every minute he was with Noah Higgins, and on many occasions outside of the experiment as well. She tells a different tale of their relationship.

TAYSHA WILLIAMS: Everybody is going around saying, "Oh, Judith Higgins and Delton Hayes…they're this big miracle team." But I'm telling you right now, they hated each other at the start. Screamed at each other. Couldn't stand to be in the same room together.

BROOKE On Camera: Judith Higgins has gone from a woman who intensely disliked the man her son was paired up with, to the mother who picketed out in front of this prison every day desperately seeking his release. What was it that caused her change in attitude?

JUDITH HIGGINS: You have to understand, at the beginning I was concerned about my son being a part of this program.

BROOKE: Then why be a part of it at all?

JUDITH HIGGINS: It was something my dad said to me…he talked about…basically the idea that no one excels in a comfort zone.

BROOKE: So when did your feelings change about Delton specifically?

JUDITH HIGGINS: My feelings slowly changed throughout the program. When I came in each day, Delton had studied the night before and had some new thing planned for Noah. But the day Noah walked in and spoke his first words…I was convinced that Delton was a miracle worker.

BROOKE Voice Over: This is the room camera footage of the moment Judith was talking about.

RECORDING AUDIO: My man.

BROOKE Voice Over: Noah Higgins enters the room, walks over to Delton and speaks the words, 'My man,' like he has been saying it every day for a year, when in fact, these are actually the very first words little Noah has ever spoken.

RECORDING AUDIO: My man.

BROOKE Voice Over: But that remarkable moment was only the first. Noah's time spent with Delton Hayes was filled with unprecedented growth. In other recordings we can see and hear him asking questions, requesting different toys to play with, and even hear the laughter as Noah experiences moments of sheer joy.

RECORDING AUDIO: Noah's laughter.

BROOKE Voice Over: So who is Delton Hayes—the enigmatic figure who was imprisoned for armed robbery, shows dedication and tenderness for a child, and is now portrayed as a cold-blooded killer?

TAYSHA WILLIAMS: He's a young man who cares to the extreme. And that deep concern and passion for those he cares about can lead him to make wrong decisions.

BROOKE: What do you mean by that?

TAYSHA WILLIAMS: Just look at why he's in prison in the first place. They call it armed robbery. But he didn't rob a convenience store because he was trying to score a few bucks. He robbed it for a few cans of SpaghettiOs and some cookies because his sister was crying from being so hungry, and his mom had spent the last of their money on a fix.

BROOKE Voice Over: Rena Blossom is a Marmont graduate student. She was part of the Two Rivers project, and the individual assigned to Noah Higgins and Delton Hayes. It was her job to watch and record the interactions every minute the two were together. She is not only a fan of Delton Hayes', she is a staunch defender of the man.

RENA BLOSSOM: He was good to Noah and he was good in the program. When he wasn't with him, he studied hard on his own to be the best guide… companion…teacher, that Noah needed him to be. He connected with Noah, and it wasn't just some miracle connection. Delton struggled a lot at the beginning. Delton worked at forming a connection. He worked so hard at it. And I think that's why they were so good together. Delton wasn't just putting in his time every day. He put Noah first every single minute.

BROOKE On Camera: This is the building where the Marmont project took place. It is an abandoned office park on the outskirts of Two Rivers. This is where Delton, Noah and the other nine pairs met every weekday for just over two months. And where Rena

Blossom watched the interactions. When she said Delton struggled in the beginning, she was putting it mildly.

BROOKE Voice Over: In this video, Delton is seen trying to restrain an obviously upset Noah, and a guard enters with his gun drawn. And then, in walks Judith Higgins. Rena Blossom explained that what Noah was experiencing was called a meltdown, which has the potential to be dangerous for an autistic child.

RENA BLOSSOM: Noah started screaming very loudly and hitting himself. When this happens, it is important to restrain the child or they can hurt themselves. Taysha had called Miss Higgins and asked her to come back. A guard heard the noise, looked in, and thought Delton was hurting Noah. We tried to tell him that everything was fine but he didn't listen; he went in and pulled his gun. That was right when Miss Higgins showed up. So you could understand how a mother could be a little bit freaked out about the situation. But up until that point Delton was doing everything right.

BROOKE: Explain a meltdown.

JUDITH HIGGINS: Oh…you saw the video too.

BROOKE: Yes, and I want to know the difference between a meltdown and a tantrum. Why doesn't someone just give an autistic child a timeout when they're acting so badly?

JUDITH HIGGINS: Okay, well, they're completely different. An autistic person doesn't understand how to process their emotions, and quite often they can't process outside stimuli either. Things like loud noises, or…they don't even have to be that loud. Large crowds, lots of flashing lights, and lots of movement…those kinds of things can take an autistic child over the edge. It's like taking a bottle of soda and shaking and shaking it. All that pressure builds up and there's no rational way to release it. And just like a plastic bottle can't keep the top from blowing off, an autistic child can't keep from blowing either. It's not like a tantrum, where they're whining because they didn't get what they want. An autistic child has no control over the explosion. And they lose the control until all the pressure is released.

BROOKE Voice Over: This video is from just last week. Noah joined Judith during one of her pickets in front of the Two Rivers Correctional Facility. Noah's meltdowns become very self-destructive, so it is important that he is restrained to avoid causing any serious injury to himself. To the onlooker who doesn't understand autism, this can look a great deal like child abuse, when in truth, it is exactly the opposite.

BROOKE On Camera: So how did Delton Hayes handle the situation? Well, as Rena said, he studied everything he could get his hands on about autism spectrum disorder. He made sure that he was ready, so when the situation inevitably arose again, he would know exactly how to handle it.

BROOKE Voice Over: Here he is with Noah, days later. Noah is upset, begins his meltdown, but Delton is ready. He prepares a tool he discovered in his studies: a beach blanket to create a special hammock that wraps around the child to help soothe him.

JUDITH HIGGINS: I didn't tell him about that. And neither did Rena or Taysha. That was something he figured out on his own by studying. And I thought 'hmm...you know, maybe this kid has his _____ together after all.'

BROOKE On Camera: So how did this caring and

capable young man become such a brutal killer behind bars? Well, just like the image of him restraining young Noah was not all it seemed, so too is the image of him as a murderer.

BROOKE Voice Over: Hector Sanchez was a good friend of Delton's on the inside, and he was there when Rick Simpson was killed.

HECTOR SANCHEZ: It has been totally misrepresented. Delton was attacked by Rick Simpson because he squealed on him.

BROOKE: Squealed about what? Drugs?

HECTOR SANCHEZ: Yes. Rick was getting drugs from the mother of his kid in the program, and Delton was worried about the kid. So he told the powers-that-be, and got Rick thrown out of the program. Well, in prison they don't like squealers. So Rick and some of his buddies attacked Delton and cut him up real bad. But Delton fought back, and Rick slipped and fell on his own blade and killed himself. Delton didn't even kill him. But they had to lock Delton up by himself to keep him safe, and they had to stop the program because...I don't know, liabilities, I guess.

BROOKE On Camera: Far from the drug-crazed madman that the media has tried to make him out to be, Delton Hayes was, once again, trying to do the right thing, and it turned against him. He has recently been transferred to El Dorado Correctional Facility in Kansas, under the guise of protection, but many believe it was to get Judith to stop picketing out here. We requested the opportunity to interview Delton and were turned down. But we were granted the opportunity to talk with the young man over the phone.

BROOKE: How are you doing today, Delton?

DELTON HAYES: Same as yesterday and the day before.

BROOKE: Just wondering what's going to happen?

DELTON HAYES: Pretty much.

BROOKE: We understand you behaved pretty remarkably during your time with Noah Higgins.

DELTON HAYES: Well, he's a pretty remarkable kid.

BROOKE: Why do you say that?

DELTON HAYES: I got a chance to know him. There's a lot of life in that kid. You just gotta know how to get to it.

BROOKE: And you now know how?

DELTON HAYES: Yeah. He taught me a lot.

BROOKE: From what I understand, you did a lot of the learning on your own.

DELTON HAYES: I did. But it wouldn't have happened without meeting him first.

BROOKE: Tell me about your relationship with him.

DELTON HAYES: It took work, but I think that's what made it all so special. I think the reason people don't necessarily hang around with autistic people is because it actually takes work. You can't just have a conversation with them like you can with anybody else, you feel me? It ain't always easy, and people only want to do what's easy for them. But if you put in the work it takes to get to understand them, it's a pretty great experience.

BROOKE: So you liked your time with Noah.

DELTON HAYES: Probably one of the best experiences of my life.

BROOKE: And how is it, now that you don't see him every day?

DELTON HAYES: It's like…living life without…joy.

DR. WARREN FITZPATRICK: Quite honestly, Delton Hayes' experience was what I was hoping for when I first proposed this project. I wanted a truly transformative relationship between two people, and the story of these two…is just…I'll call it a win.

RENA BLOSSOM: He was definitely the right person for Noah and even after all of this, I'm glad I had him with me.

BROOKE On Camera: And so Delton Hayes remains

locked away in another state, as he said, in a life without joy, wondering when and if he'll be released. On the outside is a little boy on the spectrum, very depressed because he can no longer spend time with the best friend he's ever had. And a mother, who is losing everything in her fight to help free the man who can rescue her son once again.

BROOKE: I understand you lost your job over this.

JUDITH HIGGINS: Oh well, yeah, but…they had always had problems with Noah.

BROOKE: What do you mean by that?

JUDITH HIGGINS: The leadership at Fillmore National never really tried to understand what it took to raise a child on the spectrum. Anything that took your full attention away from the task at hand meant you were a slacker and not really serious about your job. So when the first major bump in the road hit, they had had enough.

BROOKE: What will you do now?

JUDITH HIGGINS: Keep fighting the good fight.

BROOKE: Why keep fighting such an uphill battle?

JUDITH HIGGINS: I'm too scared not to. I'm too scared about what will happen to Noah if I stop…so…I won't stop.

Chapter Fifty-Two

"Wake up, Noah. We need to get you over to Aunt Dar's." Judith reached in and flicked on the switch in his room, then walked into the kitchen to get his cereal out of the cupboard. She heard two little feet thunk to the floor, and pad on into the bathroom.

Judith knew she was no closer now to getting Delton out of prison than she had been two weeks ago, before the entire GINfo crew showed up to do their story, but somehow she felt a little more hopeful this morning.

The segment on Noah had appeared the previous night on the GINfo show, Deep Dive, and it had turned out better than Judith could have hoped. In the twenty-minute segment, Brooke Winthrop had done an excellent job explaining the project and sharing her concerns. And Brooke had never mentioned that they had garnered a phone interview with Delton. Perhaps that occurred after they left. It surprised and delighted Judith to hear that Delton missed Noah as much as her son missed him. But if she were to describe the piece in one word, it would have to be, "validation." The GINfo segment validated the project, the struggle of parents with autism, the plight of autistic children, and especially who Delton was, and his impact on Noah's life.

Her phone chimed in the pocket of her robe. She pulled it out to see a text from Neil. "Watched you on TV last night. Very proud of you." Judith put her hand on her heart and gulped at the cry that tried to break free. The last person who ever said he was proud of her was her own father, and when he passed, she thought she would never hear those words again. With all the dealings with Noah and the fight for Delton, those four words seemed more important to her right now than the three words a woman normally wants to hear. Judith wanted to hit dial and tell him that she appreciated him, and wanted nothing more than to be near him forever.

But now was not the time. The fight wasn't even close to being over, and she couldn't handle that kind of distraction. She flipped off the phone and slipped it back into her pocket, only to have it start ringing. She pulled it out to see Darlene's smiling face on the screen. "Hey, Dar. What's up?"

"Jude, turn on the TV. Now!"

Judith hurried over to the remote. "What's going on?"

"Just turn it on to GINfo."

Judith clicked on the TV to see aerial pictures outside the prison. Hundreds of supporters were jammed into the parking lot waving signs and shouting. The ticker on the bottom read: "Hundreds show up in support of Delton Hayes, and Noah Higgins."

"What the hell is this?" Judith said.

"It's amazing, is what it is." Darlene laughed. "Sister, you little rebel. You're making a difference."

Judith turned up the volume on the set. Tom Boyer and Jenna Hanson hosted the GINfo morning show Sunnyside, and Jenna, blond hair shining brilliantly as always, was at the news desk talking to the camera. "…is just the tip of the iceberg. We have heard that Michigan Governor Mitchel Anderson, has been watching this story closely for quite some time. And it's been reported that after he watched the Deep Dive presentation last night, he put in a call to Kansas Governor Cahill, to get extradition started for Delton Hayes. And sources in Two Rivers have confirmed that both Marmont State College and Two Rivers Correctional Facility have received calls from Governor Anderson this morning. So it appears that the Michigan Governor is intervening in this situation. But with all the supporters outside the prison, something needs to…"

The phone buzzed in Judith's hand. She pulled it from her ear and saw it was a call from Lansing, Michigan. "Dar, I'm getting a call from Lansing. I think the governor's calling me, right now."

"Oh my God. Call me back." Dar hung up and the phone rang again. Judith punched the screen. "Hello?"

A strong, firm man's voice answered her. "Is this Miss Judith Higgins?"

"It is."

"This is Governor Mitch Anderson. How are you doing today?"

"Uhhh…okay?" Judith rolled her eyes and stomped her foot, upset she sounded so stupid.

"Glad to hear it," the governor responded, forging ahead with the business at hand. "I saw the video GINfo did on your son last night. I've also been watching your situation for a while now and I'd like to discuss it with you. If you're willing to, that is."

"Ummm, sure. Let's do it."

"Great. Is it possible to come to my office at around 11:00 this morning? I'll have some people here, and we can round-table this thing."

"Thank you, Governor. I'll be there."

"Excellent. See you then."

Judith clicked off the call just as Noah wandered aimlessly out from the bathroom. "Noah," Judith said. "Mommy's going to talk to the governor today."

Noah plunked down into a chair and stared, confused, at

his empty bowl.

"Oh, sorry." Judith hurried over and prepared his Captain Crunch.

She had lived in Michigan her entire life, but when she parked in front of the ornate Capital Building, Judith realized she had never been in Lansing before. She dumped every last coin she had into the parking meter, then headed across the street to the governor's building.

She was required to empty her pockets and go through the scanner before she could even reach the information desk. The clerk directed her to the fifth floor, and when the elevator doors opened, an attractive young redhead met her, and escorted her directly into a posh conference room with a large wooden table.

A meeting was already in progress, and she was surprised to find that she knew most of the individuals around the table. Dr. Fitzpatrick sat closest to the door next to a man in a business suit with thin gray hair. Taysha Williams gave her a cheery smile from the other side of the table. She was sitting next to Warden Luzynski.

At the head of the table sat Governor Anderson with a young Hispanic woman sitting on his right and an Asian man on his left. The governor's suit coat was off and his sleeves were rolled up. He looked every bit the part he portrayed in his political ads three years ago. "Ah, here she is." Governor Anderson raised a hand and gestured her toward a seat at the far end of the table. "Join us."

Judith took her seat. "I'm sorry. I didn't think I was late."

"You're not late, Miss Higgins," the governor said. "I just wanted to get a head start so I completely understood the issues before you showed up." He glanced around the table. "I'm assuming you know most everyone in attendance?"

Judith looked over at the man next to Dr. Fitzpatrick. He

nodded at her. "I'm Dr. Philip Baden, President of Marmont State College."

She nodded at him. "Pleased to meet you."

He smiled politely and nodded back.

The governor pointed to the two people flanking him. And these are my assistants, Gina Villarreal, and Stuart Shin."

"Nice to meet you." they both said, and nodded in her direction.

"Nice to meet you, too." Judith said.

"Miss Higgins, I don't want to waste your time," Governor Anderson said. "We've been talking for about a half hour now on the idea of a pardon for Delton Hayes."

"That would be wonderful," Judith said.

"Would it, though?" the governor said, sitting back and crossing his legs. "Nobody denies he's been terrific in Dr. Fitzpatrick's program. But he has been taken care of during that time." The governor leaned forward and flipped through some papers in a folder on his desk. "But as I scan the parole board's review of him, their greatest concern was that he didn't have any way of supporting himself, nor the education to do so in the real world. With no job, and no place to live, he was destined to be a 'back-slider,' as they say."

"So the answer is to keep a good man locked up because he doesn't have the education?" Judith said.

"Honey," Taysha interrupted. "In order for the warden and I to feel comfortable for him to get out, we would have to know he has a place to lay his head at night."

"He can start on my couch," Judith said. "And that's only until I get a bigger apartment, so he can have his own room."

"That's what we needed to hear," Taysha smiled, and patted Warden Luzynski on the shoulder. "Isn't that right, Warden?"

Warden Luzynski nodded and cleared his throat. "Yes. That's right. If he could stay with you, that would help his transition a great deal."

"Done," Judith said. "What next?"

"There's still the matter of education," Dr. Baden said. "And that's the reason Governor Anderson has asked me to this meeting. I have agreed to see to it that Delton is given the support and opportunity to get his G.E.D. once he's released. And then I'm required to give him a scholarship into the program of his choice."

"And will you?"

"I will give him a two-year scholarship, nothing more than that. I have to be concerned about precedents."

Judith looked over to the governor. He shrugged. "That's where we were when you walked in. Still in the negotiation phase, if you will."

"Negotiation over," Judith said. "Where do I sign?"

"Hold up," Taysha said. "I think Delton deserves more than that."

Judith shook her head. "I am confident Delton will be happy with that. The goal here is to get Delton out, on his feet, and together with Noah again. Anything beyond that is a blessing." She looked back at the governor. "Where do I sign?"

Governor Anderson chuckled. "Gentlemen and ladies, it appears we are going to make this thing work. Now I need the room with Miss Higgins, to finalize the deal."

Without another word, everyone stood to exit the room except the governor's assistants. Taysha passed by, not looking too happy with Judith's agreement. But that was okay, Delton was getting more than anybody else in his position, and if she needed to Judith would help him the rest of the way.

When the door closed, Governor Anderson stood. "With an agreement like this we don't require signatures, Miss Higgins. We can handle the whole deal with a simple handshake." He walked over to her end of the table. "But it's going to require a little more effort on your part." He stopped in front of her, sat on the edge of the table, looked down, and smiled.

Judith didn't smile back. "What kind of effort are we talking about?"

"We're coming up on an election year, Miss Higgins, and I won't deny that I like how this whole thing will make me look." He drew in the air in front of his face. "The whole, 'defender of the persecuted' looks pretty good when it's attached to a guy like me. I'm not going to lie, I want that."

Judith shrugged. "So what is it you want from me?"

"The simplest thing in the world, really." He leaned down to her. "When the election craziness gets kicking into high gear, all I want from you is your undying support. I want to put you on stages and commercials, selling the voters on how I'm the answer for those who are struggling. When Delton was in need, it was me who heard the cry, and decided to give him another chance. Is that something you can do?"

Judith looked up at his smile, which looked so plastic now. She considered if this was akin to selling her soul to the devil. But she decided it was a small price to pay for Noah. "Yes," she said. "I can do that."

Governor Anderson held out his hand.

Judith didn't reach for it just yet. "But I'll need one more thing from you."

The governor leaned back and crossed his arms. "And what might that be?"

"Delton has a sister living with a foster family. I want her pulled from them and moved in with me too."

Governor Anderson narrowed his eyes.

"You do that, and I will shout the virtues of Governor Mitchel Anderson from Detroit to Iron Mountain."

The governor smiled. "Done," he said, and held out his hand once more. "Now, Miss Higgins, let's get your man out of jail."

Judith took his hand firmly, and shook it.

The governor turned back to his assistants, clapped his hands and rubbed them together. "Stuart, get Governor Cahill on the phone."

Chapter Fifty-Three

"Delton Hayes was returned to this facility last night, and we're about two hours away from the arrival of Governor Anderson," Brooke Winthrop, the famous blond reporter for GINfo stated.

Judith wrapped a towel around her wet hair and ran out of the bathroom. She grabbed the remote off the arm of the couch, and turned the volume up.

Brooke Winthrop was standing in front of the Two Rivers Correctional Facility sign, amongst a large crowd of people, carrying Delton Hayes signs, and waving to the camera from behind her. "His people have confirmed that he is planning to sit down with Delton Hayes to discuss the situation, with the intention of pardoning the young man."

"The place looks crowded around you." The well-groomed anchorman said, from the comfort of his studio.

"The crowd is massive here this morning," Brooke said. "In fact, if we can take a shot from the copter overhead, you can see that there are literally thousands more people here than there were yesterday."

The shot was from way overhead. It showed people filling the parking lot and beyond. "We see it now," The anchorman said. The camera zoomed out to see the crowd down the road surrounding the fencing. "Oh my goodness, Brooke. The place looks like it's under siege."

"It kinda feels that way, Doug."

"Have you seen any sign of Judith Higgins?" Doug asked.

"She hasn't arrived yet," Brooke said. "But when she does get here, she will be able to pull in to this parking spot." The camera panned off Brooke to the direction she was pointing. "The police have kept all cars out of the prison parking lot today, and are only planning on letting certain ones pass. Obviously the governor and his security team," the camera panned back to Brooke. "And Judith Higgins. This is where we're camped so when she arrives, we'll see her."

The scene cut back to Doug in the studio. "Yes, I'm just hearing that she has not emerged from her apartment. So we'll be able to let you know when that happens, and she's on her way."

The shot cut to an image of a familiar-looking building. It took Judith a moment to realize that was her apartment building. She got up, and pulled the front curtains back to see news vans and busses pulled up in front, with rows of cameras pointing directly at her. Realizing she was still in her robe with her hair wrapped, she screamed and yanked the curtains closed again. "Shit, Judith." she said to herself. "This is what you wanted. Now you've got to deal."

Her phone rang and she rushed back into the bathroom, clicking mute on the TV as she passed. She picked up the phone and tapped the call, even though she didn't recognize the number. "This is Judith."

"Hello, Miss Higgins, this is Jeff Taggert, down at Fillmore National."

"Uhhh...hi?" Judith fumbled for words. Of all the people to hear from this morning, the CEO of Fillmore was not the call she would have expected. "How can I help you?"

"You can help me stop the bleeding," Mr. Taggert said.

"Since your fifteen minutes of fame the other night, our little firm here has been inundated with emails telling us how awful we are for treating our employees so badly, and investors are walking away, saying it's embarrassing to be involved with such a backward company as ours. Our analysts are calling it the 'Higgins Event' and they say it could be one of the worst financial disasters our company has ever faced."

Judith had her hand over her mouth, in case she were to laugh out loud. She moved it slightly to speak. "I'm sorry to have caused you so much trouble."

"I'm thinking your sincerity is questionable but that doesn't matter. I want to make it worth your while to help us out."

"And how are you planning on doing that?"

"By doubling your salary if you'll agree to come back to work for us."

Judith shook her head. The thought of dealing with Bernie another day wasn't worth it. "I'm sorry, Mr. Taggert. You could triple it, but I can't work for Bernie…."

"I'm not asking you to work for Herbstreit. We don't want you in that department. We want to make use of your real talents, down in public relations."

The news took Judith's breath away. It took a moment to regain it so she could utter, "Are you serious?"

"I'll tell you how serious I am, Judith. There's a ten thousand dollar bonus in the deal if you let the news media know today, that Fillmore National has rehired you with assurances that your son's needs are not only your concern, but ours too."

"Ten thousand dollars?"

"Ten thousand dollars," Mr. Taggert said.

Judith looked back at the curtain. "Mr. Taggert, I'm standing here in my robe, wet hair, and no make-up. If you make it twenty thousand, I'll go tell them right now."

There was a commotion on the other end of the phone.

Judith could hear Mr. Taggert tell someone to turn the TV up. Then he came back on the line. "I've got GINfo on the TV here. I'll watch you do it. Twenty thousand, if you go out there right now."

"Pleasure doing business with you, Mr. Taggert. I'll see you week after next." Judith clicked the call off, and walked to the front door. Unwrapping her head, she let her wild wet hair string down in all directions. She chuckled as she pulled open the door and walked out.

As soon as her foot hit the porch, the numerous cameramen jumped to their cameras, and had them pointed directly at her. Reporters ran to their side, holding up recorders to capture her every word. Judith smiled with satisfaction at what she hath wrought. "I just received some really good news and wanted to share it with somebody."

"And what's that?" One of the reporters shouted from the mass.

"I just got a call from Jeff Taggert, CEO at Fillmore National Life," Judith said. "He's offered me a job, and he told me they are enacting a policy of support for single parents, especially those with children who have special needs. And he's asked me to consult in the construction of the program." She turned and stepped back into her apartment, but then decided to use her soapbox to extend the conversation. She turned back to the cameras. "I think other companies should take this as a challenge, to be as forward thinking as Fillmore National." Then she stepped inside, and closed the door.

Judith ran over, grabbed the remote, and turned up the volume to hear Doug. She was surprised to see a picture of herself in her bathrobe already placed in a box above his left shoulder.

"…to hear, as Fillmore National has been taking a beating on social media the past couple of days, since Miss Higgins stated she had been released from the company because of their lack of compassion over her autistic son. So this apparent turn in their collective company consciousness is refreshing and, from what it sounded like, long overdue."

Judith's phone chimed, and she pulled it out of her pocket to see a text from Darlene. "I'm leaving the house now. Will pick you and Noah up soon. Get dressed and stop prancing in front of the cameras half naked! Have you no shame, girl?"

Judith looked in the kitchen and saw Noah staring at the box of Captain Crunch. She smiled. He looked so sad, but she knew he would be happy by the end of the day. She went into the kitchen and gently nudged him by the shoulders. "Come, Noah. We need to get the best day of your life started. Go get your clothes on." Noah slid out of the chair and she followed him to his room, then she slipped into the bathroom, took out the phone and dialed Jack. It was up to her now to make things right. He had held up his end of the bargain—in fact he had done far more. It was up to her to do the same.

"Hey, Judith. It looks like you've got a big day ahead of you."

"Noah does too, thanks to you."

"I just called in a few favors. I'm glad it worked out."

"You did it for your son, and I thank you for that." There was silence on the other end of the phone. "Jack, I want you to know that by being a good man, you've taught me a big lesson. You've taught me that I shouldn't try to do it all alone. I don't have to have all the answers, or be the strong one all the time. In fact it's better for Noah, and even myself, if I'm not. You taught me that. If it weren't for you, Delton would not be getting out today. So Jack…I want you there."

"You what?"

"If you're going to be a part of Noah's life, you need to start by meeting his best friend in the whole world. So meet us at the prison, and start being his dad today."

"I…." There was a pause and then a breath. "Thank you, Judith. I would love to be there."

"See you in an hour or so?" She asked.

"See you then." His line went dead.

Judith slipped the phone back into her pocket, looked into the mirror and smiled. "You just did a good thing, Judith," she said to her reflection. "You got this, girl." Then she could've have sworn she heard her father's voice. "Judith, you know you're not done."

"What are you talking about?"

"You have one more phone call to make."

Judith shook her head. "Now is not the time."

"Now is exactly the time," her father said. "You just told Jack that it's better for everyone to let others be involved. So get out of your own way and make the call."

Judith sighed like a ten-year-old school girl and slipped the phone out of her pocket. She hit dial quickly before she lost her nerve. "Hello?" Neil Keating's sweet voice said on the other end.

"Hello, Neil?" Judith said, tentatively.

"It is you," Neil said. "I was afraid I was being butt-dialed. And that would have been tough to take. So to what do I owe the pleasure?"

"Delton is getting out today."

"He is?" Neil said. "Oh wait, I think I did hear something about that, on every single channel known to man."

Judith giggled. She suddenly felt stupid. This is the kind of energy she needed in her life, and she had been keeping it at arm's length for far too long. Not anymore. "So here's my question. What do I have to do to get you to hold my hand at the prison when he's released?"

"You just did it," Neil said. "I'll see you there. I know where you're parking." Then the line went dead.

Judith sat with Noah on the couch watching GINfo, while they waited for Darlene to show up. They had cut back to Brooke who pointed out the governor's car was arriving. She watched as Governor Anderson got out of the car, towering over the crowd like a modern-day Lincoln, and waved to the cheering masses with his bright smile. Then he went into the front entrance of the prison to meet with Delton Hayes.

The cameras cut to Judith's apartment again just as a blue SUV pulled up with big white letters on both sides which read "Hayes-Mobile." The cameraman walked to the back of the car to see a dozen tin cans on strings dragging behind it with the words "Just Freed!" scrawled across the back window.

Judith laughed and clicked the TV off. "Come on, Noah. Aunt Darlene's here."

Chapter Fifty-Four

Two armed guards accompanied Delton, hands cuffed, through the prison. He was weary and ragged. He hadn't been able to get much sleep since he had been flown back to Michigan in the middle of the night, and delivered back to Two Rivers early in the morning.

Delton paused as a set of barred doors were electronically slid open. He was nudged into an area of the prison he'd never been in before. This area looked more like an office building than a prison. The floors were carpeted, the walls were clean and not sticky, and the doors were made of wood and not metal. He was led into a large conference room, where Taysha Williams, and two white men in business suits sat around a long conference table. The man at the far end stood. "Well, here's the man behind all the trouble." He was tall; like six-foot-five kind of tall, with graying hair. He stepped forward and held his hand out to Delton. "Governor Mitch Anderson. How are you, Delton?"

Delton shook it. "You the governor of Michigan?"

The man smiled down at him. "Yes, I am."

"You the one who brought me back here?"

"I am. I want to have a discussion with you, and perhaps

see about getting you out of here." Governor Anderson pulled out a chair. "Have a seat, and we'll talk."

Delton turned and sat down. It was then he noticed the TV on at the far end of the room near the door he came in. The picture showed a helicopter shot looking down at thousands of people around a building complex. Delton saw his name scroll by at the bottom of the screen. "...-derson has arrived to talk with Delton Hayes." Delton pointed at the TV. "Where's that?"

"That's right outside this building." The governor took his seat again at the end of the table. "Your friend, Judith Higgins, has been very busy on your behalf."

Delton looked over and saw Taysha. He waved to her with one hand while the other hand hung from the cuff. She smiled back, winked and nodded.

"I understand you already know Taysha Williams," the governor said. "I'm not sure if you've met Warden Luzynski."

"We have not," the warden said. He stood and reached way across the table to shake Delton's hand, then sat back down.

Delton looked back at the TV. There were closer shots of the crowd. He couldn't believe his eyes were actually seeing signs that read, "Free Delton Hayes," and "Noah needs Delton." "So why do you say I'm the troublemaker?" Delton asked.

"Pardon?" Governor Anderson said.

"When I walked in here, you said I'm the man behind all the trouble." Delton looked back at the governor.

Governor Anderson nodded to the TV. "That. What's going on outside this building right now."

"But didn't Miss Higgins do all that?" Delton said.

"Delton, now's the time to hush," Taysha said.

"No, no." Governor Anderson said, holding up his hand to quiet Taysha. "Delton, she did that on your behalf."

"But I didn't do it," Delton said. "So I'm not the troublemaker."

Governor Anderson's brows drooped with his head. He was beginning to lose some of his fake swagger. "Miss Higgins did it because you couldn't keep yourself out of trouble in here. And now I'm dragged into the middle of all this nonsense because of the shit you pulled."

Delton put his cuffed hands on the table. "What shit did I pull?"

Taysha cleared her throat. "Delton, that's enough."

Governor Anderson threw his hands in the air. "A man's dead."

"I didn't kill him," Delton said.

"And yet you were there when he died." The governor rested his hands on the table. "Right in the middle of trouble again."

Delton narrowed his eyes at Governor Anderson. Here was a man who was judging him without even knowing him or caring to. He was just another white man who was writing him off as a menace, without seeking any truth. Which only left Delton with one question. "Why did you bring me back here again?"

Governor Anderson leaned in. "To pardon your ass. You have a problem with that?"

"But why would you want to pardon a man you think is a troublemaker?"

Governor Anderson looked over at Warden Luzynski, who shifted uncomfortably in his seat.

Taysha dropped her face into her hand, and shook her head.

Governor Anderson looked back at Delton. "It's all about the boy. We want to help little Noah Higgins. He's suffering without his best friend, Delton Hayes."

Delton looked back at the TV. The picture cut to a shot of a big blue car pulling up with the words, "Hayes Mobile," across the side. The text below read, "Judith and Noah Higgins arrive." All Delton had to do was shut up and he would be free to walk out the door. He could see Noah again, and spend time with his sister once more. He looked back at the governor. "I don't believe you."

"What?" Governor Anderson said. His head snapped back and forth from the warden to Taysha.

"This isn't about Noah, or me. This is about you, and how you will look to all of the thousands of people out there and who are watching this thing all over the country. This is about you running for president someday, or some damn thing like that. And I'm not going to be part of that shit." Delton stood slowly and looked down at the governor. "You see, I've had time to think things out. I'm a good man who made some really dumb moves in his life. I done my time for those decisions and then some. I'm capable of doing a lot a good for a lot a people in my lifetime. I know that for a fact. My work on Dr. Fitzpatrick's project showed me that. And I'll be honest, I can't wait to get out of here so I can get my life started. But I can't do it like this—you letting me out just so you can look good for the world. I'm sorry, but this thing here, right now, has to be about me being good enough, not you trying to get votes for helping out some poor black dude too stupid to help himself. And if you think I'm nothing but a troublemaker, then it looks like I'm not ready to leave yet anyway. You can pardon me when your mind has changed about me."

"You pretentious little prick." Governor Anderson stood and looked down on Delton. He pointed to the TV. "What the hell am I supposed to tell all those thousands of people out there waiting for your ass to walk out the door with me?"

Delton shrugged. "I don't give a shit what you tell them. They're your problem, not mine." He turned to the guards. "Send me back to Kansas."

Chapter Fifty-Five

They had made it through the mass of people to their parking spot, but there was no getting out of the car. The crowd was too thick and too loud. Judith sat in the back seat next to Noah on the ride in. She couldn't believe the number of people that had shown up in support of her son and Delton. Cars were parked along the road for the two miles prior to the prison, with license plates from Indiana, Ohio, and Illinois, along with Michigan.

But the noise was what was concerning her now. Noah had his head buried in his hands and was moaning his discontent.

"Darlene, this is not good. With all these people and those helicopters, Noah is going to have a meltdown right here, before Delton even gets out. I don't want that on the national news."

"I got this, Sis. You sit tight." Darlene unbuckled, opened the door and slipped out of the car as quickly as she could. She squeezed her way through the mass of people to a police officer. "Sir, I'm Darlene, Judith Higgins' sister and Noah's aunt. And I need a megaphone."

"For what?" The officer asked.

"I gotta quiet this place, or little Noah's going to blow a gasket in front of the cameras and everybody."

The officer nodded. "I get it. I was here the last time that happened. Give me a minute."

"Bring it to the car," Darlene said. "I'll meet you there."

The officer nodded and headed in the other direction. Darlene turned and worked her way to the TV lights. Brooke was there, facing the camera, microphone in hand, speaking to the thousands of people who were watching live. Darlene moved in as close as she could when an arm reached in front of her and a brute of a man said, "That's far enough, lady. We're live right now."

Rather than try to explain, she just put her hands to her mouth and screamed. "Hey, Brooke. I'm Judith Higgins' sister." Then she waved her arms over her head.

"Stop that," the brute said. But Brooke looked over, then pointed in her direction. The cameraman panned the camera as she walked over to Darlene. "...going to talk with Judith Higgins' sister who has just showed up." Brooke tapped the brute on the shoulder and he let Darlene pass. Brooke spoke into the mic. "So Judith and Noah are in the car?" She held the microphone out to Darlene. "Yes, that's what I need to talk to you about."

"Oh, what do you need to say?" Brooke asked.

"The copters above are freaking out Noah," Darlene said. "I know they're getting good shots and all, but they have to leave or he's going to get ugly. Can you make that happen?"

Brooke looked up to the camera, like a deer in headlights. "Ahhh...," She put her hand on her ear for a moment, then she nodded. "Yes. We can do that right away."

"Thanks," Darlene said. "And Brooke, I'm a fan. I think you do a great job. I've been watching all day and I love that scarf. I'll be in touch and you can tell me where you got it." Then she turned and wriggled her way back to her car. The copters had flown off by the time she made it back. The police officer was there with the megaphone.

"Thanks," Darlene said. She took the megaphone, stepped up on the bumper of her car and then onto the hood. "People, I love your enthusiasm, but we need to keep it down."

The crowd did not seem to notice or care that she was speaking. She pulled the trigger and screamed. "Peeeeeeeeeople, please. Quiet!"

Many in the crowd hushed and turned in her direction.

Darlene looked into the front window of the car. Noah was rocking back and forth with his hands in front of his face. Judith was rubbing his back and talking to him. She looked up at Darlene and gave her the thumbs up. Darlene continued to talk to the crowd, much quieter this time. "Noah is in the car, and he can't handle large crowds or noise, so this is absolutely the worst place to bring him. But we wanted him to be here when Delton got out. So if you could all just whisper, and not cheer, Noah will be able to stay. Please explain this to people near you who couldn't hear me."

The crowd grew very quiet. They turned to others and began whispering. Darlene stayed on the hood of her car listening to the crowd grow quieter in an ever-expanding circle.

Chapter Fifty-Six

"Now hold on just a minute," Governor Anderson said. "Just what is it that has your panties in a bunch?"

Delton looked back. "I'm not doing this, Governor. I'm not going to live the rest of my life with a cloud over my head that I'm a murderer, but you took pity on me because a boy was sad without me. When I walk out those doors, it will be with a clean reputation."

"So what is it you need from me?" the governor asked.

"You can start with an apology."

"Oh, Lord have mercy," Taysha whispered.

"For what?" Governor Anderson asked.

"For assuming that I'm the cause of all the troubles, even before you have said one word to me."

Governor Anderson stood up straight, put his hands on his hips, and stared Delton directly in the eye. There was a long pause before the governor spoke again. "You know what?" He nodded. "You're right. You have reason to be upset, and I apologize." He gestured to the chair. "Can you sit down now?"

"One more thing," Delton said.

Taysha scooted her chair out, crossed her legs, and looked

angrily at the wall.

"Name it," the governor said.

"When you talk about all of this to the press, and I know you will thousands of times, you will say I was pardoned because I acted in self-defense, not because you took pity on me. If we don't agree to that, we have no deal."

Governor Anderson scowled at Delton. Delton could see he was weighing his options at this point, wondering if it was even worth the trouble of a pardon now. Finally the governor reached his hand out. "Deal."

Delton shook it firmly, and took his seat.

Governor Anderson sat down and looked at him. "You're a first for me, Mr. Delton Hayes."

"How's that, sir?"

"Before today, I've never respected a man behind bars."

Delton smiled. "Thank you, sir."

Taysha picked up the pad of paper in front of her and fanned her face.

The two men chatted a few minutes more. Delton explained why Rick Simpson was angry with him, and how the fight went down that led to his death.

The governor let Delton know that arrangements had been made for him to stay with Judith and Noah, and that his education would be covered for the first two years by Marmont. Delton was surprised and grateful for both pieces of news.

"Okay, let's get this done." Governor Anderson opened a folder that had been on the table in front of him the entire time. He took a pen from his coat pocket, and scrawled his signature across a line on the bottom. A few in the room clicked photos of the moment. The governor then looked over to Delton. "Delton Hayes, you are a free man. Gentlemen, please uncuff this citizen."

One of the guards walked over and removed Delton's cuffs. As soon as they were off, Governor Anderson shook his hand.

More photos were clicked.

Taysha walked up and hugged him. "Son, I think you just took a full year off my life."

Governor Anderson slapped his shoulder. "Well, innocent man, there's a little boy who would love nothing more than to see you again. Shall we go make him happy?"

"Yes, we should. Thank you, sir."

Chapter Fifty-Seven

Judith and Darlene leaned against the side of the SUV. The crowd was eerily quiet for the large number of people. It seemed more like a crowd that would be gathered at the death of an important figure, rather than one celebrating the freedom of a wrongly incarcerated man.

"Whew, I had to park like three miles away," Neil Keating said, squeezing out of the crowd to appear beside her. "I didn't think I was going to make it."

Judith looked up into his kind eyes and smiled. She reached her arms around his neck and pulled him close. "Thank you so much for being here."

"Thank you for asking. I'll always be anywhere you need me to be." He leaned in and kissed her.

"Hello again," Jack Brody said. Neil looked up and Jack held out his hand. "Jack Brody, we met briefly once before."

Neil gripped Jack's hand, and shook it firmly. "Neil Keating, nice to see you…again."

Jack put his hands in his pockets and sighed. "I wasn't sure we were going to make it."

"We?" Judith said.

Jack nodded his head in the direction of the building. "Yeah, Kate wanted to come with me. She's in her wheelchair, up on the sidewalk."

"Kate's here?" Judith asked. "Should I go say hi?"

"That probably wouldn't be a good idea," Jack said, shaking his head.

The doors to the building opened, and the crowd murmured. All the signs shook wildly. Darlene, megaphone in hand, ran through the crowd whispering, "Stand aside. Make a path for Noah." She walked all the way through to the building, clearing an aisle so Judith could see the doorway through the parting of the bystanders.

There stood Delton, next to Governor Anderson, who towered above him. Both men smiled and waved to the crowd.

Judith put her hand on her heart, and tried to hold back tears. Seeing Delton now, brought a feeling of joy that was almost overwhelming. All that work and worry, with little to no hope that this day would ever come. Neil reached down and held her hand.

Jack leaned in. "Judith, shouldn't Noah see this?"

"Yes, thank you." Judith turned and opened the car door. Noah was in his car seat, calmer now, playing with a rubber band. "Noah, you need to come out here." She reached in, unbuckled him, and lifted him out of his seat. Noah moaned loudly and squirmed excitedly, clutching at his seat. "Noah, this is important." She stood Noah on the pavement, and knelt down. He buried his head in her shoulder and moaned. She whispered in his ear. "Noah, Delton is here, and he wants to see you."

Noah stopped moaning. He pulled back slightly and looked her in the eyes. She smiled at him and nodded. Then she pointed in the direction of Delton.

The place was silent. The wind whispering through the chain link fence was the loudest noise.

Noah reluctantly looked around. He saw the hundreds of

people lining the path and buried his head again.

"Noah, Delton is over there, and he wants to see you."

Noah lifted his head once more. This time he let his gaze travel down the path to the doorway. The change in his expression was distinct, and immediate. The fear in his eyes faded at the moment of recognition, and a sparkle glimmered. The tension in his cheeks and neck softened. Noah stepped away from his mother and took a step toward the door—toward his best friend.

The crowd took one collective breath as Noah passed them by, his awkward steps surely making everyone nervous, for fear he would fall on the hard cement. But Noah didn't fall. As he drew closer to Delton, each step seemed to come a little faster, and the terror of the crowd around him dissipated, eclipsed by the excitement of seeing his friend once more.

Delton knelt down. Noah completed the last few steps to get to him, held out his fist and yelled, "My man!"

Many in the crowd chuckled under their breath, others threw their hands over their mouths so as not to startle the boy, and still others, mostly women, wiped tears from their eyes.

Delton smiled, and fist-bumped Noah. Then he stood, took Noah's hand, and guided him back to the car.

Judith had streams of tears by the time the two made it back. She threw her arms around Delton and hugged him tightly, almost afraid to let go.

"Thank you for all of this," he said in her ear.

"Delton, this doesn't even begin to thank you for all you've done for Noah," she said.

They pulled apart, and he smiled at her. "So I understand I have a couple of roommates."

"You do," Judith said.

"What about Danna?"

"We're getting her too. She'll be living with us soon."

Delton choked up, and hugged her again.

"I hope you like spaghetti for dinner."

"I like anything that ain't prison food."

Darlene slapped him on the shoulder. "This is my sister's cooking. Don't expect it to be better than prison food."

They chuckled and climbed into the car. Darlene stepped up on the bumper and held up the megaphone one last time. "Okay people, let's hear it for Delton and Noah!"

The crowd erupted, and waved their signs. Darlene stepped down and tossed the megaphone to the officer she'd gotten it from. Then she hopped in the car and drove off, tin cans rattling on the road behind them.

The following is an excerpt from the article "Special Needs + Special Rehab = Special Circumstances," written by Dr. Warren Q. Fitzpatrick, of Marmont State College, and published in "American Psychology Magazine," October 2019.

This is the part of the article where the researcher discusses the findings based on the data collected. However, in this instance, this article was not written with the findings in mind, but rather a chance to tell our end of things, as it were.

As the world is aware, the project was terminated the day Rick Simpson was killed, which was just two short months ago. We have begun the arduous process of sifting through notes, videos and interviews with the remaining parents, but we are still in discovery mode, and not ready to form a hypothesis at the time of this writing.

There is one outcome I can take the liberty to discuss, and I feel that it would be wrong if I did not do so. Though many opinions abound on Delton Hayes, and his culpability in the death of Mr. Simpson, there is an important message that I cannot iterate enough. Noah Higgins spoke, due directly to the intervention of Delton Hayes. That is a fact that is undeniable and irrefutable. Delton remained devoted to Noah throughout the project, and spent his own time creating new ways to reach the boy.

No matter what people are saying this young man did, or didn't do, I need to make it clear that I have pages of transcribed notes and hours of recorded sessions to conclude that when given a chance, Delton is as good, or better than anyone out there who feels privileged enough to judge him.

In conclusion, I will state proudly that if all the data were to mysteriously evaporate overnight, Noah Higgins saying loudly, "my man," is all the proof one needs to declare this project a resounding success.

Thank you for reading!

If you are finished with the book, please take a moment and leave an honest review on Amazon. It would be greatly appreciated.

For more information on upcoming books please stop by my web page, **rob-edwards.net** and sign-up for updates. I will be sending out a newsletter with updates every few months. You can also connect with me on Facebook at **@robedwardsstoryteller**, on Instagram at **robedwardsstoryteller**, or on Twitter at @ **robedwards5000**.

And watch for the second installment of the *Threads of Life* series, *I DO OR I DON'T*, coming in 2021!

Acknowledgments

This book has been dedicated to three of the greatest encouragers in my life. I don't think they comprehend how much their words have motivated me over the years. Even though my father is gone from the planet, he instilled in me a belief that the first step in achieving a goal is to simply give it a try.

I still hear you, Dad.

A huge thanks go out the editors of this book, Louise Knott-Ahern, and C.D. Dahlquist.

Louise was instrumental with defining crucial elements of the story, and C.D. Dahlquist did another outstanding job with the copy editing work.

Another contributor was Dr. Mary Sharp, M.D. Highly regarded for her work with developmental disabilities, autism in particular, Dr. Sharp made sure I had all the facts straight regarding ASD.

And I would be remiss without mentioning another important contributor, my late father-in-law, Dan Ostrom. A retired state trooper, he spent a warm, sunny, summer afternoon discussing all the legalities of this story with me when it was nothing but a glimmer in the back of my mind.

Thank you to all of the beta-readers who took the time to give their honest feedback. Your input was invaluable.

The cover art benefited from the photography work of Victoria Borodinova, and Spencer Selover. You can find both at pexels.com. The third picture was taken by my wife, Dayna Marie.

Thanks to a great writing community in the mid-Michigan area. I have gained a great deal of advice and support from the Capital City Writers Association, the local NaNoWriMo Chapter, my writing group the Skaaldic Society, and the annual Rally of Writers.

Thanks to Anne Stanton, Doug Weaver, and Heather Shaw

at Mission Point Press for their support.

And finally - thanks to you, the reader. I hope you continue to follow the threads of life with me!

Made in the USA
Middletown, DE
22 June 2020

10544911R00215